STEVEN J SMITH

THE PATH TO REDEMPTION

Foreword

This novel has been in my mind for the best part of three years, after reading and studying the history of the Crusades and the lasting issues and problems we still have today, connected with the 'Holy Land'. In general, I have tried to keep the clothing, food, arms and such like as identical to the reality of the middle ages as much as possible and the time line of the various conflicts and factual historical characters are prevalent and factually correct in the story.

However, it is a created story and James Rose is a fictional, if unconventional central character to the book. Along with Aisha, Alessio, Thomas and a multitude of others you will meet and become involved with, during the reading of this novel; all have been created from my own brain; albeit some may have characteristics of people who are known to me. I leave it to my friends and family to decipher those familiar traits as they read but my lips will always remained sealed on this! I truly hope you enjoy my creation.

Gloucester, April 2013

Dedication

For Clair, for your love, support and
understanding....always, not just in the creation of this
book. Thank you.

Chapter 1

The Desert Trail

11ᵗʰ February 1145, 2 miles from Acre

The high-pitched scream shattered the silence. Shielding his hazel eyes against the glaring sun; James twisted his lean body on the back of the ebony stallion and scanned the golden sand in all directions. Stroking his three day old beard with his left hand, the outlander looked over at the twelve year old Jacob and did his best to look reassuring. Jacob's azure eyes were wide and the Jewish boy was scared. The cloak of fear had covered the poor child for most of his short years and he moved his chestnut mare to his guardian and held out his perspiring palm for support.

"Relax Jacob, now go and help Aisha barter with that old skinflint; Abdul. We need decent grain at the house"

Tousling the mop of russet brown hair and keeping his voice light, he urged the boy west across the sand towards the distant figures of Aisha and the huge bulking frame of the merchant. Nodding silently, the apprehensive child moved his horse forwards and James watched the boy trot and then gallop across the bleak landscape. Casually unfastening the leather harness on his French handmade mahogany crossbow and checking the short sword was in its scabbard at his waist; his mind began to count the reasons for a female scream beyond the dunes to the north in the simmering summer heat of Outremer. Not one of the four or five assumptions invoked comfort and as the figure of Jacob began to blur out of focus, he felt the uncomfortable presence of perspiration trickling down his spine.

"Come on Merdlan, old boy"

He nudged his left boot against Merdlan's flanks and the horse grudgingly trotted towards the dunes. Moving carefully to the base of the highest of the dunes, James dismounted and patted his faithful steed softly as he strode past him and pulled out the crossbow; loading an iron bolt into the loading mechanism as he studied the lie of the land. A second scream, followed by hysterical screeching caused the crossbowman to sprint up the sand dune as quickly as possible in the scorching heat. Reaching the crest, he threw his body to the sand and pointing his crossbow forward, looked over the brow at the unfolding scene below.

A covered wagon lay on its side across the desert trail that classed as the merchant road from Acre. A number of arrow shafts remained in the wooden frame and from the dead horse that lay beside it. A second horse was dying slowly and painfully nearby, an arrow shaft embedded in its neck and James inwardly cursed. The driver of the wagon and presumably the guard, from his armour and weaponry were also lying on the golden sand; unconscious or dead. A woman, clad in the silken layers of a style worn by wealthy Egyptians, waved a scimitar wildly in front of her as three robed figures taunted and abused her in Arabic as they circled her, toying with her. One held a short bow with arrow notched, as the others held short curved swords and the onlooker swore vehemently as he recognised the favoured weapon of the secret cult of Hashini from the mountains of Persia. Closing his right eye, he aimed the crossbow and fired.

The third scream erupted as the man to the left crumpled in a heap; a sharpened iron bolt smashing at speed into the back of his neck; killing him instantly. The two remaining protagonists froze momentarily and whirled around; seeing the newcomer some seventy yards away at the summit of the dune. The first sprinted towards him as James calmly reloaded from the leather pouch at his waist. The second man headed to the fresh corpse and frantically tried to grab the bow and reload

7

the arrow that lay on the ground. He managed to hold the arrow in his left hand before he was punched back to the ground, struck in the chest, a little below his heart and piercing the leather breastplate he wore as protection. Grunting, the man was thrown backwards and lay on the sand, wounded and dazed. James, with much rehearsed precision reloaded his crossbow, his eyes watching the swarthy assassin closing in on his position with alarming speed. The man was fit and determined and was within 20 yards when he was hit in the stomach; the bolt stopping him in his tracks and dropping his sword; he grabbed limply at his wound; vainly attempting to stem the flow of blood. As the man forced himself unsteadily to his feet, the second bolt ended his life, a direct hit to his forehead.

James forced himself to calm down, moderating his erratic breathing and rose from his squatting position. The woman was peering up at him in confusion and still held her scimitar before her as he strode towards her; his hazel eyes on the moving third assassin who was crawling to one of the three well groomed desert horses, who stood obediently at the edge of the trail. Reloading his cross bow as he walked down the sloping sand; he paused only to shoot a quarrel into the spine of the wounded enemy, ending his pathetic attempt at leaving the scene. Content that all three adversaries were dead, James tossed the crossbow over his shoulder by its strap and held his hands outwards in a show of peace to the stricken woman, who still bore the weapon and a face contorted by panic.

"It is over. I mean you no harm."

He used Arabic as the dark skinned woman was clearly of Egyptian descent; his accent was poor and his vocabulary limited. He knew English and Italian fluently; French and Arabic less so but the words at least caused the scimitar to lower. James approached slowly and smiled.

8

"It is ok. Really. I am not going to hurt you."

The woman stared into his eyes and dropped the sword, suddenly dropping to her knees and sobbing silently into her hands as she looked over the five corpses around the roadside. James wiped the perspiration from his hands, face and neck and allowed the woman the dignity of crying alone; moving to the injured horse who was now flailing its hind legs and whinnying pitifully. In pain and dying slowly, James stroked its mane and spoke softly to it as he unsheathed his sword and sliced the keen blade across its neck in one fluid motion; ending another life, albeit this one being an innocent one. Wiping his short sword on the blanket that covered the beasts back, he studied the scene before him; unanswered questions assailing his mind. Rubbing his stubble, he viewed the horizons for signs of more would be assassins but seeing nothing; he looked down at the carriage driver and guard. Both were dead. The livery was definitely Arabic but did not look Egyptian and yet the attackers were also Muslim. There may be an uneasy peace between the nations in the Holy Land right now but it was still one of the most dangerous places in the world.

A figure appeared on the dune from where James had fired and his hand slid to the shaft of his crossbow. The woman, who had ceased her sobs and was watching him warily now, also saw the figure and he heard her sharp intake of breath. He recognised the lithe figure of Aisha and grinned as he saw the loaded short ash bow in her hand; even from this distance he saw the look of concern in her pretty young face. He waved as she lowered the bow and spoke to some unseen being behind her. She was flanked by the immense frame of the overweight merchant, who lumbered breathlessly into view, carrying a throwing axe in one hand and the fearful Jacob in the other.

"They are with me. It is ok."

James spoke to the woman, whose breathing was becoming broken and ragged once again. He smiled warmly and moved to the woman's side, offering her his hand to help her up. Suspicious eyes watched him carefully but she allowed him to help her to her feet. James studied the dark skinned woman closely, hoping his easy smile looked genuine as his eyes registered the facts. In her early twenties, dark ringlets of hair covered half of her face, which was striking rather than beautiful. She looked rather feline to James and cats could never be trusted.

"Thank you…Thank you for helping me."

The voice was heavily accented but spoken in perfect Arabic, the *Mamluk* dialect. Her eyes were oval and dark brown and were studying him just as much as he was studying her. Growing concern was building within James and he realised his forced smile was fading in front of her.

"No problem at all, are you hurt?"

"I am Kallissa and no I am not."

A thin smile flickered across her face showing perfect white teeth and the image of a panther leapt suddenly into his mind.

"I am James, pleased to meet you."
He responded haltingly and nodded in the Mamluk manner.

"Are you ok James?"

Aisha spoke in English behind him, having moved swiftly to the scene, concern and a hint of confusion in her voice.

He turned and nodded, embracing the girl as she rushed to him.

"I am fine Aisha, just fine."

Pushing her gently from his frame, he stroked her cheek and traced a finger across her nose. Aisha smiled and nodded and then looked over at Kallissa, appraising her instantly and blurting out her observations.

"Mamluk noble, see the Egyptian silk? Clearly not welcome in these parts. So why only one guard?"

James nodded at his ward's swift understanding.

"Are they Hashashim do you think?"

He asked Aisha pointing to the three men he had killed.

"Yes they are and we had better leave the area right now in case there are more around."

Abdul's deep, booming voice answered for her.

"You do not want to make enemies of those people James."

He added cradling Jacob's tear stained face in his hands and looking towards the woman pointedly.

"You do not want to involve yourself in whatever this is, my friend."

Abdul warned, shaking his head.

"I could not let them just kill her or whatever they were going to do."

James responded evenly, casting a quick glance at the silent Kallissa.

"And I cannot just leave her here Abdul. She is in shock I think."

"Okay, let us all go to my home; I will see to this with my brothers later. I will make sure the honourable are buried and the others are burned. We want no knowledge of what happened here to get out James. Get your answers from her later, now let us go."

Within minutes, the small party; enhanced by the assassin's horses, which Abdul would sell on discreetly at a later date, crossed the desert and made their way in the fading light to Abdul's well-presented homestead on the outskirts of the multi-cultural city of Acre. The wealthy merchant led James, Aisha, Jacob and Kallissa through his gates and past the toiling workers in his vineyard; who watched the unlikely group move past with interest. Stabling the horses, Abdul barked orders at his servants to bring food and drinks for himself and his guests. Directed into the dining area, they were seated on low benches at a wooden table and sat uncomfortably in silence as ice cold fresh water, white wine, various olives, hot bread, grapes, figs and dates were brought in hurriedly. The simplistic meal was eaten in the same awkward quietude and James was the first to speak as the clay bowls were cleared away.

"Aisha, will you take Jacob to the guest room upstairs; it is too late to ride home tonight and it has been quite a day. For all of us."

His smile was forced and as he bent down to kiss the young boys' cheek, he nodded to the teenage girl; a motion he hoped would prevent any discussion or argument. It did and he smiled more genuinely as Aisha stood and led Jacob out of the room, through the hallway beyond. Both sets of young eyes stared at Kallissa as they left the dining area; Jacob's with interest and Aisha with barely concealed suspicion. James waited for the soft footfalls on the stone stairs to subside before he leaned forward and looked into the stranger's oval, dark eyes.

"Are you ok to talk now?"

"We can speak in English if you prefer."

The woman replied fluently to the halting question in Arabic and James grinned easily and nodded, reverting to his father's native tongue.

"It would make the conversation easier."

"I need to reach Damascus, could you or your friend who lives here arrange to escort me or get word to my betrothed. My family will be worried about me. I can pay you of course."

James held up his hand to stem the flow of words from the woman and smiled.

"I am sure Abdul will be happy to arrange an escort for you. So, who are you Kallissa and why would assassins be sent to kill you?"

The woman's lips curved upwards into the very essence of a sardonic smile.

"You are very direct for a Frank."

"I am not a Frank."

James responded curtly yet his brusqueness barely made an impression.

Kallissa smirked mischievously, clearly her brush with danger easily swept aside.

"I did not mean to offend you James but to my people, all white men are Franks."

She paused as if to await an answer and James kept his mouth closed, the realisation that he did not like this woman the only thought in his head. The pause lengthened into discomfort and as James shuffled on the uncomfortable seating and rubbed his forehead; Kallissa merely stared directly at him; her dark, almost opaque eyes boring into his.

"My mother was a Venetian seamstress and my father was an English knight, they met in Tyre and I was born in Acre so this land is my home. I am not a Frank. Now, I have been more than patient so please....."

The explanation tumbled from him but the woman interjected abruptly.

"Thank you for aiding me, I will repay you but I do not know anything about those men who attacked me or who may or may not have sent them. I am the daughter of a minor noble family in Egypt and was on my way to my betrothal ceremony in Talien, near Damascus. That is all I can tell you."

Her eyes avoided his own and she placed a soft goatskin pouch of coins upon the table.

James smiled thinly; disbelieving every word that had so carefully been chosen and merely nodded, ignoring the offering.

"Now, do you know where I may be able to freshen up; the dust from the road you see?"

Suddenly feeling as if he was eleven years old again and dismissed by his overworked and emotionally crippled mother; he shook his head and shrugged.

"I will arrange it with Abdul's wife."

He said simply and left the room, closing the heavy ornate door behind him. Striding to the kitchen he found Fatima baking some heavenly smelling almond cakes and the rotund middle aged woman hugged him tightly, a cacophony of melodic Arabic spilling from her ample lips. James extricated himself politely and grinned at Fatima. Eventually reassuring his oldest friends' wife that he was uninjured, he arranged hot towels for Kallissa and the firm acceptance that Abdul would sort everything out and he was not to worry. Accepting the large goblet of Cypriot wine from the benevolent hostess, he left the obnoxious stranger in Fatima's capable hands and climbed the stairs to check on Aisha and Jacob.

"What did she say?"

James reached the top of the staircase to see Aisha standing on the landing with her hands on her slender hips and he was reminded of his mother for the second time in a matter of minutes, an image he did not hesitate to replace instantly with something else more welcoming.

"Not much at all."

He stated flatly and shrugged his shoulders.

"Well I didn't like her."

Aisha declared and James agreed.

"She called me a Frank."

Aisha chuckled, knowing it was a pet hate of her guardian's.

"She spoke perfect English to me and her clothing and jewellery is worth more than our house. How would she know to speak English to me; you Saracens always think us foreign white devils speak French!"

Aisha chuckled at the teasing.

"Hey, I am but a lowly Seljuk from Syria; Jacob is a Jew from Antioch and you are the strangest mix of all! You tell me where the three of us could possibly fit in!"

James smiled genuinely and kissed her gently on her cheek.

"The three of us may be the strangest family in the entire world but I love our family and I would not change any of it for all the grain in Egypt."

Aisha blushed and headed inside the bedchamber with a shy smile, where Jacob lay curled on the enormous four poster bed; sleeping soundly and snoring loudly.

"Is he ok?"

"He is good, apart from his hideous snoring of course."

Aisha grinned childishly and sat down on the bed.

"He was worried about you; we both were James. You have to look after yourself. What happens to us if anything happens to you?"

The grin had disappeared, replaced with a look of haunted dejection and James approached his teenage ward and wrapped his arms around her, cradling her slight frame to his own, stroking her soft hair as her tears fell across his tunic.

****

Four hours later, Abdul knocked softly on the door and opened it slightly to peer inside. His large saggy face grinned as he saw James sat on the bed with Aisha sleeping soundly across his lap and Jacob curled into his side, happily snoring like an injured camel. Motioning for his friend to head downstairs to talk, Abdul headed back to the kitchen as James carefully extricated himself from his predicament without waking the children and followed him down the stone steps. The two men hugged briefly in line with their usual greeting and Fatima handed him a second glass of wine with a broad smile and he accepted it readily and graciously.

"Are the children asleep, James?"

He nodded in response and thanked Fatima as she bustled upstairs to check on Aisha and Jacob.

"Have a seat my friend, we need to talk."

James winced inwardly at the seriousness of the tone and sat heavily on the low stool near the embers of the fire.

"My men have escorted that woman back along the road to Damascus and the scene in the desert valley is sorted. The assassins bodies are now ash, their horses are heading south to the markets and the covered wagon has been burnt. Tracks have been erased so nothing will lead anyone to any of us."

James smiled and leant over to grasp his friend's wrist.

"I appreciate it Abdul and sorry for bringing this on you and your home."

Abdul waved away the apology as unnecessary.

"You did what was right. Allah moved your hand."

The Muslim smiled at his friend's discomfort at the mention of Allah and continued.

"To pay three Persian killers from the mountains costs hundreds of Bezants; only a few options there. Your friends in Jerusalem perhaps?"

James shook his head dubiously.

"Peace is holding; barely. They are too busy building

17

trade routes with the West; a war with the Ayyubids would ruin everything for them. The Christians do not want war; slaying a noble woman from Egypt is murder; that could create enough trouble to start another conflict."

"So, one of the other factions; Mamluk or Seljuk?"

"But what would they gain from a war between Muslims?"

"We have no overall leader James, when my people unite, that is the day for the Christians to worry. The Seljuks want to lead, the Mamluks want to lead, the Ayyubids cling to power. What can I say? May Allah help us all if Zengi takes control; he is an animal to all, regardless of race or religion."

"In Acre, the Venetians are saying Zengi must be stopped. His power is growing and conquering Edessa in the north has worried the Kingdom of Jerusalem."

Abdul drained his wine and poured another, topping up his friend before putting the bottle back down heavily on the table.

"We all have a lot to fear from that man. He has bribed, assassinated and conquered to become the Atabeg of Mosul and Aleppo. His armies grow with mercenaries from the Kurds and Turcoman tribes. Zengi promises 'Jihad' to strengthen his Muslim credentials but every single one of us know he craves Damascus. Since he took over Homs and massacred the local Muslim population, he rules only by fear. "

James stroked his stubble and sighed.

"We live in a strange world Abdul; waiting for an inevitable war. By the way, didn't she leave a pouch of coins on the table....I do not seem to see it anywhere."

Abdul shrugged, grinned, winked and drained his glass.

"Pah, enough of this talk. I have my contacts checking out this noblewoman to find out who she is and why her death would be so important to anybody? I will know by tomorrow – now, let us get drunk together and then in the morning, we will have forgotten rude nobles and dead Persians!"

"Amen to that."

James concluded and the two clinked earthenware before draining the sweet alcohol in unison and both reaching for the bottle at the same time, chuckling together like naughty children.

Chapter 2

Past and Present

The woman who had called herself Kallissa strode through the elegantly decorated hall to the inner chamber. Her shadow danced eerily behind her as the flaming torches leapt in the whirl of her direct, forceful movement. The Arabian spearmen who guarded the approach all made absolutely certain they did not look upon the robed woman's face as she stormed past; her face a mask of pure vitriol.

****

James closed the heavy door and stripped wearily before gingerly stepping into the heated, scented water that filled the oaken bath tub. Murmuring an expletive as the heat turned his skin pink instantly, he swiftly washed his aching body with the almond soap and then settled back to relax. It had been 24 hours since the incident on the desert trail and he had not heard any news at all from Abdul. Presumably, this meant there was nothing of interest to tell but James was unsure of this. Abdul had many sources across the Holy Land and generally found out the information he required within a few short hours. A lingering sigh brought this train of thought to a sudden end, already boring him with the endless amount of speculation about the attack. Everything had been cleared up without witnesses so there was no possible retribution. It had been an unfortunate incident and they had hardly been the first men he had killed in the East and sadly, it seemed unlikely to be the last.

Dropping his shoulders into the water as it cooled in the ground floor marble and polished stone room, his drifting thoughts meandered to Jacob and

Aisha. Neither had reacted badly to the event, which was pleasing after the hardship both had experienced in their short lives and the 'family' unit had returned this morning with the trade goods from Abdul and set about the daily tasks without issue. The word 'family' caused instant pain and he sank his head below the water for a few seconds before breathing again. His mood darkened. The main reason that he had took on Jacob; the orphan and Aisha; the runaway, was that everybody deserved a happy childhood, no matter of race, creed, religion or circumstance. He truly believed that; due to the fact that his own childhood had been sad, lonely and filled with melancholy. Wiping his face, he attempted forlornly to wipe away the creeping memories that seeped into his brain.

Images of his mother sobbing on her husband's slain body swiftly morphed into the harrowing scene of his elder brother's funeral. At just eleven years of age, he lost his father and brother to a holy war, a meaningless crusade against the heathen. His father; Jack, a strong, devout man from middle England died at Sarmada, the battle that ended the initial victories of the Christian forces and eventually brought the two sides to stalemate and a grudging peace. His brother; John, just sixteen years of age had accompanied his father as his page and the arrow head that had wounded him, slowly and painfully killed him in his mother's arms a few weeks later. The Field of Blood, the survivors from the battle had renamed it after Ilghazi of Aleppo had savagely destroyed Roger of Antioch's tired and outnumbered knights. It meant that the lonely childhood which James had already struggled with became almost totally unbearable.

His mother; Maria, born in the squalid streets of the innumerable poor in Venice had arrived on one of the very first Venetian ships carrying the hopeful populace to their land of plenty. She settled first in Antioch and then in Jerusalem, where she met and married Jack. A son was born nine months later and when the coastline had become settled and the region of Outremer had been created; the family moved to Acre, where James was born a few years later. The religious conflict ebbed and flowed all around the Holy Land and the family, led by their father were pious and Christian. When Jack and John died, his mother became enslaved to Catholicism; retreating from motherhood and settling into the role of bitter widow; spending more time with the dead than with the living. A Frenchman; Georges; invalided out of the Knights Templar due to his left hand being hacked off in the eight month siege of Antioch, who himself, had lost his wife to illness, spent time with James and taught him everything he knew. In the young boy, he found a willing and eager pupil and James quickly learned to ride, to fight with a sword and knife and how to read, write and speak English, Italian, Latin, Arabic and French.

His greatest achievement and his favourite subject was the use of the crossbow. From an early age, James had excelled in archery but despite his English ancestry, he was drawn to the crossbow; loving its power and its workmanship, the simplicity of its mechanical action and beauty of its design. Drifting into manhood, he saw very little of his mother who preferred the church or graveyard and he became friends with Georges, looking after the old man as the years proved difficult to cope with for him. Georges arranged for James to enter the elite Knights Templar and all the tests had been passed convincingly before his final conversation with his mother ended this commitment. His mother, hysterical and emotionally unbalanced made the sixteen year old James swear on the souls of his father and brother that he would not become a knight and in a confusing mix of family loyalty and honour; the young man agreed.

For the next few years, he remained at Acre, with the support of Georges, becoming a wine trader; his natural charm and personality helping the flow of funds and the gathering of assorted friends; regardless of nationality or religious connotation. Abdul became a close friend and opened up the trade routes to the Saracens and James made considerable wealth, supporting Georges and his estranged mother with bequests and enjoying a carefree lifestyle of hedonism. War became more distant and more Europeans flooded into Outremer, keen to pursue a better class of living in the new world. Life was easy and shallow; lovers came and went and wine, friends and money were plentiful. Georges died, a peaceful death of old age after three score and ten and James gained his house and all worldly belongings, including his ornate crossbow, handmade by artisans of Paris. As overcrowding and religious fervour began to increase in Acre, James decided to sell his business and the house; moving beyond the Southern walls and into the relative wilderness of the rugged coastland. With his plentiful funds he constructed a wooden cabin of his own design, complete with stables and a well; purchasing a vineyard and enough land to breed horses. Abdul provided the skilled labour and the dwelling was built inside a year. With a cursory wave, James left the Christian city of Acre and established himself in his own private piece of heaven.

The loud knocking at the door shook his mind from the thoughts of yesteryear and he smiled as Jacob poked his head around the door.

"Aisha said I should bathe too as I stink badly."

James chuckled as he watched Jacob say the words with contempt but then sniff his own tunic and contort his face.

"Give me ten seconds to get out and it's all yours; I will fetch you some more hot water though; it is tepid now."

Jacob grinned boyishly and murmured something unintelligible but appreciative and his head disappeared back behind the door.

James grabbed a towel and stood in the tub; placing the soft wool around his naked form before stepping onto the cold marble floor. Using a smaller hand towel to dry his hair and face, he called Jacob in and collecting his discarded clothing; he left the boy to bathe; padding to the room next door where he grabbed a large bucket of heated water from the burning coals and warmed the bath. Leaving Jacob to his leisurely soak, he headed into the kitchen barefooted and through it to the wooden staircase which led to the three bedchambers upstairs. Trudging upstairs; he finished drying his toned body and dressed in tight fitting Arabian pantaloons and a deep green sleeveless tunic embroidered in the Venetian style. Keeping his mind clear of memories, he focused on the mundane tasks ahead of him to maintain his vineyard and horse farm running. With thoughts of watering vines and hay bales distracting him, he smiled as Aisha knocked softly and entered his bedchamber.

"Can I accompany you to the docks in Acre tomorrow?"

James had expected the question all day and smiled, agreeing happily as he had not spent much time alone with Aisha in recent weeks; the endless amount of work on his land occupying the vast majority of his time.

"Sure, it should be really busy. New traders are due to arrive from Sicily and Malta so plenty of material, clothing, weaponry, armour and people. Possible buyers for horses and wine as well."

"Clothing, material?"

The young woman's eyes widened in undisguised excitement and James grinned.

"Yes and as you have been wonderful with

Jacob recently, we can even go and see Zachariah in the marketplace."

Aisha rushed over and hugged him, knowing that Zachariah was the elderly Jewish owner of the precious gems stall and known as the greatest jeweller in the whole of Acre.

"Thank you James! I will pack everything tonight for us and sort the horses in the morning – you riding Merdlan?"

"Actually, I thought I would take the new mare; see how she copes with crowds."

He considered thoughtfully, smiling as Aisha interrupted him.

"You mean Chestnut; it was Jacob's turn to name the new horse."

The smiling youth needlessly explained and James chuckled throatily as Aisha headed out of the door, her mind a myriad of thrilling possibilities about the morning at the docks and markets of Acre. His mood brightening, James headed back downstairs to the kitchen and grabbing a handful of dates, wondered out into the evening; the intense heat of the region lessening as the fiery sun was slowly sinking into the placid Mediterranean before his eyes. Hearing the two Nubian freedmen herding the horses into the stables in the paddock to his left, he strode towards them to help his workers undertake the unenviable task of coaxing eight horses of very different personalities into the stables for the night.

For two arduous hours, James, ably supported by Aboulias and Jamaal locked up the animals carefully with fresh hay, grain and water. Bidding goodnight to his workers, he made a final round of his lands; a low stone wall marking out the perimeter, before heading back into the kitchen to be greeted by Sharla, his keeper of the home and mother to Aboulias and Jamaal. The hard working, permanently positive African woman in her fifties basically ran the home; cooking, cleaning and educating Jacob but generally mothering all. Due to one of the many conflicts in Nubia; her homeland, during the Egyptian conquest of her peoples; she was taken prisoner and enslaved with her two boys. Drifting through the slave markets, the three poor individuals found themselves in Arsuf where Abdul bought them at a bargain price; setting them to work on his farm. During a drunken game of dice; James gained victory over the Arab and never betting with money; James freed the family from slavery. However, with no home and no Bezants to their name; hundreds of miles from their birthplace; freedom actually meant a new life of incredible hardship. Learning harsh lessons in this part of the world, James reacted by granting jobs and a home and never made a better decision. All three relished their freedom, working hard and becoming an integral part of the homestead; supporting James in building his businesses and family.

In typical fashion, Sharla offered him the strong herbal tea and James accepted gratefully; four years of drinking the beverage had created a liking for the sweet, aromatic taste.

"Are you sure Aisha should accompany you to Acre?"

The admonishment was clear and James nodded, sipping the tea.

"She deserves a treat; she is a young girl who works harder than any girl should. Aisha has been so good with Jacob; they are already bonding like brother and sister. It is much more than I could have hoped."

Sharla smiled proudly and nodded slowly.

"Well, do not spoil her. She is growing into a young woman and will not be a girl for much longer. But you are correct, it is beautiful to see. When you brought that poor boy back from the north years ago, I was worried. He had seen such things and could have affected us all, especially Aisha, who had finally found contentment herself."

"We are blessed Sharla and life is good. We are all healthy, the vines are growing rapidly and the horses are coming along nicely."

"And I thank all of our gods every day; all of my children are well and I mean all five of you. Goodnight James. "

The woman bustled out of the kitchen, kissing James on his forehead as he sat at the low table drinking, heading to the log cabin near the entrance of the compound, where she lived with her two grown up boys. He smiled as Sharla left him alone to his thoughts. Thinking how fortunate he was and how his life had changed immeasurably richer in the past few years in so many ways; his smile broadened as he listened to Jacob's chuckling as the boy played some imaginary game in his bath in the adjacent chamber. Upstairs, Aisha was giddy with excitement at her trip to Acre's plentiful markets in the morning and he drained his tea in contentment. His mother, in the earlier and happier days of his childhood, used to have an Italian phrase that she used often. 'Vita e bueno.' It was a simple, beautiful statement and he echoed his mother now as he closed the door on the golden red sun setting on the placid Mediterranean.

"Life is good."

****

The man known to his fanatical followers as Imad Ad-Din Atabec Zengi Al Malik Al Mansir hurled the goblet of Syrian wine against the ornate rug that hung against the wall of the great chamber.

"Why is Allah punishing me? The dogs in Damascus still will not accept me as their master, what more must I do? If I use all of my forces to destroy this city, I risk the Christians attack in the west or the Armenians or Byzantines in the north."

The aged advisor; Mahmud, remained stoically silent, hoping his expression of understanding was apparent enough to avoid the contempt and aggression of his Emir. Eighteen years of service as his right hand taught him many things and staying alive was chief among them.

"I have taken Edessa from the Christians to prove my strength and what do the cowards claim; this will incite the Franks to attack us and they fear them! I proved to them at Homs and Baalbek, if my own people turn on me, I will annihilate them!"

The shrill voice became more high pitched and hysterical as the glass fruit bowl and cutlery followed the goblet at speed against the wall.

"Fear the Westerners? Fear them? All they have done for the past 10 years is build walls and castles to hide inside. I offer my own people Jihad and they are too frightened to take up arms! The Egyptian scum are stirring to the south, our spies tell us the Caliphate is building his own army of Mamluks and they refuse to accept my authority. Byzantium sits in the north biding its time as we all kill each other and now you inform me the Christians are still crossing the sea to our lands. You tell me that they will attack if I move against any more of their cities. The Armenian campaign has robbed me of troops and money; my Kurdish mercenaries will happily fight against me if someone paid them enough. What do I do? How can I prove myself anymore to my own people to prove I am

28

the One who will unite all our brothers and sisters?"

Zengi spat out the words and slammed his fists on the intricately carved table and tried to reign in his vehemence. His dark, almost black eyes narrowed as he studied the tall, emaciated frame of his only trusted advisor and controlled his rage.

"And now, you tell me that they failed. These Shi'ite warriors that never fail did not do what I paid them to do. You said they never failed."

Concern rippled through the advisor as those penetrative eyes of darkness stared at him and he coughed apologetically.

"Sire, they have advised that they will amend their mistake as soon as is physically possible and they offer complete apologies for this most unusual failure. They are investigating how this could have happened as they expected only token resistance from her one bodyguard."

The Atabeg swore under his breath in response to what he perceived as a weak excuse.

"Get word to these people not to bother and to refund my gold. Immediately! I will do what I should have done all along and take care of her myself. Find out where she is and give her my concern; I need to get to Armenia with money for the mercenaries. Some Frankish knights slaughtered a troop of Turcoman archers and now there are rumours of deserters I also need to check on the Kurd; Naim al-Din Ayyub; I gave him control of Baalbek and now his Kurdish mercenaries class him as their leader and not me."

"Leave it to me Sire, I will pass on your concern and find out what exactly happened and see to it that no stone is left unturned."

The advisor bowed his head as Zengi strode around the table towards him.

"I want you to personally make sure that my gold is returned, find out how she survived and make sure she is here waiting for me on my return. I want to deal with the traitor myself. "

With the menacing words ringing in his minion's ears, he abruptly turned and left the room, screaming for his guards to prepare for his journey.

Chapter 3

Acre

The expedition commenced badly. Jacob was upset that he was being left behind to be tutored rather than being treated to presents and Sharla had made her feelings well known on the subject of Aisha accompanying him to the heavily populated port, creating numerous images of doom over a simple breakfast of bread and honey. Relieved to leave the gloomy atmosphere behind them, James soon regretted his decision to take the skittish young mare instead of his trusted Merdlan. The journey became arduous in the extreme morning heat of the desert trail as James constantly coaxed, harried and abused the horse into submission, much to the amusement of Aisha; who seemed immune to the array of tears, complaints, moans and forebodings that had been thrown, rather unfairly, her way that morning.

The journey to Acre improved as James felt the burden of responsibility ease with every mile they travelled away from the homestead and Aisha was good company; conversing freely and easily with her guardian; sharing hopes and ideas. The older rider in turn, his usual persona returning, openly discussed his plans for the future with Aisha, trusting her implicitly with details of finance and time frames. His vision of developing and growing the vineyards, creating olive groves as Abdul had excitedly described these as 'black gold' and improving the stables to include breeding. Aisha was proud to be included in these plans and the two of them conversed deeply and happily until the high walls of Acre loomed in the distance.

The two riders followed the roughly hewn stone path through Patriarch's Gate and towards the inner harbour and the dockside market in the Venetian Quarter. James knew the port intimately as his entire childhood and much of his early adult life had been spent in the overcrowded, badly built city. Only the extensive walls and towers that defended Acre had been planned and well-built with excavated foundations and skilled craftsmanship; utilizing the artisans that flocked to the Holy Land from all corners of Europe; England, France, Holy Roman Empire, Austria, Poland, Hungary, Sicily and the various Italian city states. The churches had multiplied in the past two decades and now Acre had no less than six places of Christian worship within the city walls. These ornate, elegant buildings sat unhappily amidst the hurriedly and haphazardly built homes of the booming population; increasing at an alarming rate with every Venetian, Genoese or Pisan galley bringing more citizens to Outremer.

James watched Aisha as her young eyes widened at the sheer scale of the city walls, towers and churches and her face scrutinised the crowds around her. Robed French priests, armoured English knights and Genoan sailors mingled freely with Moorish peasants and Muslim traders, their differing languages creating an incomprehensible chattering which assailed the ears. As the two figures stood silhouetted on the dockside with the morning sun blazing in the azure sky behind them; they watched as a caravel bearing the coat of arms of Pisa across its sails unloaded a dishevelled array of new arrivals of all ages; their eyes wide with wonder, excitement and fear at the 'new world'.

Safely installing the horses in one of the many stables which punctuated the quayside; a whole bezant was paid to the grinning boy, who promised to groom and look after both animals personally, James explained the reasoning for the arrivals.

"They come from every squalid, poverty stricken corner of Europe – desperate for the better life the Pope has promised them. This is the New Land; God's Realm; where they hope to find salvation from their previous sins."

James stated as he watched the newcomers get ushered onto the cobbled streets by the sailors, eager themselves to find a tavern or other form of entertainment in the bustling city.

"And what do they find?"

Aisha asked, squinting in the haze as her eyes followed the steady stream of bodies leave the calm Mediterranean Sea and rush headlong into the alien environment of Outremer.

"Who knows Aisha? Some may find a better life, most will not. Some will remain in poverty, just in a different part of the world. Others will die fighting for their various gods and beliefs."

The girl contemplated for a moment and then spoke quietly, choosing her words carefully.

"If the Christian God is omnipotent and benevolent and the Jewish God is the same and the Muslim God is the same. Why is there so much death in the name of these gods?"

James looked at his young ward and his smile widened as a youthful bald man wearing simple robes strode from the docks holding forth a wooden cross; his face contorted into a grimace as he mumbled through some form of prayer.

"Aisha, you are the brightest, most intelligent girl I have ever known. Honestly. Now let us go visit Zachariah! If life is so short in this damned land of ours – let us enjoy it."

Aisha's dark, oval eyes widened, more than a

little bewildered by the effervescent compliment but more than a little excited by the prospect of the jeweller's wares. The finest crafted gemstones in Acre and perhaps in the whole Kingdom of Jerusalem itself awaited her. For that very moment, she was overcome by love and affection for James and rushed to him, hugging him tightly to her slender frame and kissing his pale cheek softly.

"Thank you."

The older man was touched by the sentiment; knowing the young Syrian was not prone to sudden outbursts of emotion. He smiled and held her close, surprising himself with the sheer force of his own love for her. Stroking her ebony hair and soft olive cheek, he stepped backwards from the embrace.

"You deserve a treat Aisha. You have helped me so much; with the home, the vineyard, the horses, the stable and especially with Jacob…he adores you."

He paused and Aisha held his strong, calloused hand, her countenance expectant; waiting.

"You are my daughter in all except blood. You are the closest person to me in this world and I love you with all of me…"

The words became brittle, choked with feeling and James twisted his tanned face to look over the crowded fish market, confident that the ever moving sea of faces was unconcerned with their emotive conversation. Aisha felt the wetness of tears on her cheeks and she wiped them swiftly away with her free hand.

"I love you too. And Jacob. And what we have built from nothing. Our home…our family."

Her lyrical voice trailed off and both suddenly

smiled at the other.

"Just look at the state of us? Come on, let me spoil you."

"And Jacob."

Aisha almost admonished and James laughed heartily, feeling alive in the middle of the docks of Acre, surrounded by the market traders calling out their wares in Arabic, French and Italian; the warm sea breeze caressing his skin.

"Yes, and Jacob. And don't forget Sharla, Aboulias and Jamaal – today, we all get gifts!"

The girl laughed gleefully and literally skipped with pleasure along the low stone wall of the port, skirting past the Venetian quarter and into the densely populated, antiquated area of Acre where the Jews existed. Their wooden one storey, one room homes packed uneasily between the Genoan and Venetian quarters. The shrill sounds of the Italian hawkers abated as the streets narrowed and became little more than cramped alleyways.

"James, my boy and Aisha, you beautiful vision of womankind!"

The booming voice spoke in heavily accented English, which the elderly Zacharias knew both patrons understood and he opened his corpulent arms wide as they approached his garishly coloured store.

"It has been too long."

He grinned showing a distinct lack of teeth, even for a man of more than sixty summers as he shook hands vigorously with his male guest and hugged Aisha.

"And how are you sweetness? Does he look

after you as he should?"

Without waiting for a response, he clapped his hands and a boy, no more than twelve years old appeared with glasses of iced water, a delicacy in the arid lands of the Holy Land.

James and Aisha took the elegant glassware gratefully and sipped the refreshing drink, ducking under the crimson cloth canopy and entering the confined store. A conspicuous guard, clad in a shiny suit of scale mail armour and holding a longsword, eyed the visitors warily from a stool in the dimly lit corner. Zacharias nodded sagely to the swordsman and James drained the glass, narrowing his eyes as he studied the guard evenly.

"We have come to see your jewels my friend. Not your usual cheap imported stuff from Cyprus or Armenia. We want to see your handcrafted items; this is for Aisha."

The aged owner smirked.

"But of course, something exquisite for the young lady."

Turning his avaricious eyes to Aisha, he bowed slightly.

"And what are you seeking? I have gold from Egypt, bronze from Syria, silver and copper from Byzantium…."

"A necklace with a golden chain I think…"

Aisha interrupted, exchanging a knowing glance with James, who smiled warmly. Zacharias clapped his hands again and barked orders in Hebrew to an unseen servant. Within a matter of mere seconds, a different boy appeared with a polished onyx tray, an array of delicate gold chains with a variety of gemstones and precious metals interwoven in intricate designs. The young, thrilled orbs studied the necklaces carefully, eventually picking out an elaborate chain with a single blue sapphire pendant.

"This one."

She stated as James nodded in response to her questioning gaze.

The vendor pursed his lips, nodding in agreement.

"Aaah... that is a beautiful piece is it not? That however, is one of my favourite necklaces but is also one of the most expensive items."

"I thought it may be you old rogue. Is 30 Bezants enough for you?"

James stated with a wry smile and pointedly ignored Aisha's worried glance.

Zacharias nodded his balding pate enthusiastically.

"For you James and because I knew Georges so well, I will grant you the artefact at that outrageous price, though it is almost theft."

He bowed slightly and James stifled a chuckle, mumbling that outrageous was indeed the correct word as he counted out the agreed price and lifted the necklace, carefully placing it around the girl's sleek neck, stepping back to admire its well-crafted beauty.

"It is an excellent choice. Simple but effective design in only the best gold with a sapphire from the mines in southern Egypt."

The seller said proudly and James winked at Aisha.

"A pleasure, as always my friend. Now, we have many more purchases to make. Until next time Zacharias, you take care now."

The Westerner clasped hands and the two men embraced quickly.

"Peace be with you both. Are you going to see your mother while you are in the city?"

Aisha smiled and followed James out of the small shop but sensed her guardian stiffen suddenly and he turned his head to the Jewish owner. The usual gentle hazel eyes flashed with anger and he replied simply.

"No."

Various questions meandered through the teenager's inquisitive mind as she strolled in silence and as they moved back into the Venetian Quarter, she chose to stifle the burning desire to understand the history and background of James, instead asking a simple question with a smile;

"Where to next?"

"Alessio's; for the riders cloaks for Jamaal and Aboulias. Hopefully his sister; Maria will have some of the silk scarves from Syria; Sharla deserves something nice."

James smiled but Aisha knew it was forced and the hazel eyes were dulled. Her need to ask questions was almost bursting out of her but she managed to focus her attention on something else, wondering why every woman of Latin origin seemed to be named Maria. As the unlikely duo strode through the busy streets, her young eyes widened at the sights and sounds they encountered. Street hawkers called out their wares in Italian; figs, oranges and wheat from the lands in Outremer itself, saffron and cinnamon from the Turkish territories to the east, apricots and plums from Armenia, olives and lemons from Sicily, apples and grapes from Greece and Cyprus, wine from Italy and the Judean Hills, mead, ale and cider from France and England. The sheer variety of foodstuffs excited her senses as James passed them by, apologising and smiling at the vendors as he did so. Moving past the street vendors and into Silk Street, they headed to a brightly coloured shop with deep red awning; the colour of the Venetian Quarter itself.

Entering the store was like entering an exotic, enticing realm as lengths of silks, wool, satin and cotton of every conceivable colour were out on display and in every garment of clothing imaginable and some that Aisha had never imagined. Hundreds of bolts of fabric lined the wooden shelving across every wall. The small, dark haired woman in her thirties looked up and smiled genuinely as she recognised James and Aisha watched her rush around the counter and hug him tightly.

"James! Alessio did not say you were coming? Oh it is so good to see you."

Pulling away to appraise him she turned her flushed face to Aisha and crouched down to kiss her cheek.

"Aisha, you have grown. How old are you now? You are turning into a beauty, but your clothes, we must dress you properly!"

"Fifteen." Aisha mumbled, suddenly self-conscious as she looked down at her riding breeches and her favourite tunic, which seemed dull and worn in such a store.

"Fifteen! You are practically a woman Aisha. I could make you something perfect for your shape. So slim, you are so lucky!"

James smiled at Aisha and he pushed the melancholic thoughts of his mother out of his mind as he saw Aisha blush at this well-meaning but embarrassing Venetian onslaught.

"Stop embarrassing her Maria, we do not live in Acre and attend parties like you and Alessio; we live and work on the land. Where is Alessio anyway?"

"I am not embarrassing you, am I Aisha?"

Maria beamed, rubbing the girl's cheek and causing yet more colour to rise; the polite fifteen year old shaking her head although her eyes screamed out for the seamstress to stop. Stifling his grin, he looked around, repeating his question.

"He is where he always is these days. 'The Caravel'."

The final two words were almost spat out and James winced. 'The Caravel' was one of the largest taverns in Acre and had established itself in the Genoese Area of the port, its reputation was poor with a brothel upstairs and card games in the cellar rooms. Few nights passed without violent incident and it instantly brought back memories of yesteryear for him as he had frequented the very hostelry throughout his late teens and early twenties when he lived with Georges. Since leaving Acre, seven years ago, he had not been back but rumours of money lending and criminal activity still made their way down the desert trail. His instincts told him to be worried for Alessio, who had been a constant drinking and gambling partner all those years ago and who, had the unfortunate ability to get involved in trouble whenever the opportunity would arise.

"Aisha, are you ok to stay with Maria for a while. I need to go and see Alessio. Choose the riding cloaks and scarf for me, you have better taste anyway and if you want a new outfit, go for it but do not let Maria bully you into anything you do not like."

He winked at Maria and kissed Aisha briefly on her forehead and exited the store.

"So is James still not married then...?"

Maria smiled broadly at Aisha and the girl giggled at her obvious statement as the Venetian strolled to the door and closed it, rotating the sign to 'Closed'.

"I think we are just going to have the best afternoon! Now, think pretty!"

Pausing to hear the laughter from behind him in the haberdashery, James grinned and was pleased that at least Aisha was in good hands, he headed to the inn in trepidation, knowing that at mid-morning, a man who spends his time at such an establishment was a drunk, a gambler or something much worse. Sighing audibly, he instinctively felt for his short sword and wished he had not left the comforting feel of his crossbow with his saddlebags at the stable.

****

The aged, emaciated soothsayer shook the worn leather pouch and scattered the contents onto the bronze plate; her wild eyes staring at the assorted teeth and bone splinters that came into contact with the metal and fell haplessly in the fresh animal blood that covered the salver. Peering closely at the human shards, she scraped the lifeless grey wisps of hair back from her forehead and stared gleefully at her Mistress.

"Mistress Nadirah, the omens are auspicious. He who tried to slay you shall he himself be slain within one year. His kingdoms will be split asunder but the Lion of Islam will come to unite our people and claim victory over the outlanders."

The weeping eyes glazed and Nadirah watched the seer in tense quietude; the sweltering heat of the small room creating beads of perspiration to appear across her covered forehead.

"Your funds have helped His father claim His ascent to power but we must watch over him Mistress. He is but seven years old and a feeble boy. The prophecy will be fulfilled but there are dangers."

"Dangers?"

Nadirah whispered hoarsely and the elder woman nodded gravely; picking up the contents of the tray and dropping them delicately back into the pouch before emptying them on the metal again. Spreading the blood with her elongated brittle fingernail, she studied the signs and gasped an oath.

"The Frank! The one who saved you from the assassins… Mistress, he crosses your destiny."

Nadirah smiled slowly.

"The life of one miserable Outlander does not concern our prophecy. We need to continue to destroy Zengi's power first, starting with that old fool Mahmud. I will enjoy dealing with him myself."

"And the Frank, Mistress?"

"Forget about him…for now at least. If he still appears in your visions, I will deal with him when the time comes."

The wizened crone cackled shrilly as Nadirah pulled the cowled robe around her slim shoulders and departed the chamber.

Chapter 4

Il Caravel

With the mid-morning sun blazing overhead in the cloudless Arabian sky, the lone figure trudged westwards across Acre, passing the newly built Christian church of St Marks, passing the fortified harbour and headed into the Genoese Quarter. As with all men of Italian blood, although part of the Latin peoples who had worked and fought together in hostile territory to create Outremer with the support of the French, English and Northern Europeans; James's mother was Venetian and therefore, he naturally distrusted those of Genoan or Pisan ancestry. James knew this was a ridiculous and simplistic insult, a sweeping generalisation but even a man of his intellect felt this emotion deep within him. In truth, he preferred those of Venetian ancestry to those of Genoan and as he walked through the dusty streets of their Quarter; he felt tense and acutely aware that he did not belong nor indeed, actually want to be there. Musing over why his Father's Anglo-Saxon bloodline did not dilute these feelings, the large wooden sign depicting a turn of the century Caravel bearing the flag of the Genoan city state loomed into view. A dilapidated timber frame building, in need of restoration and repair, standing not a stone's throw from the Holy Church of St Lawrence was the disreputable hostelry with its gambling dens in its cellars, a brothel upstairs and a bar in the centre whose clientele included every smuggler, thief and bandit imaginable.

Scowling and blinking through the dust kicked up from a troop of fully armed Knights Templars who trotted past in an obvious display of power and pride; James crossed the street and opened the rickety door, pointedly ignoring the hired guard who sat lazily on a stool in the shade beside it, his toned and bronzed chest on display and a wooden club close at hand. A foul mixture of acrid smoke, stale ale and a veritable array of human odours struck his nostrils as he entered the gloom of the tavern and strained his eyes to try and locate his friend. Unsurprisingly at this time of day, the bar was relatively quiet with an elderly man supping from a tankard at the far end and a very young man in his early twenties vainly attempting to sweet talk the solitary female worker, whose expression swapped from boredom to amusement and back again repeatedly as she listened to his tall stories of bravado.

Only one of the eight tables was occupied and James barely glanced at the four mariners who all stared in his direction upon entry. Mariners had a fearsome reputation in two areas of life; drinking copious amounts of alcohol and in all types of fighting and James had no wish to test either part of their reputation today. He nodded and smiled warmly to the serving woman; in truth little more than a girl; barely eighteen years James would have guessed and wearing only a thin tight fitting leather tunic which pushed her ample cleavage almost to her chin.

"What will it be Sir?"

Her voice was musical and light, a smile danced across her red lips.

"Ale please and some information if you would be so kind?"

James responded in Italian and placed a bezant on the stained and uneven bar.

The deep ocean blue eyes narrowed with suspicion and she stole a glance towards the other patrons as she poured the murky brown ale into a dented tin tankard. Placing the drink before James, she deftly removed the coin and leant on her elbows and

45

leaned forwards.

"I can try?"

A playful smile adorned her quizzical expression.

"Do you know a man named Alessio?"

The woman's face clouded momentarily and she nodded, motioning to the spiral staircase, which led beneath the floorboards in the far corner. Without expanding, she moved to the older man and refilled his tankard without him having to ask. James mouthed some thanks silently and sipped his ale in trepidation, a little surprised at how good it tasted and he gulped around a third of the liquid and turned to watch the young man fail to impress the serving girl yet again. In his peripheral vision he could see the Mariners taking an unhealthy interest in him and as he was contemplating leaving his drink unfinished and just heading downstairs, one of them stood and approached him. Cursing inwardly but showing a distinct lack of interest, James sipped his ale and looked at the wall opposite where a large crucifix was fixed with nails into the wood.

The man loomed over him, a few inches taller than his five feet and eleven inches and James turned his face to look at the unwelcome newcomer.

"Not seen you here before stranger..."

James sipped his ale again with a forced expression of disdain and he shrugged.

"It has been a while since I have been here."

He replied simply and evenly, acutely aware that the rest of the room's residents were now staring openly at the unfolding scene.

46

"Gianni…leave him alone."

The young woman stated with a smile and the hulking Gianni threw a dismissive look at her and turned his focus back to James.

"There is no trouble here Francesca, this nice gentleman was about to buy me and my friends a round of drinks, that's all. Isn't that right, friend?"

Gianni grinned showing blackened and broken teeth and James smiled at the woman, glancing over at the aggressor's companions, who remained seated, nudging each other and clearly enjoying the show. Deciding to call the man's bluff, James turned to the woman and stated slowly.

"My apologies but the man is mistaken."

A look of discomfort crossed Francesca's youthful features and as her eyes widened, James turned back to Gianni, a moment too late to avoid the huge fist striking him hard in the cheek, sending him flailing backwards, his spine striking the bar and his limp body bouncing awkwardly on the dirty paved stone floor. Snapping his body taut, he rolled away from the incoming boot and scuttled backwards, wincing as a loud mocking burst of laughter greeted his obvious retreat.

"All you had to do was buy us a drink. Now I am gonna have to break your nose."

Gianni grinned manically and moved forward slowly, both hands forming fists as he approached James, who eased his aching body to its feet and stood his ground.

"Leave him alone Gianni…"

A deep authoritative voice boomed like a cannon and the pugilist stopped abruptly, his face snapping into the direction of the order. James followed suit and his heart sank as he recognised the owner of the voice; the face more lined and the muscled body turning to fat since the last time he had seen the man but he would know Francesco Corelli anywhere.

"I was just about to teach the stranger some manners, Francesco. He was asking about Alessio. I thought he could have been one of those Temple types."

"He is no stranger Gianni. His name is James Rose; or is it James Vittorio... I forget. It has been a long time. You went off to live with the Muslims I heard, breeding horses or some such. Became respectable."

James said nothing as the conversation about him drifted throughout the silent room. He had hoped that Francesco had died or sold the tavern by now or at the very least, that the one time in a number of years he came back into 'The Caravel', he would not meet him. The pain emanating from his bruised cheek and his lower back instantly forgotten as the unwelcome feelings of discomfort and fear stirred within.

"Francesca, pass me a bottle of the Cypriot wine will you. James and I need to have a little chat downstairs about old times. Give Gianni and the boys a round of drinks on the house and whatever you do, don't tell your sister; Sophia, who has popped in for a drink."

Those unwelcome feelings intensified as Francesco Corelli patted his shoulder and literally pushed James towards the metal staircase.

"So what are you doing in my establishment James? I am guessing this is no social visit after the last time you were here. How long ago was that now, four years?"

James did not turn his head to look at the tavern owner as he reached the bottom of the metal stair case; instead he studied the badly lit, cavernous chamber that stretched out before him, sensing danger and murmuring simply;

"Almost five years now."

The elder man pointed to an empty table, well away from the two tables where games of dice and cards were being played by stern looking, perspiring men; their faces masks of intense concentration. His fleeting glance failed to locate Alessio and he sat heavily on the wooden stool as Francesco placed two wine goblets on the table and filled them with expensive, sweet smelling Cypriot wine. Seating himself opposite James, he raised his drink and said with a smirk;

"To reunions!"

James half-heartedly raised his goblet in response and forced a smile, choosing his words carefully.

"You look well Francesco; business must be good."

"It is my boy! Wine, women and gambling; mankind's greatest sins, all under one roof. What more could any man ask for? So tell me; which sin are you here for? I seem to remember you used to like them all!"

James looked over at the gambling tables as a brief splutter of excitement occurred with colourful language and the banging of wood.

"I am not here for any of those things. I am here to find Alessio."

He levelled his eyes at the older man and held the amused stare evenly.

"Alessio? Yes, he works for me now."

"He works for you?"

James replied dubiously.

"Yes, he is quite a useful enforcer is your old friend; Alessio. He had some trouble on the tables and no way to pay off those mounting debts. It was unfortunate but I offered him a deal to work for me instead, that way, he pays off his debt to me gradually."

Biting down his revulsion at the situation Alessio had found himself in, James smiled warmly.

"How much does he owe you?"

Francesco chuckled mirthlessly.

"The gossip is true then; you have become the Good Samaritan. My, how you have changed from the lascivious little drunkard who was lucky at cards."

The tone hardened and James winced inwardly, trying not to give away his discomfort and to keep his voice pleasant and accommodating;

"That was many years ago Francesco, I am sure everybody has regrets from their youth."

"She was my eldest daughter. She was engaged to be married. To nobility no less. She was pure. Innocent. You took that away from her. It could never be replaced."

The words were hissed vehemently and James responded calmly, attempting to retain his composure.

"And I deserved the beating your associates gave me. I was young and I was foolish. It was a long time ago. I am sure Sophia has forgotten it and moved on with her life."

Francesco clicked his fingers and James ceased talking, eyes widening as a well-armed bald man sauntered over; a livid scar running down the right side of his face. Without turning his attention from the horse trader; he ordered the man to find Alessio and bring him to them. James sipped the wine and welcomed the refreshing warm taste of cinnamon and lemons on his tongue. The wine was good and he cleared his throat, deciding now was as good a time as ever to broach the subject.

"You are a businessman Francesco. How much does he owe you? I can perhaps pay his debt to you in full and add a few coins for your benevolence?"

The man opposite him smiled thinly, drained his wine and belched loudly.

"Selling horses to the Saracens must make good money, young James. "

"I sell to anybody, whatever God they worship. I do not judge nor care."

Francesco stared balefully at him and refilled his drinking vessel, nodding as his guest refused further refreshment.

"Alessio owes me a lot of money, hence the arrangement we have. His luck with cards and dice failed him and of course, he likes to frequent the girls upstairs."

The last remark was followed with a low rumble of laughter and James forced a false smile in response.

"What will it cost me to release Alessio from your employment?"

"Who says I want to release him from our arrangement? Who says he wants to owe you rather than I? Are you his father? What do you care what happens to that sorry excuse for a Venetian?"

James left the questions unanswered. He already knew that Francesco would accept the offer as the man was the most materialistic and covetous man he had ever met. Silence descended on the table as both men awaited the next stage of negotiation, neither wishing to play their hand too soon.

Francesco sighed audibly and for dramatic effect.

"So you like to help poor unfortunates; be they Muslim, Jew or Christian? How very noble of you? Still, what do I care for your reasoning? One hundred bezants and we have a deal, not a piece less."

"Deal."

James drained the magnificent wine and held out his right hand to finalise the agreement, aware that the price was no doubt an inflated one but to save his oldest friend from the life he was now living, it was worth every coin. Pointedly ignoring the gesture, the elder man merely shrugged, asking;

"You have the funds on you?"

The horse and wine trader turned as the tall, scar-faced man strode from the staircase; a gaunt, puzzled looking Alessio beside him.

"James?"

The Italian's tanned features broke into an

attractive grin and James stood to accept the welcoming hug.

"What are you doing here?"

He asked, looking down at a smiling Francesco; his own grin vanishing swiftly.

"He is paying off your debts Alessio, so you will owe him rather than I. For some reason, James here thinks this will be favourable to you. I cannot imagine why? Maybe he likes the look of your breeches!"

The same low rumble of laughter followed on from the last word and the scar faced underling joined in the humour and James nodded to Alessio's ashamed yet hopeful expression and placed a leather pouch of coins on the table.

"There are fifty bezants. I will need to get the rest from my home. I will get it to you tomorrow, if that is acceptable to you, Francesco?"

"I am a reasonable man, you know that James. I will be here tomorrow but am opening another tavern in Tyre so will be there for some time after that."

The threat was real and ill-concealed and James nodded gravely.

"Until tomorrow then my affluent young friend."

Happy to be so obviously dismissed, James headed for the staircase and an appreciative Alessio followed suit. Striding up the stairs, they moved into and quickly through the tavern's bar and out into the fresh air and blazing sunshine of Acre's streets. Alessio grabbed James and hugged him again.

"Thank you. You have no idea how much I owe you for this. I will pay you back I promise."

James grinned and clapped Alessio on the back of his thick ebony hair.

"Let's just get back to the shop and away from here and we can talk about what the hell you have been up to, getting on the wrong side of that man. I mean, look what happens to you when I am not here to look after you!"

Alessio cursed and then chuckled.

"Come on, I can tell you the whole sorry state of my life at home. I need a drink in my hand first though!"

The two old friends laughed together and headed east across the port to the relative comfort of the Venetian Quarter, both happy with the outcome of their meeting.

"By the way, what happened to your face?"

James smiled with self-effacing grace;

"I got caught off guard!"

****

Francesco counted the coins out on the table carefully and smiled at Aldo, his most loyal worker and most effective enforcer.

"Follow them. Young James has done very well for himself it seems. I need to know exactly where his home is, in case we want to pay him a visit one night. "

Aldo smirked as his superior erupted into mirth, bellowing out bursts of laughter as the underling nodded and exited the chamber.

****

By the time James and Alessio sauntered into Silk Street, they were both in good humour; bawdy recollections of youth being brought up at regular intervals. Heading inside his sister's clothing store, Alessio called out her name and smiled as Maria turned to welcome the two men.

"I thought you had got lost or started drinking in that tavern!"

The admonishment was clear but the affable woman continued, unable to remain upset at her brother or James for long.

"Well, we have been really busy here. Aisha has chosen a beautiful pair of Egyptian cotton cloaks for the workers and a scarlet silk scarf in the Seljuk tradition for their mother. She really does have a good eye for detail; you should bring her more often to see me, she is in her element with the bolts of silk, satin and velvet. Oh my lord, what happened to your face?"

James nodded amiably and rubbed at the sore cheekbone, a dark bruising already becoming apparent.

"I slipped. To be fair, it would not hurt her to have some different female company from Sharla. I am sure your conversation is more interesting than her conversations with Jacob and I."

"Of that, I have no doubt."

Maria teased playfully and winked at James who scowled in reproach, continuing gaily.

"Now, come on through, Alessio can open a bottle of wine and you two can witness a revelation. Aisha has chosen a dress; I have amended the style and shape to fit her body perfectly and she looks absolutely beautiful. Come see, come see!"

The two men smiled knowingly at one another and meandered through to the back of the shop, where a door led into the cramped private quarters of the Piero siblings. Moving into the main room, which served as a kitchen and dining area, all three sat down and Maria shouted through to the adjoining area beyond an archway, for Aisha to come in. There was a momentary pause as all three sets of eyes stared at the opening, awaiting Aisha's entrance and the awaiting onlookers exchanged glances as Maria called out Aisha's name again.

A shuffling noise could be heard and the Syrian girl appeared; clad in an exquisitely fitted dress, popularised by the affluent women in Byzantium. Ephemeral layers of violet gauze covered a shimmering deep purple satin, which clung to every contour of her slender youthful body. Alessio whistled softly and grinned as his sister, who had worked tirelessly to create the vision of beauty in front of them. Aisha stood awkwardly and her eyes sought out James; desperately waiting for his impression and hoping it would be positive. Maria turned to her left to observe the reaction and smiled as she could see his face soften, emotion flickering across his gentle smile.

"You look so beautiful Aisha."

The words were hardly audible and his ward beamed and hurried to embrace him. Burying her head into his shoulder, James held her tightly and looked to the dress maker, thanking her and complimenting her skills.

"Bah, the dress would be nothing without Aisha; I would eat camels alive to have a figure like yours my girl."

Maria stated happily and the emotive tension collapsed into natural laughter and the four figures embraced and kissed each other in turn; seating themselves and embarking on an afternoon of humorous anecdotes from the many chapters of Alessio's and James's early lives in Acre. Maria's eloquent stories of their escapades and misdemeanours brought riotous laughter from Aisha, bemused embarrassment from James and guilty pleasure from Alessio in equal measure. Eventually, Maria took Aisha to the back room to remove the dress and pack it carefully for the journey on horseback back to the homestead and Alessio took James by the arm and led him back to the store, out of earshot.

"Thanks for what you did today, my friend. I will repay you, every single coin."

The other man listened, nodded and shook the offered hand, gripping each other's wrist as they used to do as children in more innocent times.

"Come back with me. I need help and you would be wise to leave Acre for a while. Do some proper, decent work for a change. Keep away from that old thug at 'The Caravel' and keep your head down. Even you cannot get into trouble at my place on the Desert Trail."

To his surprise, Alessio nodded his head gravely.

"Yes. It will be good to clear my head. I will. I will speak to Maria and then I will come out to yours for a few days."

"Excellent. I will take Aisha back once we have finalised our purchases and then when I come back tomorrow to pay off Francesco, you can come back with me then. Say midday?"

Alessio nodded again and agreed heartily as the two women reappeared, Aisha once again dressed in her dowdy travelling clothing.

"Do we have to go back so soon James? I was having such a good time."

"We have much to do yet and we have to get back before the sun sets."

"You can come back anytime and as often as you want to."

Maria said hurriedly, diffusing the situation simply and Aisha hugged her tightly, thanking her profusely and promising she would.

"How much do I owe you for the dress and the other gifts?"

"Nothing, it is my gift to you both, for what you have obviously done for my brother."

Maria said softly and kissed James on the mouth gently.

"You have always been a good man, James."

Gripping the neatly wrapped packages, James and Aisha departed Silk Street after more emotional hugs and moved back to the busy dockside markets. With the dwindling supply of funds; James purchased iron tipped bolts and a length of expensive hemp to strengthen the tension of his release mechanism for his crossbow from a French weapon smith, fresh saffron from the Judean Hills as requested by Sharla, peaches from Araby as a treat for all and a very personal gift of a cask of ale from a newly arrived English trader. Finally, a wooden toy falchion was purchased for Jacob, as carefully selected by Aisha before they headed southwards, out of Acre along the desert trail on their refreshed and watered horses in the early afternoon baking sun of the desert. The pace of their return journey was slow as an animated Aisha excitedly repeated the events of their time in the port; eager to tell James of her conversation with Maria. In her element, her flushed youthful face grinned as the words flowed and the man indulged her; making the right facial expressions and murmuring relevant answers when pressed but his mind was agitated. The repressed memories churned through his thought processes and images of yesteryear forced themselves to be confronted and therefore resolved.

Chapter 5

Shifting of Power

Mahmud wiped the perspiration from his receding brow and sat heavily on the cedar wood chair in his bed chamber. He cursed repeatedly under his breath, rasping out expletives as he placed his head in his hands. The elderly advisor to Zengi slumped in the chair and felt the urge to scream in frustration. The days since his master had headed north to deal with the problems of his army were the darkest ones he had experienced since he had accepted the role of chief advisor to the Atabeg himself.

He had been ordered to gain the refund from the Assassins for the failed murder of the Egyptian noble; Nadirah and this was not going to happen. His contact through which the Hashini had been paid had disappeared, only to re-appear this morning; face down in the poor Muslim alleyways of Damascus; with his throat cut, slain presumably by the killers themselves to prevent any further discourse. Unable to contact this most private of groups and unwilling to send messengers to their likely deaths into their protected independent lands, he would have to inform the increasingly intolerant Zengi of the bad news when he returned in the morning.

To add to his woes, the news from Armenia had been concerning; with rumour of the prospect of Christian and Byzantine alliances reaching his ears. The initial victories over the Armenians had stalled and with Byzantine gold recruiting western and Greek mercenaries; Zengi's own mainly mercenary army had been gradually beaten back. His enraged leader publically executed the mercenary general as a warning to others that he would not brook weakness but this had failed to instil the anticipated resolve in his troops. In fact, hundreds had simply immediately melted away;

some to their own enemies' larger purse strings and others to the talismanic Kurdish general; Naim al-Din Ayyub, who ran the town of Baalbek, ostensibly under Zengi's rule but this was a man of vision and men of vision worried Mahmud. Ayyub had his own regiment of mercenaries, loyal only to himself and his power and influence was growing at an alarming rate. This was also the man that Nadirah provided funds to and a man who would ultimately need to be brought to heel or slain.

The Atabeg was with Ayyub at this very moment and Mahmud's spies had already been sending back reports of Zengi's hostility and arrogance in comparison to Ayyub's calm and welcoming approach. This shifting of power worried Mahmud as he reached across his desk and found his favourite deep blood-red wine from Syria and poured a large amount into the bronze goblet. Rubbing his aching temple, he thought of the many varied Islamic nations and peoples, who had spent so many decades fighting and killing each other. It was in this maelstrom and power vacuum that the Outlander Christians had come upon their lands like a dynamic force of nature, slaughtering all of the Chosen in their path and building Outremer; the Christian nation that now stained Allah's realm. Mahmud took a large sip of the refreshing liquid and remembered Zengi, the bold holy warrior in his prime, building an army of fanatical Islamic soldiers; creating a united Arabia to blunt the swords of the European settlers. Charismatic and brave, his master attempted to unify the Arab tribes to defeat the unwelcome infidels and his ideals were as great as his ego. However, the years had brought more wars and battles against fellow Muslims as the unity failed to last and Outremer developed into a nation which traded and allied with several of their own peoples to secure their sovereignty.

Zengi had been the best chance of the races of Islam to lead them to glory but as Mahmud drained his wine and refilled the goblet; he realised the dream was over and another's time was coming. Maybe Ayyub would manage what Zengi had failed to do and send the Outlanders back across the sea or maybe the Egyptians would find themselves a heroic leader. The adviser gulped the alcohol down and realised he was being watched from the doorway. A lithe form, half hidden by the shadows of the doorway studied him in silence.

"May Allah be with you, Mahmud? May I enter?"

The elder placed the goblet back on the desk and nodded, the heavy alcohol dulling his senses and he failed to completely mask the fleeting look of disdain as he recognised Nadirah's voice. He merely waved acceptance with his hand and the attractive Egyptian glided into his personal chamber and smiled easily at him; her lips pouting and her teeth perfect.

"And to what do I owe this pleasure?"

Mahmud asked, forcing politeness into his question and Nadirah strode forward to stand before him.

"I came to thank you again for your concern over the mysterious attack on my being. I am so pleased that our illustrious Emir was so worried for my health."

The sarcasm hung heavy in the words and Mahmud tried to ignore it and reached for his goblet of wine. His left hand snaked out towards it but he felt a sudden pang of pain in his throat and he coughed heartily, feeling the unpleasant taste of bile in his mouth. He swallowed hard and blinked as the exquisite features of Nadirah's face came closer.

"What is the matter old man? Something you drank, perhaps? Maybe if you adhered to the scripture and refrained from the poison?"

Her shrill, mocking laughter echoed around the curved walls of the chamber and Mahmud looked to the goblet of wine and tried to stand. His vision was blurring and he felt nausea sweep through him and he retched violently, vomiting next to his desk and staggered to his knees.

"You should have chosen your sides more carefully you fool. Zengi is teetering on the edge of insanity, seeing enemies all around him and trusting nobody. What will he think when his only trusted adviser will be found dead, murdered in his own bed chamber, surrounded by his personal guards. Oh my Mahmud, will that drive him over the edge?"

Mahmud vomited a second time and saw the dark colour as blood mixed with the liquid that projected from his mouth. He tried to respond to the scorn but his senses were failing and all his brain could focus on was that he was dying.

"Zengi will join you soon, do not worry. To think I thought that pathetic mad man was the Lion of Islam."

The sound in Mahmud's ears reminded him of being underwater and his third period of vomiting was pure blood and phlegm and he groaned in agony as he rolled into a ball on the stone floor. As his vision failed him, the last sight he saw was Nadirah's triumphant grin of what seemed pure ecstasy. The woman watched the man thrash slightly before dying with sordid interest and content that he was no longer mortal, she chuckled throatily and strode from the room.

****

The powerful black stallion carried its rider easily and gently across the desert trail as the sun rose in the east, casting a warm golden shadow across the silent realm of Outremer. James had left the outpost before any of his extended family had woken; the inability to sleep creating anxiety and the anxiety creating tension. The leather pouch of bezants bounced uncomfortably at his waist, tucked into his belt was sufficient to pay off Alessio's debt of honour to Francesco but it did leave a slight concern over available cash with the slave auction coming up at the oasis near Jaffa this weekend. The plan has been to purchase two more slaves and liberate them, giving them freedman rights of a wage, food and shelter. This had worked so well with Sharla and her sons and with so much work looming in the near future; the timing of Abdul's offer of companionship to the event seemed fortuitous. As an Outlander, any price from a Muslim owner would be doubled but with Abdul's knowledge and religion; the trader would bid on his behalf and get the best price available. The agreed deal with the Knights Hospitalliers temple at Acre for six mares was not to be completed until fourteen days hence so the availability of funds would mean that only one adult male slave of any worth could be purchased.

Sighing as he entered the stables at Acre's city gates, his mind churned through the other numerous concerns as he absently stroked Merdlan's flanks and went through the motions of paying the stable hand and trudging through the deserted Venetian Quarter, heading for 'The Caravel,' eager to rid his agitated brain of Francesco and the bitter memories his very name instigated. Pushing the elderly rogue from his thought processes momentarily, he heard Sharla voice her worry over Jacob's teaching and that a tutor was needed as had been done for Aisha. The basic education that Sharla, Aisha and he had provided was no longer enough and the naturally intelligent boy needed a more formal learning structure. Aisha also caused trepidation; the vision of her in the dress Maria had created proved to him beyond any doubt that she was a young woman and could not be treated as a girl any longer. The difficult conversation about future hopes and dreams that James had been putting off for months needed to be addressed and he told himself that this afternoon, when they would be together working; watering the vines, he would definitely broach that very subject.

Subduing his creative mind, he found his feet had found the tavern in the Genoan Quarter and he swore inwardly, took a deep breath and rapped on the door. A few moments of waiting in awkward trepidation ensued before the door opened inwardly; a heavily tanned man motioning James into the dark interior with a curved dagger in his left hand. With all of his senses on alert he strode uneasily into the empty bar; directed by a wave of the gleaming knife blade towards the staircase and he headed across the room and down the stairs as the sentry closed the entrance, the sound of the access being locked reverberating around the walls in the silence. Stifling his rising fear, James proceeded to the cellar where the card and dice games took place and as his eyes adjusted to the shade; he made out the outline of two figures at the table in the far corner. As he approached warily, the figures became more distinct and he recognised Francesco sat sipping something from a tin cup with the bulk of Aldo stood behind him.

"You are very early James."

The owner of the establishment said simply and James smiled thinly, nodding as he sat opposite Francesco.

"You have the money?"

He nodded again at the direct question and placed the pouch of coins on the hard wood. Taking heed of an almost imperceptible nod, Aldo picked up the leather purse and counted the coins out onto the table behind them. The seconds lengthened into minutes and James shifted uncomfortably under the intense stare of the older man. Aldo eventually completed his mathematics and confirmed the agreed amount to his employer who grinned briefly, his dark eyes flashing as he spoke.

"I knew you wouldn't let me down James. Your horse trading must be doing well. Selling horses to the Muslims and us Christians must be more profitable than I thought."

James stood and ignored the barbed comment, remaining calm.

"I think that concludes our transaction."

Francesco narrowed his eyes as the man opposite him stood before the conversation had ended and his brows furrowed. He despised rudeness and to compound the insolence, James turned on his heels and walked swiftly away from the table and up the staircase.

"You know where he lives?"

"Of course, Sir."

"Good. Keep an eye on him. I do not like that man and never have. He ruined my daughter and now he treats me with disdain. He will know manners that one! I need to know the layout of the grounds and how many men work for him. I don't want any nasty surprises when we decide to visit James and relieve him of all his money."

Aldo nodded in understanding and grinned, revealing the blackened husks that had once been teeth. Francesco looked at the mound of gold coins and smiled, wondering how many more mounds of bezants lay hidden in the log cabin, south of the port; where James had made his home with his motley array of black Africans, Jews and Muslims. Aldo scowled broadly; he despised these races. The whole reason the Christians had come to the Holy Land all those decades ago was to destroy the heathen. Pope Urban II himself preached the divine right of the Christians to rid Jerusalem of the unholy and now, just fifty years later, pathetic individuals like James were trading with these people, befriending them and even taking them into their home. He thudded the table with his clenched fist, causing the drinking vessel to topple over and the old man scratched his chin as he imagined the younger man's painful demise at his hands and the scowl changed to a manic sneer.

James reached the top of the stairs and let out a deep breath; his heart was thumping hard in his chest and perspiration covered his palms. He headed quickly to the door and laid his left hand on the rust laden handle and twisted, pausing when he heard his name spoken behind him. Releasing the mechanism, he recognised the soft voice and his body stiffened as he turned to face the oldest daughter of Francesco.

"Hello Sophia."

He stated nervously, unsure what to say to a former lover of some years ago and he looked on the Genoan woman in a state of awkward agitation.

"You look very well. Time has been kinder on you than I."

She spoke, the Italian accent strong in her gentle tone.

The man blushed slightly and raised an eyebrow, before responding with an easy smile.

"Your sight is failing you too in your old age I see."

The brunette in her thirties giggled coquettishly.

"Same as ever then James, always ready with a jest."

"You look the same as ever Sophia."

"No I do not. It has been ten years since you have seen me but thank you for the compliment."

The woman tilted her neck to look over James and her face became serious.

"You must take care. My Father. He hates you. He is a dangerous man."

The words tumbled from her as she looked fearfully over her shoulder at the staircase.

"I am not overly fond of Francesco either but the deal has been done. I do not need to bother him nor does he need to bother me in the future. What was done is past. Our paths do not need to cross again. I thank you for the warning though."

Sophia rushed across the bar and placed a hand on the man's shoulder.

"I mean it, James, be careful."

"I will. You do not need to worry about me."

The man smiled fleetingly and patted the offered hand gently.

"You take care too, Sophia."

With that he opened the door and strode out into the glorious sunshine onto the dusty street beyond, the warning ringing in his ears and he knew Sophia had reason to concern herself. Walking through the market traders and early risers of Acre, he remembered the hateful stare the tavern owner had given him as he stood and left the table and knew this was not to be the end of this matter. Trying to shake the impending feel of disaster from his head, he trudged past the Knights

Templar's impressive temple and to the docks where the first of the fishing boats were coming in across the placid easternmost part of the azure Mediterranean. His mind cleared as he watched the impressive skills of the fishermen, bring in net after net of fresh fish; their finely spun nets bulging with wriggling sea bass and tuna. As he watched the mixture of repatriated English, French, German and various Italian go about their business with the local Christians, Muslims and Jews; he wondered if there was hope after all for Outremer and his mood lifted momentarily until his keen eyesight spotted the hulking frame of Aldo; sat on the stone wall of the quayside. Francesco's henchman was a known criminal; having allegedly left Northern Italy for the crusades instead of facing the death penalty for murder and robbery. An enforcer and bodyguard, he rose swiftly through the Genoan underworld in Acre and was now clearly Francesco Amoretti's right hand man.

Ambling slowly through the market stalls of fresh food; James purchased a large fresh orange and peeled it carefully, loving the sweet taste of the ripe juice that flowed against his parched tongue. Taking his time to let the onlooker know he had seen him and knew he was there, James meandered his way through the Venetian Quarter and eventually arrived at Alessio's and Maria's cloth store, the brightly coloured awning already on display, indicating the shop was open for business. Entering the establishment, he found Maria discussing the positive aspects of Egyptian cotton with a middle aged customer and exchanging smiles; James moved through to the rooms beyond the shop and found Alessio drinking a heated herbal drink in the kitchen area.

"You are early!"

He exclaimed, placing his clay cup onto the table and clasping hand to wrist with his oldest friend.

"I wanted to pay off Francesco as soon as

possible."

"Understandable."
Alessio remarked with feeling and offered his guest the herbal drink. James politely declined, taking the secondary offer of cold water instead, sipping the liquid eagerly.

"I thought it would end the affair but Sophia warned me about her father and his pet; Aldo, has been following me since leaving the inn earlier."

Alessio swore under his breath.

"Aldo is no pet...more a wild beast and you spoke to Sophia? How did that conversation go?"

James attempted to ignore the flush that came to his own cheeks and the foolish grin his companion wore as he asked the second question.
"It was brief...awkward. I don't know why, it was so long ago. Have no idea why the old man cannot let it go."

Alessio's broad grin erupted into mirth as he explained in good humour;

"Oh I have no idea James? His first born daughter who was betrothed as a virgin to a member of the royal family of Outremer, a man who could have become the King of Jerusalem himself and you, my most esteemed friend, decided to make love to this woman and get caught in bed with her by her own father..."

The mocking explanation would have continued but Maria's appearance at the doorway to the kitchen stifled Alessio's appraisal of the past events.

"Leave it alone Alessio, it was 10 years ago now and I was not much more than a boy; younger than her and full of ale."

James defended his actions and Maria grimaced, saying vehemently.

"Are you two really talking of that whore; Sophia?"

"Now, now, sister of mine. I believe Sophia is the madam who looks after the establishment, not one of the ladies themselves."

"Does she work in a brothel?"

Maria demanded and Alessio shrugged and nodded his head, opening his hands in appeasement; knowing that when discussing the subject of previous lovers of James; his elder sister's emotional attachment would rear its' ugly head.

"Can we stop talking about this now...please?"

James said, looking to each of the sibling protagonists, continuing once he had received curt nods in return.

"I am more concerned as to why Aldo is following me when the transaction has been made and our business is over."

"The old fool thinks he owns Acre these days; his ego is immense. Let the beast follow us if he wants; this is not his port and if he breaks the law, I will happily arrange for the authorities to know exactly who is to blame."

Maria answered evenly and James smiled in response.

"Anyway, I am all packed; let me start repaying you."

Alessio stood, draining his cup. Hugging his sister, he whispered some genuine loving words and ducked into his bedchamber to pick up a large backpack. James hugged Maria briefly.

"Thank you for this. Look after him please, he may be an almighty pain, but he is all I have."

James acknowledged the hushed request with a smile and told the woman not to worry.

"Any problems get word to the Knights Hospitallers; I have dealings with them or Zacharias in the Jewish Quarter, he can get word to me through one of his sons. Alessio and I will come see you this Sunday."

"May God go with you both."

Maria said crossing herself as the two men departed for their four hour journey across the desert.

Chapter 6

The Prophecy

Imad Ad-Din Atabec Zengi Al Malik Al Mansir wiped the fresh blood from his curved dagger on the clothing of the dead guard and stood to his full height of six feet, his eyes glistening with impotent rage. Sheathing his blade at his waist, he kicked the still twitching corpse at his feet and screeched to the nervous on looking guards to remove the body immediately from his throne room. Seating himself wearily on the cushioned, elaborate chair on the raised dais, he surveyed the chamber with a baleful stare. Two men dragged their comrade from the room in obedient silence and every other occupant carefully and deliberately avoided his gaze.

Bellowing another order to leave him alone, he watched the various underlings file out in ill-concealed thankfulness and alone in the flickering glare of the numerous burning braziers; he mumbled a prayer to Allah, calling for his support in these dark times. He had returned three days ago from his trip to maintain the support of his mercenary forces in the north and this in itself had been an unsatisfying visit. Not for the first time in the past twelve months, he wondered if Allah had forsaken his people. The Muslims appeared more content to kill each other than to ally and defeat the infidel. His own generals and advisors urged their own very personal plans and ideals, dependent on their own history and race and he was tired; tired of the constant bickering and inaction. He was not blind to what was happening and he knew the time was near to either succeed or fail in his quest. There was no middle ground or alternative. His army was fracturing in Armenia; weak generals, demanding terrain, heavy losses and the reliance on mercenary troops had taken *its toll and without his constant presence, it was void of leadership. The Kurd general; Naim al-Din Ayyub had proven his worth and had been rewarded with control of a town but the devout loyalty of his warriors and his natural charisma worried him immensely. He needed him more than ever now against the Christians, who would not allow Edessa to fall without retribution, but the future ultimately would bring the death and destruction of the Kurdish horsemen once they had been useful. No man could be allowed to challenge his authority, however good a general that man may be. There were also his secret liaisons with the Egyptian snake; Nadirah and she was a woman no man could trust.*

For the hundredth time since his return, he wished his oldest and trusted adviser; Mahmud was here to discuss his next course of action with. In truth and only in his death did he realise how important the elder man had been to him over the years and he scowled darkly. Mahmud was dead. Murdered in his bedchamber in the home of Zengi himself and allegedly protected by handpicked guards. Even the Hashini themselves could not infiltrate his tower so clearly it had been somebody on the inside who had slain the aged counsellor. In the maelstrom of the emotive need to find the killer quickly; every guard and slave was questioned by his 'Immortals', his elite force of fundamentalist Islamic warriors. Strangely, it was the suspected traitor; Nadirah, who spotted a new Syrian slave attempt to flee the tower the following morning and the archers ended the miserable, pathetic life of the murderer.

The personal guard of Mahmud was tortured but could give them no information and was executed for failing to protect the advisor; slain by Zengi's own hand in full view of the other guards to show that this treason and incompetence could not be accepted. An intriguing conversation with Nadirah yesterday evening had yielded definite results and he thanked Allah for allowing the woman to live for however, untrustworthy she may be, she was a woman of uncommon intellect and insight. Mahmud had believed her a traitor to Zengi and arranged for the Hashini to assassinate her with his blessing. However, all that had been actually proven against her was that she had visited the Kurd general; Naim al-Din Ayyub and her explanation yesterday made some sense. A proud woman; Nadirah, replaced as a lover by another in his bed, needed to be away from the tower as she was hurt emotionally and advised by her soothsayer; the grotesque caricature of an old woman who called herself; Kalaama, to see Ayyub, who due entirely to Zengi's excellent choosing, was now one of the best generals in the vast powerful army under the Atabeg. Whether this was true or not did not really warrant the death sentence inflicted upon her and in this instance, he believed Mahmud's protectionist policy had been ill conceived.

More importantly was the simple fact that the hideous Kalaama had undoubted skills of prophecy. For months, his own dreams had been infiltrated by visions of failure and his own death, at the hands of an unknown but definitely Christian slayer. Mahmud had brought in every seer in the vicinity and beyond and none had dared to tell him the truth, claiming the dreams were merely stress induced or evil signs sent from the priests of the infidel. Pressing Nadirah to force her pet soothsayer to read the entrails for Zengi himself, Kalaama calmly informed him of his impending death within the year, slain at the hands of a Christian swordsman. Ignoring the hollow feeling of panic enveloping him, he pressed for information on how to avoid this destiny and his cloak of fear evaporated as the solution was simply pointed out to him. Slay the murderer before the prophesised time and destiny will change accordingly. Finding use for the witch and happy that Allah had protected the untrustworthy but useful Nadirah, he ordered Kalaama to find out using her talent who the killer was. Ordering every weird and wonderful ingredient required by the mystic for this purpose, he had awaited the result impatiently and unable to sleep; he passed the time by studying the maps of Outremer and studying the perceived strength of each Christian town, port and castle.

The two women returned after six hours of foretelling and divination and Zengi was advised that he was to be slain by the Infidel who saved Nadirah from the Hashini. The irony was not lost on the Atabeg and he could not prevent the smile at the Almighty's sense of humour. Clearly a professional killer of some skill to slaughter three trained assassins alone, this problem was an easy one to solve as Nadirah's eyes sparkled in the gloom advising him that she knew exactly where a man called Abdul lived, a traitor to his own people as he was a friend of the Outlander even though he was a Muslim. With some persuasion, this Abdul would obviously give up all he knew of the Westerner known as James. With a sense of power welling inside of him, he had bid the two women goodnight and slept like a baby for the rest of the night, for the first time in many months.

Now, as the early afternoon sunshine streamed through the glass paned windows of the chamber in the upper part of the tower; he studied the fresh blood stain of one of the guards who had failed to stop the murdering servant from fleeing on his polished stone floor and smiled broadly. The tide was turning at last in his favour and his smile broadened as Saddiq's muscular frame entered the room. Saddiq was the leader of the 'Immortals', Zengi's best and most awesome warriors; his elite fighting force who slaughtered all non-believers at his request.

"Ahhhh...Saddiq, come closer, have some wine, I have a little task for you; you will only need only a few of your men but I want you to lead the mission personally; it is of the greatest consequence to me and to the whole of the Islamic world that a certain Outlander's life is ended, as swiftly as possible."

The dark eyes narrowed and he removed the

black silk scarf from his mouth and chin and the man nodded simply.

"He is an infidel called James and I want him to die a most painful death Saddiq, a most painful death…."

The response to this chilling command was a thin smile and the formidable Arab moved forward to get the detailed orders from his Master.

****

Sharla passed a tankard of ale to the man who had given her a true sense of worth and bustled away back inside the cedar wood log cabin. James accepted the drink gratefully and smiled as she headed inside for her next task and wondered how he had ever coped before he had brought the North African woman and her two sons into his home and his life. Retaining the smile, his hazel eyes moved back to Alessio and Jacob who were pretending to be knights with wooden toy swords; the young boy giggling and squealing in pleasure as Alessio fell to the ground with a theatrical tumble, rolling over and over.

"I am the King's champion!"

Jacob jumped with his arms in the air, turning to the watching James and Aisha with a triumphant boyish grin adorning his features. The teenager turned to her guardian and chuckled happily;

"I am glad Alessio has come here; the past three days have been such fun."

James watched his old friend rise from the sandy earth and lift the laughing boy into the air with a flourish.

"Alessio shares Jacob's maturity level so life is

all about having fun to him. He has always been the same; nothing really brings him down."

A slight sense of envy washed over him and he quashed it instantly, replacing it with pride in his friend.

"Jacob adores him. It is so good to see him so happy."

Aisha said softly and James agreed as the girl stood and headed into the kitchen to help Sharla prepare the evening meal of chicken and vegetable broth, leaving the man to his thoughts. James rubbed his freshly shaven face and looked beyond the two figures playing to the rows of vines; stretching from the cabin for two hundred yards eastwards where the low boundary of a wooden fence marked out the territory he had bought from the authorities of Acre; almost five years ago. His knowledge of the wine trade, cultivated under Georges and aided by his French contacts in Acre, Haifa and Caesarea meant that he was to plant his own vines and produce his own wine. This being a long term project and without regular funds at his disposal, James used his love and natural expertise with horses to trade them between European settlers and the Arabian peoples to ease his cash flow initially. However, the need for horses became immense and within twelve months, James had built a good reputation and by buying foals from the various Bedouin tribes and training, grooming and preparing them; the lure of making substantial sums proved too much and he invested in a stable and a rudimentary irrigation system complete with a fully operational deep stone well. This created a sandy earth more suitable for the vines and horses and now both projects were bringing considerable wealth to the owner.

Sharla's loud call for Jacob to come and wash before supper brought the expected disappointment and cursory objection, prior to Jacob hugging both Alessio and James, before heading inside. The Venetian lowered himself down next to James and sat cross legged beside him and sipped the other man's ale, grinning cheekily.

"You have a good thing going here. The kids are great, your workers are loyal and your home is beautiful. A long way from living in that tiny house with Georges next to Montjoie."

"Seems an age ago now Alessio, but it was the best choice for me."

"I can see that; you are a different man now James. It suits you and you have done so much good. Georges would be very proud you know?"

James clasped his companion on the shoulder in a gesture of appreciation.

"I hope so. He taught me so much. I don't mean just the business stuff, I mean about life, religion, family and about Outremer itself."

Alessio nodded in understanding and raised the tankard of ale and stated simply;

"To Georges."

Passing the remaining ale to James, he repeated the vow and drained the alcohol.

"I need to check the horses before supper."

James added and rose wearily; it had been a long day and his limbs ached. A sudden unwelcome thought of his age forced itself upon his brain and he masked the scowl from his companion.

"I need to clean up before the meal."

Alessio grinned and the two men parted as the Italian headed inside, leaving James to stride to the main gate as the sun began to set dramatically on the horizon. He closed and locked the solid wooden gate and began his nightly stroll around the perimeter of his small holding; the four feet barrier marking out his land. Keeping his eyes wide open on both sides of the partition; his thoughts drifted to the events of the past three days since he and Alessio had returned from Acre and he smiled. The worrying attack on the unknown woman had receded into his memory and the widespread fear of total war between Christian and Muslim once again, had also seemed to dissipate over the past week. Zengi's assault and massacre at Edessa had not been followed up with any major battle and news from the northern realms of Outremer advised his Islamic troops had been defeated in a number if skirmishes and if rumour was to be believed; his own generals and warriors were unconvinced with Zengi's violent and authoritative leadership. If the Knights Templars and the more reckless religious leaders could be controlled by Baldwin III, drastic bloodshed could be avoided.

Looking over the beautiful landscape that drifted in artistic sand dune formations towards the azure Mediterranean to his west and the verdant, lush vineyard immediately behind him; he hoped this land could avoid another all-encompassing war, which could destabilize the entire region. Striding around the barrier, his mind moved to events closer at home and how even in the smallholding itself, things were better than ever. His conversation with Aisha about her future brought only joy to him as her response was direct and unequivocal; her immediate future was here with James and Jacob. Sharla was happy as Alessio had sorted out a Jewish tutor in Acre for Jacob; free of charge as the elderly man was lonely and relished the prospect of performing a useful act. Alessio had organised Maria to provide his four daughters with handmade outfits so no funds were needed for the three lessons a week. Jacob was happy as another man was now spending time spoiling and playing with him and Aboulias and Jamaal were happy as the heavy burden of their work was substantially reduced with Alessio's involvement. James ceased walking suddenly and realised that most of the improvements were down to the arrival of his Venetian friend and he grinned; a rush of pleasure on behalf of Alessio pumping through his veins. Completing his daily routine in high spirits, he entered the kitchen less than fifty minutes later; embracing the warmth of the crackling log fire and the even warmer sense of love and companionship as Alessio, Jacob, Aisha, Jamaal and Aboulias sat waiting for him as Sharla fluttered around them with drinks. Closing the door, James thought only of his mother's favourite saying; 'Vita e bueno.'

The rich, perfectly spiced broth was accompanied by freshly baked unleavened bread and followed by a plethora of ripened fruit and the conversation was brisk; positive and good humoured. By the time the North Africans had retired to their own cabin for the evening and Jacob and Aisha had headed reluctantly to bed; Alessio and James were halfway down their second bottle of Syrian wine.

"So why no wife James, that is probably the only element missing from this Eden you have created."

Alessio asked directly, the wine loosening his tongue and he chuckled as his friend blanched visibly.

"Do I need a wife...do I not look happy?"

The evasive response failed to stem the tide however.

"Okay, why no lover? We all need love and not just that of our workers and children."

James drained his glass and refilled both, giving his mind the time needed to find a suitable answer that Alessio would accept without further questioning.

"There have been lovers but never really the one you know, the special, eternal one that everybody speaks of."

"Pah…stuff for women and priests. We all need a lover and you need a wife as well. Look around Acre James, how many married couples do you see jumping for joy? They are contented in their own way but they need each other. Are all those married couples in a permanent state of excited bliss; I think not."

James grinned.

"Well now that you have explained it to me in those terms, why would anybody not want a wife? Anyway, you have no wife so why dictate terms to me?"

"Ah, but I am a shallow, selfish man who is alone in this world. I have no need for a wife; I have not built a home, built a business, taken on children, employed workers. I have no need of a wife, but you my friend, you need a wife. There are options you know. You are not old, how old are you by the way?"

In a state of humorous disbelief, James responded simply that he was twenty nine and let the partially intoxicated Venetian to pursue his intended course.

"You are fairly wealthy and not bad looking."

"I never knew you cared in that way Alessio!"

Pointedly ignoring the sarcastic remark, the Italian barely paused for breath.

"Now what about Maria? She has adored you for years, since we were boys. Her torch for you has never expired and she is unmarried. True, she can be annoying with her sarcastic sense of humour and she has a sharp tongue but she is a good looking woman."

"Are we really having this conversation?"

James spoke feigning indignation but he knew the conversation needed to be concluded or this could last until dawn.

"There is nothing wrong with Maria; she is clever, witty, caring and beautiful. But...she is like a sister to me and I already love her in that way. And, she is actually your sister and that would make us brothers by marriage and I do not think I could cope at all with that."

Alessio frowned at his companion's levity and progressed, undeterred.

"Okay, what of Sophia? You have already experienced her...ahem...talents shall we say and she is keen I feel. Otherwise, why warn you of her father if she did not at least care?"

"You are unbelievable! It was almost a decade ago and it was a very brief affair which ended in me being beaten by her insane father's thugs. Why would I want to be related to the vilest man in the whole of Acre, perhaps Outremer itself?"

Taking a deep gulp of the sweet wine, he did his best to glare at Alessio but his attempt at putting the man off his stride failed miserably.

"Hmmm...I suppose I can understand that. Shame, she is a very striking woman. Okay, well if you are not going for looks alone, what about Sharla?"

The throaty chuckle that came after the statement continued as James laughed with him, abusing his comrade in the most colourful of ways.

"Sharla is in her early fifties I believe but that is not to say she does not have her charm and I do indeed love her dearly. She does more for me and our home than you could ever imagine in your twisted little mind! Now, let us discuss something else."

"Okay, okay, enough on weddings but I will take it upon myself to find you a suitable wife; it is the only thing missing in your life."

James smiled but finally managed to lead the conversation back to the coming trip to the slave auction, outside the Kingdom of Jerusalem and that caution was required as they were heading into the Saracen lands beyond Lake Tiberius and Jacob's Ford, the accepted boundary of the Outremer and the numerous Arab states. Alessio accepted the warnings readily as unlike many of the immigrants from the West, the Venetian had no radical Catholicism and although a believer in the Christian doctrine; he accepted people on their own merits and worth, rather than the skin tone or religious persuasion. This rather unusual trait in Alessio had always matched evenly with James and had brought them close together, even as teenagers in the Venetian Quarter of Acre. Brought back to serious conversation once again, Alessio asked about Abdul; knowing him vaguely and only through the trade and business dealings, James had had with him on previous occasions.

The twenty nine year old explained that he had known Abdul since becoming a wine trader and he had aided him immensely in building and expanding the small holding, had made trade possible with the various Muslim factions and indirectly; through losing card and dice games, provided James with Sharla, Aboulias, Jamaal and his favourite mount, the powerful stallion; Merdlan. In short, James admitted, with the death of Georges and the estrangement from his mother; Abdul had filled the gap of mentor and advisor, if not exactly a parent. Alessio nodded in comprehension through heavy eyelids and he stood, swayed a little and then held onto the back of the chair for balance.

"So, to which God do you pray James? You seem more Muslim than Christian, out here, away from the safety of the city gates with Arabs as neighbours."

"I have no God, Alessio."

James said seriously, finishing the wine in his glass and placing it carefully beside his hand.

"We all pray to some God, be it the Christian one, the Jewish one or the Muslim one…or any other one for that matter."

Alessio seemed genuinely puzzled and James smiled to ease the tension he instantly felt when discussing religion.

"There is no religion here in this dwelling. It is due to religion that my family exists here. Think about it, without the Pope demanding Jerusalem be brought into Christian hands, my father would never have come here and never met my mother. Without the Egyptian Muslims expanding all across the deserts of North Africa; Sharla, Aboulias and Jamaal would never have been enslaved and brought to this land. Without the misguided attacks on Jewish settlements throughout Outremer, Christian gangs would not have destroyed Jacob's home and murdered his parents leaving him an orphan to be sold as a slave, destined to fill the Mamluk slave army or worse. Without the Muslim atrocities of Zengi against his own peoples; Aisha would not have had to flee a massacre when her village was put to the torch just to feed his army when the elder refused the order to give over all their food supplies. It was religion that created our very family here but I will not allow religion to destroy it."

The usually placid eyes blazed in the candle

light as James clenched his fists as he spoke earnestly. Alessio thought better to say anything contradictory and nodded, bidding him goodnight but padding to his bedchamber with a touch of fear at the blasphemous words he had heard. Crossing himself, he prayed forgiveness from God for his friend and undressed for bed in some distress for his oldest friend's soul.

Chapter 7

Knights and Slaves

James welcomed the permanently affable Abdul and his three eldest sons happily on the clear, warm morning of Saturday the 18th February. Introducing Alessio to the four; a cacophony of greetings in various languages and clasping of wrists, backs and patting of shoulders ensued. Too early for all the denizens of the small holding to be wake with the obvious exception of Sharla who waved the six figures off out of the gates; her own concerns about the trip hidden behind her smile.

Abdul's sons led the way up the desert trail towards the port of Acre but then across the well-trodden trade route, which ended at the southern crossing of the River Jordan, which was heavily guarded by knights from the King of Jerusalem's army and which marked the end of his rule and sovereignty. Beyond that crossing lay the deserts of Syria and the various rival factions of the Islamic peoples. Although slavery was tolerated in Outremer, it was far from welcomed and thus the slave markets existed in Muslim territory as in the Arabian world, slaves were currency and more slaves simply equated to more wealth. Alessio frowned upon slavery but saw its place in the foreign world he now called home and in truth, was intrigued to see a slave auction in process. James despised the very concept of slavery and was convinced that a free man who had a home and food would work better than a man enslaved. All of the six men who travelled knew that the Outlander would purchase a slave today and then free them instantly, risking his funds as the slave may well simply flee the smallholding at the first opportunity. This very conversation was developing between the three older riders who meandered some way behind the leading

87

pack when those ahead halted and waved frantically for their attention. The talking immediately ceased and all kicked their horses into a full gallop to see what the development was.

James reached the three young Arabian men first, the powerful stride pattern of his ebony stallion easily beating the smaller mares his companions rode. His eyes followed the outstretched arm and finger and narrowed his eyelids as he strained to see through the sun's haze into the distance. On an arid stretch of scrubland, a pathetic array of goats and sheep grazed away on the tiny amount of vegetation, a little way from a teenage herdsman who was clasping his face and sat on the ground, shaking his head at three armoured men who wore tunics bearing the emblem of a red cross on a white background.

"Knights Templar...."

He whispered almost inaudibly as Alessio and Abdul reigned in their mounts either side of him.

"Having some fun with a goat herder...."

Alessio grimaced and spat on the earth below, indicating his obvious distaste.

"Not our business James, come on."

Abdul nudged his companion and pulled the leather harness for his horse to avoid the scene and progress along the trade route. His sons moved to follow him but James had already kicked his heels softly into Merdlan's flanks and was trotting towards the knights and the herdsman. As all observers watched one of the knights kick the boy as he sat on the earth, the trot became a gallop and Alessio cursed loudly and followed suit. Sighing and nodding to his sons, Abdul urged his own steed into pursuit and the six riders kicked up a dust cloud as they galloped across the barren wilderness.

James kept a steady gaze on the three knights who turned to see him advance rapidly and noted the drawing of their long swords as he reduced Merdlan's speed, shouting a greeting in French and removing his keffiyen to show that he was of European descent. Pulling up the stallion for dramatic effect a few metres short of the protagonist, he stared at the man's surcoat with a look of disgust.

"What is the meaning of this?"

James spoke in halting French and pointed to the boy, whose face was cut and bleeding profusely.

"None of your business, Monsieur."

The fluent, blunt response was stated coldly by the man who placed the tip of the sword gently onto the ground and watched the five other men pull up their animals beside the European man who was dressed as a Saracen. Noting that four of his companions appeared to be Muslims, suspicion immediately transformed into arrogant hostility.

"Do not involve yourselves with affairs of the Temple."

James laughed sardonically and pointed to the cowering teenage boy.

"The Temple sends its knights to beat teenage goat herders now does it...how times have changed?"

The knight's left eye twitched unconsciously and he glared at James balefully.

"The boy is no more than a thief, we offered to purchase one of his sheep at a good price and he refused, wanting a price more befitting a horse. I was merely teaching him some Godly manners."

James ignored Abdul's warning look and Alessio's calming hand on his forearm, spying a decapitated sheep near the silent pair of knights. Without moving his fixed stare from the swordsman in front of him, he calmly asked Abdul to ask the boy how much he wanted for the animal. Abdul translated and the fearful teenager advised five silver pieces.

"Is that a fair price for such a sheep?"

James asked flatly and Abdul agreed that it was indeed a good price in the current market.

"Pay the boy five silver pieces for the animal you have slain and five more for the damage you have done to his face."

"And why should I do that?"

The man snarled and turned to look at his two fellow Templars for support.

"Because as Knights Templars you are to show an example to us all how to behave and you certainly should not steal from and beat up those who are younger and weaker than you."

The Frenchman merely snorted and turned abruptly, heading to his horse as the other men also mounted their great beasts that bore chain mail coverings themselves. James loaded his crossbow swiftly and raised the weapon, pointing it directly at the aggressor, enjoying the look of abstract panic contort his features as he wheeled his horse around.

"Give the boy a bezant right now or I swear to your God that I will shoot you down as a common thief and bully."

Abdul swore inwardly and shifted uncomfortably on his blanket as the knight slowly allowed his impotent rage to subside. Tossing a solitary bezant, worth ten silver pieces to the ground he said with a bitter smile;

"I will remember your face and we will meet again."

"I look forward to it monsieur."

James shrugged in reply as the three Knights Templar slowly cantered away from the area. Alessio dismounted and helped the boy to his feet, bending to pick up and hand him the bezant.

"You pick your enemies most unwisely James."

Abdul stated as he watched the three knights depart.

"Maybe so but they embarrass themselves and their Temple by acting as they did today. "

The older trader nodded thoughtfully and spoke in Arabic to the herdsman who approached James and bowed slightly.

"I thank you kind sir. I too will remember your face and I pray to Allah we meet again for me to thank you properly."

Touched by the boys' warmth, James nodded and waited for Alessio to sit astride his horse once more, before they all continued eastwards, leaving the young herder elated with his coin, his cut face forgotten amidst the jubilation of relative wealth. Waving to the Outlander, he watched the men ride off eastwards where the arid landscape turned to desert until he could see mere dots on the horizon. Only then did he gather his animals into a rough circle and move them north along the rough pathway towards the sparse Bedouin camp he called home.

The group rode across the barren landscape swiftly and in silence; all lost in their own thoughts and all scouring the sand for any further signs of trouble. Abdul watched James ride ahead of him and was worried for the man. He was a good man with a fine heart but he always seemed to make people choose to be his enemy or his friend. In any land, that was a dangerous way to behave but in this land, it was the quickest way to meet Allah. Abdul had seen first-hand what religion had done to the Holy Land and simmering hostility raged everywhere under the surface. Christian hated Muslim. Muslim hated Jew. Christian hated Jew. Muslim loathed and betrayed Muslim. Christian loathed and betrayed Christian. However, when the war came and come it would certainly do; you had to belong to one side or the other and the man who rode so casually ahead of him did not seem to have a side. Clearing these depressing thoughts, he concentrated on his riding skills and marvelled at those shown by the man in front. James was a naturally skilled horseman and although he used the leather saddle to maintain balance as all white men did; his ability was better than most Arabs who had been born and bred on horses. His eyes lowered to the dark stallion that he sat astride and inwardly cursed as he marvelled over the beauty, strength and grace of the beast. To think that animal had been his once and then lost, gambling him in a game of chance; humility was learnt that day and a great price had been paid for pride.

The party stopped to rest their horses and partake of a much needed drink of cold water before continuing to the fortified river crossing, where they succumbed to a lethargic search of their saddlebags and a series of mundane questions as to who they were, where they were going and what they intended to do. Truthful answers were provided to the bored and listless guards and they passed into an area of the world ruled by Zengi, or at least provisionally ruled by his mercenary bands and various independent Emirs, who paid token allegiance to the Atabeg's rule. At Abdul's advice; brightly coloured Keffiyah were worn around their heads to give the impression all of the group were locals and thus, deter any unnecessary and unwelcome interest in them.

For four arduous hours, with infrequent and fleeting stops for water, the six men cantered across the well-worn path through the desolate tract of land to the Im'yah Oasis, a place the various Bedouin tribes congregated and it had become synonymous as one of the greatest trading posts in all of Syria. Abdul frequented the place regularly and was well known to many of the Bedouin elders as a fair merchant, fond of haggling but ultimately a man of honour who always paid a reasonable price. A man could purchase anything he desired at Im'yah on market days; from the most mundane tool or food to the most exotic animal or spice. Garish tents and blankets filled with bizarre weaponry, outlandish clothing and colourful gem stones mixed with the religious artefacts, historical scrolls and vellum parchments which provided information from ingredients for soup recipes to love potions. However, throughout the Muslim world, the oasis was best known for its monthly slave auction and whether you wanted a man, woman, boy or girl for work or pleasure; a healthy specimen would be found here. No questions were ever asked or answers required, if you had the coin, you could purchase a human life. Today, this monthly event was taking place and the six faces exchanged glances as they pulled up and stabled their mounts at the outskirts of Im'yah. Hundreds if not thousands of people were present, crowding the market stalls and shattering the silence of the desert with the noise of laughter, haggling, shouting and swearing. The huge frame of Abdul led the others through the mass, oblivious to the heaving crowds and the calls of the stall owners, intent on gaining a good position at the slave market and to be able to have more than a brief glance at the merchandise before bidding.

Following his companions, James strode through the heaving multitude, his inquisitive eyes looking upon the vast array of products available; far more choice than at the markets in Acre or Caesarea. He thought of Aisha and how she would love this place to browse and barter but this was no place for a young girl and as he squeezed past a tall Saracen, James noticed the suspicious glance in his direction as his pale skin and hazel eyes were viewed.

"We are in luck, my friends, there are many to choose from!"

Abdul exclaimed excitedly, the merchant in his element in such surroundings and the six figures emerged from the host of potential customers and into a circular area with a raised wooden stage in the centre. To one side of the stage was a covered awning where the slaves stood, nervously awaiting their turn to be put on display by their current owners. Armed guards loitered nearby, watching the proceedings with impassive faces. A short, overweight man in purple robes; complete with an effeminate high-pitched voice talked excitedly to the assembly; pausing only to poke or move the poor young man who stood next to him in nothing more than a loincloth to cover his modesty. Abdul nudged James in the ribs and pointed to the area in the shade where the slaves were lined up and all of the party headed over to view the human specimens.

Alessio looked at James momentarily with eyes that showed the same sense of distaste and James nodded in understanding. Their older comrade was sharing his experience at such events, droning on about what to look for in a slave; the state of a set of teeth, marks of beatings or whippings and so forth but neither of the Westerners really listened as they viewed the array of mortal offerings. The men and women either looked void of emotion, hostile and angry or just plain terrified. There were many ages, shapes and nations represented from black Nubians, wiry Kurds, Arabs of all skin tone and race but none of European ancestry. James raised this with Abdul and he shrugged; claiming that they were too near the border with the Kingdom of Jerusalem and any excuse could be used for war right now. The only Christians you would find were Syrian Christians; persecuted for their beliefs by Muslims and abjectly ignored by the European settlers who distrusted them as 'Saracens'.

Abdul was seeking a helper for his wife to undertake household duties and James was seeking a strong healthy male to help Aboulias and Jamaal with the physically demanding work connected with the horses and around the small holding, enabling him to concentrate on the vineyards and the wine selling. Alessio would not stay forever; his incessant need for adventure would make the place tedious to him in a few short weeks. The extra pair of hands had proven invaluable however and therefore a ready replacement was required. Uneasy at looking people over as he did horses, James walked the line of the next group up for auction and wondered what personality type to bid for. He believed that the ones who stared back at him balefully would flee at the first opportunity once he had granted them freedom and yet the ones who looked void of emotion generally looked weak and pathetic, as if the very essence of life had already been extinguished. Focusing on the ones who looked fearful, James believed this category would fit in better; if treated with respect and care and given a home, food and a wage, hopefully they would react as Sharla and her boys had done.

A series of blank or hostile faces met or purposefully avoided his gaze and as he moved around the other buyers; he took note of three separate fearful looking young men. All were of Arab extraction and all looked relatively fit and healthy although it was hard to tell with a brief appraising glance. Nodding to Alessio who lingered behind him that he had the little information he was likely to get, they moved in unison

95

back to their companions, who stood within a larger huddle of men. The heaving mass surrounded the female contingent of slaves and significant attention seemed to be on the five terrified looking young women; dressed in diaphanous robes, leaving little to the imagination.

"Girls from the East. Soon to be concubines it seems."

Abdul's deep voice said as if this explained everything to the Westerners, who merely exchanged puzzled looks. The 'East' to those of Syrian, Egyptian or Palestinian birth were the oceans of sand that stretched for hundreds of miles under scorching skies known to all simply as Arabia.

"Beautiful are they not?"

James masked the look of dismay from his features as Abdul asked him a direct question and he tried to ignore the lascivious bidders, who clamoured around the frightened women, held at bay only by the armed guards who protected the slaves prior to sale. Muttering his agreement, his eyes met the almost pitch black orbs of one of the enslaved women, whose haunted look seemed to be screaming out in silence for some form of salvation. The victim, no more than eighteen years of age was of slim build with dark ringlets of hair which cascaded onto her shoulders; oval almost charcoal coloured eyes bristled with hurt pride. Her skin was dark olive in hue and the smooth perfection of it bore a soft sheen of perspiration, caused by the heat and fear in equal measure. She was not beautiful as such to James but certainly striking and almost enigmatic in a way he did not fully understand. As he turned he saw Alessio stare open mouthed at her in undisguised lust before dropping his eyes in embarrassment.

"The bidding starts on the woman I want in a

moment; stay with me James, I need you to nudge me when you wish to bid."

Abdul reminded him and he turned his attention away from the woman and moved nearer to the raised dais where a dark skinned nervous African had just been purchased by an opulently dressed Egyptian. Alessio and James remained vigilant and silent for the next twenty minutes as poor unfortunates were paraded on the grim stage to the baying crowd and bought for varying amounts of coin. The merchant showed his eye for a bargain by purchasing a plain looking female slave approaching middle age for a very small sum, content that she would have the skills and experience to support his household without concerning his wife with beauty or youth.

The first of the Eastern women was then put on the platform and the bidding was brisk and fierce as affluent traders competed for the pleasures such a female could bring to an owner. James observed the type of bidder with scorn and a deep feeling of sadness and pity for the slave, whose future looked incredibly bleak.

"Your choices will be up after the girls."

Abdul explained quietly and James hoped they would be; his first visit to a slave market would also almost certainly be his last. The second woman; pushed heavily into the maelstrom of noise, was the one he had watched earlier and a great deal of early hands raised the bidding to a high level swiftly. He felt a pang of emotion he could not fully quantify as a morbidly obese, elderly man in flowing azure silk seemed to be winning the auction much to the amusement of his fawning entourage. Seeing the primitive desire in his bulging eyes, James prodded Abdul who merely raised an eyebrow at his friend before raising his hand. Alessio watched in growing concern as the value of the stake increased and eventually, at a price more than double that of the first girl, the corpulent Muslim shook his head and James had gained his new addition. In mystified silence, Abdul handed over his own and his companion's money to an ecstatic auctioneer and the two female captives were handed unceremoniously over to him.

Cutting a swathe through the enormous gathering, the motley band made their way to their horses and as Abdul's sons purchased some freshly cooked spiced meat for all; the trader shook his head at James and advised the younger slave who she now belonged to in Arabic.

"I am not sure Abdouleye and Jamaal are going to be thrilled with your choice in new worker."

Abdul grinned and Alessio stared at James with humorous derision, murmuring that they may well be very thrilled with his choice of slave.

"I am not convinced she is going to be able to help them with the heavy labour and long hours outside."

James swore and smiled apologetically.

"What do you want from me? I did not want to imagine what would happen to the girl if that old lecher got his hands on her; she can help Sharla out and support Aisha and Jacob. It will be fine. I will explain."

The two men who faced him laughed at the hurried and stuttering explanation. The eldest man of the three grinned wanly and patted the flushed speaker on the shoulder.

"It is up to you what you spend your money on my friend. If you want a pretty girl to warm your bed, who are we to argue?"

Winking at Alessio who chuckled at the righteous indignation that spread across the small holder's expressive features, Abdul roared with laughter before holding his hands palm side up.

"We are teasing you. She looks healthy and has intelligence behind those eyes. I am sure she will be useful. It will help your Arabic too as she probably only speaks our language."

Taking his leave of the two men of Outremer with a slight bow; the merchant led his own slave away to where his sons congregated, crouched on the ground eating the saffron infused meat.

"I did it for the right reasons."

James said earnestly to Alessio who smiled affectionately.

"I know James but you cannot save everybody you know, especially in this world. Now I will get us some provisions while you sort out the girl and let us get away from this god forsaken place!"

James watched him saunter off to a nearby stall selling hot breads and other unknown local cuisine and turned to smile at the nervous woman who stood alone. Heading to Merdlan, he stroked the great beast's flanks gently and removed a thin olive green cape, used to protect from desert storms and approached the slave offering her the garment. The dark eyes narrowed suspiciously for a moment before taking the cloth and thanking him in Arabic, before placing it around her, covering her modesty. Practising his rudimentary Arabic in his head before speaking, James commenced the stilted conversation.

"I am James. I have a home near Acre, in Outremer. You will come with me. I am not going to harm you, in any way."

The woman stared into his eyes as he spoke hesitantly, trying to pronounce the words as accurately as possible. Her head moved slightly showing understanding but said nothing. James asked her name and offered her his water skin, seeing the grazes on her flesh around ankles and wrists, where chains or rope had held her captive.

"I am Jaeda."

He smiled and asked if she spoke any other language and winced inwardly as she shook her head. Deciding not to discuss the details of what he was offering Jaeda in what was his fourth language; some distance behind English, Italian and French; he knew he would have some explaining to do back at the cabin but as was his way, his brain was already believing Jaeda would be a better addition to the household than another male worker. The positives of helping Sharla with cooking and cleaning, supporting Jacob and Aisha and adding whatever individual skills she may have soon overwhelmed his initial concerns and as Alessio strolled back languidly with honey glazed bread, he was convinced he had made the right choice.

"This is lovely."

Alessio grunted as he chewed the food, sharing the warm, freshly cooked bread with James and Jaeda. The Venetian understood even less Arabic than his compatriot so the three ate their fill in uncomfortable silence. Introductions were made and vague smiles exchanged but the woman clearly remained frightened about the future with these foreign men. Unable to master the language enough to appease her viable concerns, James remained quiet, feeling Aisha and Sharla would be better equipped to ease the fear in the young woman. Completing their simple meal, James waved to Abdul and the group began to mount their horses and commence the return journey. As Merdlan was by far the more powerful horse than Alessio's young mare, Jaeda would ride behind James. Wishing to leave the slave market as swiftly as possible, he sat astride his faithful horse and helped Jaeda to clamber behind him; waiting for the girl to adjust her clothing to sit as James did with legs either side of the leather saddle. Tentatively, she placed her arms around her new owner's waist and ignoring Alessio's broad grin, James nudged Merdlan into a slow trot, bringing up the rear of the assembled party as they moved away from the noise and smells of the gathering.

The return journey was uneventful and the group rested only briefly to water themselves and their beasts of burden. Jaeda was quiet and James used the silence to get his explanation in order for the others who were awaiting him at home. Finding answers for any prospective awkward questions and balancing the positives and negatives in his mind, he was content that his decision remained sound and when he bid Abdul and his sons a fond farewell at the stone bridge, which crossed the placid tributary of the Abuja River; he remained convinced of his choice. Reluctantly agreeing to Abdul's offer of an evening of cards and dice the following day, much to Alessio's excitement, he knew he owed the merchant for today and to refuse would be seen as impolite by the venerable trader. His smile broadened as the two horses approached the physical boundary of the small holding just two miles beyond the bridge and he saw Jacob and Aisha waving to them from the orchard, where Sharla had clearly had the children watering the vines from the well. The easy smile and confidence decreased somewhat however when he looked at the faces of Sharla and Aisha as he dismounted inside the wall and helped Jaeda from Merdlan.

"I know, I know…Give me a chance to explain."

Aisha's surprised expression softened and she kissed James briefly on the cheek and hailed the newcomer with a smile and a fluid Arabic greeting. Sharla maintained her suspicious gaze but this was fixed at James and not Jaeda before she too smiled and welcomed the girl to her new home.

"Can you show her the cabin and see if she needs to bathe or freshen up or whatever Sharla? I will see to the horses and then be in."

Jacob ran up and hugged his stomach and James tousled his hair briefly as the boy then hurried over to Alessio to do the same gesture. Alessio immediately picked up the boy and tossed him around bringing whoops of joy and much giggling. Sharla led Jaeda inside gently and Aisha grinned at him.

"Will finish the watering off and then be in, I cannot wait to see you and Sharla sort this out!"

Calling for Jacob to follow her and eventually, he acquiesced, albeit with much complaining.

Alessio clapped his thoughtful companion on the back and chuckled as the two men led the horses to the stables for the evening and where the North African brothers were working on fitness and obedience training for the three young colts.

"I thought you were sure this was a good thing?"

"I was...I mean, I am. It's just I had not thought where she could sleep. The new man was going to go into the spare bed in Abdouleye's and Jamaal's room in their cabin."

"So what choice is there? In with Sharla?"

James grimaced outwardly at the twinkle in his friend's eyes and he swore abjectly.

"Fortunately, she has a tiny room so that is not

even an option, which is good, for all our sakes!"

Alessio sniggered through his nose.

"Sometimes, I am just not sure who runs this place. You? Or the slave woman you freed?"

James grinned boyishly.

"Well that's easy, she runs this place. I just happen to own it."

The two old friends laughed together and stabled their mounts, removing bags, blankets, harness, reins and saddles before brushing and providing a mixture of straw and hay. Fresh water was poured into the stone basins and the wooden doors were closed before the conversation commenced again.

"Ok, so what choices do you have?"

"There is room for her to go in with Aisha but I am not sure how Aisha will take that, it wasn't that long ago that I gave her independence from Jacob to prove to her I was accepting her growing up!"

"She can sleep in my room."

"You are unbelievable, I save her from one unsavoury, indecent……"

Alessio burst into laughter and cut him short.

"I meant, she can have my room, I will go in with Jacob, in Aisha's old bed in that room. It doesn't bother me."

James smiled and thanked his friend as the two men strode into the kitchen area to be greeted by the intoxicating smell of fresh blue fin tuna roasting over a bed of aromatic herbs and spices. Washing the sand

and dust from their hands and removing their riding cloaks, the two men sat down with two mugs of ale as Sharla entered the kitchen from the interior door.

"She is bathing."

The sentence was terse and Alessio half smiled knowingly towards James who cleared his throat.

"Sharla, I intended to bring home a worker to help your sons but I have brought home a worker to help you and Aisha. I thought you would have been pleased?"

The woman placed a dish of olives for the men and stared blankly at the landowner, awaiting further explanation.

"She was going to be sold to the most odious disgusting man; you know what she would have become."

Sharla's impassive features contorted in understanding and she nodded.

"You are a good man James. But, where shall she sleep? What will she wear? What can she actually do? Can she cook? Can she even speak your language? Life is more than a grand gesture. I have to think of the practicalities."

James quelled his initial response, swallowed and responded gently.

"I know and you run this place amazingly well and I could not be without you."

Alessio saw Sharla's expression soften again and excused himself, explaining that he needed to move his things into Jacob's room, heading rapidly upstairs, ale in hand.

"Alessio will share the room with Jacob for a while; he will not be here forever. Aisha's old bed is still empty in there. Jaeda can have her own room next to Aisha, who will also keep her independence. Clothes are an immediate problem but Maria will sort her out as soon as we can get her to Acre. She is not that much taller than Aisha so I am sure she can borrow something for now. "

Sharla nodded, apologised for her hasty reaction and James continued, accepting the words graciously.

"I think she only speaks Arabic which will be a challenge for me and Alessio but for the rest of you is fine. We will have to find out her skills in time but you can teach her to assist you in most things I hope."

"Fine. Well, it will be good to have another female in the place. As long as Aisha gets on with her, it will be a positive thing I am sure."

James rubbed his chin as he pondered Sharla's final words on the predicament and drank deeply from his tankard.

"There is just one thing I need you to do for me."

The dark skinned woman turned back from her cooking and smiled as James explained that Jaeda needs to know she is no longer a slave but a worker, as Sharla and her sons. She will be expected to work hard but will be paid, fed and housed. Sharla listened and her smile broadened,

"To be granted your freedom when you have been a slave is one of the best feelings in the world James. I will be honoured to give this girl that feeling."

And so the evening went remarkably well, everybody seemed happy when darkness fell and they had eaten a truly sumptuous meal. Jacob was elated that he would share his room with Alessio; Jaeda seemed to relax as she digested the news and once Sharla and Aisha had understood what would have been the alternative for the girl, both spent much of the evening chatting amiably in Arabic to her. Abdouleye and Jamaal accepted the decision without issue as Alessio was already helping with much of their work currently anyway. James was also happy that the kneejerk, emotional decision had worked out so well and by the time he had patrolled the boundary of his land and retired for the evening, his mind was at peace and he was truly content.

Chapter 8

The Price of Friendship

James wiped the steaming water from his cheek with the rough towel and put down the flat bladed knife, he had used to shave off his four day old beard. The day had been long and he felt exhausted but it had been a most productive twenty four hours. He had received a message from the Knights Hospitallers in Acre that they would like to bring the transaction for the six mares forward to tomorrow and if he could arrange this, an extra twenty five bezants would be made available for the inconvenience. Such good fortune was welcome indeed, especially as the young horses in question were ready and in perfect condition. The vines were progressing well and the small holding was developing exactly as he had planned and hoped.

Sharla had spent the morning explaining to Jaeda how things worked in her new world, the tasks involved and her part in the extended 'family'. The girl's response to being freed from slavery was encouraging and she worked hard on various chores with Aisha and the North African woman for most of the day. James had given the three females some time to themselves for the evening and he smiled as he heard the excitable Arabic chattering below him in the kitchen, interspersed with giggling and eruptions of high pitched laughter. Tomorrow, he had promised the two teenagers a trip to see Maria in Acre and some new clothes while Alessio would take Jacob to his first lesson with the venerable Jewish tutor he knew.

"Thank you."

He rotated his head slightly to see Alessio in the doorway to the small bathing chamber, his right hand holding up a small cloth bag of coins.

"You have earned it."

James said simply, shrugging as he did so and dropped the hand towel, carefully placing the leather belt around his waist, to which he attached the battered scabbard containing his short sword.

"Expecting trouble?"

The Venetian stated, eyeing the weapon.

"Not at Abdul's no but we will be returning at night. The patrols never stray too far from the walls of Acre after dark and there are dangers. Just being careful."

Alessio nodded gravely and moved into his room to collect his keenly edged dagger and hid it within the sheath at his side. Secreting a throwing knife within the inner folds of his tunic, he returned to his friend and grinned.

"I am ready now."

The two men chuckled softly and headed downstairs to bid goodbye to the three women; Jacob was already asleep and Abdouleye and Jamaal had retired to their own dwelling. Ten minutes later, the two men were riding through the gloom along the desert trail having extricated themselves past the high spirited females and their good fortune wishes. Riotous laughter filled the dining area as Jaeda managed to say 'thank you for freedom' in English to James, which considering the extremely brief tutoring in the language from Aisha, proved at least some intellect on her part.

Enjoying the sensation of riding at full gallop atop Merdlan as the slight breeze caressed his freshly shaven face; he chuckled silently as Alessio fell behind, the young mare he had chosen as his mount, no match for the power and speed of the sable stallion. Patting the horse's sleek neck, the rider slowed to a canter to allow his companion to catch up and the two men enjoyed a cavalier banter as they rode side by side to their destination. The walls of Abdul's isolated home eventually came into view and the jovial conversation ceased as the two animals trotted through the main gate, which stood wide open and void of guards. James's brow furrowed as his eyes strained in the darkness to make out any movement as they passed into the grounds.

"Alessio. Wait."

He hissed and brought Merdlan to a shuddering halt.

"What is it?"

Alessio asked in surprise as he reined in his dappled mare.

"Listen!"

James whispered as only the echo of silence greeted their ears. Alessio unsheathed his dagger and leapt deftly from the saddle, tying it around the shaft of a young olive tree. James dropped to the earth and loaded his crossbow, his eyes darting around the perimeter wall and towards the carefully laid stone pathway, which led to the impressive building. His heart sank as he saw the first of the bodies, crumpled in a heap beside the gate. Even in the shadowy half-light, a mortal wound was visible across his chest. Touching Alessio's arm, he pointed out the corpse and the Italian swore harshly as another body was spotted, lying face down across the pathway. James inched forward, his palms beginning to perspire as he held the crossbow before him. His partner now held the tip of the throwing knife in one hand and his dagger outstretched in the other as he moved across the sandy earth beside James.

A third corpse lay in a pool of his own blood before the open doorway and the men stood either side of the opening, pausing to make eye contact before rushing through into the grand hall. Seeing nothing untoward, they stood back to back and slowly moved into the kitchen, which also proved to be totally void of life. James pointed to the closed door from the hall, which led into the main heart of Abdul's home, the spacious dining area. Moving as quietly as possible on the cold stone floor, the two men listened at the closed entrance to the room and then rushed inside to view the most horrifying sight of their lives. Alessio dropped his eyes immediately, not wanting his brain to recall the image before him as James tried and failed to avert his gaze from the gruesome scene.

In the centre of the chamber, Abdul's lifeless body lay outstretched on his back, a grotesque look of abstract fear across his usually amiable features. James felt a surge of nausea wash over him and he doubled over, retching violently and vomiting against the wall. Alessio looked over at his friend and felt his pain, turning his back on the dining room and focusing on James. Spitting out the unwelcome bile, James rubbed his watery eyes and forced himself to study the carnage. Abdul's sons had appeared to have been lined up on their knees and beheaded. His wife lay in a foetal position, with a multitude of cuts across her semi naked body. Four more bodies lay scattered in the far corner, limbs having been crudely hacked off and piled up haphazardly on top of each other. Alessio watched James wipe his mouth and enter the room and his guts tightened as his compatriot walked to Abdul's dead body and looked down on his erstwhile friend.

"They tortured him before killing him."

The words were hoarsely whispered and James flicked his stare from the merchant onto his wife; one of the nicest individuals he had ever met, she had never been anything but kind hearted and loving towards him.

"They assaulted and tortured Fatima."

A solitary tear trickled down his strained face as he turned his attention onto the three men, who had been forced to kneel with their arms behind their back and then beheaded; their faces all contorted in fearful surprise.

"Who would do this? And for God's sake…why?"

James turned to face Alessio who mouthed the obvious questions. Unable to give an answer and without his voice breaking with emotion, he shrugged. Wiping the tears that had commenced falling, he knelt beside Abdul's body and cradled his lifeless form.

"I will check the rest of the house."

Alessio said simply and left his friend to say his dignified goodbyes and moved cautiously up the staircase, knives at the ready. James looked over Abdul's body and saw the single sword thrust through his abdomen which had killed him. Bruises and cuts where he had been beaten around the face prior to this concerned him and he knew that what had happened in this room was more than a mere robbery. To beat somebody and then to assault and torture his wife in front of him, while servants and sons were held hostage in some form meant that somebody wanted information. To then kill every single person indicated that those who had done this preferred to remain anonymous. James closed Abdul's eyes and moved to Fatima's body, whom he clothed fully and laid next to her husband, before closing her eyes also.

"Nobody here."

Alessio said as he reappeared in the room, adding;

111

"You ok?"

James stood and rubbed his eyes, smiling thinly and nodding, his words barely audible.

"We should bury them."

The Venetian shifted uneasily before responding.

"I agree but...what if they are moving from each homestead to..."

He ended his sentence as James flashed him an angry stare, the grim realisation suddenly coming into his mind.

"Yes you are right. We need to get back to warn them. There is nothing we can do to help them now anyway."

James stood and touched right hand to his breast in a mark of respect and strode from the macabre spectacle into the hall. Alessio crossed himself and murmured a prayer for the departed souls before following a visibly emotional James out into the pitch darkness. Mounting their horses in grim silence, the pair hurtled themselves through the inky blackness; Alessio shocked at the sheer scale of horror he had just witnessed and James feeling strangely numb, as the mixture of concern over his loved ones' safety merged uneasily with the primal need for vengeance on those who had committed this atrocity on some of the most beloved of people he had ever encountered.

****

Saddiq watched the two horsemen depart swiftly from the dead merchant's house with little interest from the low hill of scrubland, four hundred yards from the main gate.

"Should we kill them Sir?"

The toned body of the leader of the Immortals shook his head and watched the riders disappear into the night.

"No, we have left no sign of who attacked the traitor's house. It could be bandits, Bedouins, Infidels, anyone."

"Very good, Sir."

The cowled figure drifted backwards as silently as he had crept forwards.

"Get some rest Asif, we will scout the buildings at dawn and attack before noon. I want to take back the Infidel's head and place it at our Atabeg's feet before nightfall."

Saddiq lay his prayer mat down and sat cross legged upon it, to give thanks to Allah for his help in destroying the enemies of Islam. There was no worse enemy than a man who claimed to be a Muslim but who held Allah's true enemies as his friends. Cursing the very soul of the merchant named Abdul who had refused to give the information he sought, despite a brutal beating and as he recent memory surged into his mind; the curse twisted into a sneer as he knew every man has a weakness. Bringing in his three sons and threatening to behead them in front of their mother was enough to make him think hard about his decision. Removing his wife's clothing and threatening to give her to his men to enjoy in front of the husband and sons made him tell everything he knew. Of course, they had to be slain anyway but true to his word, he had made the final death blows as swift and as painless as possible. They could then make their peace with Allah for their betrayal.

He viewed his temporary camp fleetingly as the nine members of the holy warriors began their prayers, all still wearing their ebony leather armour, keffiyah and robe; the uniform which inspired hero worship in the

East and fear in the hearts of their enemies. The Immortals were the personal bodyguard of their overlord; Zengi himself. To become one you had to show honour, bravery, swordsmanship, horsemanship and be a devout Muslim. You never surrendered and followed every order without question. Zengi promoted Jihad and the Immortals owed their very existence to their leader. Saddiq only placed Allah himself before his Master and nobody else mattered. This land was holy land, Islamic holy land and his entire being had been designed for one purpose only – to annihilate all enemies of Allah.

The attack had been a complete success, the few inexperienced guards had been completely taken by surprise and then the servants and family had been rounded up as they prepared for their evening meal. The prevalence of alcohol and the setting of a card game proved their unworthiness to the scriptures, in living in the realm of the Infidel merely to gain money by trade and friendship with the outsiders showed disrespect to Saddiq's Master, who had so gloriously gained a crushing victory against the Franks at Edessa. The merchant and his family's honour were non-existent and their deaths did not stain his soul. Not one of his nine holy warriors had been injured in the assault and tomorrow, they would plan their attack on this enemy of his people. This James Rose; who had attacked and slaughtered three Hashashim on his own and worried even the great Imad Ad-Din Atabec Zengi Al Malik Al Mansir himself piqued his interest. A worthy opponent perhaps, a man he will actually enjoy defeating. Settling his thought patterns and beginning his holy chant, he gave himself completely to his god.

Chapter 9

Death of a Dream

The soft rose hue of dawn broke through the veil of darkness and James welcomed the faint illumination, as he surveyed the surroundings with tired eyes. His hands gripped his loaded crossbow firmly as he had done for most of the night and he moved his vision over the scrub and sand that lay before his carefully created small holding. The nightmarish images from Abdul's home invaded his mind and he was grateful to stay awake and alert, meaning Morpheus could not haunt his dreams with pictures so stark and so vile that he feared closing his eyes. The events of the past seven hours drifted through his thoughts as he recalled their flight from the scene and their explanation to the horrified listeners; whose worried faces all turned to him for guidance. He loathed himself for having no answers to alleviate their anxiety. All he could do was to send Aisha and Jaeda into Jacob's room for relative safety as Sharla sat outside their bedchamber with a carving knife in her shaking hands.

Downstairs, the four men collected every item of weaponry within the dwellings and stood staring out into the open space around them. Alessio strapped his five throwing knives to a belt, which he tied diagonally across his chest for easier access as Abdouleye placed his great axe across his lap and simply waited. Jamaal stood motionless in the doorway, a spear and shield held steady and James looked proudly at them all. In the horrendous conversation last night, nobody wanted to run. Every one of them agreed to stand and fight and if these murdering creatures were coming, they would need to be prepared to die this day. All of the horses were saddled and ready to leave in the stables and if the possible battle went badly, all those who could, would get to the mounts and ride for Acre as fast as they could.

As the seconds turned agonisingly slowly to minutes and the minutes had gradually become hours; the four men dared to believe there would be no battle. This act of callous butchery had been an isolated incident or Abdul had upset the wrong person and had paid the ultimate price. Alessio voiced these possibilities and the North Africans were quick to respond with hopeful positivity, creating various reasons for such an assault but James remained quiet. Something inside him told him these devils were coming. Some deep, dark part of his soul screamed out the danger and somehow, he knew they were coming. What he did not know was why.

The murky grey morning cloud broke effortlessly above them and bathed the statuesque figures in the warm glow of the bright dawn sky and it was then that James knew he was correct. Pointing beyond the first ridge of scrubland towards the desert trail and the open sand; a black clad shape of a man sat motionless on an Arabian brown and white horse. From this distance, James could not make out the detail except that he wore a flowing ebony cloak and that he was staring directly towards the cabin.

"Warn them upstairs."

James ordered flatly as he watched the form raise his hand and wave to something unseen behind him. Feeling the cold sensation of fear creep over him as he counted the dark riders one by one as they moved into position behind the leading man, the landowner placed the quiver, which contained twenty four iron tipped bolts on his shoulder and checked his short sword at his belt. There were ten riders and the odds were certainly not in his favour. He saw the same fear in the stark faces of the African workers and he struggled to find some words to inspire them.

"Only ten? Less than I thought!"

Alessio exclaimed as he reappeared from the stair case, peering out of the window. James grinned in spite of their predicament and watched the riders canter slowly towards them, working out the range in his head as to when he can lower the odds with his crossbow.

Saddiq led the Immortals at a slow pace, knowing from plentiful experience that the small group who huddled around the doorframe would be feeling, at best; uncomfortable and at worst; terrified for their lives. Whatever their thoughts, the sense of discomfort would increase with every passing second and this helped the forthcoming battle. A confused, frightened enemy was dead before he even attempted to fight. The patrol of the outlying lands and the layout of the Westerner's home gave them all the advantages they required. There would be no help and there were very few adult males to engage in the battle. Of course, Saddiq would give the Outlander the chance to save his family and home in return for his personal surrender so a battle could be avoided. The Immortal Champion hoped he did not. It was a perfect morning to kill.

James watched the tall, broad leading rider stop a few feet short of the range of his crossbow and he scowled, understanding that the Saracen was an experienced veteran of battle. Seconds passed in complete silence as the ten mounted men faced the cabin from outside the perimeter of the small holding. The four men looked on and could do nothing but wait. A heavily accented voice broke the solemn quietude with a simple sentence in Arabic.

"We only want James Rose. The rest of you will not be harmed. Nor will any building be destroyed."

The owner of the name blinked and rubbed his forehead, immediately thinking of both options and their plausible consequences.

"Don't even think about it James! Look what happened at Abdul's; they have to be the same murderous scum who did that."

Alessio grunted with feeling and unsheathed the first of his knives. James looked to the grim nods of the other two workers and made his decision.

"When they charge, I can get one at range and then another close up. Alessio make sure you take another. We then let them come through the door and all four of us will be waiting."

Three men nodded as one in agreement and James approached the door gingerly to respond.

"Be on your way. We have no wish for violence here."

His voice was hoarse but he was pleased it did not break.

"So be it."

The leading man shouted back and unsheathed his large scimitar, holding it aloft and then forward. After a momentary pause, the nine horsemen kicked their horses into action and charged at pace, beyond the orator, drawing the enormous curved swords as they neared the wooden fence.

James moved fluidly out of the cabin and aimed his crossbow briefly, before pressing the mechanism to send the first of his bolts hurtling through the air at immense speed and accuracy. The quarrel struck the fastest rider in the chest and the thin leather breastplate was no match for the sharpened iron head and the man was punched back off his horse and onto the ground, dead before he hit the sandy earth. His three companions assumed position outside of the cabin's walls, content in the knowledge that the unknown assailants were not carrying bows or spears; Alessio mentally noting the arrogance of the enemy to risk their lives in hand to hand combat and he smiled grimly, balancing the razor sharp throwing knife in his right hand, a second blade already in his left. Abdouleye balanced his feet and held aloft his great double bladed axed and awaited the charging enemy. His brother stood to his left and stared out over the shield, the spear held ready to throw with all of his strength; a sharpened hand axe in his belt.

Saddiq watched the battle unfold before him and immediately realised he had underestimated the opponent, who had already slain Usamah with one telling release of his crossbow. However, he had absolute faith in his men and knew that when the initial charge was over and they had dismounted and fought hand to hand, victory was his to savour.

Narrowing his eyes as the horsemen thundered over his fencing and through his home; James reloaded the weapon smoothly and knew he would have time for one more shot. The sable clad Islamic host rapidly approached and then as one, wheeled their horses in an arc; showering the defenders with sand and dirt as the hooves ground to a shuddering halt. Leaping from their hand woven blankets that served as saddles, the dark robed warriors attempted to form a semi-circle around the adversary but the well-rehearsed and somewhat obvious tactic failed badly. The two central riders had barely landed deftly onto their feet when a crossbow bolt shattered the cheekbone of one and a flat knife sliced through the neck of the second. Both crumpled to the ground in a shower of blood and gore; one lay perfectly still as the other writhed in panic and agony. The Africans had also waited for the perfect moment to act and as a swordsman gathered his poise from the sudden dismount, Abdouleye hurled himself towards him, his axe high above his head. The Arabian took a step back to steady himself, backed into his horses' flank and raised his scimitar to parry the blow that smashed through the weak defence and embedded

119

into the man's chest heavily; tearing through vital organs. Jabaal allowed the enemy to land and take position, feet spread wide as he crouched with the blade outstretched before him. Grunting loudly, the freedman threw the spear with all of his composed strength and the athletic foe attempted to spin away from the spear and he almost managed to; the head of the thrown weapon striking his abdomen as opposed to his chest and the man staggered backwards. Jabaal picked up the hand axe and dived forward to provide the killing blow but the superior numbers of the robed Muslims began to tell.

Saddiq watched in growing apprehension as his fabled Immortals enacted the famous circle of death and dismounted. No sooner had they landed on their sandaled feet, half of his men collapsed, either dead or badly injured and he prayed to Allah for support against the infidel and allowed himself a slow teasing smirk as the remaining well trained warriors clashed with the enemies of his lord.

Abdouleye hauled the axe head out of the dead man's chest with a sickening sucking sound and as he lifted the heavy weapon, searing pain stretched rapidly from his left thigh and he looked down to see a gaping slash across the top of his leg, blood pouring from the deep gash. The momentary, fearful glance down sealed his fate, as the scimitar which had wounded him, hacked into the back of his neck and severed many arteries and veins. The axe dropped from numb fingers and the man twitched twice before dying. Jabaal lunged forward with his hand axe but a glancing blow to his left caught him off balance and although it bounced harmlessly off his shield, he staggered momentarily and a second strike caused him to drop the shield and stumble into the attacker. The swordsman was surprised but recovered with lightning reflexes, cutting Jabaal's left forearm where the shield had previously been. Yelping in pain, the African hacked savagely with the hand axe into the man's body, landing three flesh wounds and pushing him backwards. Regaining his composure but losing large quantities blood from the various wounds, the warrior slashed wildly at Jabaal, catching his hand and severing the tips of his three middle fingers. Howling in agony, he had no time to prevent the thrust to his stomach, the blade moving inside his body to do as much internal damage as possible and he fell, the scimitar still attached as he crashed to the ground, his life force fleeing his broken body.

James swore as his second shot had missed its intended target and merely injured the enemy and pulled forth the falchion and turned to face the next black garbed adversary, who moved with ease around him, his longer sword giving him the crucial advantage of reach. Around him the battle raged but he closed his ears to the sounds and focused on the figure before him; a man who wanted to kill him and if he died, every one of the people in the cabin behind him would undoubtedly die. Maintaining absolute composure, James awaited his opening, moving lightly on his toes. The horseman's scimitar snaked out towards him and James parried the attack easily. The longer blade flicked out a further three times and each time was blocked but each time the scimitar edged closer to his body and he knew that in a fair sword fight he would inevitably lose. Feinting with his own direct lunge, the Arab smoothly clashed blades to prevent the obvious strike and this led to the opening. As the scimitar parried, James hurled the crossbow into his surprised face and although the heavy polished wood only bruised the nose of the warrior; the defence was open for the short sword to slice through the exposed chest and the man dropped like a stone. Retrieving the crossbow, James scanned the gruesome scene and watched in impotent fury as first Abdouleye and then Jabaal fell. Alessio was in a face-off with another of the bandits, the swordsman unwilling to move forward as the Italian held a knife in his right hand, poised to throw. The slayer of Abdouleye moved towards him from the left, a sickening grin across his swarthy features. Four enemies definitely lay dead and three others were wounded, one it appeared fatally and the battle was lost if they stayed where they were in the open ground.

Screaming in Italian to his friend to get back inside, he sprinted through the open door as Alessio backed away, his knife ready to throw at the numerous swordsmen who pressed forwards. None of the Muslims risked the charge though and as Alessio passed over the threshold, James slammed the heavy door shut and forced the iron bolt across. Both men rushed to the interior door, which led to the staircase and bathing chambers and James reloaded his crossbow as Alessio patted him warmly on his shoulder.

"They come through that door, your knife and my crossbow takes another two out. "

James whispered and Alessio nodded, both grim faced and stoic in the face of the considerable danger.

Saddiq shouted an order in Arabic for his troops to halt and back away from the locked door, fearful that the wily Christian could use his crossbow from some unseen aperture. His warriors backed away and their leader took stock of the deadly skirmish. Four of his elite warriors lay dead and one more was mortally wounded. Only two were unhurt and of the other remaining two, one had bled considerably from various wounds across his chest and abdomen but was able to fight; the other had major damage to his face; his cheekbone had been smashed entirely and fragments of bone were visible and his left eye had been torn entirely apart, rendering him incapable of serious fighting. Studying the cabin, he knew that a frontal attack would bring more casualties and enough of his men had already died this day. Within a minute, his stern face creased with a knowing smile as he knew the weakness of the building and he remembered the unfortunate, traitorous merchant's words, which told him the weakness of this James

Rose, who had proved a worthy adversary indeed. He would slay him personally and slowly, to bask in Allah's honour at destroying a potent enemy of Islam itself.

Heavy breathing filled the tense kitchen area as the two men of Venetian origin awaited the final stage of the battle. Fingers ached as they remained stationery, poised to throw a dagger or squeeze the trigger pulley mechanism of the French made crossbow.

"What are they doing?"
Alessio's voice was cracked and James shrugged, attempting nonchalance but failing badly. They faced the locked door, reinforced with the heavy table now; hoping the few extra seconds would mean an ability to throw a second knife and fire a second bolt before the melee commenced. Lapsing into silence again, the two men awaited the inevitable. There was not to be a long wait.

High pitched screams from upstairs erupted at the same time as the thumping on the door, the cypress wood holding firm initially.

"Will be back in a minute! Stay here!"

James blurted out as he could recognise Aisha and Jacob's panic stricken voices above him and ran to the staircase.

"Throw your knives and then get up the stairs as quick as you can when they break through. I need you to stay alive Alessio, no heroics."

Alessio nodded as he watched his friend rush up the stairs and looked back to the door, which was beginning to splinter under the incessant hammering.

Sharla ordered the three young ones out of Jacob's bedroom and through to Aisha's bedchamber and stood in the doorway with the carving knife gripped in perspiring palms but there was no fear. Her life had been one long trial and the past few years had been the best of her life and she intended to protect those she looked after as a mother. Aisha, her face ashen but determined, pulled a terrified Jaeda and Jacob through to the hallway and into her own room.

"Close the door and push the bed against it."

The elderly woman said calmly and smiled reassuringly as Aisha worriedly closed the door behind them. Sharla watched the huge axe smash a hole through the ceiling timbers above the Jewish boys' room and steeled herself as a leering face peered through the gap in the roof and mocked the rotund African woman, the face grinned showing blackened teeth and he dropped through the wooden frame onto the floor. Sharla cursed his very soul in the language of her youth and stepped forwards, the knife stabbing into the air. With well-rehearsed skill, the man avoided the slow, clumsy lunges and hacked the scimitar into her arm, forcing Sharla to drop the makeshift weapon and screech out in horror as she watched blood pump from her exposed flesh. Eyes wide with agony, Sharla did not even see the sword slash through her upper chest, ending her brave attempt at protection.

Hearing his fellow warrior drop down into the room behind him, he moved slowly out of the door and stepped over the fresh corpse into the hallway. Turning at the sudden noise to his right, he stared down the staircase into the loaded crossbow and his scream gurgled in his throat as the quarrel tore through his windpipe. James reloaded the weapon swiftly, his eyes fixed on the top of the staircase where a trickle of blood began to seep down the steps from the dead body. There was no noise from upstairs at all and only the door splintering asunder below him caused him to turn around, indecision created momentarily in his brain. A low moan emanated from the kitchen area followed by a piercing shriek and Alessio rushed through the hallway and appeared at the bottom of the stairs, only one throwing knife left attached to his belt.

"One more hit, not sure if he's dead though."

Alessio informed James as he placed a foot on the stairs.

"Killed another but may be more upstairs."

James pointed to the prone body and heard the door being smashed apart and the table being moved. Alessio bounced up the stairs two at a time, his last throwing knife in his right hand as James crossed the hall rapidly and appeared in the kitchen. The first robed Muslim was resting against the inner wall, removing the knife that had penetrated deeply into his collar bone as a second warrior, who bore the disfigurement of a smashed cheek and a shattered eye socket moved warily through the gaping hole in the door. James released the bolt upon sight and the trajectory was slightly low as the deadly quarrel hit the swordsman in the pelvis and he bent double in shock and pain, dropping his scimitar with an anguished cry. Tossing the missile weapon carelessly to the floorboards, James drew his falchion and charged at the injured men as another cowled figure eased his muscular frame into the room.

James's short sword hacked at the crouching Saracen, who was gripping his reproductive organs, in a vain attempt to stem the flow of blood. Cutting wildly through sinew and muscle around his shoulder and upper arm, James whirled around to thrust his blade deep into the chest of the man who had finally managed to remove the knife with a profusion of swearing and bleeding. Removing the sword, James faced the man who was the last to enter and he looked at the two dying bodies and merely smiled, commenting in the tongue of his blood.

"You are indeed a man worthy to be killed by my own hand. Come let us fight gloriously under Allah's gaze."

Hatred burned in hazel eyes as James watched the man step casually back through the damaged door and back into the sunlight beyond. Needing to know answers to too many questions and the sickening images of Abdul and his family rushing into his mind, he followed the enigmatic Arabian out into the blood-stained courtyard with dead bodies of friend and foe scattered around the ground.

Alessio bounded onto the small landing and stole a quick glance at the body to make sure it was not breathing and looked from one closed door to an open one. Knife poised for flight, Alessio leapt into Jacob's chamber, with the clear opening and saw the deft movement too late. With his back upright against the interior wall, the Islamic warrior drove the scimitar across the Venetian's chest and a scarlet line immediately appeared through his thin tunic. Diving to the ground, he lost hold of his knife and the assailant kicked him harshly in the exact location of the wound and Alessio groaned out loudly in pain. Lashing out with his boots, he drove the man backwards out of the room and into the hall. Staggering backwards, his feet stumbled over the corpse of his countryman and he struck the closed door with force, falling into the chamber beyond.

Flailing in mid-air as the door swung inside, Jacob screamed as he stood behind Aisha who unleashed the arrow she had strung in her short bow. The arrow lodged itself firmly in the man's left upper arm and he swung wildly with his scimitar as he struggled to his feet. Jaeda hurled a clay pot at the Immortal and he groaned as it disintegrated into pieces of his forehead. Dazed, he forced himself forwards, swinging his sword in a fervent arc before him. Aisha attempted to parry the deadly blade with her bow and the scimitar scythed through the wooden shaft, cutting the bow into two pieces and rendering it useless. Tumbling back across the bed to avoid the secondary blow, Aisha rolled frantically away as Jaeda threw a carved jade elephant at the groggy swordsman. The man growled in indignant pain as it whacked against his chin and his continuing undisciplined attack struck an opponent as his weapon hacked through flesh.

Aisha watched the blade slice through Jacob's young body and she screeched in horror, leaping onto the bed and at the attacker, her nails scratching through the exposed flesh on his face. This sudden and unexpected onslaught caught him off guard and he dropped his hand weapon as he pushed the girl forcefully away from him, hurling her slight frame across the bedchamber. Wiping the blood from his slashed cheeks, he bent to pick up the sword but Jaeda had snatched the scimitar from the floor and swung it with all of her might into the body of the Arabian and as the horrendous sound of metal slicing through flesh and bone filled the room, he opened his mouth to scream but he only managed a throaty gurgle before crashing to the floor. A deathly hush swept over the proceedings and Aisha picked her bruised and battered body from the floor to see Jaeda drop the bloodied blade and sink to her knees, sobbing uncontrollably. Aisha looked to Jacob and rushed to his side, slapping his soft plump cheeks and checking for a pulse. Tears welled and fell as she felt nothing and cradling his head to her breast, she wept with emotional suffering.

"Who are you?"

James asked directly as he picked his way through the deceased bodies on the ground to face the powerfully built man, halting around ten yards away from his opponent.

"My name is Saddiq. I am the leader of the Immortals. You, I presume are James Rose?"

James looked over the dead bodies around him and confirmed the question as he said with a sardonic expression;

"Immortals?"

Saddiq frowned and removed his sable cloak, exposing a black leather breastplate and showed off his impressive, toned physique. Not an ounce of fat adorned the man's body but years of training and warfare had honed his body to its muscular frame.

"How do you know my name? I do not know who you are."

"I have been sent to destroy an enemy of my lord. That is all I need to know. You are a threat to him and therefore to my nation."

James watched him slice the air with his curved sword in an elegant pattern, loosening his shoulders and moving his head sideways, easing his neck muscles.

"I am no threat to anyone and certainly no nation."

Saddiq smiled with cold eyes.

"Enough talking infidel... Are you ready to die?"

James positioned himself on the balls of his soft leather boots and looked around the arena of combat, locating possible sources of aid and fixed his stare at the approaching hulk of a man, at least six feet six inches in height.

Saddiq would not underestimate this Christian again as the scattered remains of his Immortals proved and he immersed himself in the concentration of being at one with his blade; slowly easing forward before suddenly charging at the Westerner, slashing towards his knees with his first attack. James parried the stroke comfortably and circled at a steady pace, lunging and parrying as needed in the scorching heat of the morning desert sky. Saddiq studied the man's tactics and knew he must have been trained as a knight, his poise and use of tried and tested manoeuvres was clear to see. A worthy opponent indeed but the leader of the Immortals had bested over twenty such men in one to one combat and as the contest progressed, James began to defend and parry more and more, the extra physical power and skill of Saddiq posing a troublesome problem.

James changed tactics as much as he could, using his considerable athletic prowess and quick reflexes to avoid the numerous sweeps, lunges and slashes but his limbs were tiring under the continuous bombardment. Spinning away, he found Jabaal's discarded shield and attempted to push the Immortal backwards with the implement as he stabbed from the side with his sword. Saddiq was momentarily caught off guard but his superior strength turned the situation to his advantage, grabbing hold of the iron ringed wooden shield in his left hand and forcing it from the other man's grasp, sending him spiralling away, stumbling onto the earth and losing his grip of his short sword, as he dropped next to the corpse of his erstwhile worker.

The Immortal leader strode forward and raised his blade high above his head, grinning as he prepared for his death blow. The pretence of the fall was all James needed and as he dived to the ground, he gripped the shaft of Jabaal's spear and spun on the ground, driving the weapon deep into Saddiq's stomach and rolled away to safety. The muscled warrior looked in absolute shock at the spear; its barbed iron head doing irreparable damage to his insides. Hitting only sandy earth with his great scimitar as James had scuttled across the ground and was now standing, with an Immortal's curved sword in his hands, a few yards beyond the length of his blade. With a herculean effort, the man yanked the spear out of his stomach and

129

placed a hand to stem the flow of blood and guts that poured out of the wound. Staggering forward, Saddiq swung frantically and James casually side stepped the clumsy act and crouched low, slicing tendons in the back of his right leg. Cursing in confused rage, the man lost balance and slumped into a half-crouch, the taste of bile and blood entering his mouth.

Alessio staggered through the hallway to view the scene in Aisha's bed chamber and averted his weary gaze as he realised the danger was at least momentarily avoided but Jacob; beautiful, innocent boy that he was, lay dead in Aisha's young arms. Stifling his own bleak emptiness that pervaded his mind, he thought of James and picking up a dead Arab's scimitar, he headed carefully down the staircase and into the kitchen to help his friend if he was still alive or to protect the two women if he was not. The shattered corpses on the floor proved that James had certainly come through this way and the sound of clashing metal outside drove him onwards, opening the damaged door and blinking in the bright sunlight, he covered his eyes and watched James look down balefully at the wounded Saracen who responded with utter bewilderment written across his face.

James turned to see that it was Alessio and not more danger and pausing only long enough to whisper;

"For Abdul and his family."

The scimitar swung true and Saddiq's proud head bounced without dignity from his neck; the body jerking for a brief moment before crashing to the earth. Turning to his friend, he wiped his mouth and spat onto the sand;

"Everybody safe inside?"

Alessio could only shake his head and mouth that he was so very sorry as James sprinted past him and up the staircase, two steps at a time. Of all the repulsive scenes that had unwillingly entered his subconscious over the past twenty four hours, the vision that he faced in Aisha's bedroom was the worst of them all by far. Dropping to his knees, he opened his mouth to scream and at first, no sound emanated but when the sound came; it was an unearthly shriek of abstract pain.

Alessio heard the noise and placed his head in his hands and knew that his friend would struggle to come to terms with the losses of the past twenty four hours. Abdul had been a mentor and confidante, a man who helped him build the small holding and supported its growth. His family had welcomed James into their home. Sharla was more like a mother to him than his own mother had ever been. Abdouleye and Jabaal were loyal workers who he respected and liked. These would be hard to take but the loss of Jacob would be almost impossible; a young boy, who had watched his parents butchered by fervent Christians and offered protection and love by James. A young boy now dead, slain needlessly by fundamentalist Muslims, who came here seeking James by name. The Italian wiped his eyes and knew he had to remain strong for the sake of all who survived. A golden dream may have died under the morning sun today, but he prayed to God Almighty that there would be a day to come, when dreams would be available again. Sighing deeply, he retraced his steps up to the room and steeled his soul against the destructive sight he would find there.

Chapter 10

Repercussions

Alessio studied his friend's drawn, pensive face and sighed inwardly. It had been thirty six long and arduous hours since the unprovoked attack on the small holding and James had still not really reacted in the way, Alessio had believed he would. After the initial shock, there had been no explosion of emotion or angry outburst, merely calm introspection. It was now early evening and the desert air had cooled considerably from the intolerable afternoon dry heat, and they sat in the quiet tavern in the Venetian Quarter of Acre, overlooking the docks and the serene, azure Mediterranean Sea. They sat in silence and due to the hour of the day; 'The Holy Crown' was almost empty. Alessio ordered a fourth round of drinks, even though James had not finished his third and wondered for the hundredth time what he could say to bring his oldest friend back from the brink of melancholia.

James muttered his thanks as the ale tankard was placed in front of him and then immediately drifted back into the morbid coldness of his thoughts. He felt more than double his thirty three years and he was weary and tired. He envisaged the battle as it had happened in slow motion stages and the shocking, irrevocable results of it. Jacob was dead. Sharla and her two sons were dead. Aisha would probably never be the same again. Literally everything he had worked for; emotionally and professionally, had been damaged and James was not sure how to fix the first of these issues and if he even now had the inclination to rebuild the other. Rubbing his left hand over his unshaven face, he drank deeply from the tankard and pictured yesterday's events after the deadly skirmish had ended. Alessio had taken control of the situation and organised everything

132

in a composed manner; taking time to calm the remaining three survivors down and explain what needed to be done. The arrival of the patrol of six Knights Hospitallers, who had arrived to complete the business transaction for the horses, had been most welcome. The Sergeant who led the troop; a French knight in his mid-thirties, named Etienne; was brought up to date by Alessio's strained explanation and took control. The bodies of the Muslim warriors were stripped of all weaponry and armour; taken deep into the desert and dumped unceremoniously for the carrion to feast upon; a just response to such an unprovoked and disgraceful act. On instruction from James, the bodies of Sharla, Abdouleye and Jamaal were carefully washed and laid in white linen. In due respect to their North African ancestry and age old tradition, the corpses were then burnt and their ashes spread in all directions of the compass.

Sending men back to Acre to make their report to their Temple and to Abdul's home to investigate further, the remaining knights helped Alessio and James dig a shallow grave and bury Jacob. The boy was buried near the vines, where he used to play and flat stones were used to mark the final resting place; stones taken from the Kishon River, where James had taught him to swim and to fish in happier times. Eventually, after hundreds of tears had been shed and the sun had departed; the cabin was thoroughly cleaned and partially mended to make it secure and the four survivors headed under escort to Acre, to the warmth of Maria's embrace and her unconditional love. The agreement for the horses was concluded and the ample funds were paid by the Sergeant of the Knights Hospitallers.

James knew he could not thank Alessio's older sister enough or ever repay her for how amazing she had been in dealing with the four shaken and devastated people that walked into her home yesterday evening. Immediately closing the shop as a mark of respect, Maria comforted the two young women and catered for their every possible reaction by listening to the pain and supporting with kind words, with patience and with assurance. Jaeda, a woman who on her first full day of freedom from slavery; experienced a most devastating, frantic, pitch battle; supported a distraught Aisha, who resiliently hour by hour improved and coped with the tragic loss. Leaving Alessio, who tried in vain to support James, Maria became a rock of sensibility for the young women.

James, however, knew he did not want to be supported or helped in any way. He knew he needed to wallow in this tortured sorrow for a while and simply held every grief stricken thought inside. It had been hard to leave Jacob behind and unable to sleep last night, James had slipped out, taken Merdlan from the stables and rode hard through the darkness to sit next to his make shift grave through the night; speaking for hours about the past and the future but not a word about the present.

"What do you think the Hospitallers will want from us tomorrow morning?"

Alessio's first direct question startled James from his reminisces and he shrugged listlessly.

"The messenger said it was important and they have information they need to discuss with us."

He continued, not to be put off by his companion's shrug.

"Who knows Al? The rumours will be flying around before long and they are supposed to protect Outremer's borders from attacks aren't they?"

James said testily and Alessio nodded with understanding and diverted his attention back to the pretty barmaid and lapsed back into silence, leaving his friend to continue his musings.

"Sorry, I don't mean to be offensive. I just need to be alone awhile; I don't want or need your company."

Alessio looked into his friend's eyes and smiled weakly, patting his shoulder in friendly concern. He had found James sat next to Jacob's grave and he had brought him back to Silk Street, much to the joy of a distressed Aisha and a concerned Maria. The Italian gulped his ale, finishing his drink swiftly.

"Fine, I will be at the shop. Come back when you are ready."

Exiting the tavern, Alessio disappeared into the crowded street; wishing he could get through to the man and get him to understand that the living needed him more than the dead. Lost in his troubled thoughts he failed to notice the hulking scar-faced man, who watched his movements closely from across the street, half concealed by the awning of a weapon smith. The spy remained stationery as Alessio strode out of view and he grinned suddenly. The rumours appeared to be true and his superior would be very interested to know that James and Alessio were back in Acre. Clearing his throat noisily, he hawked and spat onto the ground, whistling out of tune as he made his way to 'The Caravel' to inform Francesco of the news.

James began his fourth drink and drifted back into his self-imposed misery and tried to make sense of the unbelievable mess he found himself in. He wanted to return to his home and use the funds from his deal with the Hospitallers to improve the facilities and increase security. Hiring some workers from Acre, he could extend the buildings and purchase more land and continue what he had established before the attack. However, it would not be that simple and he muttered an oath as his mind lurched back to Jacob and acute pain assailed his heart as he thought of the boy's smiling face. Aisha was certainly not ready to return and there was a distinct possibility that she would never wish to go back at all. He had avoided this conversation or in fact, any conversation at all with his ward since Jacob's murder and he condemned himself for this avoidance tactic. It was weak and pathetic to avoid the one person who needed him most and he silently swore; absently sipping his ale.

He made a mental note to speak to Aisha at the first opportunity and to apologise for his weakness and his abject failure at protecting the home and his family. His mind's eye paused over the use of the word 'family' and he cursed violently again, taking the Lord's name in vain. There was now no family at all; just Aisha and he, thanks to the robed Saracen murderers. His brows furrowed as he thought of the tall leader of the killers; a skilled swordsman who had come for him. A stranger, of some standing and power, who knew his name and therefore; Jacob, Sharla and her sons all died because of him. James sighed deeply as this heavy burden clarified in his brain and a stomach churning feeling struck him and he struggled to find a name for the tightening in his guts. It came to him in a few seconds and his attractive features contorted into a look of grim satisfaction as he digested the word that described the alien feeling; 'Vengeance.' This was his need and he welcomed the annunciation with cold comfort.

"It is still early days, Alessio. Give him time."

Maria spoke softly as she entered the kitchen to see her brother sitting listlessly at the dining table, his eyes betraying the sense of impotence he was feeling.

"I just cannot get through to him. He seems to need to keep his emotions inside himself."

Alessio responded with incredulity in his voice.

"His Father was English remember and you

have met his mother; she is hardly a typical Venetian!"

The man grunted an affirmative response and failed to see Aisha drift quietly into the doorway.

"Maybe he should see his Mother, maybe she could help him?"

Maria continued, ending her statement swiftly as she noticed the girl.

"Are you mad? His Mother is the last person he needs to see right now. He is in a bad enough state as it is...."

Alessio said forcefully and stopped abruptly as he turned his head to face his sister and spotted Aisha.

"Is he okay?"

The three words were stated with such concern that it almost broke Maria's heart and she nodded her head in reply.

"James is fine. He just needs a little time, he keeps his emotions in check you see and he thinks too much. Always has."

The brittle exterior of calm on Aisha's pretty features dropped momentarily and she struggled to retain her composure, prompting the Venetian seamstress to move beside her and cup her olive face in her hands.

"Honestly, he will be okay. We promise."

Maria added, holding the young shaking body to her own and looked to her sibling for support.
"Maria is right. James just feels responsible for the deaths, it's ridiculous but he somehow feels he failed Jacob and the others."

Aisha broke away from the hug and rubbed her tear stained eyes.

"It's not his fault! He tried to save us all, as did you. It was their fault; the bandits who attacked us!"

Fresh sobs ended the screeched response and Maria threw a glare at Alessio as she wrapped her arms around the girl once again.

"I didn't mean to upset you Aisha. I am not saying it is anybody's fault."

The sobbing became incessant and Alessio closed his mouth and watched his sister lead the distressed Syrian back to her bedchamber. Swearing under his breath as he was left alone once again, he wondered how long the omnipresent gloom would remain hanging over the house. It was not often the easy going, carefree Italian was worried but his concern was palpable. The rumours were already swirling around the port about the attack on the small holding and the last thing any of the occupants at Silk Street needed right now was to be the subject of gossip. The morning would also bring the meeting at the Temple of the Knights Hospitaller, arranged by the Grand Master of the Order himself; Raymond Du Puy. Alessio had no idea why this conference had been called and he did not like it. He had no time for the religious or military orders that seemed to be pervading Outremer's very fabric of society and this did nothing for relations with the nation's neighbours of differing religious beliefs; causing only distrust and animosity. Scowling, he attempted to put something positive into his mind and with a saddening realisation, he could not think of a single thing to raise his spirits.

****

Nadirah hid the smirk behind her pink silk veil, as she observed the court room of the self-proclaimed

Master of Jihad and supreme ruler of the Muslim peoples. The cowering underlings scurried backwards and forwards, attending to his every childish whim in a vain effort to stem the violent outbursts and temper tantrums. More than one slave, guard and servant had been beaten, whipped and even slain in the grotesque shows of power that Zengi was forced to undertake to cease the whisperings of his failing leadership.

If the murder of his one trusted advisor; Mahmud, had created an atmosphere of paranoia and fear in the royal court; news of the slaughter of the contingent of indestructible 'Immortals' led by the famed Holy Warrior; Saddiq had shook the very foundations of Zengi's rule. Surrounding himself with the remaining cloaked warriors of the group, he promoted only family members now regardless of age or skill, his mind creating enemies and spies everywhere. Nadirah smiled broadly as she and every other person in the Muslim world now knew the man who led them was finished and a new Lion of Islam would be needed to destroy the Infidels. It was rumoured that Zengi could not even satisfy his wives any longer and shunned them, preferring the company of his troops; terrified his army would disintegrate and leave him exposed and unprotected.

Nadirah knew she would have to leave soon as even her illustrious blood line would only protect her from the man who teetered on the brink of insanity, for a period of time. The new power lay in Baalbek in the form of a Kurdish general but he could wait; it was not his time as yet and until Zengi was finally destroyed; the Islamic warriors would not simply follow a man of Kurdish descent against the Westerners. There were plans still to make and issues to resolve. The growing issue being this Outlander called James; a man whose destiny seemed to cross her own. First, he saves her from Mahmud's paid assassins and then he invades her own soothsayer's prophecy and now he seems to have single handedly defeated one of the greatest swordsmen in Arabia and a force of the elite horsemen. Zengi had decreed him an enemy of the religion and would pay handsomely for his decapitated head. This was after he had disembowelled a well-respected seer for daring to warn the Caliphate that this Infidel crossed his own future. As the pathetic excuse of a man raged at a slave before her; messengers were scurrying forth to all of the main cities and town owned by the Christians with the news that 500 bezants awaited the killer of James Rose. This man was interesting, Nadirah admitted to herself and should she ever set eyes on the man again; she would kill him herself for nothing could cease her future plans; it was her destiny to protect and teach the Lion of Islam and it was his destiny to rid the lands of the Europeans and cleanse the Holy Land once and for all. Tightening her veil, she departed the chamber and strode to her room to write to Naim al-Din Ayyub, explaining the recent events and to urge him to continue to await her instructions.

■■

The ample figure of Francesco rocked softly as he chuckled at the news.

"So he is back. Hiding in the port like a scared rat! His Muslim friends not so friendly after all."

Another round of throaty chuckling ceased the mocking sentences as Aldo poured a glass of wine for each of them, smiling at the older man.

"Rumours are; he killed a Saracen hero; some big shot in Zengi's army so they say."

Francesco squinted as he sipped the fresh, cold wine.

"Interesting Aldo, make it your business to find out the facts not the rumours. He has a habit of collecting powerful enemies' does young James and I want to be there when he takes his fall."

Aldo nodded silently and savoured his wine and noted with grim satisfaction that his news had already reached Francesco's eldest daughter, who pretended to continue her duties behind the bar without listening but the furrowing brow and slight movement of her eyes towards them, told Aldo that she had certainly heard. This could be used to his advantage he mused as Sophia was a prize he had coveted for many a year and he grinned as he thought how very much he loved his job.

Chapter 11

Meeting with a Grandmaster

It was unusually overcast and dull as the two men trudged to the Temple of the Knights Hospitallers to meet with the Grand Master of the Order, who had travelled from the great hospital in Jerusalem personally to conduct the interview. Both men were quiet and thoughtful and the clipped conversation between the two old friends merely concerned the inclement weather. The streets and alleyways were beginning to fill with its industrious denizens even at this early hour as the Venetians headed to the fortified northern part of the port, where the quarters of 'The Order of the Hospital of St John' was located; a solid stone building, which appeared to James and Alessio; to be an uncomfortable mix, of a church and a fortress. Made of solid brick, two imposing towers stood either side of the great oak double doors, over which the insignia of the Kingdom of Jerusalem fluttered in the slight breeze. Atop each tower sat great ballista's, capable of firing huge spears into any attackers foolish enough to attempt to take the building. A series of stone steps led upwards to the entrance where six armed men stood guard, in full Milanese plate mail armour and bearing kite shields and long swords; their tunics and shields carrying the silver cross on the black background; distinguishing them clearly from the Knights Templars, whose ensign was the red cross on a white background. Approaching the Temple brought the immediate attention of the guards and an uncomfortable wait ensued as their meeting was confirmed by one of the Knights, who disappeared through the doors, only to reappear a few moments later and wave the two men inside.

Entering the building, the two men swept

intrigued eyes over the opulent interior as handcrafted tapestries and paintings adorned the walls; great urns and sculptures decorated the chambers and hallways as they walked over luxurious woven rugs. Hurried through to an antechamber, the two nervous men waited once more for a few minutes before being summoned gruffly into an oval shaped room, dominated by a large polished table, at which a middle aged man in refined clothing sat at the head. A slim, younger man stood to his left with a weak chin and a haughty expression and as the Knight who led the two men into the room departed and closed the door behind him with an ominous bang; Alessio and James were ushered to the two empty cushioned chairs, positioned directly opposite the Grand Master, who studied each man's face in turn before speaking.

"Welcome to the Order, please, help yourself to orange juice or water."

His hand waved vaguely in the direction of the two jugs and Alessio mumbled some thanks and poured a glass of iced juice; an expensive delicacy he did not wish to miss out on. James held his hand up in an effort of manners, his own hazel eyes appraising the man who led the Military Order of the Hospitallers. He knew only a little about Raymond Du Puy; a French nobleman who had become Grand Master in 1120 and had been a successful General under the illustrious Godfrey of Boullion. Rumour suggested a deeply religious man and favourite of Pope Pascall II, who recognised and blessed the order over thirty years ago. His scant knowledge ended there and he was curious to know why he and Alessio had been summoned; his business dealings regarding horses had been undertaken at a much lower level in the Order and he had no political interest in Acre.

"I suppose you are wondering why I requested you attend this meeting."

The bearded man spoke in an educated French accent as if to read his thoughts and James nodded warily as Alessio sipped his orange juice, savouring the rich flavour as his dark eyes flicked from the seated to the standing Frenchmen.

"These are troubled times and I would like to offer you both the protection and friendship of the Order."

"Thank you kindly. However, I was not aware we needed your protection, My Lord."

James spoke lightly, interrupting Du Puy much to the dissatisfaction of the man who stood to his left. The Grand Master held up a hand to stop any unwanted rebuke from his companion and smiled thinly.

"In this part of the world, we all need protection and friendship. I am sorry to hear of your loss in recent days."

Alessio felt his friend's entire body tense and was relieved to see James control his emotions.

"Thank you."

"It is unusual that such an attack would take place so far inside the region's borders and that two such attacks would be made within two days and by such a group."

Alessio shifted uneasily in his chair as he watched Du Puy and James staring into each other's faces.

"I suppose it is."

The evasive answer brought only an indignant snort and a flush of anger to the Grand Master's cheeks.

"Come, come...do not be coy. We are currently

in the most dangerous days that Outremer has ever known. The new King of Jerusalem himself has requested that I garrison frontier fortresses with my knights. His predecessor, King Fulk died in 1143 and our most trusted ally, the Byzantine Emperor; John II died the same year. Edessa fell to the Turks of Zengi just two months ago and his armies are ready to sweep us from these very shores! I am here to help you if I can but do not test my patience!"

Alessio shifted again as James said nothing in response to the outburst and simply stared into the Frenchman's face before responding evenly and softly.

"I admit that these are bad times that we live in but I do not understand as to why I am here in your Temple and what any of this has to do with us."

Du Puy poured himself some water and sipped briefly; looking up at his companion and nodding as he visibly maintained his composure.

"Do you have any idea as to who attacked your home?"

James pursed his lips as he envisaged the muscular Arabian and remembered their brief conversation before combat.

"He said his name was Saddiq and he claimed he was the leader of a group called the 'Immortals'."

He paused as the man standing beside Du Puy took an audible breath and he looked towards him for an explanation before progressing.

"Please excuse my brother, Francois here. You killed a fine warrior. A feared warrior. A famous warrior."

Alessio and James exchanged puzzled glances as the man continued.

"He was the greatest warrior in Zengi's entire Muslim host. The leader of his elite fighting force; Saddiq himself led the conquest of Edessa and it was the Immortals who slaughtered the Christians who surrendered. You have done a noble deed in slaying that man."

"Why would such a man come looking for me?"

James mused in a hoarse whisper, adding;

"He claimed he was sent from his 'Lord' to kill me as I was an enemy of his people? I do not understand. If his 'Lord' was Zengi; what have I done to such a man? I am friendlier to Muslims than most Westerners I know."

Du Puy studied the young trader and drained his glass before continuing the conversation.

"This is what I had hoped you would tell me. I have no idea why such an act would be decided upon. Our spies tell us of course that the once great Zengi is losing his grip on sanity and he has more enemies amongst his own people than he has within the West. But, that does not explain why he should send his greatest swordsman to specifically slay you if, as you say is correct, you have dealings with Muslim traders and have adopted an Islamic child I believe?"

James forcibly eased the irritation from his voice and spoke calmly in reply.

"Yes, that is so. I also took a Jewish boy under my protection but he is now dead. Murdered by the men this Saddiq brought to my home. Other friends were killed that day and forgive my rudeness but I am still in mourning."

Alessio rested a hand briefly on his friend's arm and added his first words of the meeting.

"As you can understand, Sir....this has been a most difficult time for James and for all of the survivors. We are still coming to terms with the loss and we know nothing of this Saddiq or Zengi. None of this makes any sense at all to us. We are simple merchants."

The Grand Master switched his attentive stare to Alessio's handsome, angular face and nodded sagely.

"I do understand young man. I know loss all too clearly and feel it deeply. I apologise unreservedly for rushing you into our offices but there is much danger to the entire kingdom right now. The Knights Templars clamour for a larger Kingdom and another crusade against the Saracen hordes. Every week, many of the King's advisors support an assault on our neighbour's in retribution for the loss of Edessa and the atrocious slaughter of the prisoners afterwards. The new Pope; Eugenius III, who was elected just last week was elected based upon his demands for another Holy War and is already finding willing European leaders to pledge military support. Louis of France is young, idealistic and extremely pious and it is reported that he will definitely 'take the cross' and lead a French army of Christian Knights against the East. Conrad III of the Holy Roman Empire has also indicated an eagerness for battle with the infidel."

Du Puy paused and rubbed his eyes before continuing with a resignated sigh.

"There are Priests in England, Denmark, Poland, Austria and Sicily promoting the abolition of all sins to the man who kills a Muslim in the Holy Land. I fear war is coming and I am seemingly alone in trying to stop it."

James smiled ironically, warming to the honest nobleman but fearing that he was another idealistic fool from the French aristocracy who naturally believed themselves superior in intellect to any other race and their view was therefore, the only correct one.

"There will always be religious wars between Christians and Muslims, My Lord; nobody, not even God himself can stop that."

Francois stiffened at the hint of blasphemy but Du Puy merely chuckled softly.

"Maybe so but one should always try to do what is right. I do not want war for war's sake but I have no love of our natural enemy. However, it is clear to all that Zengi's power, despite his victory in Edessa is failing and as we know from our very creation of Outremer; a disjointed enemy is a weaker enemy and one we can exploit and dominate. If we attack Zengi now, the Saracens will unite behind him and every Arab, Syrian and Turk will fight for him against us and they could defeat us so utterly that we could be back in ships heading west."

James nodded in agreement, concluding;

"So you play for time. It makes complete sense in the circumstances."

"And this is where you two fine fellows come into my line of thought. The rumours are already flying around like locusts in the summer breeze that you have killed Saddiq in hand to hand combat. This is a fine thing, a noble thing and even I can commend your skill and bravery. However, such a story in the wrong hands will make you a folk hero and a Christian Knight; a trader who fought and defeated the enemy's best man. Ahhh, it is almost biblical is it not; David and Goliath perhaps?"

The man's eyes twinkled as he watched James squirm in his padded seat.

"I am no hero or Christian Knight. The man was

sent to kill me and my family; I saw what he had done to Abdul and his family. It was fear that drove me to kill him My Lord. I was scared and fought desperately for my life and the lives of my family and friends."

The Grand Master's face became stern once again.

"But you see how easy it would be to contort this into a recruiting tool. It makes them look weak and pathetic. Easy to defeat. I want to offer you an alternative to being a saviour."

"I am listening."

"Play the situation down; maintain a low profile around the city. Help me stifle this need for revenge and retribution. In return, I will protect and repair your home. The deal for the horses you provided will be renewed as often as you wish and you will have my friendship and support for all time."

Alessio looked sideways at his companion and prayed that he would make the correct decision and he was not disappointed as James barely waited five seconds before responding.

"Agreed My Lord. I have no wish for honour or praise. I was protecting everything that I hold dear and any man would do the same. You have my agreement but you are, if I may say so, wrong about one thing."

"Oh?"

Three faces stared apprehensively towards James as he explained.

"I have no wish for another war or for retribution regarding Edessa, a city I do not know or have ever visited, I do want vengeance for my boy and you say that this tyrant 'Zengi' must have sent his band of 'Immortals' to slay me for some unknown reasoning, then I want that man dead. I want to kill that man."

Du Puy began to smile but on seeing the man opposite and his utter belief in what he was saying, his smile died on his lips.

"He resides in a heavily fortified Tower on the outskirts of Damascus; a city he has coveted for years. It would be impossible to get to him but he will die, do not trouble yourself. He has more enemies than friends and if we can avoid this looming war for long enough, his own people will depose him and in the dissolution of power; then will be our time for war."

James remained impassive and the warmth he had temporarily felt for the Hospitaller, dissipated completely and silence ensued.

"So, we have reached an agreement?"

It was Francois who spoke in a heavy Provencal accent and James agreed and stood from his chair, quickly followed by Alessio.

"Thank you for your time, My Lord and I thank you for your kindness and hospitality."

"My pleasure and I will honour my commitments to you James Rose."

The meeting ended and the two men were led back out under the cloudy sky and strode in silence for a few yards, away from the imposing building before Alessio, convinced he was out of earshot spoke.

"Well, that wasn't so bad. What do you think?"

James smiled and clapped his friend on the shoulder.

"The arrangement is good but what did you think of Du Puy?"

"Typically French."
Alessio grumbled and grimaced, adding;

"Haughty, arrogant but better than most of his kind. You?"

"Oh, I would say that if Zengi is bordering on insanity; old Du Puy in there is not far behind. That man will lead his Knights into war once the Caliphate is dead. His body will not be cold and he will be charging towards Damascus to increase his power and prestige. "

Alessio smiled knowingly and nodded but shrugged in typical Venetian style, putting the thoughts out of his mind and diverting his attention to the smell of hot bread baking on a nearby stall.

"I am beginning to think everybody in this damned place is a little mad."

James stated more to himself than to his friend who had left him to peruse the baker's wagon a few yards to his left. The man smiled and shook his head and whispered to himself;

"And I mean everybody."

Chapter 12

Family Matters

The setting of the sun was a beautiful natural event wherever in the world you are but when sat on the edge of a rickety wooden quay, overlooking the Mediterranean Sea with the orange and amber reflective illumination dancing across its placid sapphire surface; one felt truly glad to be alive. This exact feeling surged through the veins and arteries of James Rose as he watched the sun sink beneath the horizon across the vast expanse of water and smiled as Aisha sat beside him, close enough to hear her breathing and for the first time in a few days, he felt a brief glimpse of happiness.

The hours following the meeting with the Grand Master of the Knights Hospitallers had been both productive and enlightening. He finally had the deep and meaningful conversation with his surviving ward about the future, the present and the past; about Jacob and Sharla, about their home, their business and a whole host of other topics. The conversation drifted through tears of disconsolate despair, sad melancholic smiles, fond memories and all their hopes and fears, with every conceivable emotion interspersed throughout the hours of the early afternoon. By the end of the poignant afternoon, both individuals had taken on-board the other's point of view, reasoning and needs and had moved, if only slightly, away from the awning chasm of despair and were strengthened and invigorated by the other. Now, as he sat on the damp cedar wood planks to watch one of the miracles of natural beauty, James felt his confidence rise and he processed the earlier discussion points through his mind. Jacob was dead and nothing could be done to change this terrible fact; Aisha wanted revenge just as badly as James did but she also needed time to grieve and mourn his loss. The young woman wished to think of the good times with the child she regarded as her younger brother and feel love and affection for the boy, undiluted by hideous thoughts of vengeance and violence. Jacob, she told him, deserved that; deserved their undiluted love and James could hardly argue with the simple, beautiful statement.

Sharla's loss had also keenly affected them both more than they had previously admitted. As close to a loving mother as either of them had ever known; the North African had one of the most pure souls you could ever hope to find. Life was simple with her and you always knew where you stood; a hard worker who was honest and loving. James learnt that Jaeda was counted as a friend by Aisha and someone, who had supported and helped her in the past grotesque two days. Interestingly, whilst James had sunk into introspection and isolation; Jaeda had blossomed in Acre, helping Maria in the shop and proving to be popular with the patrons and having an aptitude and talent with material and clothing. Maria was apparently close to asking James if the young woman could help her permanently in the trade and become a type of apprentice to the Venetian seamstress. Aisha had also confessed that she had overheard Maria and Alessio talking about James and the loving concern they both felt for him and that he was lucky to have such people around him who genuinely cared. This open discussion had also provoked questioning from Aisha who had heard pockets of conversation relating to Sophia, to Georges and to his mother and unwilling to lose this closeness between them; answered the questions honestly.

He explained to Aisha about Sophia; their relationship, and the repercussions of it. He explained what happened to his father and his brother and how his mother became obsessed with God; alternately abusing and ignoring James. As a young man, he found a father figure in the retired Templar; Georges, who taught him many things in life; not just his skills with a crossbow and sword; but horsemanship, manners, etiquette, learning, languages, business and self-confidence. The conversation regarding his mother was brief and hurt emotionally, surprising that something so deeply hidden could still provoke such excruciating pain. Aisha's advice had been simple and direct as most things in life are to teenagers.

"Go and speak to her. She has suffered loss as you have; make peace with her. There is too much hate and not enough love in this world."

Eventually, after much debate, James had relented and promised he would go and talk to his mother and to end the impasse with which they now found themselves at and basking in her moral victory; Aisha had led him hand in hand to the position where they now sat to watch the sun set and the Syrian had embraced the Outlander, whispering that she loved him and she was elated that he was alive and could at least smile again. Unable to mask his happiness, smile he did.

Returning to Silk Street, under the darkening sky; Maria greeted them with a dazzling smile and a veritable feast of spiced lamb stew, unleavened bread and potatoes, freshly bought from a Cypriot trader that afternoon. For the first time since Alessio's return to Acre, the meal was a happy one with laughter and simple conversation and he smiled at his sister knowingly across the roughly hewn table and thanked God that life was returning slowly back to normal. James advised all that Jaeda was free to do whatever her heart told her to do and so, his thankful sister gained an apprentice to help with the huge amount of work running a business created and in turn, the former slave was overcome with gratitude and kissed everybody around the table as she wept tears of happiness. All agreed to visit Jacob's grave the following day and to make sure that the Knights Hospitaller were undertaking what had been promised in rebuilding and guarding their home. At the end of the evening, as the three women headed for their beds, James offered to buy Alessio a drink; the first tentative step towards making up for his morose behaviour in recent days. Never a man to refuse such an offer, Alessio gratefully accepted and the two men drifted into the night to head to the nearest tavern; 'Il Tavelletta', a simple, traditional establishment owned by an elderly Venetian called Gianluigi Pelare; where their friendship was renewed over a number of bottles of cheap wine from the distant hills of Lombardy.

The following morning was to be a difficult one. Unable to face any trace of food; his stomach growled angrily as James walked towards the Church of St Sabas on the edge of the Genoese and Venetian Quarters; set deep within the alleyways of the poorer residents. The saint was one of the early martyrs of Christianity; slain by the Romans during one of their persecutions of the religion hundreds of years previously. He had always been a favourite of his mothers and he remembered her telling him and his brother the story of his death and how he was tied to a tree and shot with arrows, all because he would not denounce Jesus Christ. It was perhaps fitting that his mother worked under this patronage and from Maria's constant information, James believed he would find his mother at this church, as Saturday was a day of cleaning and preparation, for the holiest day that followed with its long sermons, mass and confession. He had to duck under various open shutters and awnings as he weaved his way into the maze of back streets; little more than a series of interwoven dusty alleys in actuality and more than once, he had to retrace his steps to seek out the Church; a small, simple building; built and designed for the purpose of its religion and not a grandiose statement to other religions of how much power and wealth the Christians had; as was the case in many of the imposing cathedrals that were being erected across Outremer. His soft leather boots halted outside the basic entrance and with a deep breath, he moved warily into the gloom of the interior;

his senses on alert to the silence within and the smell of burning incense and candle wax that pervaded the close musty air. Taking a moment for his eyes to adjust to the half-light within in comparison to the stark sunshine outside, he carefully strode through the antechamber with its many candles of remembrance, prayer beads, bronze crosses, bibles and notes of parchment with names and messages for lost loved ones and peered into the main chamber beyond.

Great stone pillars held the ornate, decorated ceiling in place, many feet above his head and many wooden benches lay in neat rows; a flimsy purple runner inlaid with the cross and verses from Psalms in Latin, laying in the centre of each pew. Mosaic floor tiles led through the pews and James followed them, heading past the shrine to St Sabas with its' depiction of his dying body peppered with arrows against a great tree and towards the holiest part of the building where the enormous marble altar stood, flanked by the baptistery containing its ornate stone font and the brass lectern. Behind the altar, an ambulatory presumably led to the bell tower, chapels and vestry and his eyes scoured the chamber for signs of life or movement. A figure, half hidden and remaining absolutely stationery, stood near the confession and under the shadows of the pulpit; her simple black dress merging with the darkness and he stepped closer to see into the icy grey eyes of his mother.

"Hello mother."

The greeting was almost inaudible and James wondered why he always believed he should whisper in a house of God as his mother moved out of the shadows and into the flickering illumination of the candles in the brass candelabra on the altar. Her body was slightly heavier set from when he had last seen her and wrinkles were set deep into her brow and around her eyes, which remained fixed onto his. Her face was set in an expression James could not distinguish between surprise and pain.

"I thought you were the ghost of your brother sent to me."

The words were spoken in the soft Italian dialect he remembered as a small boy, before the fall and collapse of their family and he winced visibly at the first words she had spoken to him in more than five long years.

"No, I am no ghost. How are you?"

Maria Vitelli's attractive features creased into a bitter smile and she shook her head as she spoke; the once raven hair cut shorter and streaked with grey.

"I am old but I have the strength of the Lord in my body and He will not forsake me."

She crossed herself and looked briefly upwards. James followed suit but saw only a decorative ceiling and focused back on the woman with refined cheekbones and a high bridged nose before him; in her mid-sixties now but still retaining poise and grace.

"I just thought maybe we could talk. It has been so long and well, things have happened and I just thought...."

His words tumbled from his nervous mouth quickly and lacking co-ordination and he ceased his garbled explanation as his mother nodded, adjusting her outer robe slightly.

"Your home was attacked and people died. Just because you left me when I needed your love most does not mean I do not care what happens in your life. It is all over Acre how you killed a great Saracen warrior, a champion of the hateful race no less."

Struggling to respond in time to the words almost spat

out at him, his mother continued.

"At last, you have done something of which I am proud of you."

James stifled his abrasive reply but stepped back as his mother approached him and raised her hand to touch his cheek, as she had done when he was a child. His own eyes narrowed and a flash of anger was noted by his natural parent.

"Always the same sensitive little boy."

Scorn was clearly evident in the six mocking words and James smiled thinly.

"I knew it was a mistake to come and see you but I made a promise to someone important that I would."

Maria snorted in indignation.

"Someone important? In your life; let me guess. The pathetic wastrel or his love sick sister, who still carries a torch for you and still you ignore her?"

James shook his head and turned to leave, thoughts of his hideous teenage years and growth into manhood flooding into his mind, obliterating the few repressed golden memories of childhood with his brother; when his parents were happy and kind.

"As I said, always the same boy. Runs away at the first sign of any trouble."

His footfalls stopped echoing around the church and he looked over his shoulder with a derisory stare.

"Why do you hate me mother?"

The question caught her off guard and she chewed the

inside of her mouth before retorting.

"I do not hate you James, I never have. But..."

The pause unlocked the unpleasantness in the mind of the son and he laughed mirthlessly.

"But I am not John and I am not my father and you would rather look after the dead than the living. Because the dead can never let you down can they and nor can they answer back. You stand there and tell me I left you when you needed my love the most? How dare you? I was a boy, a child of seven years when my brother and father were killed. I needed you. It was your job to look after me. You were the adult, you were my mother. I was lost and you did not bother to find me. I came a lowly third and you can never compete with the dead."

Emotion spilled into his mouth and his hoarse voice cracked as he spoke rapidly and viciously. His mother stood motionless; her face imperious and impassive and he nodded in understanding.

"I am sorry for bothering you in your Lord's house. I lost a child, a sweet, innocent boy and I thought you would understand that loss and help me take away the pain in my heart but I was mistaken. "

James controlled his tone and turned back to leave as his mother spoke again.

"You can never understand the loss of a child. I gave birth to that boy and he was perfect in every way. You lost some orphaned Jew who you pitied and brought up."

He stopped again and turned around slowly, fury building within his mind and his heart ached in his trembling body; struggling to keep his voice low and calm.

"You are empty. A mere shade of a mother. I will not come again. When my father and my brother died, so did my mother to me."

Whirling around, James quickened his pace and almost ran out of the church, oblivious to the tears trickling down his face as he burst out back onto the narrow streets and hurried towards the south wall and the stables; needing to get out of the city and ride Merdlan out into the sanctuary of the desert to be at peace with himself.

Standing alone in the dark, Maria Vitelli watched her only remaining family member leave the sanctity of the Church of St Sabas and turned to kneel at the altar, her body heaving as she sobbed and begged the forgiveness of her benevolent deity.

Chapter 13

Thomas Holdingham

James returned from his solitary ride through the lush valleys of wheat fields below Mount Huron refreshed and at peace with himself once again. The introspection had been completed as Merdlan's hooves thundered past the Muslim and Christian farmers, who made the verdant valleys their home; one of the few stretches of arable land in Outremer. He felt at one with his great stallion; it was as if he merged with the beast, becoming one. Unlike the Christian Knights, James sought no dominance over his steed and unlike the fierce destriers of the Crusaders; Merdlan was an Arabian horse; larger than the typical Turcoman or Egyptian breeds but of their placid temperament. He was a joy to ride and his owner adored him. James was a skilled horseman; for a man of European blood, he was truly gifted and had trained hard to be a talented rider but in comparison to some of the Saracens, who seemed born of the animal and who rode bareback before they could actually talk and who could shoot a bow from a galloping horse in their early teen years; he knew he would never be a master of the art. However, he also had a natural affinity with the breed and his development and training of them had been a success, both financially and in terms of personal contentment. No horse was deemed unworthy and James treated every animal with respect; building up a relationship of equal standing and getting the best from every mare or stallion. Of all the horses he had owned or rode in his thirty three years; Merdlan was his favourite by far and after five years of ownership; both animal and rider knew each other perfectly; to such an extent that James did not use stirrups any longer and his saddle was specifically designed of the softest leather and the harness had been simplified so the usual mouthpiece

161

had been discarded. Merdlan did not need to be kicked, pulled or poked to be more aggressive as the Christian insisted nor did he have to be coaxed into subtle obedience as the Muslim required; James treated him as he did any friend. The relationship was pure and like any good relationship, was built on trust and equality and like any true friend; after an emotional morning and after two hours of company; James felt revived and had consigned the parts of his past that brought him pain, back into the darkest recesses of his heart.

Returning to the loving bosom of his eclectic group of friends; his spirits soared as the entire group rode to the banks of the Kishon River, near the Desert Trail, which led to the small holding two miles in the distance. Maria, Jaeda and Aisha prepared the various dried fruits, goat's cheese, assorted breads and various other delicacies on the woollen blanket as Alessio and James tethered the horses to a lemon tree, near the reed grasses where the three horses could graze happily.

"How was the meeting?"

Alessio asked quietly as he tied his dappled mare to the sturdy trunk of the fruit tree and James groaned audibly.

"Sadly, that woman is as bitter and twisted now as ever."

The Venetian chuckled softly, smiling at his friend's look of resignation.

"Well, did you really expect any more from her? Maria goes to her church and says she is the same as ever."

"Hmmmm...well, possibly not...anyway, I made good my promise to Aisha and my conscience is clear."

James shrugged and smiled as he basked momentarily

in the fact that he had managed finally to find the higher moral ground than his mother. Alessio gripped his forearm and spoke earnestly.

"Your mother does love you James; she always asks after you with Maria and follows your life's journey from afar. Loss affects people in different ways..."

James smiled warmly and nodded in understanding, chuckling as he moved back towards the others.

"She was complimentary about you too, Al!"

"I bet she did! What did she say? Am I still leading you astray? I mean, you are in your thirties; I cannot believe I am still getting the blame for your mistakes..."

Aisha grinned as she heard Alessio's continuous whining and all three women laughed as James explained the reasoning for his friend's moans and complaints. The same joyous vein flowed through the afternoon with laughter, self-deprecation and humility enveloping the group; as they ate, conversed and enjoyed the men's appalling and ultimately futile attempts at fishing with bare hands in the gentle river. The afternoon ended with the trip to the small holding, where they all visited Jacob's final resting place; Maria offering silent prayers to God, Jaeda offering silent prayers to Allah, Aisha picturing the boy's smiling face as he played, Alessio remembering their sword fights and wrestling matches with fondness and James struggling to recall the good times as he knew he must but the blackness of his soul devoured the beautiful images and he was left with the shattered, lifeless corpse as his final memory.

Masking his pain from his companions, he thrust the need for vengeance back into the part of him he did not like to unleash and together, with Alessio, they chatted to the patrol of Hospitallers that were guarding the buildings and seeing to the vines and horses. The main cabin had been expertly repaired and no sign of the attack could be seen. As everybody assembled to return to Acre; Aisha approached him solemnly and placed a leather pendant in his hand; the base of the jewellery a simple silver bar which bore the name 'Jacob' in Hebrew. The man's stomach lurched as he looked into her oval, dark watery eyes and he wiped the tears before they fell onto her olive hued cheeks. Aisha showed him her left wrist which had a new leather bracelet adorning it; the same silver bar and the same inscription.

"Maria organised it; I owe her a days' work in the shop. I thought it would be nice...that we had the same. He loved us, James. This way, we will never forget him and he will always be with us."

She struggled to get the words out and they tumbled out in a staccato fashion and James placed the gift around his neck, kissed the girl and nodded slowly.

"It is a beautiful thought. I love it and I will never take it off."

Hugging his ward briefly, he waved his thanks to Maria who watched smiling a few yards away and the emotional group travelled the Desert Trail back to Acre in relative silence, each of them meditating on their own feelings as they entered the great gates of the port and stabled their mounts at the Knights Hospitallers Temple stable; another part of the agreement between James and the Grand Master. As usual, it was Alessio who broke the subdued contemplation with his innate charming tongue.

"I say that James and I go to the fish market and get a fresh tuna for tonight's meal whilst you three head back."

He beamed at his sister; knowing that she and the girls

would like to bathe and cleanse the dust and sand from their bodies and he was eager to maintain the positivity within the household; he knew James remained in a difficult paradoxical position and Aisha was still vulnerable. The tuna was a special treat as only few fishermen drifted that far into the Mediterranean to spear them and so were expensive, but it was also the favourite meal of his friend.

"Sounds perfect, give us a couple of hours to prepare ourselves and then bring it back so I can cook dinner."

Maria said gently and grinned at her two favourite men as they said goodbyes and drifted into the crowds. Aisha chuckled to herself as she saw Maria stare wistfully after James and Jaeda's eyes sparkle as she watched Alessio's sinewy frame disappear. Maintaining a modest silence for approximately five seconds, she blurted out her observations and soon all three were giggling as the initial indignant refusals diluted into shared secrets before they had even reached Silk Street.

The two men strode past the arsenal and the Patriarchate along the outer harbour's wall, moving swiftly towards the fish market; located in the inner harbour's walls in the Genoan Quarter of the city. Alessio chattered incessantly about people's clothing, new stalls that had appeared, a new cog bearing an enormous catapult on its stern deck and flying the flag of the newly independent Kingdom of Sicily in the docks and other miscellaneous observations, to which James responded with affirmative grunts or nods when pressed, but he had no interest in the idle gossip and chatter of Alessio. A man had been following them since they had arrived back in the port and he was following them still. Worse than this, he knew the man and disliked him intensely. The scar running down the length of his face and the height and breadth of the man was hard to disguise. Aldo was a dangerous man, the leading henchman of Francesco, personal bodyguard to the old owner of 'La Caravel' and a known brigand, smuggler and murderer. A man who delighted in inflicting pain and a man, James had always been wise to avoid and as Alessio witter on like an old woman; his thought processes failed to find a reason for Aldo to be following them. The deal over Alessio had been concluded in full and he had not provoked any further argument with Francesco at any point in the past few days.

Reaching the oval shaped fish market, the air became filled with its multi-lingual shouts from the numerous proprietors of the stalls and the overwhelming stench of the sea's bounty. James pointed out the usual trader he used; an elderly man of Tuscan ancestry and Alessio began to head towards him before stopping and turning to James.

"I don't have any money."

James swore under his breath as he had expected the sentence to come from his comrade and he flicked his eyes to the heavens as he passed Alessio a mixture of bronze and silver coins. Thanking him, Alessio moved away again as James stood in the centre of the marketplace and scanned the area, locating his obvious spy, leaning against the wooden frame of an unknown man's fish stall. Steeling himself, he strode slowly towards Aldo, who watched him approach; a sardonic smile spreading across his tanned features. Cursing the fact that the larger man of ill repute merely stood casually, waiting for him, and his mind whirled with what to say to Aldo.

"Good day to you Aldo."

He chose a pleasant tone in Italian and the man stared down at him with a curt nod.

"James."

"You would not be following me would you?"

The question was direct but dripped with a sarcastic humour. Aldo stood upright and stated matter of factly.

"Possibly and if I was?"

The response threw James off guard and he struggled to find a swift retort without looking weak and foolish.

"Why would you do that?"

"That is my business."

The uncomfortable conversation attracted the attention of the nearest vendor and four of his patrons and James flushed under their scrutiny. The pause lengthened as James and Aldo stared at each other balefully.

"What's the matter James? The great Christian hero who killed the Muslim champion is now scared of a lowly ruffian like me?"

His voice grew louder so his speech could be heard and a ripple of excitement murmuring echoed immediately around the stalls. James gritted his teeth and turned and walked towards Alessio, who he could see was purchasing his chosen tuna across the marketplace from him.

"And I thought you loved Muslims more than Christians, guess I was wrong!"

Aldo shouted after him and James grimaced as a man hurried towards him in a cloth robe, obviously some holy preacher or priest of some kind.
"My son, my son! Are you the one who killed our enemies' champion?"

The words were asked loudly in Italian with a French accent and James kept his head down and ignored him blatantly, pushing past him and the crowd of hawkers and buyers, who were now all turning to study the unfolding scene. Aldo followed, bellowing at the holy man that James was indeed the man who defeated the man known as Saadiq, the leader of the Immortals and the Champion of the Caliphate Zengi himself. Trying to avoid the cheers and claps on his back, James heaved his ways towards Alessio, who was now looking at the commotion with a puzzled expression adorning his face.

"You have done a wonderful thing, my son. God be praised. The Gates of Heaven await you for your devotion to God Almighty."

The priest and Aldo strode behind him, each in turn calling after him and many of the men and women around him called after him, praising him and asking for details of the heroic battle.

"Leave me alone!"

James roared as strangers hand grabbed and rested on him from all sides and he pushed his way through the heaving mass to get to the street, Alessio already heading towards 'Harbour Street', which led to 'Via Casa' and back to the relative sanctuary of the Venetian Quarter.

"You are a hero of God my son. You have shown the way in which we must deal with the heathen. Death to all Turks and unbelievers!"

The priest's voice became louder and more high pitched and he clung to the shoulders of James, who darted left, ducking under the feeble grip and the man fell, flailing to the ground.

"He struck the priest!"

Aldo shouted, pointing to the retreating James and repeating his sentence over and over again. The marketplace became a hostile venue; angry words between strangers leading to punches being thrown and a brawl soon developed, with men fighting and others pushing and shoving to avoid the confrontations. James reached Alessio and the two men attempted to reach the cobbled street which exited the fish market when a middle aged man, screeching insults in French punched James in the back and the horse trader fell heavily onto the ground and would have been stamped on by the same raging individual had Alessio not struck the man full in the face with the carefully wrapped tuna, sending the irate Frenchman sprawling backwards, disappearing into the surging crowd. Laughing at the sight, James scurried across the ground and exited the market with Alessio, still gripping his makeshift weapon in both hands, running behind him. The laughter ended suddenly as the great bulk of Aldo appeared before him and his hand shot out to grab James by the throat and pick him physically off the ground in one hand. In his other hand, a curved knife glinted in the sunlight and he smiled sickly at Alessio.

"You want to try and hit me with that fish?"

Alessio snarled in reply, ignoring the men and women who streamed past them away from the fighting that had suddenly and violently erupted in the centre of the market, concentrating only on the man in front of him, ignoring the various cries, oaths and screams as people were hit and stalls damaged in the melee.

"What do you want Aldo? We have done nothing to you."

James twisted violently as he felt the blood rush to his head and his booted feet kicked out at Aldo who laughed at the struggle. Alessio threw himself into Aldo's left side, grabbing his forearm in both hands to protect both James and himself from the knife and Aldo had to drop his one opponent to concentrate on the other. James fell heavily to the cobbled street in a heap

169

and coughed heartily, stroking his tender throat with his hand as he struggled to rise to his feet. The sounds of hooves came suddenly to his ears and he realised the guards were heading this way to end the riotous behaviour and he swore as he watched Aldo toss Alessio against the crumbling wall of the inner harbour and raise the knife in one sweeping arc. Before his legs could move, a fist struck the muscular immigrant in his stomach and as he turned sharply to face the unknown assailant, a second punch cracked off his chin. A third hit his left cheek with immense force and Aldo yelled in defiance, loosening his grip on the knife and Alessio, who crawled across the ground like a crab, out of the way of the pugilists. A fourth punch shattered the man's nose and James shuddered as he heard the bone break on the sheer force of the impact. Aldo collapsed, blood spraying from his nostrils.

"Come on! We need to get out of here!"

Alessio shouted above the cacophony of noise as the armed guards began to ride into the marketplace to quell the violence. James pointed across the street to a slim alleyway, which led to the Jewish area of the port and the stranger who had broken Aldo's nose followed Alessio and himself into the alley, where they paused to watch Acre's guards begin to clear the market and some of the rioters were arrested and held at sword point. Alessio grinned as they all watched a dazed Aldo be greeted by three guards who bundled him into the centre of the fish market with several others as the brief explosion of violence dissipated.

"Let's get out of here."

James smiled and led the others down a series of stinking lanes and finally out into 'Via Tempia' where they relaxed their pace to a stroll.

"Well, my friend, what is your name?"

Alessio drawled with a beaming smile at his saviour. The stocky man, in his middle forties shrugged his muscled shoulders and spoke in English back to Alessio's question in Italian.

"I don't speak anything but English."

James smiled at the accent, which reminded him instantly of his father and he translated Alessio's question into English for the stranger.

"Ah, good, a fellow Englishman. My name is Thomas Holdingham and I am pleased to make your acquaintance."
James shook the man's large, calloused hand and introduced himself and in turn Alessio and they too shook hands.

"Well, Thomas Holdingham, my friend and I would like to buy you a drink as a gift for your fine right hook."

Thomas scratched his balding head and one of his pale blue eyes winked.

"Lead on boys, you can each buy me one!"

James laughed and translating for Alessio and Thomas in turn, who spoke none of the other's natural language, the three men strode through the Genoese Quarter in glorious sunshine.

"There's a bar. Drinks are on you."

Thomas said heartily and trudged to the tavern he had pointed out. The two men halted behind him as they saw the sign 'Il Caravel' and Alessio shrugged his shoulders, grinning as he followed the Englishman to the door.

"Aldo will be kept in a cell overnight so we will

be fine! Don't worry, nothing will happen!"

James watched the two men disappear into the inn and groaned audibly, a sudden feeling of dread passing over him as he stepped inside the bar room. Alessio was already ordering at the bar when James reluctantly entered and felt immediately relieved that there was no sign of Francesco. Sophia's younger sister was serving and already feeling the force of Alessio's charm and complimentary language. Thomas and James found a small, rickety, round table near the grime covered window, away from the other drinkers and Alessio joined them with three flagons of ale.

"You actually bought a round of drinks Al, I am impressed."

James said with heavy sarcasm but Alessio promptly chuckled in reply.

"Well, if you want to be truthful about it, it was your change from the tuna that bought the drinks."

James could not help but laugh and translated for Thomas, who had perhaps the loudest most raucous laugh, he had ever heard in his life. In fact, during the ensuing conversation, everything about Thomas was loud. He was a mercenary from a small village named Great Drayton, near the town of Shrewsbury on the Welsh borders with England and had earnt his money and learnt his trade fighting the bands of rebellious Welsh, who refused to kneel before the English King Stephen. More money could be made fighting in France so Thomas moved to where the battles raged, as fighting between the feuding lords and barons was plentiful. Eventually he migrated south to where the Aragonese Royalty were throwing money at mercenaries to defeat the Muslim Moors of the Almohad dynasty and he took part in a series of victorious battles against the infidel. A chance encounter with a group of English knights, who had stopped in Southern Iberia, on their way to the holy land, brought him here as passage was provided on their ship, which was bound for Acre. Thomas advised his avid listeners that the new Pope has decreed all sins will be abolished for those who atone for these sins by fighting against the Saracen in the Holy Land and he who kills in God's name will go to heaven.

"So you have sinned?"

Alessio asked with interest and the answer was hard to read.

"Many, many times. I feared for my very soul but now it seems, even God will forgive me."

James was bemused and could not understand the Papal logic.

"But why would killing Muslims here be any different than killing Muslims in Navarre or Castile?"

Thomas turned and studied James for a moment before replaying evenly.

"Because this is where Christianity was born, it is Christ's land and because the holy Pope himself has decreed it so. Now James, do you know more than the Pope himself about God's will?"

"I am not sure if I even believe in God any more Thomas, this land has destroyed my faith not improved it."

The blue eyes of the Englishman softened and he nodded gravely.

"There is violence and death everywhere and I have seen my share but if the great God himself can forgive my mortal sins by killing Muslims in this land; that is what I will do."

173

James partially translated to Alessio who mumbled a non-committal response, his mind already filtering away from the conversation as he had seen one of the working girls from upstairs come down to replenish drinks for their guests. The woman saw Alessio and grinned, acknowledging him with a sultry pout.

"Alessio! You have not seen me in weeks! Have you come to see me?"

James turned to see a young woman in her early twenties he did not recognise but was wearing a tight fitting long dress, open at the bust to show an appealing amount of powdered cleavage. He turned back to grin at Alessio who ignored him and stood, to kiss the woman's cheeks.

"I will be up in a few moments Teresa."

A throaty giggle was the only response as the woman headed back up the staircase with a tray filled with wine, mead and ale.

"Do not judge me, I have not.....for many days. I am not married; there is no shame in it."

Alessio wriggled under the gaze of James who opened his arms passively.

"I have not said a word, she seems a lovely girl and I am sure she has many hidden talents!"
"Not that hidden!"

Thomas exclaimed with another burst of guffawing.

"By all things holy, you are as bad as Maria. Keep your moral high ground, some of us have needs."

Both men erupted into a bout of chuckling and James struggled to translate for Thomas, whose own eyes widened in delight, at the thoughts of what was happening upstairs and James had to translate a most disconcerting conversation between his two fellow drinkers about pricings and types of women, available in the chambers above. Fortunately, a friendly voice stopped the uncomfortable translation as Sophia appeared behind James, the tight fitting white dress, girdled at her waist with a black braid, showing off every curve of her body. Used to the lascivious stares of men; she flicked the soft ringlets of her brunette hair from her shoulder and spoke to James, her eyes not wavering from his.

"Back so soon James? You need another round of drinks?"

James struggled to maintain eye contact and nodded, looking to Alessio who winked at him and declined.

"Not for me, I have an...an...err mm...appointment with Teresa."

Sophia smiled broadly, her full lips curving wickedly upwards but her charcoal painted eyes did not leave the face of her former lover.

"Ahhh, I see and your new friend, will you not introduce me James?"

James murmured an affirmation and repeated the words in English for the mercenary. Thomas stood immediately and undertook a slight bow with a flourish.

"Thomas Holdingham, at your service ma'am."

Sophia clucked a soft giggle and imitated a curtsey, speaking in faltering English.

"Pleased to meet you kind sir, I am Sophia and I look after the girls upstairs. Are you joining Alessio? And you James?"

The alluring eyes had left him momentarily but were back within a second and James shook his head, stammering under the beguiling gaze.

"No...no...I am just fine here."

Alessio masked his humour at the discomfort of his friend and stood, motioning Thomas to follow him. The Englishman needed no secondary encouragement and rose; straightening his tunic and breeches as he followed his new found Venetian friend up the staircase and into the pleasure palace beyond. James shuffled his backside on the basic wooden chair as Sophia stood, smiling into his eyes.

"May I sit? I could take a break, it is unusually quiet today."

The horseman stood, agreed and moved to the bar to purchase another tankard of the brackish ale and a spiced wine for Sophia, which he hoped she still enjoyed. Moving back to the table with the drinks, Sophia grinned and gratefully accepted the alcohol, complimenting her one time suitor on his memory.

"So, you are quite the famous swordsman it seems? Is it true? You killed some Champion?"

James blanched openly and shifted his weight on the uncomfortable chair.

"I killed a man who attacked my home, Sophia. It is nothing to be proud of; his men killed Jacob and my workers."

The Italian woman rested her elegant hand gently on the fingers of James and sighed audibly.

"I heard that too James, I am so sorry. How is your girl?"

Not for the first time since returning to Acre, James wondered if everybody knew his business and felt spied upon, his personal life violated in some way.

"Aisha is ok, she survived."

Sophia removed her light touch, sensing the rebuke and sipped her wine.

"Sorry, I don't understand any of this, I am no hero. I killed a killer, defending myself. If I had not, he would have slaughtered me and everybody else. I have no idea why he even came to attack us; I have done nothing to bring such a man to my home."

His earnest words brought back the hand to touch skin again and Sophia leant in, whispering conspiratorially.

"I do not understand any of this either but you need to be careful. I overheard Aldo and my father talking about you; they have been watching you; they know you are back with Alessio's sister. You know how they feel about you...."

James pulled his hand back and gripped his tankard to take a deep draught, wiping his mouth afterwards and leaning back in his chair.

"Your father hates me for what happened between us, I can almost accept that but Aldo, that man is an animal. He hates me because he wants you, he hates me because he loves to hate."

Sophia grimaced and muttered a filthy oath.

"That man is evil and will never touch me. I see his eyes on me, always have and he is vile but he is also dangerous so keep your eyes open. Whatever powerful enemies you have found James, watch your back with Aldo and my father."

"Aldo stirred up trouble for me this afternoon in the fish market. I have no concept of an idea as to why but a riot erupted. Fortunately, Thomas came to our aid and broke Aldo's nose and then he was taken by the city guard."

James explained and his hazel eyes sparkled with a glint of humour. Sophia chuckled loudly and with a wistful smile upon her Latin face, she spoke.

"Now that I would have liked to see. Remind me to tell the girl; Thomas is with to offer herself freely. I wondered why he had not returned."

James joined in with the laughter and looked over at Sophia's beautiful smile, swiftly averting his stare as the woman caught his admiring gaze.

"We shall have to go soon; I wouldn't want to be here when Aldo returns!"

Sophia let her fingers dance lightly across the man's sensitive skin of his upper cheek and grinned.

"Don't worry my hero; I will protect you from the big, bad man."

She teased playfully, continuing with a mischievous twinkle in her eyes.

"Anyway, if the girls are to be believed; you will have a long wait for Alessio!"

James spat out the gulp of ale he had just taken back into the earthenware tankard, screwing up his face in a look of absolute horror.

"Please, please don't tell me that."

Sophia smiled warmly at the mock derision.

"Well, I was amazed that the Venetian was actually good at something!"

James made a gesture of defiance at the teasing woman of Genoan descent.

"I have Venetian blood and he is my friend, I am the only one who can abuse him!"

Both laughed in unison and the other patrons of the tavern turned to stare at their uproar.

"Well, well. How touching, the sweet reunion of teenage lovers touches my heart."

The laughter ceased abruptly as James twisted sharply in the chair to look behind him as Sophia's eyes widened in alarm at the man who had silently walked into the establishment. James had no time to register that Aldo had strode in, when he was physically seized in a vice like grip by his shoulders and heaved across the bar room floor, skating across the dust and dirt of the floorboards and striking the solid oak bar with a heavy thud.

"Leave him alone! How dare you...in my father's bar."

Sophia stood, shaking with a mixture of indignation and fear as she looked upwards into the man's broken and battered features.

"I am going to enjoy you watching me teach this whelp a lesson he has had coming for a long time."

Aldo's eyes were void of emotion and the woman feared for James, screaming shrilly to gain the attention of her father and other guards, who she knew were stationed downstairs where the gambling tables stood. James breathed heavily, clutching his stomach and crouching into a squat position. Winded, he stood groggily and turned in time to see Aldo bearing down on him, a

179

twisted smirk adorning his bloodied, demolished face
and he staggered backwards into a table, where the
skittish locals who had sat there, edged away nervously.
James swung his fist as Aldo neared him and struck the
hulking Genoan on the chin with a glancing blow. Pain
erupted across his knuckles and his pride also took a hit
as Aldo threw his head back with a snort of derision as
he punched James with force in his abdomen; sending
the man flailing backwards onto the table where he
rolled onto the wood and slumped onto the floor.
Bracing his prone body for the kicking that was about to
commence, James covered his head and genitals with
arms and knees; until an unlikely saviour stopped the
bar room brawl with two words.

"Aldo. No!"

Francesco's portly frame shuffled into the bar and Aldo
immediately ceased his onslaught. James unravelled
his limbs slowly on the floorboards and using a chair for
support, raised his aching body to his feet to see
Francesco, Sophia and Aldo before him as Thomas
bounced down the stairs behind them.

"Not here, not now. You, get out of my bar."

Francesco grunted unhappily and thrust a stubby finger
towards James. Forcibly pushing Aldo towards the
winding staircase that led to the gambling den below,
the owner of Il Caravel shuffled away, murmuring
something to his eldest daughter, who, with a last caring
glance at James, followed her father and Aldo down the
stairs. Two armed guards pointed to the door and
James nodded as Thomas joined him.

"You ok? What did I miss?"

James forced a smile and said.

"Nothing much, just our old friend returning
early from the guard house."

"Oh, I see."

Thomas replied, watching the backs of the three figures disappear down the stairs in the far corner of the room. Alessio appeared at the landing above them, fastening his breeches and his shirt wide open, and boots in hand.

"Trouble?"

James looked at his lustful companion and said simply.

"We are leaving."

Alessio struggled to put his boots on and trotted down the stairs, seeing the armed guards open the door for them. Filing outside, the three men walked wearily down the pathway towards the Venetian Quarter.

"Well boys, spending time with you is certainly never dull!"

Thomas stated and roared in laughter, his booming voice echoing off the walls of the densely packed terraced buildings as they moved off.

****

The unremarkable face of the bounty hunter broke into a slight smile as he watched the events in the tavern from his position by the roaring fire. Unrolling the vellum parchment with his dexterous fingers, the man read the words again and confirmed the name of the man wanted dead by the Muslim despot; Imad Ad-Din Atabec Zengi Al Malik Al Mansir and licked his lower lip as he stared at the purse on offer; 500 Bezants. An incredible sum for the death of one man and such an easy kill to locate. It had taken him less than a day to find this back street den of inequity. The man allowed his smile to broaden as he rolled up the parchment and replace it back into a large leather pouch at his waist. Easing back in his chair, he watched the flames of the fire dance as he contemplated what he could purchase with such a sum and wondered if this should be his last kill. The men, known only as 'Il Falco' sipped the most expensive Italian imported wine the inn had to offer and allowed himself to drift into a series of pleasurable dreamscapes.

Chapter 14

A Brief Respite

      James was awake, long before the dawn of the early morning sun streamed through the wooden shutters of the small, nondescript bedchamber on Silk Street in the largely Christian city of Acre. It was a Sunday and for many of the residents of this port, the church bells pealed out for the holy to congregate and listen to, in the opinion of the man who was casually waking; the various tedious oratories and sing the banal hymns to their omnipotent and benevolent God. Beyond the flimsy door, he could hear Maria and Alessio preparing to leave for their chosen sermon and he groaned and rolled onto his back, staring up at the cracked ceiling and trying not to remember the hideous nightmare that had woken him hours previously. Not for the first time in the past few days, he wished that he was a believer and could get some support from the Christian faith. If reading the Bible and listening to old men talk of sacrifice and commitment, equated to him feeling less guilty and depressed over Jacob's loss; he would join the gathering throngs heading to the numerous churches right now. Unfortunately, the man of mixed English and Italian blood merely lay back and focused his mind on recreating the beautiful moments he had been fortunate enough to share with the boy and not the grotesque visions of his death that haunted his dreams. Rolling his aching body out of the bed, he trudged wearily to the cold water that sat on the floor near the door, in an earthen clay bowl and he splashed the water over his face and shoulders, the icy temperature numbing his skin momentarily but succeeding in reviving and invigorating his body, bringing him out of his lethargy instantly. Using the metal ladle to pour the lightly fragranced water over his hair and forehead, he allowed the freezing rivulets to run down his entire frame, shaking his naked body as he shivered involuntarily.

Pulling on his linen undergarment, which covered his modesty, he threw his simple cotton tunic over his head; absently touching the pendant that dangled from his neck as he did so. Seating himself on the bed, he tugged on his breeches and short stockings, easing his feet into the soft leather boots and then standing; he added the thick leather belt and then opened the door, striding to the kitchen area to break his fast. The dwelling was empty and he recalled Aisha telling him yesterday that Jaeda and herself were heading to the Muslim market outside the ports walls as the spice camel train from Egypt would be passing through before the muezzin would call Allah's faithful to their own prayers. Alone, James searched for something to eat and he settled on some goat's cheese and unleavened bread, as this was simple and quick, hurriedly washing it down with two cups of fresh water. Left to his own thoughts in a silent room; he cleaned his platter and smiled as he remembered the events of yesterday and how Thomas, the English mercenary had thrust himself into their lives in such a dramatic fashion. James had managed to get the man lodgings at the Hospital free of charge for a few days and he wondered when he would see him next. His meandering thoughts drifted onto Sophia and he envisaged her obvious and very sexual beauty and wondered what held him back from making her his once again. Incomprehensibly, Maria's softer features appeared in his mind's eye and he scratched the stubble on his chin and filled his brain with less enigmatic musings by heading to the basin and using his flat bladed knife, he removed the unwanted facial hair from his jaw, neck and cheeks. Completing the daily chore, he wiped his face with a rough cloth and wondered what to do with his day. He had forgotten how tiresome Sundays were back in Acre; the stalls did not trade, taverns did not open and religion was thrust firmly into the forefront of life. At his home, Sundays had been the same as any other day and tasks were performed with equal vigour and religion did not play a part in the life cycle of the cabin and its inhabitants. Again, the smiling face of Jacob thrust itself forcefully into his mind and he grimaced, as the negative emotive feelings of loss and blame reacted with the image. James needed to perform some activity and as always, when at a loss, he decided to visit Merdlan at the Hospitaller stables and head out into the open ground for a ride to clear his recurring thought processes.

Less than a mile away and at exactly that moment, Thomas Holdingham was rudely awakened by a French knight who rapped his steel gauntlet off the oak door continuously until the Englishman roared out an array of expletives, which halted the banging and brought about a harsh order, rasped in heavily accented English.

"You are wanted by the Grand Master. Immediately!"

The man grunted acceptance and rubbed his forehead as he heard the man's retreating footfalls on the flagstones. Sitting up instigated another groan as he felt sharp pain in the knuckles of his right hand. Memories flooded into his brain of his exploits yesterday and he looked around the small bedchamber; James had managed to get for him to stay in free of charge temporarily. It was austere but satisfactory and the only negative in such an arrangement was that he seemed to be surrounded by Frenchmen in the walled Order of the Hospital of St John. Thomas stood upright and washed his face in the basin of freezing cold water that had been left for him and he swore under his breath. He had met many nationalities and being typically English; despised most of them. Celts were no more than painted savages, Flemish were tedious and without humour, Spaniards were weak and ineffective, Italians could never be trusted and the French; they were the most odious of all God's creations; arrogant and rude to a man and right now, he was surrounded by members of this annoying breed. Dressing quickly, he opened the door and followed the stone hallway to the main dining area and from there, through two ante chambers and paused momentarily at the closed door of the Grand Master's private chamber; glancing at the armed guards on either side of the aperture. Stealing himself, he knocked on the door loudly and was greeted with an ejaculation in French he did not understand but presuming it to be a form of welcome, the mercenary opened the door and strode into the opulent surroundings of Raymond Du Puy, the current ruler of the Knights Hospitallers.

"You wished to see me, My Lord?"

Thomas sat down as Du Puy, dressed in a fine satin shirt with the coat of arms of his Order emblazoned across the chest, waved his hand casually towards the basic wooden chair.

"You must forgive me, my English is not that good."

The Knight commenced in perfect English and Thomas smiled thinly, feeling belittled already as it was apparent that he spoke no French and thus, the Grand Master had to speak in the one language they both understood.

"Whilst a friend of James Rose is a welcome guest at our establishment, grave news about your friend has come to our attention."

Thomas bent slightly nearer and listened intently at this unexpected and very direct conversation, as he had been merely expecting a time frame for his stay to be discussed.

"You are familiar with the Tree of Knowledge, in the very centre of Acre Monsieur?"

Du Puy continued as the blank expression on the Englishman's face told him all he needed to know.

"Well, it is an old Cypress tree with a huge trunk, which has been here for decades; before even we came and conquered this realm. It is used as a message board of sorts, where people place notices or requests for help; finding a loved one, workers required and such things."

Thomas nodded as the man paused to make sure the conversation was being followed accurately, clearly not entirely confident of his knowledge of the English language.

"Yesterday, notes were found on the tree in Arabic, Italian and French; offering a large reward for the death of James. His description and both his Venetian and his English surnames were mentioned."

The mercenary could not mask his shock at the statement.

"Why would anybody want James dead? He is a trader in horses."

The Grand Master clasped his hands and looked directly into the eyes of Thomas before responding, unnerving the recipient of the gaze somewhat.

"Well, I am not sure how much you know of your friend but it is common knowledge that he has slain the leader of the 'Immortals', a Champion, if you will, of the mad tyrant; Zengi himself. Indeed, it is Zengi's crest upon the notes."

Thomas shifted in his seat and reminded himself to have increased respect for the man he met yesterday.

"And what, pray tell, would James have done to instigate the wrath of such a man?"
The Frenchman opened his hands and shrugged in typical Gallic fashion.

"Obviously, these notes have been removed and destroyed but we cannot be sure how many are in circulation. Your friend is in danger and I would like you to advise him of this danger and perhaps advise him to leave Acre. The reward is substantial and the port will be filled with bounty hunters and assassins if this gets to a wider audience."

"Of course."

"Good. If James would like to see me, please arrange it with my advisor."

Feeling dismissed, Thomas made sure before risking offence, his mind still whirling at the shocking news.

"Are we finished?"

Du Puy nodded and the English swordsman rose and left the chamber stiffly, closing the door behind him gently. Once outside the door, Thomas moved through the luxuriously decorated rooms without even a passing interest in the colourful tapestries, elaborate artefacts or exquisite paintings as he was interested in the man called James Rose and all of his thoughts were directed at the man he met yesterday. The Grand Master had not mentioned an actual fee but the word 'substantial' was used. This was indeed intriguing and with a lighter step, the mercenary headed to his chamber to collect his remaining belongings and to seek out this most extraordinary individual who had a very rich, powerful Caliph wanting him dead.

The search was short lived in the extreme. Thomas exited the main corridor of the Temple and headed into the spacious courtyard where sword practise and horse training took place and there at the stable entrance was the man, he had been requested to converse with.

"James!"

Thomas called out above the incessant din of metal striking metal and hurried over to clasp forearms with the horse merchant. The initial easy smile he had been greeted with faded as the conversation ensued swiftly; Thomas repeating verbatim what he had been told by Du Puy himself. James did not respond to the information immediately and his face clouded in confusion and frustration.

"I need to think this through. Thank you for the message but I need some time to get to grips with the news."

The brief answer was stilted and muttered and Thomas felt sympathy for the man, who seemed to have the weight of all the many problems of the Holy Land on his shoulders.

"I am going to take Merdlan out. Will you be here when I get back?"

Thomas blinked in the morning sun, which streamed over the sand of the courtyard and shaded his eyes.

"I could ride with you?"

James nodded and shrugged listlessly.

"I am probably not going to be much company and I thought you were a religious man? You will have prayers, hymns, and sermons today?"

"God and I have made our pact through a priest back in England. I know what must be done for me to atone for my sins. This I will do to enter the Kingdom of Heaven. Until this is done, there is naught to be said."

The words were solemn and stated with conviction and James nodded again and let the matter pass without further explanation. The men moved inside the gloomy stables and as James mounted the ebony stallion,

Thomas awaited for a black and white gelding to be readied for him by the young groomsman. A few minutes later, the two men rode their mounts hard along the dusty track out of the city gates and across the road that led northwards, snaking its way along the coastline, giving glorious views of the Mediterranean Sea, had either of the riders the inclination to look.

James gave Merdlan the opportunity to gallop and the mature beast of a horse responded happily; leaving the younger gelding in his wake as he raced over the dust, sand and dirt, eating up over two miles of the rough terrain without tiring. Eventually, as beads of perspiration covered both horse and rider, James eased Merdlan down to a canter and then a trot, stroking his neck and whispering compliments into his flattened ears. Approaching the outskirts of a Christian village, he located the well and dismounted, leading his mount to it. Heaving the bucket filled with cool water up the stone shaft, James shared the refreshing liquid with Merdlan; taking his fill and then leaving the bucket for the stallion to continue drinking. Resting against the outer wall of the well, he ignored the curious glances and stares from the few inhabitants of the village who were not at their local church service and awaited Thomas, whom he presumed was causing the dust cloud a few hundred yards to the south. He patted Merdlan, praising his constitution and stamina and removed some grain from a leather bag, which hung from the partial saddle and fed the ravenous animal from his cupped hand. His hazel eyes observed the horse and rider approach and his eyelids narrowed as the cloud of dust and sand clouded his vision as the Englishman pulled back on the reins with a raucous 'Hah!'

Thomas dismounted heavily, his hardened leather boots striking the ground with a shuddering thud.

"Christ Almighty, you can ride!"

James grinned at what he believed to be a compliment

190

but to be honest, he was not entirely sure. Passing the man some water from the ladle, he watched the mercenary's flushed cheeks retreat to their natural colour and his breathing regulate as Thomas gulped down the refreshment.

"So where is this?"

He continued, staring at the five or six mute locals, who cast uneasy glances in their direction.

"Welcoming kind of place isn't it?"

James flicked his eyes in the direction of the villagers and smiled thinly.

"They are scared, that's all. They do not the thick walls of Acre to protect them out here."

Thomas cursed fluently, hawked and then spat in derision.

"I came from a God forsaken village like this, it's up to a man to be able to defend himself and a man who can fight should not be scared."

The younger man smiled and looked away from his companion, he had no wish to enter into a debate with the Englishman about the politics of the Holy Land. Thomas clearly had a black and white approach to every topic of conversation and such superfluous commentary would merely confuse his beautifully simplistic approach to life. James suddenly realised that he envied this way of living; void of problems, issues or complications and his smile widened as he looked into the other man's weather worn features.

"Why did you ride with me, Thomas?"

The man avoided eye contact and answered rather evasively.

191

"I didn't want you to do something stupid. You seemed upset."

James nodded and grinned.

"I am fine. I was confused. I am no longer. I know exactly what I need to do."

Thomas scratched his head and his face remained puzzled; seating himself besides James he asked if he would like to share the enlightenment.

"I am going to do what nobody in the world will expect me to do."

The elder man raised an eyebrow quizzically.
"Which is?"

The horseman paused to reflect, choosing each word carefully and stating them with purpose.

"I am going to kill the man responsible for destroying my happy existence. I am going to assassinate Zengi himself."

Thomas bellowed in laughter and sensing his companion's tense seriousness, stifled his frivolity to a chuckle and then to an awkward silence.

"Are you mad? It is impossible. You may as well take your sword right now and put it straight through your guts."

James remained impassive and waited for the man to cease his negative chattering.

"It is perfectly plausible and makes complete sense. I have no idea what I have done to this man but so far he has slain one of my closest friends and his entire family, he has taken an innocent young boy from this world and he has slaughtered three people I cared for deeply. All in my name. All because of me. He has tried to kill me and now he has put a price on my head so killers and glory hunters from all over the lands will seek me out and murder me."

Thomas nodded slowly, listening to the softly spoken words and James progressed.

"This man has caused permanent damage to Aisha and myself with his actions and now if I stay in Acre, I put her in danger again as well as Alessio and Maria. Perhaps others who know me, who knows? So, I have to leave Acre to protect the innocent; I am not having any more blood spilled in my name."
The mercenary nodded with more vigour.

"This is all true and well and good. I think the Hospitallers expect you to head to Cyprus or Byzantium not into Zengi's army!"

"Let me finish, I have not lost all my senses. It is the last thing anybody would expect; it can be common knowledge that I leave for Cyprus and from there to Italy and then I will head alone into the east. Du Puy will have maps of Zengi's territory. I can speak Arabic and alone, I will not arouse suspicion. Once I get to Damascus, I will blend in with the minority Jewish and Christian communities there and work out how to get into Zengi's stronghold. It is not madness. Dangerous yes, perhaps, some would say, it is unlikely that I will succeed."

"Some would say?"

Thomas repeated with a shaking of his balding head.

"So, you of all people, Thomas. You expect me to run away. Like a coward, leaving loved ones behind who may be killed. So you would run would you?"

The pale blue eyes of the Englishmen met the hazel

eyes of James and understanding was soundlessly communicated.

"As plans go, it is weak and highly unlikely."

Thomas eventually said with an exasperated sigh and James agreed.

"To be honest, it only came to me when I was riding. I admit it is in its infancy as plans go."

"There will be many infidel enemies of Christ on this quest?"

James chuckled throatily.

"Almost everybody I will meet will be Muslim and most of them will want me dead I imagine."

"Good. In that case, as long as you pay me a decent rate of pay and provide food; I will come with you. I have a quest that has to be conducted and it seems your insane mission will accommodate both our needs."

Finishing his statement, Thomas watered his horse and ignored the protestations that erupted from James and with a struggle, clambered back onto his mount.

"Shall we return? We will need to speak with that Frenchman and you will need to talk to Alessio."

James placed a hand on the horse's forelock and looked up at Thomas.

"You don't have to do this. I appreciate the sentiment but I am probably better off alone."

"I am a grown man James and I have made my decision. I need my retribution just like you do. You can fool yourself and those around you with your noble ideals and that you are only embarking on this to protect your loved ones. It matters not to me how you say it. However, I know you are like me more than you would like to admit and deep in your heart, you want to kill the man who killed your boy. Now, I understand that more than noble words. Whatever your reasons, the plan, defective as it is, fits in perfectly with my needs and I am coming with you."

Before James could even develop an answer in his mind, Thomas wheeled his horse around and cantered back along the trail towards the great port of Acre, its whitewashed walls evident in the far distance. Lapsing back into thought, James leapt deftly onto Merdlan's great back and whispering instruction to his mount; followed the Englishman at pace.

 The simmering heat bore down on him as he gave Merdlan rein to choose his pace and the stallion cantered briskly along the vague trail southwards. As the horse led its rider back towards the walled port, the rider allowed his mind to question the wisdom of his reactive decision. In truth, he knew he had always wanted to embark on this action as the guilt he felt for Jacob's death far outweighed any other feeling in his being and it gnawed away at him; invading his thoughts and contorting his dreams. Man is a simple, base being and no matter how much one can be educated and righteous and want to do the sensible or the right thing; the raw emotions eradicate the carefully developed filters of human consciousness. James knew he craved vengeance and as he allowed himself to admit it to himself, a feeling of warmth and acceptance washed over him.

Chapter 15

Explanations

James sat uncomfortably in the small chamber, which had been built for Knights to pray, contemplate or write letters to their families, who awaited news from the Holy Land of their loved ones. He placed the expensive quill pen down upon the smooth polished wood next to the three letters he had written and sighed audibly. Stroking his forehead and hair, he looked absently at the large cedar cross which dominated the far wall and folded the paper, writing Aisha's name across the back and he placed it carefully with the other two documents. The hardest part of this quest had now been taken care of, with the Grand Master of the Order of the Knights of St John himself; after much persuasion, granting support to the assassination attempt. In an argumentative and heated meeting, James and Thomas had finally answered all of the many questions relating to their requests and satisfied Du Puy that their intentions were honourable and viable. The Grandmaster and his advisor listened to the basic outline of the plan and agreed that getting to Damascus was possible but incredibly dangerous with various bandits, Zengi's troops and mercenary bands prevalent and once at the Muslim city, to connect with Jewish or Christian inhabitants would provide greater more localised information. It was known that Zengi had slaves of all religious connotation and by becoming or imitating one may well get them into the tower itself but from there, the 'Immortals' protected the Caliph and to find a moment to slay him would be almost impossible, certainly unlikely if their own survival was important. James replied simply that he understood all the risks.

The Grand Master eventually acquiesced to agreeing to continue to look after his home and the loved ones he left behind in Acre; the Order also provided weaponry, armour, extra horses, blankets, provisions and most importantly, a map and pertinent information about the distance, peoples and problems the duo may have to face. Du Puy had proven himself to be an ally and James was genuinely thankful. However, even though he dismissively predicted their chance of success as 'negligible', should the mission prove to be a success; the Muslim host would disintegrate and factional fighting would immediately occur as other leaders clamoured for power. This would not only weaken the natural enemy of Outremer but also provide the perfect opportunity to win back Edessa and expand Christianity eastwards and northwards. With the new Pope adding religious fervour to the French King; a new crusade was brewing and hundreds of fresh knights would be coming from Europe. Du Puy may well believe that James is off to certain death but if the Islamic leader died, the timing for the Christian armies to march to holy war, would indeed be ideal.

Shrugging heavy shoulders, James scattered his morbid thoughts and picking up the letters, he headed towards the stables where Thomas was to meet him, having organised the provisions and equipment from the Knights Hospitallers. As agreed with the Grand Master, he left the letters with the Captain of the Guard, who would be passing through the Venetian Quarter in approximately two hours' time and he would arrange for them to be hand delivered to Silk Street. Attempting to lift the feeling of abandonment and assuring himself that he was choosing the correct path, he checked through the plentiful miscellany that Thomas had commandeered and smiled thinly at his companion.

"Are you sure you want to go with me?"

Thomas clasped hand to wrist with him and with his other hand, he clasped his shoulder.

"Deus Vult, my friend. God wills it."

James returned the gesture and loaded Merdlan and the other three horses with the various equipment, preparing his mind to leave Acre to face an inhospitable wilderness and impossible odds in grim determined silence.

****

"You think me over generous, Louis?"

The Grandmaster asked his long standing advisor as he removed his heavy fur lined cloak of office.

"Forgive my manners, My Lord, and I mean no offence but yes. This is a fool's notion surely. These two...'mercenaries' will never make it to Damascus alive, let alone enter one of the most heavily guarded palaces in the Holy Land and murder the Caliph Zengi. It is pure fantasy. A suicide mission."

Du Puy pulled on his greying beard and mused for a few seconds.

"I am inclined to agree with you yet, this man has proven himself already against a potent foe and Holdingham; a fearsome reputation with a sword and veteran of the wars against the infidel in Spain and Portugal."

"But still, two men, against the massed armies of the Saracen. My Lord, we are sending them to their certain deaths."

The nobleman sighed and placed his hands on the great desk between them and smiled enigmatically.

"Was that not said about those that marched on Jerusalem? The Lord God moves in mysterious ways, Louis and if these two have God on their side, it is for He and He alone to decide their fate."

The tall advisor remained passive and nodded his head

in response, realising it most unwise to continue the disagreement after his superior had used God's name for his cause.

"Anyway, should this foolish notion actually work and the French and German armies do reach us before the year is out, we could expand our borders two fold and provide security for a century here. However small the possibility of success, surely, with this in mind, a wager is necessary."

The advisor nodded and bowed, exiting the chamber, leaving Du Puy to pour himself some blood red French wine and to his glorious contemplations.

****

The Sicilian man in his early forties sat on a low wall across from the tavern he had frequented last night and rubbed his eyes with a yawn. It was unusual for the man to drink so much wine in one evening and he had forgotten how he struggled for decent sleep afterwards. The boarding house had been basic and clean, yet he had failed to get more than three hours sleep and now he was tired, his head throbbed and his limbs ached. Weariness was not a condition which suited his profession and he gulped some more of the cold water from his rabbit-skin container and advised himself against drinking wine again this evening as an address was required from the victim's lady friend. Scowling as a further wave of nausea struck the pit of his stomach, he told himself that by midnight, the man would be dead and he would be riding across the desert trails to collect his 500 bezants and with it, leave this hideously war ravaged land and travel back to Europe, a wealthy man.

****

The acrid stench of the burning entrails filled the room as the emaciated, elderly woman peered through the smoke and tossed the symbolized bones into the charred remains of the unfortunate animal. The dreamscape had been so intense that she had woken from her deep slumber in fearful panic and the soothsayer had to know the truth. Had her nightmare been created by a fevered mind and her breaking nervous system or was the stark image a devastating real issue. The aged, cataract ravaged eyes squinted through the gloom and she read the signs that the seven bones offered her in the burnt carcass. A high pitched shriek erupted involuntarily from her throat and she hunched over, wrapping her skeletal arms around her frail body as she rocked panic stricken on the stone floor.

The Egyptian noble woman; Nadirah, uncharacteristically rushed into the chamber having heard the scream and her heart sank as she saw the seer on the ground, muttering and cursing through tears. The awful smell was overwhelming; a pervasive mix of incense, smouldering lamb, cinnamon, nutmeg and blood. Swallowing hard to ignore the foul odours, she rushed to the mystic and cradled her almost bald head, stroking the wisps of hair as one would a new born baby.

"What is it? Kalaama? Speak to me, what have you seen?"

The ancient woman ceased her incomprehensible ravings and stared wide eyed at her mistress.

"Death."

Nadirah's stroking hand stopped and she held the bony shoulders gently.

"What do you mean?"

Kalaama wiped the drooling spittle from her bloodless lips and coughed into the back of her hand.

"I have seen death and he is coming across the desert – his body is fire and his eyes are as black as night. He is consumed by hatred and comes to kill all before him."

****

The house was empty when Alessio and Maria returned from the church service and sat at the kitchen table.

"Where do you think he has gone?"

Maria asked her younger brother as she removed her liripipe from her head and smoothed her hair back from her eyes and brow.

"Probably out on Merdlan; Aisha and Jaeda will be at the Muslim caravan until mid-afternoon at least."

The naturally attractive woman looked at Alessio, who was younger by only twelve months but had always been the baby of the family and when their father had died and their mother returned to Venice; she had taken the role of carer and even now, found herself worrying on his behalf.

"He is okay? Getting better?"

Alessio opened his arms wide and shrugged listlessly.
"I think so but he is hurting...badly. He is not sleeping and he blames himself still. I expected a dramatic reaction and his need for solitude scares me more."

"But he is talking again; he is better with Aisha and you have been out again together..."

Her brother nodded and smiled through his eyes.

"Stop worrying, he will be fine. He just needs

activity. Standing still was never his strongpoint, even as a boy. I think I need to get him back to the horses and vines."

Maria felt a pang of loss but as throughout her life, masked her emotions and said evenly.

"Probably for the best, although Aisha may not be ready to return."

Alessio grinned in response.

"Well, sister of mine, she could always stay here with you for a time until she is."

The woman could not help the smile spread across her mouth and shook her head in mock exasperation.

"Am I a mother to all of you?"

Alessio chuckled and nodded fervently and was about to add that he knew his sister secretly enjoyed being needed when a loud knock at the exterior door stopped him. Casting a puzzled glance in Maria's direction, he approached the door warily, pausing only to tuck a throwing knife in the back of his breeches.

"Who is it?"

"Knights Hospitaller, I have letters for you."

Bewilderment grew rapidly as he unlocked the door and opened it, seeing two Knights, in full plate mail and bearing the insignia of their Order across their shields and tabards. The first man nodded and handed over three folded letters and bade him immediate goodbye. Alessio watched the two knights stride awkwardly away in their armour and looked down at the parchments in his hand. His reading ability was rudimentary and so he headed back into the kitchen where Maria waited for him warily.

"What is it?"

Alessio handed the letters to his sister in answer to the question and Maria looked down upon them.

"There is one for Aisha and one for each of us!"

Concern forced the words out swiftly and Alessio rushed to the bedchamber where some of the possessions belonging to James were kept and he unleashed a guttural curse as he found the hunting robe, short sword and crossbow gone. A few items of clothing remained but it was clear he had left for some endeavour and he hurried back to Maria, whom he found looking sick with worry.

"He has gone...."

Alessio mumbled and swore again.

"What do you mean, gone? Back to the small holding?"

Alessio shook his head mournfully and then snapped unhappily.

"I don't know do I? ....just read me my letter....please Maria?"

The man forced his body to sit opposite his sister and he waited as she began to read the letter from James in a shaky voice.

'To my dearest friend Alessio,

This is a most difficult letter to write and I hope you, above Maria and Aisha will understand why I have done what I have done.

I need you now more than ever to be strong for me and

to look after that which is most precious to me in the entire world; 'Aisha.' I know she will struggle to comprehend my actions but I know not of any other way, in which I could do anything different. The Knights have found out that he who sent the assassins to my home has now put a price on my head. I am wanted dead by this despot, who I know not nor how I have offended. His men have killed Jacob, Sharla and her sons and now he wishes to kill me. The Knights believe that bounty hunters will be attracted to Acre to murder me and I cannot stay and put the people I love most in the world at risk. Aisha, Maria, Jaeda and yourself would be possible targets, maybe even my mother and others who know me. There is more than enough blood on my hands and I can bear no more.

The Knights will put the rumour out that I have fled to Cyprus and hopefully this will keep you all safe but please be on your guard and be wary. I have no idea how much these assassins know of me but everybody in Acre will talk if enough money is offered to them for information. Du Puy has promised to continue to protect my home and will post guards near to the shop.

I have taken Thomas with me and have gone into the interior. That is all you need to know. With your God on my side, I hope to come back within a few weeks but I dare not be any more specific. The less you know, the safer you are I believe.

I trust and hope you will understand my actions and one day in the not so distant future, we shall frequent a tavern and raise our tankards to our friendship once more.

Please take care of Maria, Aisha and Jaeda. I am counting on you and know you are the very best man I know and the one person I trust with an open heart.

Be well my friend and I hope to see your face again soon.

James

There was a lengthy pause whilst Alessio tried to comprehend the letter and its ramifications as Maria re-read the letter in her head and then placed a hand on her brother's, the offer of understanding and comfort clear to him.

"Does your letter tell us anything more?"

The flustered woman carefully opened the letter addressed to her and read out loud through flushed cheeks.

Dearest Maria,

I know this is going to be almost impossible for you to accept that I have left Aisha with you so soon after the loss of Jacob but I implore you to find it in your heart, to forgive my actions and see to the girl's needs.

Aisha will also struggle to come to terms with my departure but in light of the incomprehensible bounty that has been put on my head; my leaving will hopefully make it safer for the rest of you.

Please read the letter to Alessio that I have left for him and please help me when I need you most. If you can look after Aisha and Jaeda in the near future as well as you have done in the recent past, I will be forever in your debt. I know this is a burden on you that I have no right to ask.

Look to your brother for me; I feel he will be upset that I have left without him but should the Knights not do their part of our bargain, he will be needed to protect you from possible unknown adversaries.

I expect to be back in a few short weeks and until then, I wish you well.

With much love and friendship,
James

Maria concluded the letter and looked over at Alessio, who still remained in a state of shock. She chose not to read the postscript to her brother, which explained that the rights to the house and all of James's wealth was lodged with Du Puy, should he not return and was to be given to Aisha upon his death.

"What do we tell Aisha?"

The question he asked hung in the air like a stale odour as through the rear door and entrance to the actual dwelling part of the building, the sound of frivolous voices and giggling could be heard.

"Leave it to me and just back me up."

Maria hissed as Aisha and Jaeda flounced into the room, bearing a veritable host of herbs, spices and oils in sealed clay cars and garish coloured glassware. One look towards each of the faces in the kitchen halted the excitable pair and the young women exchanged worried glances before Aisha spoke slowly.

"What is it? Is it James?"

The second question was said with more urgency and

Maria stood from the chair and picked up the remaining unopened letter.

"He is ok, but you should read this."

Aisha plucked the paper from the Venetian's fingers and immediately saw that it was in the neat English hand writing of James and her mood darkened.

"Are you ok to read it, Aisha? I cannot read English; I know not the letters of the language. He wrote ours in Italian."

Maria murmured but Aisha merely nodded swiftly and sat shakily onto a chair as she opened the letter and read it tentatively as if each word would hurt her physically and emotionally.

To my dearest Aisha,

Please try to find the understanding I know you have in your heart and accept the decision I have made today. I truly believe that me leaving temporarily is the best way I can think of to keep you and the others safe. I need to undertake this task, not just for the knowledge of your safety but also for Jacob. I cannot fail you as I failed him. My only wish for Jacob was to give him a happy, healthy, full life and all I brought him was a tragic, pointless early death. He would have been better off never having met me. I can barely cope with this knowledge that I did not protect him and keep him safe. I know I could not live with myself if the same fate happened to you. If this task is done successfully, I have done what I need to do; for all of our sakes.

Do not hate me please. I could not bear that shame.

I will be back in a few days and I hope that I can make

this up to you. Alessio and Maria will stay close until I return and please do not do anything foolish.

 Please give my regards to Jaeda and please always remember that I love you with all of my heart and always will.

Forgive me? Please.

James

Aisha frowned and read the words again more slowly in her head as tears rolled down her dark cheeks. With shaking fingers, she placed the letter down onto the table and looked imploringly from Alessio to Maria.

"Where has he gone? Does he say in either of your letters?"

The voice was a fractured whisper and Maria rushed to her side, cradling her head into her chest as Alessio attempted to maintain a positive outlook.

"He doesn't really say but it is for the best. He knows what he is doing."

Aisha's voice, wracked by fitful sobs rasped again, asking for the other letters to be read again and Maria did so, again declining to read the postscript on her personal note aloud. As she completed reading both letters, Aisha blurted out a series of insults.

"Stupid, proud, stupid, foolish, crazy, stupid man."

Maria attempted to soothe the young woman's fervour but the Syrian shrugged off the kindly advances.

"He is going to kill the Atabeg isn't he?"

Alessio and Maria shot furtive looks to the other before the brother tried in vain to play the part of a naive friend.

"We don't know anything for sure. I am sure he is not. He is probably going to spend some time with Thomas looking at...at horses...or...."

Aisha glared at the man balefully, halting his explanation suddenly.

"I am not a child. Do not treat me like one."

Maria furrowed and raised an eye brow towards Alessio who placed his fingers through his thick dark hair and apologised.

"It would seem that he has gone to the interior and I can see only one reason for that yes."

"It is madness. How does he think he will get past Zengi's armies?"

The tradeswoman brought her left hand to her mouth in a state of anxiety, the realisation dawning on her at once.

"If anybody can do it, it is James, he is not insane."

Aisha scoffed openly at Alessio's defence of his friend.

"He looks like an Outlander. His Arabic is poor. He has taken with him a man more pale skinned and more foreign looking than him. He has little chance of success."

"Don't upset yourself; he is more than capable...."

The Arabian girl stood suddenly, sending the chair flailing backwards with a dull thud.

"He is many things but he is not capable of taking on an army all by himself. And if he was truly looking to our protection, why did he not hire soldiers to protect us or take us to Cyprus or back to Italy. No, he wants revenge. He wants to kill that man because of Jacob and the others."

Alessio winced as the truth indeed did hurt.

"Do not condemn him."

"I am not condemning him, I understand it. I too want vengeance, I hope that man dies a slow and painful death which is fully deserved but I do not want James to die as well....as Jacob..."

The tears flowed too heavily for the conversation to be continued and Aisha turned and ran to her bedchamber with Jaeda following her, offering ignored comfort; leaving the Venetian siblings to stare blankly at each other, neither having the ability to make the other feel any better about the stark position in which they found themselves.

Chapter 16

A New Enemy

Merdlan picked his way along the meandering desert trail which stretched roughly eastwards, towards the Crusader town of Safed, around twelve hours ride ahead. From here, according to the maps, provided by Du Puy, the densely packed sand would become sandstone and the desert trail would end. The protection of Outremer's patrols and litigation also ceased and the brutal, rocky landscape became home to criminals and bandits of all denominations. The terrain would change again near the great Lake Tiberius and the earth would become softer, with grass and dirt adjacent to the pure water. The safest route onwards from here was along the river, which snaked north to Jacob's Ford, where the travelling merchants and caravan trains would be plentiful and then there would be three days across the scorching hot desert to reach the Muslim city of Damascus. The two men who took the journey, for very different reasons, knew all of the prospective dangers and for both; the quest was worth every one of the risks.

The going along the easiest part of their travels was still heavy going as both riders had taken an extra steed, which was attached to each pommel of their lead horse's saddle by a thick length of hemp. All four mounts carried cumbersome burdens as provisions, water, miscellaneous weaponry, spare armour and shields were attached to the beasts' backs, along with woollen blankets and heavy hooded cloaks. Time seemed to pass interminably slowly although Thomas remained in good spirits, from time to time whistling tunelessly or attempting some vulgar drinking song, learned back in some poor rural tavern of England. James's face remained impassive and emotionless although his mind worked fervently; anxious at how he left and what Aisha, Alessio and Maria would think of him and also of the many and differing challenges which lay ahead. His self-confidence was low and in ever darkening mood, he allowed Merdlan rein to take the lead.

Aisha rose from the rough mattress and sniffed noisily, wiping her nose and eyes with the edge of her long sleeved white tunic and shuffled into a seating position. Across the room, sat stationary on a wooden stool was Jaeda, who stared directly at her with a genuine look of pitying concern. The younger girl managed a brief thin smile and accepted the mixture of pity and concern with a brief hugged embrace.

"It is fine. I know what I have to do. Come, I need to speak with Maria and Alessio."

She padded through to the kitchen area in bare feet and accepted the offered hug from Maria wordlessly, nodding to Alessio, who remained seated at the table with a sad, wistful expression on his handsome features.

"I need to leave now and bring him back. I need to speak to him, make him see sense. I can do this. Nobody else can, you understand? With a fast horse, I can reach him and bring him back."

Maria shook her head slowly in response and Aisha felt her emotions twist in her guts as she fought to remain calm and controlled.

"Aisha, please. James would never ever forgive me if anything happened to you. He placed you in our care. Alessio and I have to look after you. We cannot let you ride into the desert alone on some wild chase. We do not know which route he will take..."

The Syrian clenched her fists together behind her back

as she tried to compose the correct words in English. It was always difficult to communicate with Alessio and Maria; their English was limited and she had poor Italian. They had no Arabic and none of the three spoke French well enough to understand anything.

"Maria....please!"

The tone was urgent and the seamstress ceased her reasoning and held her tongue, nodding for Aisha to continue.

"I am no longer a girl. I am not a child. I know James seeks to protect me from this world but he cannot. This world is dangerous. James has taught me intelligence and practicability. I am a young woman with my own mind. Had I stayed in Syria, I would have had two maybe three children by now and be married to a man I would have hardly known. I am not stupid enough to head into the interior alone, I merely wish to leave as early as possible and catch up with James and talk to him. There has to be another way than his way to deal with all of this madness. If I leave now, I will catch him along the desert trail heading east before he even reaches the edge of your Christian land."

Maria went to speak but closed her mouth again and chewed the inside of her lip as she considered Aisha's words. Alessio frowned at his sister and spoke up, his English clumsy but his meaning clear.

"Aisha, James would literally kill me if I let you go alone. No."

A flash of anger blazed in Aisha's eyes as she focused on the only man in the room but Maria's words prevented any further debate.

"Aisha is right, as are you brother. So, you both go, right now, to the stables; take two horses, steal them if you have to and gallop as fast as you can on the

eastern trail until you reach James."

Alessio's eyes widened in surprise but seeing the pleading looks of both Jaeda and Aisha and knowing that his sister would not change her mind, once it was set, he relented and murmured assent.

"I will quickly get changed into my riding clothing and then we can go."

Aisha grinned and ducked quickly into her chamber as Alessio stared at his sister, waiting for Jaeda to follow the ward of James out of the room before hissing his opinion.

"What if he has taken some other route; what if we cannot catch him?"

Maria smiled enigmatically.

"I have every faith in you."

Alessio scowled and headed to his own bedchamber to put on an outer tunic and collect his belt of throwing knives as Maria added softly, speaking only to herself in the empty room.

"Bring him back, for all our sakes."

****

The swarthy, lean body of a man, clad in tight fitting black breeches and a soft cured leather tunic walked calmly into the tavern and ordered a bottle of deep red wine; tossing the coins casually on the simple bar and avoiding eye contact with the young woman who stared openly at him; his eyes widening as they observed the long sword attached to the battered scabbard at his waist and the curved dagger that was strapped on a leather belt across his chest. Watching the blood coloured wine being poured carelessly into the dirty, chipped glass, he smiled and studied the room. It was past midday but not by much and the bar room was all but deserted. From just two visits, he had discovered the brothel upstairs did not open until evening and the illegal gambling house below never opened before midnight. There was only one other patron; a bored looking, poverty stricken man who stared into the dregs of his cask of ale with a look of pure nihilism. The only guard remained outside, slumped on a stool in the blistering heat. The timing was perfect and he wordlessly nodded to the serving wench and sipped his wine before heading to the furthest round table, in the corner of the dimly illuminated room, nearest to the iron staircase, which led to his prey.

He sipped gingerly from the filthy glass and watched as the woman wiped down the bar and then sat back down, awaiting her next customer. Placing the glass gently down and glancing to the lost soul sat alone, he stood upright silently and padded down the iron stairs in the soft leather boots he highly regarded for such days as these. He entered the empty gambling area, lit only by animal fat candles along the bare stone walls and peered through the gloom with his excellent vision. Crouching, he made out the bulky outline of the man he had seen yesterday evening and presumed was the main protagonist of the place; a strong, muscular bodyguard, who relied on his size and ferocity to scare opponents as opposed to skill or intellect. Unsheathing his wickedly curved dagger, he stood upright and approached the man who sat outside the door, which led to the only other room in the cellar area.

"We are closed."

Aldo barked dismissively and heaved himself from the chair. Before he had even managed to stand fully upright, his chest exploded in pain as the stranger approached him quickly and he saw the glint of the sharp blade a second too late to prevent it from embedding into his upper body. His one arm failed to respond to his brain's scream to defend himself and his weaker left arm attempted to claw the assailant, who merely sidestepped the clumsy riposte and tore the dagger from the flesh; flicked his wrist and stepped backwards as Aldo's throat spurted blood in a semi-circle away from him as his jugular vein was severed by the sharpened blade. Within exactly three seconds, the once proud bodyguard and powerful brawler lay dead, his life force along with his blood pumping from him as he slumped to the ground. Wiping his weapon clean on the rough cloak of his victim, the assassin opened the door and strode into the small chamber, which was clearly used as some form of office.

"What was that noise Aldo, I am trying to sort these accounts and nothing makes sense. I think one of the bitches is stealing from...."

Francesco's tone, initially angry, faded into a passive high pitched squeak as he observed the man who now smiled into his fleshy face. There was something in the way the man moved, the way he carried himself and in that smile that unnerved him. Used to shouting at people, the sudden chill was replaced with the general arrogance and disgust he used when meeting people he did not, nor care, to know.

"Get out of my office or I will get Aldo to physically throw you out!"

The man's eyes narrowed a little and a sarcastic grin adorned his dark features.

"I do not think he will. Now, answer me a simple question and I will be on my way."

The businessman blanched openly and felt the blood drain from his face as he understood fully that Aldo was dead or incapacitated in some way, realising that whoever this man was, he was not to be treated with disdain.

"Ask your question."

Francesco replied, trying to keep his voice calm and inwardly cursing his weakness as it cracked on the very first syllabyl.

"Your daughter; Sophia; tell me where her man friend; James resides."

Interest flickered in the corpulent face of the Italian.

"Why do you want to know and he is not her 'man friend', merely an unwanted acquaintance."

The man shrugged listlessly and spoke again, quickly and with a trace of dismissal.

"That is largely irrelevant. Do you know where the man lives?"

Francesco caught a hint of a Sicilian accent and condemned the island kingdom as a whole nation in his head.

"You are a friend...or a...."

The sentence was ended with the adversary removing the dagger methodically from the sheath and the older man capitulated instantly.

"Silk Street in the Venetian Quarter. He is boarding with the owners, who are friends of his. Their names are Alessio and Maria Peroni. Their name is above the door, the awning outside is multi-coloured."

The words tumbled in a barely coherent fashion and the man's smile grew wider.

"There, that was not so hard was it?"

Francesco's broad chest heaved upwards as he

attempted to remain calm in the face of adversity.

"So that is it. You will let me live?"

The man winked and replied flatly without emotion.

"Unfortunately, not."

Francesco's broad expanse of chest tightened and his mouth opened as if to scream for help but somewhere within his brain, the fearful knowledge that Aldo, who would usually be the one he would scream for, was lying prostrate in a pool of his own blood just a few yards away. The scream became a soft gurgle as metal twisted through flesh with ease and within seconds, fifty eight years of existence ended with a muffled cry.

Sophia closed her eyes momentarily as she saw the stranger slay her father, from her hunched, crouching position in the darkest shadows; under the spiral staircase, where she had been cleaning when the man appeared initially. The clinical despatch of the vile Aldo created the urgent need to hide as best that she could in the surroundings. Fear pervaded every part of her and she knew that now was the precise time to attempt a flight from danger as if he saw her, she would certainly be the next victim. Once he turned around and strode back to the stairs, her discovery would be certain, as would be her death a few short seconds later. Snapping her pale blue eyes open, she willed her legs to respond to her desperate need as she watched the lifeless body of her father collapse unceremoniously to the rough floorboards below.

Springing forth, limbs flailing erratically, the woman stumbled swiftly up the iron steps, away from the murders; conflicting emotions assailing her mind from all sides. Horror, loss, fear, panic, despair amongst them, but, as she clambered into the bar room with the light footfalls of the killer already close behind her; the main sensory emotion registered was relief. Relief that the hated, leering Aldo was dead and that her twisted, bitter husk of a father was no more. Her life was finally her own; independent and wealthy, a life to be lived as she chose. This momentary realisation of triumph struck her at exactly the same time as the man knocked her reeling to the ground. With a shocked yelp, she struck a table edge with force and crashed to the dirty floor in a disgruntled heap. Lifting her body weight immediately on her elbows to scream for help, she cursed instead as her attacker swept from the tavern in athletic haste and disappeared onto the crowded streets of Acre.

Heaving herself to her feet with the help of her surprised younger sister, who had been cleaning tankards at the bar at the time; she quickly relayed her observations and sent the mortified girl to the City Guard, who would attempt to hunt down the assassin. Smoothing out her clothing and adjusting her hair in an elegant coif, Sophia advised the solitary guard who had watched the killer rush past him nonchalantly to lock up the tavern and await the authorities and headed at a fast pace to the Venetian Quarter. Her mind raced as she wondered why such a man would want to find James. What had he got himself into? The attack on his home and now this? It made no sense to her; she had believed James had become a good man; taking on orphans and freeing slaves; building up a vineyard and the horses. Sophia had made it her business to know what was happening in his life; if it had not been for her father, their lives may have been entwined. She had loved him so much, with such passionate ferocity, it had scared her a little; the intensity too much to cope with. It had been so long ago, a decade had passed and yet, no man had ever come close to rousing such emotions. True, she had had good lovers in that time and many admirers but she had never truly loved anyone since James and now; he was clearly in trouble and she could help him. Maybe this was the time that he would see how much she still cared and her father was gone, the tavern and wealth would be hers to do with as she pleased. She could sell it and move in with James in his home out of the port. Her feet moved her onto Silk Street and she checked her thought processes, which were rapidly spiralling out of control. Her eyes studied the people on the narrow thoroughfare and convinced that the murderer was not in sight, she approached the shop and rapped loudly on the wooden door with her knuckles.

The door opened slowly and the attractive features of Maria came into view; the smile immediately dropping from her lips as she recognised the caller.

"Sophia? Yes?"

The Genoan could not help but notice the change of expression and curt questioning but she remained composed; this had nothing to do with Alessio's sister.

"I need to see James, it is urgent. Please, hurry."

Maria's brow furrowed in consternation but did not move from blocking access within.

"I am sorry. That is just not possible."

Sophia's eyes narrowed and a silent spark of anger shot forth from them.

"Why not? This is a matter of life and death. There is a man after him....it is complicated...please, Maria, let me see him."

"He is not here. He departed for Cyprus last night for a horse trade. Alessio is with him, as is Aisha."

The calm answer shocked Sophia who could merely stare open mouthed, knowing this crushed her chances of a reunion with James completely. No words would come to her mouth and she stepped backwards as Maria bade her farewell and closed the door abruptly and finally on their clipped conversation. Sophia turned around and trudged disconsolately back to the scene of her father's murder, absorbed in her own self-pity.

****

The Sicilian assassin smiled wanly as he heard the interchange between the women and headed back down the alley towards the dockside. He knew only one ship headed to Cyprus from Acre per week and that was today. There would be nowhere for his target to hide on board a ship once it had set sail and this would make the kill so much simpler. With the smile broadening into a grin as he strode, he again allowed his mind to mentally spend the vast amount of certain wealth that was coming his way.

Chapter 17

Unhappy Reunion

James pulled softly at Merdlan's soft leather reins and stroked his beloved horse's mane and patted his neck as he dismounted wearily at the roadside inn; rather unimaginatively called 'The Traveller's Tavern' in large, painted letters; fading in the desert heat, on the side of the western wall in French. He examined the numerous stallions, ponies, geldings and mares in the open sided stable and led his own mount towards them; briefly checking over his shoulder to see the dappled grey mare follow behind Merdlan's great flanks. He had decided to call the mare; Sharla, in honour and memory of his former friend during the monotonous six hour ride from the bustling port. Thomas brought the bulky gelding to a halt beside him and he struggled from his saddle, landing heavily onto his hardened boots.

"I was not built to ride horses."

The Englishman moaned, rubbing his own rear to prove his discomfort.

"Oh well, only hundreds of miles left to go."

James winked at his scowling companion and headed to the groom, who was trudging towards them to take care of their animals.

"I could murder a flagon of ale though and I am famished."

Thomas continued, staring at the large, rather run down looking establishment before them, his expression showing a mixture of dubious distaste swiftly overwhelmed by the basic need for refreshment. James overpaid the sullen stable hand to look after the four horses; paying to use the tavern's oats and water, enabling their own supplies to remain intact. Additional coin was passed over to have all steeds rubbed down fully; the need for the animals to be in top condition was of paramount importance. The aging mercenary awaited his compatriot to return from his negotiations before entering the inn and as he opened the outer door; the distinct smells of human perspiration, urine, cooked meat and stale wine struck the visitors noses with a sudden and stark unpleasantness. Exchanging frowns, the two men strode through the hall and into the main bar, which was relatively busy with a raucous group of knights in the far corner and a selection of merchants, pilgrims, labourers and other tradesmen scattered about the vast chamber's plentiful tables and stools. Serving girls, wearing similar outfits, roamed the room removing and refilling jugs, platters and tankards as requested. A bald, pot marked man in his late fifties directed proceedings from behind the immense bar; a liveried guard at either end of it, staring suspiciously at the patrons as they held great pikes with sharpened iron tips.

"Welcoming place."

Thomas grunted and James agreed with a momentary nod and a flash of a smile as
they headed to an empty table in the far corner of the room. No sooner had they sat down, when a young girl no more than sixteen years of age appeared beside them and spoke in a strong French accent in the language of her forebears. The Englishman blinked without comprehension and James smiled and ordered a jug of ale and asked about the offering of food. An awkward conversation followed in French and English and a platter of bread, cheese and fruit was added to the order. The serving girl smiled and skittered off through the tables back to the bar, leaving the two travellers to observe the other occupants of the tavern at leisure. James watched the five men in the corner; all

223

bore the red cross of the Knights Templar and yet all were considerably drunk, judging from their loud and boisterous behaviour. The Templar's numerous vows included the fact that they would refrain from taking alcohol and James wondered what his old guardian; Georges, would have had to say about such an outrage. He allowed a thin smile to dance around his lips as he thought of the crotchety, elderly Frenchman with his brusque persona yet heart of gold. Thomas followed the eye line of his companion and raised an eyebrow.

"Drunken Templars? Whatever next! I thought they were the ones who protected travellers and pilgrims."

James murmured assent and thought well-armed and armoured, inebriated knights was no good thing anywhere, let alone in a rural tavern, far from any governable law. The rest of the crowd seemed to be of the same opinion, as a large open space had developed around the raucous group. Within moments, the French serving girl returned with the ordered drinks, advising the food would be with them in a little while. James tipped her and a genuine smile unmasked her youthful charm and she beamed at him, thanking him profusely before heading off to the next table.

Thomas poured out the luke-warm beer into the two cheaply made tankards and drank deeply; imbibing half of the contents in his first draught, grunting with contentment as he placed the drinking vessel back to the table. James sipped his ale slowly, savouring the refreshing taste on his lips and tongue and he had no sooner placed his drinking vessel on the aged wooden table when a different young girl placed the basic foodstuffs down with the briefest glimpse of a grin. His companion immediately tore the hunk of bread into smaller pieces; adding some of the cheese to a piece and eating both ravenously. Offering the second piece to a thankful James, he consumed another portion in similar fashion before commencing a third in quick succession. James watched with a wry smile creasing his lips as he ate slowly; his hazel eyes reverting back to the inebriated knights and page boys who were in turn bellowing with laughter and then hurling abuse at the other patrons. Scanning the five faces; he pondered thoughtfully as he believed he recognised one of them and then grimaced visibly as he remembered where he had seen him before. A vivid image of a young Arab goatherd being beaten and his personal intervention stopping the assault appeared in his mind's eye and the Templar who had been doing the beating now sat across the grubby tavern floor. Recalling the brief and hostile conversation they had shared; he immediately averted his gaze and looked back at his ravenous riding partner instead.

"What's wrong? Not hungry?"

The older man asked quizzically as he followed his companion's line of vision; making eye contact with one of the knights who stared back coldly. Thomas chuckled in contrast, having met hundreds of drunken men in hundreds of taverns; who hid their childish insecurity behind a threatening stare.

"Just ignore them."

James mumbled and placed another piece of bread absently into his mouth, looking towards the opposite side of the enormous room.

"Oh come on, let me have some fun...I have been bored all day."

Thomas beamed mischievously and slapped his riding partner on the shoulder heartily.

"Hey hey, the fun could just be starting...."

James groaned inwardly as he turned his head to see two of the Frenchmen struggle to their feet, one of them pointing towards him angrily. His hazel eyes met the sapphire ones of the Templar and the recognition was obvious; even at the distance through the plentiful smoke of the chamber.

"Ok, let me handle this Thomas; remember, they are Templars. We have to be careful; they are as good as the Law around here."

The response was an atypical shrug, followed by a nonchalant chew of further bread as the armed men staggered to their table.

"Well, well, well. What have we here...a Saracen boy lover if memory serves correct."

The first man spoke in French, his words slurred from the alcohol; his eyes glazed. Both knights erupted in raucous laughter at the statement and James kept his voice and tone even, responding in their own language.

"You are drunk and this is a public place. Know your station and position within Outremer and leave before you cause a further scene and further disgrace on your Temple."

"What did he say – what did you say?"

Thomas asked in English; seeing the men explode into merriment and watching as their faces changed from gleeful grins to frowns in the blink of his eye.

"How dare you? Stand up you dog!"

The first man ordered loudly, knocking over the wooden tankard of ale in front of James; soaking his tunic and breeches as the liquid cascaded across the table. The Frenchman's left hand moved to grab his adversary's resting forearm but his reactions were dulled by wine or ale and James responded with a swift, violent outburst. Using his lower back and thighs to push the stool

226

backwards; he lunged to his side, punching the knight in his midriff hard; noting that he wore no plate or chain mail armour; merely normal clothing covered with the red cross insignia on the white cloth background of his overshirt. As the man doubled over in indignant pain; James brought his knee up into the exposed face and felt the harsh connection of knee and chin; the chin coming off worse. The Templar dropped to the filth strewn floor, crying out in anguish.

His compatriot took one step towards James before Thomas stood fluidly and grabbing the man's lank, greasy hair; he brought the man's face down with immense force onto the solid table. The man's nose broke with a sickening crunch and a sudden flow of blood and Thomas pushed the screaming man onto the ground. James kicked his enemy in the groin, watching him writhe in agony, adding a satisfying tirade of expletives in French. Thomas winked at him as he watched the remaining three drunken knights make their way towards them, knocking into tables, stools and retreating patrons as they did so.

"Glad I let you handle this, my friend; not sure if it would have ended in a fight if I had sorted it out."

James pointedly ignored him as he viewed the three inebriated French Templars approaching and acknowledged the two fully armoured tavern guards screaming for everyone to stop and stand still. With no comprehension of French, Thomas picked up the almost empty tankard and crashed it into the face of the leading onrushing man, who staggered and then fell backwards into his companions; courtesy of a hefty kick from the hardened boot of the Englishman.

"Enough!"

James yelled above the din of the various shouts, screams and orders within the bar room and Thomas stepped backwards, lowering and opening his fists as the wicked pole arms of the two armed liveried tavern guards forced the two sides apart.

"Get out. You two leave. Now."

The innkeeper screeched in a high pitched nasal voice at James and Thomas. Observing the blank look of the larger man; he placed his repulsive face close to James and whispered angrily.

"Are you insane, they are Templars. Out here, they are the law! Now go; for your own sakes. Leave now. "

Pushing James backwards, he turned to the swearing and bleeding knights and began to shout about their Order and the Grand Master; the oaths immediately ceasing as the grotesque, contorted faces became more worried and James took the opportunity to nudge Thomas, and head to the exterior door; ignoring the heated argument behind him. The mercenary paused momentarily to pick up the remaining bread and cheese and followed the younger man to the door.

In silence, the two men scurried to the stables, gained their steeds and packs and cantered into the darkness of the night; James heading in front and picking up speed; flicking his head behind him to see if any horses were following, cursing himself for his foolish pride and realising that his reaction may have serious repercussions upon their return. As the pitch blackness enveloped the figures; he also had the even darker thought that they may not ever return and with this in the foremost of his mind; he kicked his heels into Merdlan's immense belly, stirring the beast into a gallop much to the chagrin of the Englishman behind whose horsemanship was much to be improved upon.

Just over three hours of hard night riding followed before James eventually halted; finding a disused, derelict wooden trading post at the side of the merchants' road. Here, he waited a few minutes for his companion to catch up and ignorant of his incessant moaning; James tied the horses and settled down in his blanket to rest before sunrise, when the expedition would continue. Thomas; getting no response to his complaints, eventually lay down beside the quiet man and grunted a simple 'good night.' James responded and tried in vain to block out the mercenary's chuckling as he observed drily;

"Tell me James, why it is that everybody you meet seems to want to kill you. It really is something you need to address."

Happy with this comment, Thomas spent the next ten minutes laughing to himself and James rolled over towards the doorway of the dilapidated building, wondering if he had already entered through the gates of purgatory and was on his way to hell itself.

Chapter 18

Lessons from History

Dusk was settling across the rough desert trail, shrouding the sand and dust in a darkness that mirrored Alessio's mood. It had been a long, monotonous day's ride. The forthcoming conversation was going to be difficult and for the past four hours; rehearsals of his speech had reverberated around his aching mind. Alessio thought that this whole episode was hopeless and ridiculous; like searching for a sense of humour amongst the Teutonic Knights Order. This joke he had shared with Aisha earlier that afternoon but it had been lost on her; she had no idea that the central European Germanic tribes who made up the Teutonic Knights were in his proven view; dour and dull in the extreme. Not that Aisha felt much like laughing anyway and the journey was tedious, tiring and largely silent. Alessio truly believed that James was capable of looking after himself and Thomas was an English Mercenary of some renown; who had fought against the Muslims in Spain or Portugal, along with Scottish barbarians, Welsh rebels and a number of other nationalities he neither knew nothing about or realistically cared. However, he was clearly a man who could look after himself in a tight situation and it made no sense to him for the two of them to try and find these men and attempt to make them return to the port. Alessio thought it prudent to return home and await news there as James had obviously requested in his letters. Aisha clearly did not and as Maria had sided with the teenager over him, he found himself saddle sore, bored and unhappy in the middle of nowhere.

He was a man who loved the city; the incessant noise, smells and visions that changed with every passing hour. He enjoyed the company of men and

230

women, old and young. He was a socialite who thought peace and tranquillity over rated in the extreme; he needed; craved in fact, excitement and variety. Thus, the bland rocky terrain which slowly transformed into sandstone and the scrubland which slowly deteriorated into endless miles of sand before him was painful to his keen azure eyes. The dark brown gelding he rode appeared hostile and smelt of an acrid mix of hay and urine and only vaguely, reluctantly at that; agreed to be ridden by the Venetian at all. Behind him; a fifteen year old girl; her face set in grim determination rode easily; trained by the accomplished James and a girl who he knew would react badly to his decision. His mind diverted immediately back to practising his speech as the dim flickering torches came into view, alerting his tiring mind that he had precious little time before they reached the coach house where they would stay overnight and return back to Acre tomorrow.

Aisha's mind in comparison was a hive of activity as her acute brain bounced from fear and love for the welfare of James, anger and frustration at the way he disappeared and trying to counteract the growing sense of futility when considering both sets of expeditions. Calming her breathing; she knew what she had to do and nodded contritely to herself as she accepted her destiny and whatever fate had in store for her young life.

The coach house was almost empty as the two bedraggled, travel worn figures walked through the door into the sparsely furnished room. Alessio used some of his little coin to purchase a basic meal, fresh water, stabling for the horses and a room for the night. Ignoring the lewd comment from the skeletally thin middle aged proprietor, who stared lasciviously over a scowling Aisha; they ate in silence and headed to the small, unkempt room with its battered bed and filth stained sheets.

"Nice."

Alessio grimaced and pointed to the bed.

"I am not really tired anyway."
Aisha murmured and closed the wooden shutters,
blocking out the rapidly cooling night air. The man
locked the door and sat down on the flimsy solitary chair
in the room. Looking into Aisha's wide brown eyes, he
sighed, rubbed his forehead and motioned her to sit
opposite him on the bed. Watching her wary eyes focus
on him, she sat on the cleanest part of the mattress she
could find and he forced a smile.

"We need to talk."

Aisha nodded mutely and smiled, relaxing her tense
body position a little.

"Aisha, this...is not going to work. Two people
trying to find two other people across hundreds of miles
is never going to happen. We will never catch up with
them and we do not really know what direction they
have gone in or where exactly they are going. I know it's
hard and I know you will not understand but this has to
stop. We have ridden all day and not seen or heard
anything of them; everybody we passed today on the
road and I mean every one of them; had not seen
James or Thomas on the trail."

He paused and sensing no real drama from the girl, he
pressed his decision upon her.

"I know this is hard. For all of us, but most of all,
it is hardest for you but I know James, better than
almost anyone and he will come back to us. I truly
believe that. I need to take you back to Acre and look
after you as he asked me too; you can live with Maria
and I for as long as it takes but let me take you home."

The teenager smiled broadly but almost apologetically
at her temporary guardian.

"I am sorry. I cannot. I know you are trying to do the best thing for me and it is what James would have wished of you but I just cannot."

Alessio scratched his day old stubble and stifled his response; he knew it was difficult for her to speak and her voice creaked with emotion. He was loathe to stop her words so he sat and merely listened as she unburdened her mind and perhaps, a little of her injured soul.

"The first days I ever remember of my life was in the village of my birth, to the south of Damascus; a place unfortunately located in the centre of many warring factions; the Christian invaders to the west, Seljuk Turks to the east, Arabian tribes to the south and Armenian mercenary bands to the north. I was taught that once my village was a happy place; Christians and Muslims lived together peacefully, there were merchants and commerce, the market filled with goods and far away from the troubles. I remember none of that. After the invasion from the West and the foreign Christian took the lands for themselves; slaying Muslims and Syrian Christians alike as they did not know the difference – all were enemy Saracens. Then before peace resumed, the Muslim factions began civil war to get stronger – defeating and slaying pashas, village elders; Shi'ite teachings became fervent; warriors came and took boys for their armies; the world of peace was shattered. This was the village I was born into. There was no peace or beauty just all-pervading fear. Our village lay untouched for the first few years of my life but there were no merchants or markets; just long hours of working to barely eke out an existence. A defeated, desperate group of Muslim horsemen; fleeing from a larger force, took out their frustration on our village when our elder refused to give them food; knowing the forces who pursued them were the new power in the region and to aid these men would bring certain death by those that followed."

Aisha paused and looked towards Alessio briefly to see his reaction and seeing only concern; she progressed, her strained voice clear.

"So he made a brave and unenviable choice. The men killed him in the street in front of the whole village and then ransacked it for stocks; animals, grain, fruit, bread, everything. Our farmers defended their supplies, fighting for their homes, women and children. They were no match for the heavily armed men and were slaughtered. Women were defiled, the old and young hid or ran; the lucky ones escaped with their lives as the homes were burnt and then simply, the men left, leaving a broken, destroyed village with no food. I can still remember the stench of death and the sounds of the dying. One of my earliest memories..."

Her voice broke and she sniffed noisily as Alessio slipped from his chair and sat beside her, placing an arm around her shoulder. Aisha dropped her head against his chest and continued hesitantly, wiping her nose with the edge of her sleeve.

"When the other warriors came, they rounded us up; there was nothing for them to do but put us in wagons and took us to Damascus, the nearest town where the old were given food in exchange for the young to become slaves; to be sold at the markets. I was bought by a merchant, who thought I would make a pretty addition to his slave harem in good time and taken to his large residence on the outskirts of the sprawling town. He was a rich man, pleasant on the outside but had unusual habits when it came to the women he bought; many came back from his bedchamber broken and bleeding; rope burns around wrists and ankles, marks on their faces from beatings....welts and cuts on their breasts, bottom and back from whips and sticks. I knew I was still too young to be taken to him but knew it was only a matter of time; when one of the older girls died from such injuries, I knew I had to escape. I worked it out, took my time, I

234

gained the trust of the eunuch who guarded us when we went to the mosque for prayers or the markets for food and provisions. I pretended I was ill and when the eunuch rushed to find a healer, I ran, hid and traded the jewels I stole from the merchants' wife for a pony and headed west towards the sea, which I believed would take me to freedom and a better world."

Her words were rushed now as the memories flooded back into her mind and Alessio kissed her hair gently, stroking her soft locks as he hoped this opening up of past traumas would in some way be helpful to Aisha.

"I rode that small, pathetic pony hard through days and nights and thought I was safe when I came upon a small community of very few souls who traded goats, chickens, sheep and horses. I used the last of my coin to buy food and water and looked around an alien world where I saw my first white European face; a man who was buying a horse with a large Arabian companion; I saw the others all happy with him and wondered how this could be; our village Imam told us all infidels were enemies of Allah and wished to conquer us all, enslaving the Arab peoples and eventually wiping them from the earth itself. I was confused but intrigued; he and his friends drank and laughed and joked. These others were Muslims and were drinking alcohol. Such things were forbidden and as I watched them the foreigner spoke to me in Arabic; in our own language, asking if I was lost in a kindly tone; and where my parents were. Before I could answer him and feeling sick with panic at being spoken to by a destroyer of Islam; two men rode into the area, bounty hunters sent by my owner, claiming me as his property. A thief who needed to be punished for the shame I had brought onto his family name. I remained silent, shaking with fear, tears rolling down my face and I am ashamed but I wet myself."

"You were just a little girl...."

Alessio interjected, stroking her shoulder gently, not wishing pain upon the teenager at these reminisces but she continued; keen to get her thoughts out of her head.

"The man went to grab me but the infidel stopped him; asking him questions; his voice calm, his eyes steady but it stopped the bounty hunter. The other one pressed forward but the infidels friends all pulled out knives and scimitars. The infidel bent down and gently asked me if I wanted to go with this man and I shook my head, unable to speak for sobbing. The infidel told the man that I now belonged to him and if he wanted to question this, he was happy to discuss it as he walked to his horse and pulled out a crossbow, slowly loaded it and as everybody watched, his friends amused and the opponents fearful, he turned it on the first man, aiming it at his head; he advised him to leave within 10 seconds and then began to count clearly. The men simply left hurriedly. The man came over to me and introduced himself as James, asking me my name. I gave him my name but could not stop crying believing that as an infidel, he would want to hurt me as a Muslim."

Alessio smiled for the first time during the monologue.

"James told me much the same story many years ago; except he described you as this dirty, scared little girl but underneath the grime, you were the prettiest, most inquisitive thing he had ever seen; your bright dark eyes watching him in puzzlement all the way back to his home."

"I remember you and Maria coming to our home shortly after I returned home with James; it was only the one simple storey log cabin where he lived alone surrounded by sand and dirt; the trickle of a stream at the edge of his small holding. He was in the process of building the worst stable I had ever seen and he had

236

only two horses; one a black foal and the other the brown and white sleek Arabian."

"Georges."

Alessio interjected with a chuckle. Aisha smiled showing her perfectly formed white teeth as she wiped a tear that threatened to slide down her cheek.

"Yes, named after the old French man who looked after him after he left his mother and put him on the 'road to recovery' as he called it."

"After a misspent youth with me he meant; James transformed from a boy to a man under Georges' guidance."

"And you never did?"

Aisha asked with an air of mischief and Alessio pretended to scowl at the girl and pushed her backwards gently causing an outburst of giggling. Sitting back upright, her delicate hand tossed the natural ringlets from her eyes and composed herself, continuing slowly.

"I remember you and Maria coming over; Maria was lovely to me; brought me a wooden carved camel; I loved that thing; I think because it was the first gift I had ever been given and she was so pretty; with her pale skin and blue eyes; her clothes exquisite and extravagant. I remember you arguing with James, there was shouting. I knew it was about me. It was about me living there in the cabin with him. James never would admit it was about me but it was. "

"I am sorry for that."

The man interrupted with a genuine look of shame adorning his tan features.

"It was a difficult time. I was younger then too and people in Acre were talking; of James bringing a very young Muslim girl to live with him in his home. Just the two of you together. Rumours were circulating; vicious rumours. I wanted him to understand how the lies could affect him; he was trying to set up a horse trading business but these rumours would destroy it overnight. The Knights and Priests in Acre held sway and if they chose to investigate, James would be ostracised by his own community and possibly worse. I wanted to protect him, that's all."

Aisha smiled at his discomfort and touched his arm lightly.

"I realise that Alessio. I didn't then, of course. I didn't like you then. It was not long after that than the man who was with him when I first met him; Abdul, brought his family to visit us and I was schooled with his children at his home. Abdul's elder sons helped James build a second storey onto the cabin and I gained my own bedchamber. Over time, a paddock of sorts developed, a wooden boundary was put around his land and the terrible stable was rebuilt completely by Venetian carpenters from Acre. Sharla, Aboulias and Jamaal came to live with us; slaves, whom James acquired from Abdul, then freed and gave them liberty but chose to stay with us. Life was truly good. We were a diverse, strange family of misfits but we were happy; friend of Christian, Jew and Muslim; Knight and Arab, merchant and traveller."

Alessio smiled wistfully, realising that at this point in time, James was noticeably absent from Acre; spending his time building something genuine rather than wasting his hours with Alessio; whoring, drinking and gambling. At the time he bemoaned James's transformation, claiming he had become dull and boring; old before his time. He now understood how truly pathetic he had been and how as his closest and oldest friend; he should have been a better and more supportive friend. This thought swirled around his mind as Aisha continued her story; clearly needing to talk of happier times.

"James brought Jacob home one day and I hate to admit it but I was jealous at first. For three years, I had been his only ward; I loved him as a father back then and did not want to share him, especially with a boy. I felt my place was threatened, I thought I was going to be usurped I think."

She stopped to giggle apologetically again; a flush of embarrassment on her cheeks as she opened her heart to the Venetian.

"I was horrible to live with at that time. I cried and cried. I made James promise me he loved me and not only that, loved me more than Jacob. That's terrible isn't it?"

Alessio paused to say no but then felt it more appropriate to remain truthful and merely agreed with a typically Italian shrug.

"Once James had promised me he loved me more, I was better overnight and Jacob was so good; so sweet and shy but so kind to everybody. Everyone loved him. He had experienced the sheer horror of seeing his parents butchered in their homes by Christian Knights and again, James's business connections with the Jewish community got him involved and brought the orphan home; away from this atrocity. It had originally supposed to be for only a few days but Jacob just stayed and within weeks; he became an integral part of the 'family.'"

Alessio nodded and smiled thinly, explaining the background to that chapter of their lives.

"I remember the time well; James caused ructions in Acre over the killings. The condemned men were Templars; who claimed the parents of Jacob insulted them and the Christian faith. It was all a smoke screen; religious disputes and beatings, even deaths were not uncommon then. It was covered up as the killers were relations of rich influential Lords back in France. James was furious, cutting all ties with the Knights Templar – this was a big step for James as Georges had been a Templar and at one time, James himself was considering joining this Order. I brought him back one night from Acre after he had been threatening violence over this; we thought he may instigate a Jewish uprising at one stage but a handful of coins changed hands between religious leaders and the whole thing was dropped overnight. James returned to Acre much less after this and only for supplies that he could not get from Abdul or other Muslim traders. He also distanced himself from many Jews, believing they had sold blood for coin."

Aisha listened intently, Alessio's observations of this time completed the story of James for her and what he went through; she felt sadness at the edge of her heart but mostly she was intrigued in this part of his life that she did not know about; it helped her in some strange way in coping with the here and now.

"After that ours and James's fortunes grew over the months and into years; he began a vineyard and planted vines in our newly arable land; our well now functioning and providing water for all of us. The stables were increased in size as James bought foals and trained them, selling them to Knights in Outremer or rich Muslims who knew of his growing reputation."

The words ceased as her eyes misted over; the glorious past approaching the grotesque future. Alessio remained silent and avoided eye contact so as not to cause more grief.

"Life was beautiful; we all became closer. I played with Jacob, helped Sharla with her chores and talked for hours with James. He discussed the future with me, his plans and his dreams. He asked for my advice and feelings. I was just a girl, a foreign, Muslim girl at that and he talked to me so openly and honestly. I thought life could not get any better and then....it all shattered; first Abdul and his family. Then Sharla, Aboulias and Jamaal and Jacob. The entire family except for James and I dead and then, when I need him most, when I need his love, he leaves me."

Her body quivered and Alessio moved softly beside her, stroking her hair and bringing her tear stained face to his shoulder; cradling her as she wept bitterly; her voice cracking as she said what she felt most in her young heart.

"I thought he loved me most....but...but...he does not."

"That's just not true Aisha, he does love you, more than anything in this world, he is trying to protect what is most precious to him and has given that task to me. To make sure no matter what, you are safe."

"I just miss him so much...."

Alessio hugged her small frame against him and allowed her to unburden her pain, sobbing hysterically into his tunic.

Chapter 19

Safed

The outlying farms of the Crusader town of Safed came into view on the bleak, monotonous landscape; a cluttering of badly built wooden buildings; the vast majority of which lay in a rickety state of disrepair. The two men had broken their fast with dry, stale bread and dates, washed down with lukewarm water and the moods of both travellers remained akin to the sparse meal. James had led Thomas and the small train of horses across miles of rolling sand which gradually compacted to become sandstone; forming a bizarre terrain to travel through. Rocky outcrops sprang from the ground randomly in twisted shapes created by the omnipresent heat and whirling desert winds. There were no sounds and no life force and the two men did not break the eerie silence as they drifted slowly through the baking, red-orange world. Both sets of eyes and ears strained to their limits as they peered past the lumps of rock in all directions; fearful of Saracens ahead and Templars behind. Nerves were fraying and neither man raised their concerns to the other; preferring the solitude of their own minds.

Despite his body's desperate need for sleep; James had spent the night in a fitful state; the deep, echoing sounds of snoring from Thomas had not helped, nor had been the discomfort of the broken wooden floor but it was the evil machinations of the darkest corners of his mind that created the void that sleep could not obliterate. Endless questioning of his actions and the reasons behind the current course of events twisted his insides painfully and his head swam as the images of the dead he could not protect, mixed scornfully with the living he had left behind; screaming insults and heaping mockery upon him. As sunrise brought illumination upon the morning; James sat cross legged and lingered in his own melancholia; hardly dissipated by the morose grumblings of Thomas as he woke; unhappy with the food, heat and journey so far.

James had toyed with the idea of avoiding the last of the Christian controlled towns as within its' walls was a Templar outpost but as theoretically, it could be the last place to replenish all supplies and to eat and sleep in relative comfort; a low profile and brief overnight stay was worth the risk. In the only conversation of the day with Thomas; the Englishman had emphatically agreed as the arduous riding in such conditions were not to his liking and he needed a town's distractions to lessen the boredom. As the four horses trotted slowly past the empty outbuildings; it was clear they were nearing the limit of Outremer's safety. Safed, which had grown from nothing to a bustling trading town after the successful Christian Crusade was now reduced to a series of taverns, brothels, stables and smiths; in existence due to the Knights and mercenaries that dwelt there behind the new stone walls, which surrounded it; its' plethora of towers and turrets blending nonchalantly with the rocks the very buildings were created from.

The only entrance into the town itself was via the tower gate; an immense structure built thirty years previously by skilled French stonemasons; which comprised of a portcullis, great cedar wood doors reinforced with heavy slabs of iron, protected by archer positions, deadly oil holes and on each of the towers; a ballista of incredible size. A brief exchange in French between James and the men at arms that guarded the entrance was all that was required to gain access and Thomas's spirits immediately increased as he saw the number of taverns and hostelries that lined the main thoroughfare of the town. James smiled as he watched the man grin like a mischievous boy and shouted above the background noise.

"Let's find a tavern with a stable; then we can

eat, drink and bathe!"

Thomas literally beamed in response.

"Forget the bath; but ale, decent food and a very bad woman lacking in morality, now that is an evening I need!"

James shook his head with a sardonic smile on his features and pointed to a large building to the left; a creaking, swinging sign bearing the words in English; 'The Royal Tavern.' Thomas's eyes followed the outstretched finger and nodded enthusiastically. Nudging the obedient Merdlan in its direction; the two men paid the stable hand to look after the four steeds as they unpacked their belongings from the saddlebags and strode into an almost empty bar room. Upon hearing the rough English accent of the innkeeper; Thomas monopolised the conversation and managed to haggle him into a ridiculously cheap price for a room for two, promising ample amounts of coin would be spent on ale and wine later. James managed to get the key for the room and headed upstairs to unload their packs and then to seek a bathhouse, leaving his friend to enjoy an evening of ale and talk of his beloved England.

The room was adequate if dirty and he dumped the saddlebags, blankets and foodstuffs on the dusty, bare floorboards; preferring to keep his ample coin, short sword, leather jerkin and crossbow upon his person; fearful of thieves in a town he did not know. Gaining direction from Thomas's new friend at the bar; he crossed the crowded street; avoiding eye contact with knight, beggar and hawker alike as he located the bathhouse and entered the building. The owner of the establishment was Arabian and James refused the offer of companionship to bathe him; interested in getting the dust and sand from his aching body and not in straining his limbs further with any of the numerous offerings; be it man, woman, boy or girl; Muslim or Christian. Shaking his head in dubious wonder at a bath house and whore house being combined, he mutely followed a pretty dark girl who led him to a small chamber; containing a simple tin bath; various buckets of water, jugs of aromatic herbs and spices, together with a pile of different sized towels. The girl began to fill the bath with hot water as James carefully removed his leather jerkin, placing it on the floor next to his crossbow, quiver of bolts, sheathed sword and riding boots. Nodding at the girl who added a handful of unknown crushed herbs to the water; which filled the room with a pleasant aroma of something akin to vanilla and nutmeg, he watched her add cold water to mollify the temperature. Stripping his tight fitting tunic from his torso, he ignored the blatant offer of the girl and dismissed her; testing the warmth of the water as she left, closing the door behind her. Content with the heat of the bath, he stripped the remainder of his clothes from his body and bolting the door, he submerged his frame gingerly into the water.

He closed his eyes and dipped his head under the surface; soaking every part of his body and hair. Spending a few minutes rubbing his body with the provided cloth to remove the grime from the two days travel, he then stretched, relaxing in the tub with his chin resting on his chest, deliberately maintaining concentration on the journey ahead; remembering the maps and conversations with the Hospitallers and mentally planned the route for tomorrow. Safed was the last town of any size that was definitely safe and protected by Christian swords. The terrain east of the town was rocky where the small party would have to walk the horses through valleys, chasms and steep inclines. Some of the more hardy pioneers had moved across this harsh land to Lake Tiberius which lay beyond; where there was enough good soil beside the great lake for farms and villages of all denominations. This area was regularly contested and frequent raiding parties of mercenaries, knights, Saracens and outlaws made it a dangerous place to live. Crossing this great lake, named after one of the more worthy Roman Emperors; would take them into their enemy's own lands and from there, the earth became a sea of sand and the most hazardous part of their journey. Miles of seemingly endless sand in hostile conditions lay between them and Damascus; the best part of three days hard riding without roads or tracks to guide them.

Slipping back under the water, a second more cursory wash with the crushed herbs took place and then he settled into a comfortable position; enjoying the tranquillity of the empty chamber; an oasis of calm in the maelstrom of recent events. Twenty minutes of peace ensued as the temperature declined and his skin tightened sufficiently for James to heave his body out of the bath and dry himself on the multitude of clean towels provided. Dressing himself swiftly in his travel stained clothing; he mentally cursed himself for forgetting a fresh change of undergarments from his saddlebag. Checking he had left nothing behind, he unlocked and exited the sparse room, paid the fee without tipping and strode across towards the marketplace; keen to pick up extra rations that would survive for a few days in the extreme heat. The sounds, smells and voices reminded him of Acre; hawkers trying to sell you their wares, merchants haggling for that extra coin, traders forcing examples of their product upon your person. To James, this reminded him of his youth in the Venetian Quarter of the place of his birth and he relished the bartering and animated conversation in a plethora of languages as he purchased olives, dates and extra water skins; made from Byzantium leather, or so he was told. Enjoying himself, he spent some time perusing the stalls and escaped the worst of the afternoon heat, sat under the awning of a fruit juice seller; tasting the exquisite and expensive luxury of ice cold pulped orange juice; listening to two local men who discussed the inevitability of another crusade and yet more violence and bloodshed.

James ignored the religious politics that became debated at length; he cared little for politics of any kind and what various nobles, priests or the Pope himself dictated meant nothing to him. Sadly, however, these people held vast power over millions of souls and it was these power hungry men who brought wars and death to the masses. His thoughts evaporated as he watched two knights in full Templar regalia stride through the crowded market, cutting an instant swathe through the milling crowd. The hazel eyes squinted in the sunlight as its rays bounced off their finely polished, field plate mail armour and watched their arrogant swagger with distaste. To him, they were losing their reason for being; no longer a breed of noble minded protectors of the weak; they were building an Empire within an Empire; independent of the King of Jerusalem; Baldwin III. The concern for Outremer as a whole was how powerful this anti-Muslim army of Christian zealots, who called for a new Crusade, would become and if their extreme doctrine would infiltrate into mainstream ideology. Draining the refreshing natural liquid, James left some coins on the table and headed back towards the tavern, hoping Thomas was behaving himself and was at least, relatively sober. There was a need for tact and diplomacy and the ability to blend into the background of Safed and he felt a distinct chill as he thought of the brash, blunt Englishman with his propensity for ale. Quickening his step, he moved swiftly to the inn.

Somewhat surprisingly, he strode through the wooden door into a scene he had not expected. Thomas sat on a stool at the bar in deep discussion with the innkeeper about England and the state of the nation back home. James nodded, accepted the offered Flemish wine from his companion and listened to the conversation with keen interest, remaining silent and digesting the facts about his father's homeland. It appeared that England was in a state of turmoil, if not open civil war and had been for almost a decade. King Stephen held the throne but the Empress Matilda held the better claim and while these fought, the barons and Lords shifted alliances and gained power and influence for themselves. Matilda had been in France at the time of her father King Henry's death and in her absence

Stephen promptly seized the throne for himself. The barons, disliking the idea of having a woman ruling over them, accepted the status quo and Stephen was duly crowned King of England on 22nd December, 1135. This was seen as treason by some as Matilda's son should have the throne by right. Matilda, who was Henry's only surviving legitimate child had been named her father's heir and prior to his death, the barons had sworn an oath of fealty to her as such. Stephen himself was among those who had sworn fealty to his cousin.

In the ten bloody years that had followed this disputed coronation, various battles and political upheavals took place, sending England into a state of terror and violence. The tavern owner, a man in his middle years and from Oxford originally, supported Matilda's claim. The rightful heir, incensed at what she saw as Stephen's betrayal, was pregnant with her third child, William, at the time of her father's death and therefore her reaction was ultimately delayed. She did eventually invade England in 1139 and was ably supported by her illegitimate half-brother Robert, Earl of Gloucester. There followed a long period during which the country was rent apart by conflict. Normandy had been recently taken by Matilda's husband, Geoffrey, Count of Anjou, but conflict in England continued between the two opposing factions.

Thomas however, supported King Stephen, believing the idiom of he who acts ultimately gains and was outraged as he described his King being captured by the 'rebel' Robert of Gloucester at the Battle of Lincoln in 1141 and imprisoned in chains by the exultant Matilda, who was then recognised as Queen, by London's populace at least. She then managed to turn the tables on herself by deeply offending the Londoners by her arrogance and pride, so much did she succeed in inflaming public opinion that she was expelled from the city by an angry mob, who clamoured for Stephen's release and flocked to his flag. The fickle wheel of fortune turned once more when Robert of Gloucester was captured by Stephen's Queen, also confusingly named Matilda. An exchange of prisoners was finally agreed upon, with no side gaining the upper hand. Matilda herself was very nearly captured while being besieged by Stephen at Oxford, but made a daring escape across the frozen river camouflaged in a white cloak.

James accepted the second glass of the indifferent wine and found himself immersed in this incredible narrative of the country his father had claimed was the illuminating light of the world, a country of peace and prosperity. To James, it sounded little different to Outremer and he continued to listen to the well informed information with wide eyes and an intrigued mind. King Stephen was still in power but was relying heavily on mercenaries and the power hungry land barons who built their own castles across the landscape of England, terrorizing the peasantry and creating personal strongholds. This fact seemed to upset both Englishmen and the commentary dissolved into a mutual hatred towards any Lord or Baron of any nationality. The bar room was becoming busier as patrons drifted into the place and after well over an hour of conversation, the innkeeper reluctantly forced himself to serve the other guests and Thomas turned to his travelling companion, smiling broadly.

"Surprised at how much trouble England finds itself in?"

James nodded at the astute question and drained his glass thoughtfully.

"I know little of England, from what I remember, my father talked of it in glowing terms; I had not expected such turmoil. To me, Stephen should not be King, if it is true he pledged allegiance and fealty to Matilda, how could he then grab the throne for himself?"

Thomas shrugged and grinned.

"A woman should not be a ruler of a country; King Stephen saw his chance and took it. I admire him and I wish him well."

Raising his tankard, he toasted the King and James smiled as he heard the friendly tavern owner swear in response and chuckle afterwards. Nodding to the man from Oxford, he placed coins on the wooden bar and purchased another round of drinks, including mead for the innkeeper. Following Thomas to the far corner of the room and a small round table with worn cushioned chairs, the two men sat and sipped at the filled drinking vessels.

"Can I ask you something Thomas, something personal?"
The middle aged man's eyes narrowed with a twinkle of interest. The nod was slight and he stretched his legs wearily, awaiting the question.

"Should I trust you? I mean, do not be offended please, but I am trusting you with my life out here in this place."

James shifted uneasily; it was an awkward moment which stretched into discomfort as the seconds passed slowly.

"I wouldn't. I have never been particularly trustworthy; I look after myself first and everybody else second. I am a selfish man and am old enough to know myself to be so. I do not have your noble soul, young James."

The response was unexpected and caught the questioner off guard, especially as it was stated in such a brusque and honest manner.

"I see."

James forced a smile and tried to mask the disappointment and alarm from his features. Thomas recognised this fleeting look and grinned impishly.

"Don't be alarmed or so sensitive. I like you but I am a self-centred to the core. Life has given me little and what I have gained, I have taken. We do not know each other well and I am not one who trusts easily; this world has more snakes in its garden than men I find. I would be lying if the thought of killing you and taking you to the enemy to get the reward on your head has not crossed my mind. It has. However, I do not believe they would let a Christian Englishman out of their palace alive so it would be for nought. More importantly, you are trying to perform a noble act of bravery and I must help you do that; we have a very small chance of success but as you know; my aim when I travelled across the sea from Spain was atonement. So do not be afraid, I am not going to cut your throat as you sleep. I require forgiveness from God and not more innocent blood on my hands. The Holy Pope himself has promised every man, no matter how bad his sins, that he will find everlasting peace in the glory of God, as long as he risks his life battling the mortal enemies of Christ. Although you are a heretic, I do not see you as God's enemy."

James sighed silently. This was a regular theme for Thomas and one he could not agree with so if the conversation progressed, it would lead to his companion becoming argumentative and he was too physically exhausted and mentally drained to embark on confrontation. Instead, the pause became lengthy as he filtered his thought processes to negate the prospect of internal conflict.

The Englishman flashed a toothy grin through his unkempt facial hair.

"You are a sensitive soul; too sensitive for this land and all of its violence and slaughter."

James narrowed his hazel eyes and studied his fellow traveller; remaining silent and intent on his own thoughts.

"Not a big talker either, I've noticed."

Thomas murmured and quaffed deeply of his ale as James fingered his glass in discomfort.

"I am too tired to debate religion with you. I hope your God forgives you for your sins, if that is why you are here with me. Whatever the reason, I appreciate your help none the less."

"Debate religion? You are a non-believer, a heretic, a pagan. Unless you take God into your heart and soul, you will be surrounded in the bowels of hell by thousands of Muslims when you leave this earth."

James shook his head slowly and refused to be drawn into the contest, Thomas could try the patience of one of his mother's revered saints with his unorthodox sense of humour and he was too tired to embark on a confrontational debate, preferring to respond to the last part of his companion's comment only.

"I will take my chances when my time is right."

"Then you are even braver than I thought young James and may God have mercy on your soul."

James could not mask his smile and he tossed his head back and looked up at the wooden boards that covered the ceiling.

"I do not see any God, I think he has left this world; left mankind to their wickedness and destruction to wage constant war and inflict suffering and death. Perhaps He was right to leave us."

Thomas raised an eyebrow and gulped another draft of ale, wiping his lips and warming to the conversation, always keen on debate.

"The difference between us is simple and emphatic; I seek salvation in this infidel infested desert and you seek deliverance. From what exactly, I do not think even you understand completely; but out there; in the far reaches of these sands; your deliverance awaits."

James smiled thinly and sipped the wine, wishing it was a better vintage but enjoying the taste of sweet citrus on his tongue never the less. A silent pause developed again as James refused to continue the discussion which would inevitably lead to a debate and then to an argument and so he stared with amusement at Thomas, whose own smirk diminished with each passing minute. He finished his drink swiftly and placed the empty pewter tankard back to the table.

"Well, before you drag me into your deliverance my boy, I am going to find a woman to make me feel like a god."

Standing, he stretched his limbs and scowled as James could not stop the retort springing from his brain.

"Tut tut....such blasphemy, taking God's name in vain."

Ignoring the vile and very personal insult that followed his quip, he chuckled into his wine and watched the man leave the establishment hurriedly. Content with his performance in the conversation, James congratulated himself by ordering a third glass, feeling it was growing in flavour and taste.

Chapter 20

The Dice are Cast

Alessio woke with a groan and slowly opened his eyes wearily. He had been enjoying a glorious dream of fervent eroticism with an unknown but beautiful woman and the stark realisation of reality was a bitter disappointment. Aisha was awake, fully dressed and sat cross legged on the worn mattress, resting her chin on her clasped hands in a thoughtful, pensive pose.

"Morning...."

Alessio managed between stifled yawns and sat upright from the uncomfortable floorboards.

"Did you sleep okay?"

Aisha remained impassive and shook her head.

"No, not really. I need to find James and get our life back on track. He needs to understand that I love him, I forgive his foolishness but to honour the memory of our family, we need to stay together and continue the vineyard and horse trading. We need to build something of value."

The Venetian scratched his itchy stubble and ran his fingers through his unwashed hair, moving strands from his eyes as he digested the words; ill prepared for such a speech at this time in the morning upon waking. Aisha stared at him wide eyed and seriously and took his silence as a rebuke or refusal, pressing on with her view relentlessly.

"You do not have to come with me. He is

heading for Damascus and I can get there alone. There is a boat that takes merchants and workers across Lake Tiberius and from there; I will be able to gain passage with traders who will be heading to the city. Once there, I can find out about James from the locals, whether he has passed through, is staying there or...."

Alessio held up his hand to stem the words which were tumbling at speed from the young woman's mouth.

"I cannot let you go alone. If anything happens to you; James will literally kill me."

Aisha dropped her eyes to her fidgeting hands, speaking softer.

"You cannot tell me what I can do. I am not your captive."

The man smiled and shifted to his feet, removing the threadbare blanket from his body and moved beside Aisha. Placing a hand to her chin, he carefully lifted her face so her eyes met his.

"I mean, if this is what you must do, I will accompany you, if you would like of course."

The teenager nodded and threw her arms around him, hugging him tightly, hiding the tears that filled her eyes as she repeated the word thank you over and over.

No more than an hour later, the two unlikely travellers cantered onwards along the trade route towards Lake Tiberius via Safed, where they would rest overnight, hopeful that as they neared the outlying limit of Outremer's safety; news of James and Thomas would be easier to find amongst the locals. Aisha was in a confident and positive mood, her spirits greatly lifted as a consequence of her actions whilst Alessio attempted confidence and positivity in the face of a growing black cloud of anxiety, which intensified with every passing mile they rode further away from his beloved Acre. The sudden need to do the 'right thing' was already wearing thin.

****

At exactly the same time as Alessio embarked on his dangerous and unenviable task, his sister struggled to retain her dignity in the face of grotesque news. The fact that this dire information was provided by the one woman in Acre she really did not want to converse with did little to steady her nerves.

Jaeda brought a clay mug of fresh water to Maria, who managed a stifled thanks before gulping the liquid down swiftly, placing the vessel on the kitchen table and using her other hand to stabilise herself as she felt nausea and dizziness sweep over her.

"Are you okay?"

Jaeda questioned in her heavily accented Italian, which she was learning rapidly with unexpected ease.

Maria nodded in a pathetic attempt at deceit and sat heavily on the chair, cradling her forehead in both hands momentarily. Jaeda cast a quick glance at the woman who stood on the other side of the broad wooden table; her angular features drawn and her dark eyes were red rimmed as she looked impassively at Maria. In her left hand, the sheet of parchment that had been taken from the great tree from one of her workers remained offered out to the other woman. The language was French and Jaeda had no idea what was written upon it but clearly something was very wrong. A mere glimpse had caused the usual stoicism of Maria to crumble into fearful emotion and she could bear the silence no longer.

"What has happened?"

The question was proposed to the stranger as Maria still

sat with her head bowed and the well-dressed woman
flicked her eyes to look upon Jaeda. Her eyes flickered
in her direction briefly and she lowered the vellum to the
table.

"It is about James. Bad news."

The words were spoken abruptly but Jaeda believed
that the stranger was not being haughty or offensive,
merely trying to keep her own emotions in check. The
voice was hoarse, cracked and brittle.

"Is he....dead?"

Jaeda paused and looked in fear to Maria before adding
the final word of her sentence and watched as her
patron looked up at her, tears staining her cheeks.

"No but he may as well be. The Templars have
denounced him as a traitor to Outremer and the King. If
he returns to the city or anywhere within the province,
he will be arrested for treason and taken into the
Knights custody."

A fresh sob halted the reply and she bowed her head
again to hide the tears that fell.

"But why? I do not understand..."

"Sophia, explain please. I need the outhouse."

Pushing herself unsteadily to her feet, Maria hurried
from the kitchen out into the small yard and out of view,
the sounds of retching carrying to the two unavoidable
listeners.

"Apparently, he and Thomas have attacked and
beaten some Knights out on the trade route."

Jaeda shuffled her sandaled feet and looked at her
toes, still not totally understanding. Sophia read the

confusion on the girl's face and expanded on her explanation.

"The Knights Templars are a powerful force here in Acre and all over Outremer, they help the King govern and rule. It is against the King's Law to attack these people and if anybody does, they are declared to be an outlaw. Not only will he be imprisoned when he returns, he will be punished and all of his possessions will be taken from him."

Maria returned to the kitchen; murmured an apology and drained a second mug of water.

"We need to get to his home; the Templars will go there soon and take whatever they wish."

Sophia added and seated herself opposite Maria, tired of waiting to be asked by the clearly distraught Venetian.

"The Hospitallers should be looking after the cabin, stable and vineyard; James made arrangements with them before he left...."

Sophia shook her head slowly which stifled Maria's words.

"This is not Antioch. In the Kingdom of Jerusalem, the Templars hold sway. The Hospitallers will not lift a finger to stop them; if we were in Principality of Antioch, maybe but here?"

Maria knew the words to be true and cursed inwardly, staring into Sophia's striking face, a woman she disliked intensely but knew that at this time, she desperately needed allies and not enemies.

"When did you find the decree?"

"Isabella saw it on the 'Great Oak' in the

Merchants Quarter this morning and brought it back to me as she recognised the name. As soon as I read it, I brought it here. We may just have enough time to get to his place. My father has...."

She checked herself, amending her mistake.

"...My father had a wagon. We can take that and fill it with whatever you feel James would want to keep."

Maria nodded, adding a Catholic blessing for Sophia's deceased father which was accepted curtly, leaving Maria to wonder which of them disliked the dead man more.

The conversation over, the three women gathered themselves, locked the shop and hurried to the tavern, where the wagon was located in its stable to the rear. Ordering the inn's guard to prepare and drive the wagon, the three women soon found themselves bouncing around in discomfort as the two horses pulled the uncovered contraption across the dirt track which meandered southwards.

It was Jaeda who saw the black smoke in stark contrast to the morning's azure sky. Her urgent exclamation and pointed finger caused both Maria and Sophia to experience the same sickening, gut wrenching emotions. The concerned bodyguard slowed the skittish mares, their nostrils flaring at the foul smells that wisped across the air towards them. All recognised the stench of burning flesh and knew they were too late even before the scene of devastation lay before them, causing tears from Maria, groans from Jaeda and colourful expletives from Sophia. Marco dismounted and drew his broadsword; checking the vicinity for any signs of life and once content, they were alone; he helped his employer and her companions to the ground and remained with the horses, talking gently to them in soothing terms.

"It's all gone. Everything he worked for, everything he built...."

Maria was stricken with overwhelming grief as she surveyed the smouldering ruins of the two storey home. Gruesome charred remains of horses were scattered amongst the debris and burnt ash of the stable. Even the vineyard, which had been so difficult to irrigate and develop had been set alight and when not all of the boughs had caught fire, axes had finished the job of total destruction. Worst of all and what brought tears to the grim faces of all; even the hardened, stoical Sophia was the final resting place of Jacob. The grave had been desecrated in the most foul of ways; dug out, the coffin had been forced open and the recently deceased body had been emptied out and trampled into broken pieces by boot or hoof.

Jaeda hugged the weeping Maria who fell to her knees, retching and vomiting to the scorched earth; inconsolable in her private grief. With Marco's help, they managed to get her to the cart where she curled her heaving body into a phoetal position and sobbed uncontrollably. Leaving Jaeda to attempt comfort; Sophia wiped her tear stained cheeks, drew on her considerable inner strength of character and collected the broken and damaged body parts of Jacob and placed them back into the box. Muttering a prayer for the poor, lost boy and vehement curses on the men who called themselves Knights of Christ, who had presumably undertaken this cowardly and heinous act; she and Marco moved the corpse away from the awful fumes of burnt horse flesh and dug a new grave with a shovel from the wagon, burying Jacob again. Adding a rudimentary cross from the cut vine branches and cotton torn from the sleeve of Sophia's blouse, the Lord's Prayer was recited and they returned to Maria who remained in a state of absolute misery; held tightly by Jaeda, their heads hung together.

In silence, Sophia joined them and nodded to

Marco to turn the wagon around and head back to Acre. Nothing more could be done here and to linger was foolishness. The smoke would bring onlookers and as the fires had only recently burnt out; the Templars who had created this act of demolition may still be in the vicinity and friends of James would not be welcomed by the powerful fraternity. Masking her own sorrow as best as she could, she hugged Jaeda and Maria in turn, desperate to get back to the port and her own bedchamber where alone, she could unleash her vulnerability and weep in solitude.

****

The man who had been born Corrado Tullius in the war ravaged island of Sicily stood at the stern of the slow moving galley, hawked and spat into the waves below. He was angry but being a solitary soul, he remained impassive externally as emotional turmoil erupted beneath the surface akin to the volcanic lava of his homeland. Born into a poor farming family in the south of the island, he was the youngest son of seven and as was the norm in many Italian families, he was a spoilt and precocious child; allowed more freedom than his elder brothers and sisters. A quick mind and athletic physique, he was determined not to follow his brothers in becoming little more than farmhands, sheep herders and stable boys. Lying about his age, he left home to follow the all-conquering hero, knight and ultimately King of Sicily; Roger in his epic creation of the Kingdom of Sicily and Naples. The young Corrado's skills at killing became those of folk tale and legend; he was born to end lives. When all Roger's foes had been defeated and an uneasy peace ensued; Corrado became restless; a man so at home in war finds it difficult to exist in peace.

As with all young men approaching the end of their teenage years, he embarked on a torrid sexual affair with a beautiful woman, quickly developing into lust and then love. The issue was that the woman who

261

he loved was married and as their need for each other grew, the husband became aware of these private assignations and his masculine pride caused the inevitable dramatic, fateful scene. Greatly underestimating the younger man, a duel was arranged and the husband was despatched with cold and satisfying ease. Corrado expected a heroic welcome in the arms of his woman, the path to true love now clear but of course, as he would realise later in life; women are far more complex creatures than men and this particular member of the fairer sex appreciated the wealth and comfort provided by her older husband in equal measure to the younger man's attention and virility.

The relationship ended abruptly and a valuable if heart rendering lesson was learned. Corrado left Sicily for Outremer, using his plentiful talents for the armies of Christ initially and as the Kingdom was gained and pacified; he became a personal bodyguard, mercenary and eventually a bounty hunter. The boy; Corrado Tullius was long dead by now and as a man, he was known only as 'Il Falco' by those that hired him. It was said by those that paid for his services that he never failed and this rumour was actual fact, something the assassin was proud of. He despised failure and classed it as a weakness, a weakness he would not accept of himself and now; he found himself tricked into losing his prey.

The unremarkable face remained void of emotion as he wiped his mouth and murmured an archaic Sicilian farmer's curse. A thin smile slowly developed on his blood red lips as he imagined meeting his victim again and how this mixed blood horse breeder would suffer at his hands before meeting his maker. Nobody would play him for a fool his mind screamed internally and his smile thickened as he envisaged the pain he would inflict on this James Rose once he found him. Chuckling to himself, he spat into the sea again as the murderous scenes manifested in his sickened brain, warming his lost soul.

****

Her dark oval eyes studied the throne room through the opening in her uncomfortable burkha with open hostility. The man she had once believed to be the leader of the Muslim peoples, a hero who would attain legendary status by defeating and ridding the chosen lands of the white barbarians, sat in contemplation on his cushioned chair, studying the great map which was spread across the table before him. He spoke rapidly in hushed tones with his newly promoted general, who now led the 'Immortals'. The black material hid her mocking sneer as she thought the one word description of the elite swordsmen rather unfortunate as their erstwhile leader; the great undefeated Saddiq lay dead, his body rotting in Infidel sand, slain by the Christian whom Imad ad-din Atabec Zengi al Malik al Mansi feared most in the world. The man, whom he had placed a bounty on his head and sent assassins to slay; the man, he had his warriors searching for across his vast lands and the man his new general; Khalim, had vowed to bring in chains to his master.

Suppressing a bored yawn, she turned from the throne room and padded in her luxuriant slippers down the well-lit passageway to her private chamber and stepped inside, shutting the door and removing her head dress. She tossed the despised item of clothing across the floor; a noble woman from the Egyptian royal family should not hide her face for the sake of a mad man's religious beliefs. With the sudden deaths of Zengi's two favourites; his aged advisor who had been with him since a child and Saddiq, who had almost single handed created the Empire with victory after victory at the head of the vast armies; Zengi initially turned to seers and soothsayers and his formidable rage exploded forth; beating servants, torturing and slaying all those that he considered unfaithful or failures. This all-consuming vitriolic violence eased after a few

263

days, giving way to thoughtful contemplation as his braver and more loyal supporters urged him to turn to Allah before his armies and power deserted him completely.

The man turned to extremist Shi'ite teachings and the palace changed overnight. Concubines were banned, his own harem disbanded, alcohol was removed and prayers were made compulsory three times every day. An Imam from the south was brought in to bring him favour from above and all women were ordered to cover themselves completely and banned from any position of power or influence. Nadirah found herself marginalised and without purpose at court and this bothered her immensely.

Three years ago she left her beautiful, plentiful home in Alexandria after Allah came to her in her dream and advised her to seek out the Lion of Islam and protect and support him in eradicating the world of the accursed Christian; sending them back to their own tainted lands in defeat. She travelled across the deserts to the court of Imad ad-din Atabec Zengi al Malik al Mansi, who she foolishly believed to be the Lion of Islam, a general of renown and the most successful of the numerous warrior leaders of Arabia since the foreign invaders had captured their lands. Seducing the man easily, she quickly became a favourite concubine and began to plant the seeds of Jihad into the man's mind. Mercenary armies were raised to supplement the Muslim troops and isolated victories raised his profile amongst her peoples. Sadly, Zengi became more interested in attaining wealth and the servitude of his own people than defeating the common enemy. Brutal treatment of his enemies of all denominations concerned her and she swiftly realised this hardened warrior was not the prophesised Lion of Islam. Seeking out the renowned oracle; Kalaama; she brought her into her service and realised she had read the portents wrong. The one she sought was a boy, the son of a Kurdish mercenary general whose skill in battle and devotion to Allah were of equal standing. Secret meetings were arranged and correspondence developed between them. Funds were sent to build his own personal guard and words to the right ears of authority were spoken. Naim al Din was growing in popularity and renown.

Never a stupid man, Zengi sent this developing threat to a small town with no chance of glory and over the months, his spies clearly found out that Nadirah had been supporting this possible usurper. His vile advisor sent assassins to kill her and in a twist of fate; this Christian enemy of her people saved her life. This puzzled her but Kalaama advised that Allah worked in mysterious ways and the way of the deity was not theirs to question. Revenge was brought on Zengi's advisor by her own hand and she admitted to herself that the vengeance had indeed been sweet. The Immortals were sent to slay the infidel who saved her life and incredibly, Saddiq himself was killed and the Christian; James Rose became a problem for the Caliphate. More prophecy became public knowledge and Kalaama, who had never been a cheap fortune teller or back street witch; saw the white man's face again and again in the same, repeated vision. Sat on the back of a giant black stallion with hooves of fire, the man stared eastwards with death in his right hand.

She ceased her restless mind's ramblings and stared out of the small window across the sea of sand and mused if the infidel was coming and wondered how their destinies were entwined. Picking at a bowl of dates at her elbow, she smiled, revealing perfectly formed white teeth and lay back on her silk covered mattress, wondering about the future rather than the past and closed her eyes to allow her brain to embrace the will of Allah.

Chapter 21

The Gates of Hell

James allowed Merdlan to find his own path on the compacted sandstone, a difficult terrain; uncomfortable for horse and man alike. Even for such a powerful stallion, travel was slow and tiresome. Merdlan was also carrying a heavy burden upon his back and flanks. Safed was now miles to the west but for the small party, it may have been the last place on their journey to gain fresh supplies of provisions and James had bought as much as the four horses could carry. Riding his favourite horse at the head of the group, he led the much smaller brown and white mare behind him; a skittish horse prone to erratic behaviour but generally of a loving temperament. For these reasons he had named her 'Sharla' after the North African woman who had mothered him for numerous years. A wry smile illuminated his passive features as he thought of her beautiful mix of abject honesty, righteous indignation and endless belief in 'goodness'. A pang of emotion cut into the pit of his stomach but he maintained the smile and tugged at the hemp rope causing the mare to quicken her pace slightly.

"Come on girl and don't whinge Sharla..."

He mumbled under his breath and the forced smile broadened across his handsome face.

Thomas Holdingham struggled to control his own steed on the uneven ground and having tied the rope to the back of his leather saddle; the stronger gelding dragged the young chestnut mare across the bleak landscape. Wiping the sweat from his brow, he indulged in a series of colourful expletives; cursing the heat, the land, his horses, his companion and a multitude of other issues. The real problem of course was more prosaic. Having indulged himself in rich food, over indulged himself on strong ale and spent much of the night exerting himself with a much younger woman; more skilled and athletic than he in the process of lovemaking. He was weary, hung over and his stomach had severe cramps. Worse than all of this however was the fact that when he finally woke, he found the woman had gone along with his pouch of coin; which contained all of his worldly wealth and more than twenty times the agreed price for the evening's entertainment. It was this affront to his considerable pride that hurt much more than his physical discomfort. He had debated seeking out the thieving whore but James had then rapped on his door, asking him if he was ready to depart and not wishing to give the rather moralistic younger man another reason to look down upon him; Thomas trotted out of the town in a foul mood intent on unburdening his growing fury on some poor soul he should meet later that day.

In comparison, James was in a much better mood; focusing on the journey ahead and oblivious to his fellow traveller's numerous personal troubles. A good night's sleep on a comfortable mattress had meant a rejuvenated, relaxed body and his mind was looking ahead and not behind. The past could not be changed but the future was there for the taking; to be moulded into what you wanted it to be. Call it revenge, foolishness or redemption; this was the course he would take and his mind was finally content with the decision, even if his heart remained in turmoil. Happily ignorant of his companion's miserable morning; James made steady progress over the hard rock, avoiding the fissures and rubble and although moving at a slow pace and having to pause numerous times to allow the grumbling Englishman to catch up; mile after mile was eaten up on their way to the great lake.

It was late afternoon and the sun had passed its peak with the heat steadily declining when the placid water came into view in the distance; the sun's rays gleaming off its iridescent gently lapping waves.

"Beautiful isn't it?"

James stated, smiling as Thomas disdainfully flicked a cursory glance at Lake Tiberius and then dismounted awkwardly. As soon as his heavy boots had touched the ground, he unbuckled one of his saddlebags and began eating some of the salted beef from Safed.

"How far?"

Ignoring the brusqueness, James gave Merdlan a handful of oats and stroked his mane as he continued to stare at the expanse of water from their vantage point on a dirt trail that had wound upwards for the past twelve miles. They now found themselves on a thin ledge, nearing the uppermost part of the ridge they were climbing.

"At the speed we are going, we will probably not make it before nightfall."

Thomas merely shrugged in response, gnawing on the tough meat and swilling it down with water.

"We need to be careful from here Thomas. From here to Tiberius, there are outlaws, bandits and thieves. Runaways from broken homes, disgraced knights, Arabian orphans forced to rob to survive, roaming mercenaries from anywhere that need food or money. We look like an easy target with all these packs on our horses."

"I thought the King's protection went all the way to the lake?"

James moved to Sharla and fed oats to the mare as he replied.

"Not for a few years, nobody really has any protection this far from the coast. It's not ruled by any Arab leader either. It's just a kind of wild Borderlands. Even at the Lake, it's a dangerous place. It is said the Atabeg has spies on both sides of the water so we cannot go on the ferry which traverses the water. We will ride northwards around the Lake and then once around its top-most point, we enter enemy territory."

The older man grunted and nodded.

"I will don my armour when we reach the Lake. Is there a settlement there?"

James patted the mare's head gently.

"Kind of. A few whorehouses, taverns, weapon smiths and the like. A dangerous place though with no law. I wasn't planning on stopping there. "

"Does it have beds? Has to be better than sleeping out here for a bunch of dirty kids to rob us and slit our throats as we sleep under the open sky."

Contemplating either of the choices, James shook his head slowly.

"No Thomas. We stick close from now on. I have not been there but Abdul called it the worst town he had ever visited. We do not need any to find any trouble. We stay close to the higher rocks and nobody can creep up on us."

He shaded his eyes and pointed to a large outcrop of sandstone.

"We can rest there and build a fire, cook some of the lamb we have and get some decent food down us for once. Pass the night away there and then we can reach the lake and make our way northwards."

"Fine James, I have had my fill of other people's company for a while anyway."

Thomas murmured enigmatically and finished the food ravenously as James looked on with a bemused look on his face. The next two hours passed in silence as the light began to fade and darkness began to envelop the stark landscape. Maintaining a comfortable distance from the settlement, the horses picked their way interminably slowly up the incline, eventually making it to the top of the stone; struggling over the broken boulders and screed.

James removed the heavy burdens from the horses, secured and watered them as his companion scouted the immediate area for enemies and wood for the fire. Finding none of either, the two men grudgingly settled down under blankets and ate a dry meal of bread and cold meat, washed down with tepid water, finishing with dates and sultanas.

"At times like these, I miss home."

Thomas stated as he placed the woollen blanket across his legs.

"Really?"
James replied, looking at the elder traveller.

"This place is so barren. It's like a wasteland. Nothing of beauty seems to exist here. England has so much beauty. Forests filled with trees, plants, streams, flowers. Fields of corn, wheat and barley. Beautiful sunny days and blue skies one moment and refreshing rain the next."

James smiled as he listened to the unusually wistful musings.

"I sometimes feel I just do not belong, here or anywhere. You know, I mean what am I? Am I Venetian like my mother? English like my father? I was born in French ruled Outremer; does that make me a Frank? All around me; friends, family, and strangers; all fighting for their land or their god; declaring and fighting wars on behalf of their opposing deities. I am not even religious – I have no idea why I was born here, of all places."

"Maybe God has a sense of humour?"

James chuckled at his comrade's question as he envisaged the concept.

"That would make the Church more bearable I think; if God was more of a jovial chap."

"Blasphemy is a sin my friend; it will not help you get into his kingdom of heaven."

Thomas responded with a solemn tone but the trace of humour danced around his blue eyes. The man met his gaze and then looked upwards towards the heavens and sighed audibly.

"I think it's time I talked to you seriously James. I mean, about why I am here and why specifically, I agreed to come with you on this journey."

An ill feeling swept up his spine and seeped into his mind as Thomas spoke.

"Go on. I hope you know that you can talk freely to me."

The Englishman nodded and cleared his throat noisily, clearly thinking through his words carefully in his brain before speaking.

"I am here to atone for my sins."

The simple declaration resonated through the still air and James remained stoically quiet as Thomas paused to collect his thoughts and continue his monologue.

"I have seen and done bad things. Terrible, terrible things; for which I am ashamed of. Things that only God can forgive."

James shifted uncomfortably at the second serious declaration, not wishing to interrupt what was clearly a difficult announcement. Remaining silent, he waited for Thomas to continue.

"Have you ever killed a man, James?"

The response was a slight nod and the man progressed warily.

"How many men have you killed?"

The unexpected question caught James off guard and he replied curtly.

"Enough. Every man I have killed has deserved it; my conscience is clear."

Thomas kicked the blanket from his legs and searched his pack for the flask of ale he had bought at Safed. Gulping a good draught, he replaced the cork back into the clay pot and offered it to James, who declined with a wave of his hand.

"Then you are indeed a lucky man. I do not know the number of men I have slain over the years. I do not even remember all of them; some were in battle, others in honourable brawls, even one Frenchman in a duel. Others, however, were killed by my hand dishonourably."

A second slug of ale ensued and James remained physically passive but alarm was coursing through his veins, He feared a revelation and he feared that he would not like what he was about to be told.

"I am not talking about killing a man accidentally in a drunken rage in a tavern. Although, that too has been done more than once in my life time. That did not bring me here to the Holy Land. What I tell you now I have never told another living soul and I do not care whether you like me for it or not, I feel you should know that is all. Only God Almighty can judge me and it is for his forgiveness that I am here with you."

James ran his left hand through his hair and tried to keep his face in a stoical expression. Thomas studied his expression for a few moments before continuing with his story; his voice low and deep.

"When I was fighting the Almohads in the pay of the Portuguese, we laid siege to the last of the Muslim fortified towns in the peninsula. The siege was long and they hid behind their walls for weeks. They eventually ran out of food and disease began to fester as we continued to fire arrows, ballista spears and boulders into the forsaken town. Their leader attempted to parley with us, requesting food and safe conduct out of the territory. Our Portuguese commanders refused, their pride requiring nothing less than a convincing military victory. With death looming, the desperate Muslims slaughtered every Christian in the town and fired their decapitated heads into our positions. You can understand what ensues after innocent children's and women's heads reign down on an army. This was too much for us to take and we breached the walls that day and what followed was death and destruction the like of which I hope I never see again. Men were tortured and killed, women were raped and slain in the streets, old men were massacred and as the children crowded in the mosque; we locked the doors and burnt it down; laughing and drinking ale and wine as their screams filled the air."

"You did nothing to stop any of that?"

Thomas glared at the look of disgust on the man's face and snapped angrily.

"I was among them, I murdered, I raped, I drank and I laughed. What do you know? You have never been in a war. You have never experienced what I did that day. I was drunk on revenge, filled with bile and hate for my enemy; they were filth to be exterminated. A disease on God's world to be destroyed totally, annihilated."

James averted his eyes from the Englishman and looked out into the darkness, his thoughts mirroring the pitch blackness that surrounded him.

"Do not take the moral high ground with me...I accept why I am here...doing what I am doing. I came here for redemption...for God....to atone for my sins and to take my place in the kingdom of heaven. I understand that. "

James threw the blanket off his body and he jumped to his feet, his own emotions heating up.

"I am here for the right reasons; a man who I do not know....a very powerful, influential man wants to kill me, sent men to kill me and has succeeded in slaying an innocent, beautiful boy who I vowed to protect and bring up as my own; who I loved as my own. This bastard also has had most of the few people I have ever cared about slaughtered and I feel I am to blame. All this is somehow my fault. I am no murderer or rapist on a quest for forgiveness – I have done no wrong here."

Thomas leant towards James and laid a gnarled hand on his forearm and his rough Shropshire accent softened noticeably as he continued.

"Do not take offence my friend. You are not to blame for any of this and I understand your loss and your pain, truly. I know this man must die for his crimes and I will ride with you into the Gates of Hell themselves to make sure this Muslim's life is ended. I also know why you need to do this. You are here for vengeance, for revenge. You feel the only way to ease your suffering is by slaying your enemy. I understand this and would do exactly the same."

"It is not just for revenge; it is to stop this shadow of death that follows me and all around me. While he lives; Aisha, Alessio, Maria and anybody who gets too close to me are in danger and that is not fair or right but I am not like you and you understand nothing of me or my life. Do not pretend you do."

Thomas removed his hand carefully and looked out into the nothingness that surrounded their small crackling fire.

"So by protecting them, you leave them alone and rush towards your own destiny; to kill or be killed, for whichever of you dies, the pain will end."

James stifled his immediate rebuke and followed his companion's gaze into the enveloping darkness and silently nodded.

"That's not fair. "

He said at last, slowly and with feeling.

"Maybe all of mankind has a blackened soul. I do not know anymore. I know I am trying to protect the ones I love. Maybe this is the wrong way of doing it. Maybe I should have taken my loved ones and scurried away from everything I know, everything I have created and worked for in my life. Maybe I am exactly as you say; maybe all I feel is hatred and vengeance and I have no choice but to act on these emotions before they eat away at me, gnawing away my soul with every passing day. I do not know Thomas."

The mercenary listened patiently as the short, sharp sentences spat out of his friend's mouth and he shrugged listlessly.

"Do not worry yourself young James; this whole thing can only end in death. Either his or yours. One way it is ended and you will find peace. Although to do that, you may wish to pray with me one of these nights. God will never forsake you."

James smiled thinly and felt the beard that was growing on his chin; rubbing the course hair between his fingers as he remained quiet. A poignant pause struck up between the two men until eventually and rather abruptly, the horseman retorted.

"Get some sleep Thomas; we ride on again at first light."

For James, however, sleep did not come and after an hour of listlessly rolling from one uncomfortable position to another, he rose and went to Merdlan, needing some form of comfort and use for his perturbed mind. Stroking the great beast with a soft brush, he had bought many years earlier from an elderly French blacksmith, his favourite steed unleashed contented snorts as he softened the hair and removed the dust, dirt and sand from his flanks and back; before concentrating on the luxurious sable mane. As he worked, he relaxed and thrust the worries and concerns from the forefront of his mind. His relationship with Thomas was brittle; their lives and experiences too vastly diverse to be capable of a bonding friendship. Trust was an obvious issue but regardless of the cultural and religious divide; James believed implicitly that Thomas was a dependable man in difficult times and whatever problems they had, he knew that when he needed him, he would come through and he would stand by his side to the end. Picking sand from Merdlan's mane carefully and methodically; he glanced over at the large man who was fast asleep and wondered about the dark side to his character; something he could not understand and nor, if he was being completely honest with himself; actually forgive. To travel alone with a man who had butchered and raped defenceless citizens in a foreign city clouded his opinion and the knowledge placed an ethereal yet impenetrable wall between them. Both men were aware of it and once it had been spoken and discussed, neither would ever repeat the facts again. James knew he that his fellow traveller would always be in pain and anguish; a man ashamed of what he had done and his almost desperate need for redemption. It was this desperate need for God's forgiveness which also scared James a little. Thomas had made it abundantly clear that he felt their adventure was doomed, a suicidal madness; a rash act of bravery in the face of impossible odds and it was this, which appealed to a man who needed to die fighting the infidels; to be bathed in God's light and taken to the promised land.

For the hundredth time on this journey he wished he had taken Alessio with him. With Alessio, he had a whole life of friendship, faith and trust to fall back upon. With Thomas; whom he had only known for a few short days; this was sadly lacking. The image of Alessio's handsome, smiling face contorted in his brain to be replaced by the dark visage of Aisha and the expectant surging emotions swept forth; love and guilt the predominant ones in equal ferocity. Muttering in Arabic that he loved her, he sighed and continued to spoil his stallion; feeling a need to do something good for another living being. As he nuzzled Merdlan's ears and kissed his nose, he heard the footfalls on the loose stone for the first time and moved lithely to his left, where the saddles and packs lay and unwrapped the crossbow from its felt casing. In the darkness, he located the quiver of quarrels with his right hand and loaded the weapon effortlessly.

"We will take that horse, she looks a beauty."

The words were spoken in Italian and belonged to a male, no older than eighteen years of age.

"I do not think so,"

James replied evenly and turned towards the voice in the darkness, his hands resting on the loaded crossbow. A second voice cackled in boyish laughter to his left and further up the slope, a third youth chuckled and spoke brashly.

"A fellow Italian; where from mister?"

Straining his eyes as they adjusted to the shadows, he made out three figures all clad in dark clothes and clearly carrying weapons.

"Thomas, get up, we have company."

He stated loudly and aimed his crossbow towards the nearest youth who ceased his laughter.

"That crossbow better shoot three arrows mister or you are dead. Now be sensible and just give us that pouch of coins at your waist. It looks heavy. As you are being silly and not playing by the rules and threatening us, I will take that horse as well."

James smiled at this and from the corner of his eye, he was relieved to see Thomas move quickly to his feet and unsheathe his broadsword.

"Tell 'Thomas' there to put his sword away before you both get hurt. There are six of us, all armed. We just want your money and that horse. You can keep your lives and the other three horses, I am being fair here. Most would have just killed you by now and taken everything from your corpses."

More chuckling from the other two figures brought Thomas alongside James and he held his sword out towards the voices.

"What are they saying? How many?"

James aimed his iron sharpened bolt towards the outline of the young man who was speaking the most and winked at Thomas, replying in English.

"Three of them, I think, not much older than boys, armed, one to the left, two straight ahead. They say there are three more but I don't think so. From what I can tell, they have daggers or short swords. They are speaking Italian so I guess they were thinking we were easy prey, merchants or such like. Leave it to me."

Thomas smirked and grinned.

"We come all this way and still get robbed by Italians; you must be so proud of your people."

The main voice prevented further conversation in English with an angry statement.

"Stop talking! Now, do you want to just hand us your money and that horse or do we have to kill you?"

James laughed heartily and placed his right forefinger on the trigger mechanism.

"I have no interest in killing you but if you take one step towards my horse, I will shoot you down right now."

He sensed nervousness and heard the shuffling of soft boots on the sandstone and smiled as he heard the footfalls retreat back down the slope. Relieved he motioned to Thomas that they were leaving and the mercenary grunted.

"Shame, I could do with a fight."

James pointedly ignored him and moved forwards, his senses straining until he was sure the young thieves had left the area.

"Go back to sleep Thomas, I will stay alert until sunrise in case our friends feel they need to visit us again."

Without being asked twice, the Englishman sheathed his sword and settled back under his blanket on the ground. Slapping Merdlan's flanks gently, James held his loaded crossbow in one hand and strapped his short sword onto his belt and settled himself next to his horse.

"Nobody will ever take you from me boy. You are one of the few friends I can rely on."

He grinned as Merdlan used his head to nudge into his back.

"I know boy, you couldn't do without me either."

Chapter 22

Into the Past

As the hazy sun rose in the east; casting out the darkness in extravagant fashion from the unremarkable realm of sand and rock; the two men led their four horses cautiously north, avoiding the borderland settlement and keeping alert for any signs of human life as in this part of the world; any sign of human life would without doubt be a dangerous sign. Keeping the great shimmering expanse of water on their left, the figures made their way from the difficult rocky ground onto the soft dirt which surrounded Lake Tiberius; moving at a swifter pace throughout the day, they paused only to feed and water themselves and their steeds; allowing the horses to graze briefly as the few scattered clumps of grass would be the last the animals would see of this for numerous days. Leaving the lake crossing settlement far behind them, the men finally rested for an hour; James bathing in the purifying water to rid his body of the unpleasant mixture of perspiration, sand and dirt as Thomas sat and prayed in silence. Conversation was as sparse as the vegetation around them as neither man wanted to bring the reasons of their journey into the arena but equally, neither man willing or able to undertake pleasantries or small talk.

Whilst the uncomfortable relationship between James and Thomas was causing friction; nothing could have been further from the truth, many miles west, as Aisha's youthful exuberance was at its height. Questions tumbled clumsily from her, directed at a bemused Alessio who rode directly beside her on the desert road to Safed. Since the Venetian had agreed to accompany the young woman on her quest to find James, Aisha's mood had struck lofty proportions; natural excitement dismissing the danger and

281

complexity of the expedition, seeing it as a grand, glorious adventure. For Alessio, the danger and complexity bothered him immensely and he had good reasons to be reticent. Should anything happen to Aisha, James would hold him entirely responsible; which at best, would ruin their lifelong friendship at a stroke. That is, of course, if James returns alive from his own travels. Doubts assaulted his brain as Aisha talked excitedly; some of her words lost in the wind created by the horses as they galloped across the bleak landscape. Nodding and smiling at his younger companion, without really listening to her garbled sentences; Alessio struggled with the concept that James could already be lost.

The following twelve hours for both travelling parties was hard and uncomfortable and only the youngest of them remained smiling at the end of the day. For James and Thomas, it would be another brief rest under the blanket of darkness after a bland dried meal and clipped, stilted conversation. For Alessio and Aisha however, the night was only just beginning as they headed slowly into the tumbledown outskirts of Safed, past the empty shells of abandoned homes. The distant sounds of voices; shouting, laughter, the occasional shriek becoming clearer as the two figures looked through the gloom at each other. Alessio smiled in reassurance to his younger companion, whose face showed the distinct trace of concern for the first time in twenty four hours. The Venetian leant precariously from his mare and patted Aisha on the arm.

"Relax, this is my territory now. I know how these places work. Stick close to me and we will be absolutely fine. We get a hot meal and a comfortable bed and at the end of this day on this horse; I need that!"

The former Muslim's mouth flickered into a brief smile in response and she thrust her shoulders back in the saddle, sitting up straight as the first citizens of this

Borderland town came into view.

Alessio opened his outer tunic to reveal the wide leather strap of throwing knives that crossed his chest from his left shoulder to his right hip. He knew of Safed only by reputation and the reputation was bad. Decades previously, the crusaders had built this town as a port on the great lake to launch future raids eastwards. After years of conquest and glory, the Western knights eventually ceased their attacks, many of them returning home as those that remained built fortifications to protect their new land; naming it Outremer although for the European invaders it was known more commonly as the Holy Land and Lake Tiberius was one of its natural boundaries. As the hordes of Europeans from all walks of life chose the path to redemption in Outremer; villages and towns grew up and a form of relative stability and growth occurred. The war ended and although battles between Muslim and Christian factions broke out intermittently; knights departed home as heroes back to France, England, Italy and across the whole of Europe; replaced by pilgrims, farmers, traders, mercenaries and a myriad of other professions who had to use other tactics than combat to cope with life in the east. Trading and alliances took place and towns like Safed became commonplace; much to the disdain of the Catholic faithful in the heavily protected cities of Acre, Jerusalem and Antioch.

Safed was now almost lawless. The King's knights and their religious law rarely came this far east, despite the fact that on any vellum map hanging in a nobleman's home; the town was part of its protectorate. Equally, every Saracen knew that to cross the great lake, would undoubtedly be seen as an act of war and bring about the distinct possibility of thousands of angry Franks swarming here from European shores. Thus, a trading town of Safed was a dangerous place for any man of any race, creed or religion. Alessio knew this instinctively but this type of hostile environment suited the Italian and played to his natural strengths. He had spent his entire life in the cramped, overpopulated poverty of the Venetian Quarter in Acre and its' underbelly of criminality and disease. Alongside James, they had spent their youth honing their skills in learning how to deal with the villainous characters that earned their dubious livelihoods in the backstreets; be they violent drunks, overzealous guards, vile pimps or out and out thieves and outlaws. His sapphire eyes narrowed in the dusky half-light and scanned the growing number of the town's populace as the horses neared the town's square; where the inns, taverns and stables were built haphazardly in the compact cobbled area.

Through his peripheral vision, he could see and sense Aisha's fears increase as the locals peered up at them on their mounts as they trotted to the piazza, where he casually dismounted and led his horse to the nearest stable. A dishevelled, teenage boy took the reins and offered coin with a curt nod, his eyes roaming all over Aisha's slim frame as she dropped her lithe body to the cobblestones expertly. Pointedly ignoring his gaze, the girl passed him the leather harness and lifted the pack from the gelding's flanks to her own shoulder. Alessio's knowing stare caused the boy to avert his gaze and turn swiftly around, heading quickly back into the stable with the two horses after the Venetian had also heaved the saddlebags onto his own back. Pointing to the well-lit tavern next door; which exuded boisterous singing, shouting and laughter; he strode past the two armed guards, who did nothing but eye him suspiciously and with Aisha in tow, he entered the 'Black Unicorn' hostelry.

He paused in the doorway and surveyed the bar room, instantly appraising the patrons and staff who filled the smoky area within. His mind raced as he ticked off the main concerns mentally; keep Aisha safe, do not drink to excess, try not to spend all the small amount of coin they had, find a decent mattress for the night and get some well needed food and rest. Approximately fifteen people cluttered the small chamber; most sat around small wooden tables talking or playing dice; an innkeeper and an affable buxom woman, who he presumed to be his wife worked enthusiastically to keep the drinks flowing with great flagons of ale and bottles of wine. Most of the drinkers seemed to be more concerned with their own preoccupations and ignored the newcomers and only the trio of armed men in the corner of the room appeared to be a possible threat. They were all in their middling years with long hair and impressive beards, wore chainmail armour and bore a plentiful array of weaponry. All briefly studied Alessio as he entered and the Venetian dropped his stare; not seeking trouble this evening. Aisha pressed close beside him and whispered into his ear;

"Trouble?"

Her dark eyes flickered in the direction of the three men in the far corner with concern. Her companion smiled thinly and shook his head, striding to the bar and waited to be served by the flirtatious innkeeper's wife; hoping she spoke Italian rather than French. She spotted Alessio and heaved her ample bosom onto the bar as she looked over him lasciviously.

"What do you need, handsome?"

She spoke in French but with the accent of one who has lived in Outremer her entire life. Alessio attempted to respond in stuttering French but the woman merely chuckled throatily and repeated the question in Italian.

"My thanks, my lady. Do you have a room available? We need rest and food if possible?"

The woman's green eyes left Alessio's face for just a second to observe Aisha beside him, before they focused again on his features.

"For you, I could find you a bed."

Her eyebrows rose suggestively and Alessio smiled warmly in return, happy to play this game and an experienced player at it.

"Ah madam, if you were not already married and I had not promised a friend to escort his daughter...."

The woman giggled coquettishly and playfully slapped his arm.

"I will arrange a room for you both; we have roast chicken on the menu tonight if you would like plates. Put your packs down; I will get my boys to take them upstairs once I have sorted the bedchamber. A drink for now?"

"You are an angel my lady."

Alessio took her hand gently and with a flourish he kissed her gnarled knuckles. The corpulent woman giggled again and a flush struck her neck and cheeks.

"Oh, you Italian boys!"

She beamed and offered the rather meagre options available for consumption.

"Ale, mead or wine; both red and white or water?"

Alessio considered for a second, judging that in such an establishment, the wine would be inferior, cheap French vinegar which masqueraded as wine so chose ale. Looking to Aisha, who had stayed silent during the conversation dutifully, Alessio asked what she wanted and in quiet, respectful Italian; she requested water of the woman.

"Such a pretty thing! You want me to flavour that

with fruit for you?"

Aisha nodded and smiled, gently dropping the pack to the dirty, stained floorboards. Alessio did the same as a worker in his early twenties appeared beside them. The woman passed him a solid iron key as he picked up both packs easily.

"Room 6 please, son."

The man nodded curtly and headed up the staircase on the left with their belongings. Alessio paid the woman from his rapidly dwindling supply of funds and followed Aisha to a rickety wooden table, taking the clay jug of cool water and tankard of frothy ale with him.

"She was flirting with you!"

Aisha grinned as they both sat on the low stools opposite each other across the table.

"Don't sound so surprised young lady!"

Alessio winked as he poured the water into a wooden cup; chunks of orange, lemon and lime splashing into the vessel also, passing it to his young charge. Aisha nodded in thanks and looked over at the three armed men who were drinking and laughing constantly.

"Don't worry about them. They look like mercenaries from northern Europe. Swedes or from the Holy Roman Empire probably. They drink more than any other race I know but generally keep themselves to themselves."

Aisha turned her attention back to the Venetian and nodded slowly.

"I wondered why I did not understand their language. Have never seen such beards; why do they grow them so long?"

Alessio shrugged with a bemused grin and sipped the ale gingerly; pleasantly surprised at its full flavour; he gulped down a third of it and placed it back to the table.

"That's better; I wasn't made to sit on a horse all day! Never understood James's fascination with them – uncomfortable beasts and where's the fun?"

Aisha smiled and drained her cup; chewing happily on the refreshing fruit chunks before refilling the small mug, before responding.

"I think James is happiest on horseback. Especially Merdlan; they adore each other. Nobody else can control Merdlan. He wouldn't even let me ride him and I used to clean him, feed him, and water him!"

Alessio nodded in understanding and thought of his oldest friend fondly for a moment.

"Do you think he is ok?"

The girl asked with the slight intonation of doubt in her voice.

"Yes I do. Honestly. James is a survivor, always has been. He could always look after himself better than the rest of us – most of the time, he looked after me too!"

Aisha sniggered and the hint of fear left her mind instantly.

"What was he like before? I mean, at my age. I have known him pretty much my entire life and know only what he has told me of his previous years. I know about his father and his brother and how his mother let him down. I know he was helped by an old French man and set him up in business and then he built our home and everything. I know all the dry facts but what was he like before I knew him. When he was a teenager; he never spoke about that and why isn't he married – has he never been in love; he never talked of such things. Whenever I asked him, he would just clam up and tell me he was too busy for love or women and he was happier on his own as he had Jacob and I to look after and his horses and the vineyard he was creating."

Alessio smirked as Aisha paused for breath and he sipped the ale again, drifting back in time in his mind to recollect a young James.

"Well, if James has not told you about women, I am not sure I should impart such things but I can tell you about him as a teenager if you like?"

Aisha shifted nearer to him on the stool and nodded enthusiastically.

"I have pretty much grown up with James; from my earliest memories we were best friends in Acre. His mother knew my mother back in Venice before either of us was even born. They moved to Outremer on the same galley after the land had been secured by the Crusaders. His mother married an English minor noble and she left Acre with him for a few years for Jerusalem I think. The two of them returned to Acre and James was born four week before me; as our mothers knew each other and we lived in the same plaza in the Venetian Quarter; we played together as young children and just became like brothers. After his father and brother died, we became even closer and into our teens, we were pretty much inseparable."

The narration was paused as another gulp of the ale was taken.

"But what was he like in his teens?"

Aisha pressed, her eyes wide and sparkling with intensity.

"Well, he was smarter than the rest of us in our group of friends but then, he had the education of the Jews that his father had instigated and then Georges had furthered his studies. The rest of us had none; we could not read or write whilst James could. He could also speak English and passable French and Arabic."

"His Arabic is still awful now."

His intent listener interjected, giggling.

"Well, it was much better than the rest of us; we struggled with Italian let alone any other language. Apart from that, I would say he was more intelligent in general but probably not as street wise as us; he was more trusting and gullible but he was funny and we had fun."

Alessio's volume faded a little as his brain created brief glimpses of their teenage years in Acre; the fights, the girls, the dares and the jokes.

"So if he was intelligent, funny and good looking; why no wife?"

The Arabian mused and Alessio grinned in response.

"I don't remember saying he was good looking?"

Aisha blushed and sipped her water to avoid the eye contact as the older man teased her.

"There were women in our later teens but I don't think it's for me to tell you that about James."

He smiled and was grateful that the roast chicken platters appeared at that very moment from the sullen son, who also passed them the iron key to their bedchamber, before shuffling away. The conversation ended as both tucked into the food with gusto, rumbling stomachs filled with the charcoal burned meat;

delicately spiced and salted. Once the large portions had been decimated; Alessio cleared the wooden boards that had been used as plates and ordered another round of drinks before patting his stomach and complimented the unseen cook.

"What about Maria and James?"

The sudden question, which had obviously been cogitating for many minutes in the girl's mind caught Alessio a little off guard and he wiped his mouth and chin with the back of his sleeve before answering.

"My sister has always loved James I think; the problem is that although James loves Maria also; it is more like a brother's love than a passionate one. When my father disappeared on us, Maria is only three years older than I but always looked after me really and she did the same for James."

"But I have seen how she looks at him sometimes, in Acre, after Jacob..."

Alessio caught the tremor in the girl's voice at the mention of her brother's name and he reached out to hold her hand across the table.

"There are many forms of love in this world. As James grew into a man, my sister's love became more than that of James, who will always see my sister as his sister. I have told Maria many times to marry and end her unrequited love."

"What about the woman at that tavern in Acre; Sophia is her name?"

Alessio shifted uncomfortably in his stool and ran his fingers through his hair.

"Well, that is more complicated and I do not think it is my place to talk about that relationship."

"But they did have a relationship?"

The Venetian chuckled at the girl's insistence and he held his hands up in a gesture of capitulation.

"Ok, ok, the shortened version and if James ever asks, this did not come from me. Sophia was the most stunning girl in the city, we all wanted her. The problem was her father was a horrible man, a violent, wealthy, scary individual so this kept most of us boys at bay. You see, her father was a man not to be crossed and he had betrothed his eldest daughter to an enormously affluent Pisan merchant's son upon her eighteenth birthday. Until then she had to remain...err mm...untouched. You understand?"

"I am not eight years old – of course I understand; she had to be a virgin upon her wedding day!"

Aisha said, rolling her eyes in mock exasperation.

"Exactly. Anyway, many still tried to breach Sophia's maidenhood so to speak as she was very beautiful and even without her father's wrath; she was a woman who could look after herself. However, where many failed, James succeeded. He courted and wooed her and in secret, they became close. They were blissfully happy until the time of the intended nuptials came to pass. As you can imagine, Sophia refused to marry this stranger and when the reasons why came out, her father was furious. He and other men found James and beat him badly; he would have probably died had not Sophia and I stopped them with threats of bringing guards. It became the talk of the Quarter for a while and the proposed marriage was dissolved. Sophia's father never forgave James or his daughter and sent Sophia back to Venice so their relationship was ended."

"That's awful."

Alessio sipped his second tankard of ale and nodded in response.

"Why did he not go after her if he loved her so much? Her father could not have stopped him from doing so and they could have been together without the fear of his retribution."

"That is something I cannot answer. Now drink up, it is getting late and tomorrow, we need to get across the great lake and then young lady, I am relying on you to get us to Damascus!"

Aisha smiled bashfully before replying.

"Don't worry, I have thought about the ideal plan for that. It is truly simple and cannot fail. I am going to make you a Muslim!"

Her giggling became a full body laugh as she watched Alessio's features change of its' own accord as his brain processed this information. She was still chuckling many minutes later as they mounted the stairs to their bedchamber much to the man's chagrin.

Chapter 23

Into the Desert

James pulled on the reins gently and Merdlan obediently slowed his pace to a standstill over just a few short yards of dirt. Letting go of the leather straps, the rider leapt from the vast ebony back and led his stallion to the water's edge for both of them to slake their thirst. Looking back, he could see Thomas in the distance, sat ungainly on his steed as it trotted towards them around the curve of Lake Tiberius. Splashing water over his face and hair, he placed a hand to cover the glare of the sun in the east and stared out at the great expanse of rolling sand which stretched as far as his eye could see. He knew from this point on, there would be no support, no food, no water and nothing they could rely on until they reached the Saracen city of Damascus; which lay around three days ride across the scorching, inhospitable desert. His stomach churned and he felt the distinct taste of bile at the back of his throat. Falling unceremoniously to his knees, he tossed water across his shoulders and chest and bent down to gulp more of the refreshing liquid, closing his eyes as he thought of the dangerous days ahead and wondered, not for the first time, if this journey would be his final one.

Thomas found his fellow traveller on his knees when he forced himself wearily from his saddle.

"You ok?"

The two words were said without emotion or feeling and James nodded and pushed himself from his knees back upright.

"We need to get all the water we can carry and make sure we have everything readily available. Once we head across that...."

James paused as he pointed to the shimmering miles of sand beyond them.

"...once we start riding over that...the only people we meet will most probably try and kill us and there will be no food or shelter until Damascus."

Thomas grunted in acknowledgement and heaved the heavy sack, which rested against the hardened leather pommel of his saddle. James watched as the Englishman opened up the sack and carefully laid out a perfectly polished suit of plate mail; complete with greaves, boots, gloves and helmet. It was expensive and the type the Knights Templars or Hospitallers would wear when heading into battle.

"You are going to wear that in this heat?"

James queried incredulously and Thomas smiled thinly, replying as he worked on removing his current clothing.

"You wear clothes underneath so the hot metal does not burn your skin. It will probably be uncomfortable sure but the idea of being hot or dead is not that tough a decision. You should think about armour yourself, the Almohads prided themselves as horse archers; I was informed that these Muslims were no different."

James shook his head and answered matter of factly.

"I have a chainmail vest and a leather surcoat; I need to be able to move easily and full armour like that just restricts my movements. Also, I do not wish to cook inside a metal container under that sun."

"I will ask you again when I pull arrows out of your body."

Thomas grinned and began strapping the various parts of the full plate mail to his body.

"It looks expensive."

The horse trader said looking over the highly decorated steel.

"I traded with a French nobleman during my mercenary days in Bretonne."
James arched his left eyebrow and stated a one word question.

"Traded?"

"Yes, I gave him immortal life in the Kingdom of Heaven and he gave me his suit of armour."

"Ahhhh....I see."

James replied and began helping his companion with the heavy armour plates, eventually passing him the box helmet with its slit cross in gold leaf from which Thomas would be able to see and breathe. Placing it on his head, he strapped it under his chin and began to move awkwardly in the field plate mail. Drawing the great broad sword and circular shield, he began to practise combat moves and James watched him with more than a little amusement. He could see the sense in full armour but he was not used to such a burden and knew he could never ride or fight in such cumbersome plate and the tight fitting box helmet would be a huge problem for him in using his crossbow. Leaving Thomas to his training, James spent the next few minutes filling each of their water skins and leather containers and repacked their supply of foodstuffs into separate portions of fruit, salted fish, bread and dried meat; happy that they would not starve at least on the path they were about to take. Checking the oats and wheat for the horses and packing the weight of the equipment as evenly as possible; he then checked all of the metal horseshoes and confident that all was as good as it could possibly be, he looked over at Thomas and pulled out a muslin cape from Merdlan's rear saddlebag. Smoothing the garment out, he approached the swordsman and offered it to him, deciding the best way to get Thomas to wear it was to lie.

"The early Crusaders used to wear muslin over their armour; to prevent the heat from the sun burning them and to negate the glare from the plate mail. That way, they don't shine like a burning beacon for all the Saracens in the Holy Land to see them!"

He grinned easily and Thomas studied the item of clothing dubiously before shrugging and putting it on.

"If it was good enough for the Crusaders, it is good enough for me."

Thomas mumbled and continued to swing his sword in an arc, sweeping from left and right. James watched him momentarily and felt bad about the deceit; muslin was used by Arabian horseman and not Christians but he had no wish to provide the enemy with a gleaming spectacle to be seen from miles around. He was also not in the mood to waste time and stated sharply.

"You ready? We need to move on."

After wisely stifling his laughter at Thomas's struggle to remount his mare, James led the small baggage train out into the desert; avoiding the merchant road for fear of discovery and using the plethora of sand dunes to attempt a hidden journey east. Keeping movement speed low in such conditions and terrain; his neck muscles and eyes soon ached as he studied the sheer emptiness around the party and as minutes turned interminably slowly into hours, the perspiration mounted on every inch of his tiring body. The travellers had agreed to ride at a comfortable pace across the rolling sand dunes and through their protective natural valleys for four hour periods before briefly halting for rest and nourishment before continuing again. Neither of them had any wish to linger in the enemy's back yard for longer than necessary.

The first four hours of the perilous journey was uncomfortably hot and intensely dull with no sign of life at all and nothing but the relentless miles of sand to look upon, through the hazy glare of the scorching sun. Without any shelter at all, they hurried through a dry meal and fed and watered the horses; James taking the time to rub Merdlan's foaming sweat from his flanks and back before heading eastwards again. As they rode, his mind wandered without any stimulus from the surrounding area to keep him occupied; his thoughts turned alarmingly to how they were actually going to find Damascus in the hundreds of miles of desert ahead of them. He had chosen not to take the trade route or the main road to the city as this would without doubt be guarded but to head in an easterly direction for three days could prove disastrous. Pushing this new item of concern forcibly from his mind, he focused on what was ahead and as the horses trotted up and down the soft sand dunes; the definite signs of a sand storm became apparent ahead of them and he cursed vehemently.

His great ebony stallion stopped upon the softest of heel kicks from his rider and he paused as Thomas brought his own steed to more problematic halt moments later.

"What is it?"

The mercenary grumbled and looked ahead at the distance, making out what looked to him as a low clouds; unusual certainly in the ocean of azure above them but nothing to cause concern.

"Some clouds?"

He questioned sarcastically and James rubbed his

stubble and shook his head.

"A desert storm I think. It's probably a few hours away at the moment. Hard to tell how big or which direction it is moving. If it is coming at us and we have to ride around it, it could add hours to our journey."

Thomas looked dubiously at the clouds ahead.

"That's a lot of 'ifs' to worry about. Come on, if we do have to go around it, we go around it."

The Englishman kicked his horse onwards, leaving James to frown at his receding figure, muttering about foreigners and their lack of knowledge or concern for obvious life threatening situations. Nudging Merdlan to follow his reckless partner, James watched the great billowing waves of sand dance in the air ahead of him get closer with every passing hour. When they finally stopped for their second meal of the day under the mid-afternoon sun in a slight incline, protected on all sides by hillocks of sand, it was clear, even to Thomas that the desert storm was in front of them and covered the entire horizon from left to right. The two men had to choose to sit and wait for it to pass, hoping it would not approach them; which in the somewhat amateur judgment of James was probable as it seemed to be heading away from them or from north to south in direction. The other options were to head through it, which was tantamount to suicide, or to try and travel around it but if this was the choice; in which direction did they head? If they chose the wrong direction of a compass, they could put days onto their schedule by following a raging desert storm which could itself take days to burn its own malevolent force out. Thomas listened to the options as he ate an apple listlessly and upon hearing all of them; shrugged and crouched down.

"I guess we wait here then. That seems to be the most sensible thing to do. You say these things can last an hour or many hours, even a day?"

James nodded as he rubbed down Sharla; the chestnut mare who was struggling more than Merdlan in the conditions. Feeding oats to the grateful horse, he looked up at the incessant glare of the sun overhead and sighed. Blowing the air from his lungs dramatically, he suddenly ceased his body's convulsion and placed a palm over his eyes as he saw something that brought bile to his throat instantaneously.

"Don't move suddenly or turn around Thomas but we have been found."

The Englishman immediately whirled around, drawing his sword in one fluid motion to look upon the western brow of the small incline. There sat on a brown and white horse was a man clad all in black, a Saracen, who even at this distance was heavily armed with spear, shield, composite bow and scimitar. The breastplate, spiked helmet and flowing cloak were all of sable colouring and he turned back to James.

"Why is he just sat there watching us?"

James eased himself to Merdlan and was carefully removing and loading his crossbow behind the great beast as he replied.

"He is one of the Immortals, he will not be alone. These are the bastards who murdered Jacob, Sharla and the others."

"Are they now?"

Thomas said slowly, moving to his horse and mounting it, edging him to face the onlooker; his great longs word still drawn and raised motionless at his side.

"I can get him from here, keep your eyes open on the other dunes; there will be more."

James spoke with authority and raised his onyx

crossbow to rest on Merdlan's rear, closing his left eye to aim at the swarthy man's face. His finger rested on the firing mechanism just as four more of the jet garbed warriors moved alongside him. Swallowing his fear, he paused in his position as in his peripheral vision, he watched Thomas unroll the blanket under his gelding's saddlebag and saw two iron javelins, of the style the Spanish and Portuguese Jinettes used when fighting on horseback and smiled grimly. The five Muslims began their move, one wheeling away and drifting from view and two lowering their ten feet long barbed spears and trotting towards them. The remaining two began to pull the composite bows from their backs and it was then that James reacted with speed and composure. He shifted his aim from one of the men who carried a spear to the man to his left, who was calmly tugging out a feathered shaft of an arrow from the quiver at his side. The finger squeezed and the sharpened bolt flew through the air and struck the man on the cheek; splintering bone upon impact and the man's bearded face erupted in blood and gore as the man was spun from his horse with an agonized cry.

Thomas swapped the sword to his left hand and raised the metal javelin above his shoulder and waited, calming the skittish animal that bore him as the two spearmen approached the Christians at increasing speed. His face was a mask of concentration as he blocked everything out of his mind except for the onrushing enemies; his eyes taking in the armour, the helmet, the shield, the spear, the horse as he waited for them to get within his killing range. One of the archers had already been taken out of the skirmish and the other was aiming his notched arrow towards James so there was no immediate danger there. The two Turcoman Horse warriors reached the levelled sand at the same time and hurtled towards the Englishman, who stretched his right bicep and hurled the javelin with all of his considerable strength into the Saracen to the right. The heavy, sharpened point embedded itself within the man's exposed and unarmoured neck, the force of the throw slicing through the soft flesh and out of the larynx on the other side. The Immortal falling heavily from his galloping horse with a muffled, strangled death cry. To his credit, the second horseman did not even check his onslaught in the face of his comrade's death. Tossing the handle of his sword back to his more powerful right hand; Thomas watched the thundering attack approach and brought his sharpened blade down in a sweeping arc to cleanly hack off the metal tip of the spear, splintering the shaft of the wood about two feet down. The broken haft of the damaged weapon struck Thomas in the chest; his plate mail armour easily deflecting the blow and as the enemy dropped the useless weapon to unsheathe his scimitar; the mercenary brought his long sword up swiftly with a flick of his wrist and hacked deep within the man's forearm, the sleeveless breastplate giving no protection. A warm, sticky jet of blood soaked Thomas as the man screamed and dropped his reins, falling from his mount as he held his other hand over the severed limb. Staggering clumsily to his feet, Thomas dispatched him with a sword thrust to his neck and turned his horse to survey the scene before him.

James, immediately after shooting had reloaded, remaining behind Merdlan as he watched the second archer draw back his bow and shoot harmlessly into the sand, a yard or so over his head, his horse rearing in fear as the man beside him fell to the ground. Bringing the crossbow up to shoot, he was distracted by the expert throw of the javelin by his comrade and his quarrel flew slightly low, striking the archer's horse in the chest. The animal reared again, panic stricken and the man was thrown to the sand. Out of the corner of his eye, he saw Thomas slay the second horseman and he tossed the crossbow to his back, the leather chord keeping it securely in place and ran up the slope, his own short sword drawn as he hurried to end the battle. The slope was steeper and longer than he had envisaged and he was breathing hard when he reached the top and looked over the stricken horse, which kicked and struggled from the ground as his life force ebbed slowly and painfully away. The sounds of Thomas urging his gelding up the incline came to him as he took in his surroundings; the one horse alive, drifting slowly away and the first Muslim, lying prostrate on the ground and then the second of the archers who rose athletically from behind the dying Arabian horse and shot a second arrow towards James, who had no time to move.

The arrow pierced the flesh just above the chainmail on his left shoulder and James grimaced in acute agony as the pain instantly emanated from the wound. Gritting his teeth, he bounded to the kneeling man and shattered his defensive arm with his first attack, killing him with his second. Dropping his sword, he put pressure against his wound and grunted as he knew the arrow head was stuck in the tissue and bone of his shoulder. Thomas appeared alongside him and dismounted heavily after he had made sure all four of the Immortals were a poor portrayal of their name.

"You ok?"

The response from James was insulting and unequivocal. Thomas grinned broadly momentarily and then his eyes focused on the arrow, which still remained in his companion.

"You fought well Thomas."

James acknowledged and attempted to remove the arrow from his shoulder, wincing in pain and a fresh loss of blood. Knowing this was beyond his medical knowledge; James broke off the shaft of the arrow just outside the wound and tossed it to the ground in disgust.

"You need to clean that and it needs to come out...."

Thomas spoke softly, looking closely at the injury with a distinct hint of foreboding before he was distracted by the billowing sand and dust heading their way.

"Damnation. That desert storm is coming in from both sides."

James followed the eye line of his fellow adventurer and swore again.

"That is no desert storm. That is the rest of the war party; these were just the scouts. See, the single figure heading towards them, screeching and shouting at the top of his voice. That was the one who left these four!"

"How many do you think?"

James studied the size of the cloud and stated grimly.

"Impossible to tell from here but at least twenty I would say, maybe thirty and I don't think we should linger to count them."

Thomas chuckled throatily and moved to his horse, clambering aboard as James sprinted painfully down the slope after sheathing his blood stained short sword at his waist.

"Where in God's name do we go?"

Thomas roared as he trotted beside the perspiring tradesman.

"Head towards the desert storm, hopefully, it is moving away from us or dying down. Go now, Merdlan will catch up!"

The recipient of the words squinted dubiously and turned to head east before moving back momentarily.

"What about the other horses and our supplies?"

James ran towards his black stallion, who watched his owner approach with intelligent eyes.

"Go! I will swap what I can but the others will have to cater for themselves, we will have no chance leading them out of here."

Thomas nodded, hawked and spat onto the ground before forcing the gelding around and cantering from the small natural desert valley, picking up speed as he did so. James headed to Sharla and removed the water skins from the pommel of her reins and thrust them onto the saddle of Merdlan. Pulling off the spare quiver of quarrels from the mare along with the leather satchel of dried meat, the man tied them onto the stallion and he heaved himself upon his back; the free flowing blood of his shoulder causing him concern and pain. He nuzzled his animal's neck and mane, whispering soothing words as his mount knew that there was trouble at hand. Cutting the hemp rope so Sharla was freed, he shouted at her and the fearful young mare cantered westwards away from them. Moving to do the same to the remaining horse, he shooed them both westwards and mouthed an apology to the stricken beasts, silently wishing them luck as they ran and jumped in confusion.

"Come on boy, let's get out of here!"

Merdlan snorted in response and hurled its immense body across the desert, the powerful strides soon leaving the valley behind and emerging into the vastness of the open, bleak landscape. Twisting in his saddle, he smiled as he saw no sign of the chasing pack although his smile faded abruptly as the figure of Thomas was rapidly becoming clearer and larger ahead of him. He had every faith in Merdlan's speed and stamina but to catch up so quickly meant that the lightly armoured horsemen behind them would also reach the Englishman before the relative safety of the looming desert storm far too easily.

305

Chapter 24

God's Breath

James drew Merdlan alongside Thomas within minutes and looked ahead at the whirling clouds of sand and dust ahead of them, his chainmail shirt and tunic already soaked in his own blood; his head aching and his eyesight blurring as he rode hard. He knew the loss of blood was too much and was impairing his senses; he glanced behind him and saw the black line of Saracens behind them, pouring forth like a swarm of dark locusts across the sand. He groaned outwardly as he lost count past fifteen and guessed the amount of riders were approximately thirty strong; much too many to fight. His brain swam as he knew they could not win a battle and nor could they reach the sandstorm that raged wildly ahead of them. The two men exchanged glances and both bore the same expression of self-knowledge; the drawn, haunted look of a doomed man.

Thomas pulled on his reins suddenly and brought his gelding around, trotting to a standstill as he calmly pulled off the muslin over shirt to allow his gleaming plate mail armour to be seen. James was caught off guard by his companion's action and he struggled to bring Merdlan about, screaming across the wind at the mercenary.

"What the hell are you doing? We cannot fight them!"

Thomas drew his sword and held his shield high, ignorant of the other man and calmly awaited the onrushing Arabian warriors.

"For God's sake man, come on."

James circled Merdlan around Thomas, his animal would not settle and the pain in his shoulder increased aggressively. He held his right hand to the arrow stump in a forlorn attempt to pacify the agony and his head dropped as the throbbing in his brain accelerated at an alarming rate. His vision was worsening and his speech slurred as he attempted to reason with the Englishman and Thomas turned and grabbed his reins.

"Tie yourself on and head to the storm. Your horse can get you there; he's the fastest I have ever known. You are weak, you cannot fight anymore today but you can tomorrow. For you, there can be a tomorrow. Please James, I came here for this very moment but this is not your time. You have to get to Damascus. For your own sake, for your own sanity and for the memory of your little boy. For myself, I had to reach the Holy Land and my task is almost complete."

As he spoke he wrapped the leather reins around the left hand of James and tied it to the pommel of Merdlan's saddle; oblivious to the disjointed attempts at arguing from a weakened James, he slapped the flat blade of his long sword onto the great flanks of the steed and watched his companion's faithful horse gallop off towards the desert storm at a tremendous pace; picking up speed like God's breath itself was pushing them onwards.

"May God go with you, James."

Thomas whispered and focused his attention back on the black riders that approached him in a horizontal line; their speed lessening as they could see their prey was no longer running away.

"Come on you beauties...take me to the Kingdom of Heaven and God's divine forgiveness."

The words were whispered hoarsely and Thomas smiled under his full helmet, kicking his brown gelding viciously to provoke the charge. Raising his blade in the air, the lone knight hurtled towards the thin line of horseman with the repeated scream;

"Deus vult!"

This was the Latin translation for 'God Wills It' which had been the original Crusading army's battle cry.

The Immortals were bemused by the suicidal charge and emotions ranged between the twenty eight warriors from amusement to honour to foolishness and the three central horsemen lowered their spears in response as the Christian galloped at full speed towards them. On the outer wings of the line, four of them pulled out their bows and slowed their mounts to allow the time to load and aim their barbed arrows. Kicking his steel heels into the beast to get the best speed he could, he repeated his war cry and with the sun behind him, he closed the gap between the horsemen in brief seconds. The Islamic riders squinted or averted their gaze as the sun's powerful rays bounced off the plate mail armour as their Master's prophesised enemy clashed with the twenty eight strong unit of cavalry. The eerie calm before the storm was inevitably obliterated as oblivious to the arrows that whizzed past him; Thomas comfortably averted a spear thrust with his shield and hacked his sword into the neck of a second man as his charge took him into and through the thin line. As the gelding galloped away, the Immortals turned and followed the Christian; leaving the stricken man clawing at his mortal wound on the desert floor, his own blood covering the sand in an ever increasing circle.

An arrow thudded into his lower back but was hardly noticed by the knight, who felt truly alive; a man who was born for battle, elementally a soul at peace when in war. The arrow dented but did not penetrate the thick, heavy armour plating and as he felt his horse tire; turned the mount to face the chasing pack; now scattered and easier to fight. The leading black clad man rode a sleek Arabian horse and his curved scimitar was held ahead of him, his elbow bent so it was adjacent to his left cheek. Thomas waited; his own sword and shield held loosely, his thighs gripped to the belly of his steed. Timing his movement to perfection, he parried the scimitars blade with his own and fiercely brought the metal shield into the fray, smashing it into his face and hurling him unceremoniously from his rearing, frightened mare. The sounds of a galloping horse caused him to twist in his saddle and bring the shield up just in time to stop a spear's sharpened point from ripping through his chest. The metal clanged and reverberated through his body as his sword snaked out in an arc and embedded itself into the Saracen's arm with the sickening noise of severed tissue and shattered bone.

Roaring out obscenities, he awaited the next skirmish and calmed his skittish horse as the experienced warriors formed a circle around him; three of their collective dead or dying on the scorched earth. Two more arrows deflected off the expensive plate mail before a change of tactic brought the inevitable conclusion of this one sided battle closer to its end. The third arrow struck his gelding's neck and as the beast snorted in sudden pain, a fourth and fifth quickly tore through his flank and underbelly. Staggering onto its front knees, Thomas stumbled from the horse as a sixth arrow inflicted the final blow into the twitching, dying animal. Dropping his shield as he lurched clumsily but remained upright, the Englishman studied the stationary men who sat out of sword range atop their small, athletic brown and white mounts. None of the Immortals moved; merely observing their mortal enemy who breathed heavily and screamed out in defiance.

"Come on then you cowards.....fight me!"

His words resonated across the rolling sand dunes; the usually stifling heat being mitigated by the whirling desert storm to their east which raged almost silently.

Thomas smiled as he could just about make out the tiny form of James in the far distance and knew there would be no catching him now. With his sword in his right hand, his left hand calmly unfastened the catch of his helmet and he removed it from his perspiring brow, tossing it to the sand. The desert was quiet and he whispered a brief prayer for his disappearing compatriot as he noticed the horses begin to walk slowly towards him all around him. Thomas grinned and gripped his sword in both hands, rotating his body in a slow circle, to look upon all of his assailants.

"Come on you bastards; send me to my maker..."

The final onslaught was as brief as it was vicious. Managing to fend off the first spear attack, he was knocked to the ground by a kicking horse from the rear and a series of bludgeoning hits forced the sword from his grasp and knocked the wind from his lungs. Flailing on the ground and exposed to the Immortals; a spear smashed through his left knee and his cries were savagely ended as a scimitar slashed across his face, opening up the flesh from chin to ear. Rolling onto his side, his attempted rise was stifled by another iron clad hoof, which knocked him onto his back and his spiritual release came when a spear shattered his temple, ending the man's life.

James lifted his weary, throbbing head from Merdlan's coarse mane and peered through the stinging wall of sand and dust behind him. Consciousness was ebbing away and as his horse thundered heroically on through the battering sandstorm, his last sight was the receding figure of Thomas falling before the black mass and falling to the ground; his head being hacked from his body and raised up in a show of abject triumph. Closing his eyes, he rested his head against the stallion's neck and allowed his faithful steed to take him into the heart of the wild storm, away from the killers of his companion.

310

Khalim removed the linen hood from his forehead and looked down on the lifeless body of the Christian devil he had been ordered to slay. He watched in satisfying silence as the defeated man was beheaded and his lips curved into a slight smile as he imagined the riches he would gain from his Master for this great victory. His men raised their weapons and whooped in delight at the wanted man's demise. In truth, it had been far easier than he had envisaged and although he had slain three of his elite warriors, the killer of the famed Saddiq; erstwhile favoured General of the Atabeg himself, was now dead. Watching the ritualistic beheading and allowing himself a seldom grin as the white dog's severed head was raised; he nodded to one of his men; whose name escaped him for the moment who had approached him.

"What of the man's servant Sire, who fled into the sandstorm?"

The leader of the troop looked across the dunes to the storm and could see no sign of the coward who allowed his own master to die alone.

"Let the sand take him. There is no need for us to risk ourselves in that storm. We have the head of our enemy and our people will be pleased. The prophecy is broken and Allah has blessed us today. Let us return to Damascus to reap the rewards."

The man nodded and within moments the Immortals headed south towards the paved stone road, with their prize safely stowed, leaving the broken, headless body of Thomas Holdingham to rot in the shimmering heat.

Chapter 25

Christian to Muslim

Alessio led his horse onto the floating vessel ill at ease with himself. Aisha followed him with a broad smile across her young features as she brought her mare skilfully onto what was in essence, little more than a few planks of roughly hewn cedar trees, with a rather pathetic railing of thin branches and twine. A rudder and two large oars made the cumbersome raft more 'boat' like but the Venetian remained unconvinced. Two young dark skinned men pulled on the great oars with a strength that belied their sinewy bodies and he looked back at the rickety boardwalk with sudden affection as it became smaller and smaller. The evening and much of the night had been spent in the bedchamber of the tavern with Aisha, who had laid bare her rather simplistic approach in getting the pair to Damascus. Alessio would become a Syrian like Aisha; his dark features naturally helped and the girl patiently taught him Arabic words and sayings; helping him with his diction and accent. They had spent the morning purchasing the relevant clothing and he now sat uncomfortably in a long tunic of linen which stretched to his knees; embroidered with cotton along the sleeves. In the same hue and material, loose, baggy pants covered his legs and his hard riding boots had been replaced with soft leather sandals. A soft length of cotton was wrapped around his head with a shoulder length veil at the back of his head, as was the Saracen custom to keep the flesh protected in the heat.

His leather harness of throwing knives hung next to his skin under the tunic and he was now also adorned with an embossed bronze handled curved dagger at his waist, sheathed in goatskin. He was to allow his facial hair to grow into a beard and to act as though he was taking his younger sister to be married in Damascus. Aisha would do the talking if questioned and Alessio would continue to learn Arabic words to stave off any suspicion. Aisha had reassured him that his blue eyes were not an automatic giveaway as many bloodlines between East and West had been mingled, either by force, for political alliances or even emotional reasons over the past few decades.

The ferryman; a thin, middle aged Arabian with a weak chin and bulging eyes rasped in Arabic in his direction as they made their way slowly across the still waters of the lake. Understanding only isolated words of the conversation, he grunted in response and looked out across the water; Aisha interjecting with an explanation of her brother's predetermined 'rudeness' which the man whom Alessio believed to be at least part weasel, seemed to accept with a shrug of his skeletal frame. The simple voyage was made mainly in silence with the exception of the constant chattering of their fellow passengers. There were only three other passengers, who appeared to be merchants in silk, from their apparel and luggage and they all spoke to each other in hushed tones at speed. All nodded in acknowledgement to Alessio who reciprocated the greeting but made himself look haughty and bored, discouraging all discussion. Aisha briefly spoke with the ferryman regarding the quickest route to the city and was advised the old Roman road was the safest and most direct method and the way merchants and traders chose to travel, as it was under the protection of the Atabeg himself and his horsemen were often seen on the stone thoroughfare.

Aisha thanked the man and sat beside Alessio to drift off into thoughts of James, hoping and praying to the myriad of different gods that he had not travelled via the main road. Resting her back warily against the rail, she feigned sleep and listened intently to the silk merchants. They were themselves on their way to Damascus to trade in the busy market there, which was

313

apparently increasing in size due to the Muslim overlord's massed army which had taken up residence at the foot of the rocky outcrop, upon which their leader had built his tower, protected by his army at the base and his Immortals in the fortified building itself. Immune to assault; a steep slope, wide enough for just three warriors wound itself in a spiral around the rock before it reached the portcullis and keep which bristled with archers. They spoke in a mixture of wondrous awe and fear of the man that her guardian was intent on slaying and she feared for his life. If what these men said was true, James could never accomplish his task and would without doubt die trying.

Alessio watched Aisha silently cry and observed the wetness on her cheeks. In quietude, he reached across and gently wiped away the tears, bringing her slight frame closer to his; kissing the top of her head as she leant her head against his shoulder. He fully understood her emotions as his own were in a constant state of flux and turmoil. Focusing on the simplistic wooden boards that acted as a docking station for the raft on the Muslim side of the water, he knew there would be no going back across this lake into Christian lands, without exact knowledge of James's death or with James alive and well beside them.

The disembarkation was completed in moments and passing through a small hamlet; the two followed a steady stream of bodies around the dusty trail and onto the ancient stone road, which the Romans had designed and built centuries ago, which led in an almost straight line to the city of Damascus. Aisha's simple plan worked perfectly as mile after mile, hour after hour; their mounts trudged ever closer and not a single Arabian engaged either in conversation or stared at them suspiciously. The two rested their horses and themselves at the various roadside watering stations, which consisted of single dwellings with stabling facilities, immense clay pots of water under huge swathes of muslin awning so travellers could rest out of the sun before progressing onwards. Some of these dwellings were large and affluent, with foodstuffs and bedding and others were basic but all were welcomed and all were busy.

For almost three days, the road was followed and the two figures continued along it ever eastwards; passing and being passed by assorted traders, families, merchant wagons and warriors of their hated enemy but no incident of note occurred at all. Nods, waves and murmured greetings were all that was given to them and for that, they were both truly thankful. By the evening of the third and most gruelling day in the saddle; their bodies sore and aching, the vast city of Damascus appeared before them in the distance. It sat on a fertile plain surrounded by barren hills with the River Barada flowing through it, bringing it the much needed life force the desert that surrounded it for miles around lacked. The city had been built wisely in its location as beyond the river and hills; the empty sands stretched for hundreds of miles eastwards. Shading their eyes, Alessio and Aisha's eyes were drawn automatically to the citadel that rose above all else to the south of the city; dwarfing even the great domed Mosque in its centre. The man who had caused all of their suffering and pain over the past month; the man who had caused the death of so many loved ones to them and the man whom James had travelled across the oceans of fire to slay; Imad Ad-Din Atabec Zengi Al Malik Al Mansir himself; the self-proclaimed Saviour of Islam was at this very moment, alive in that citadel. The rumours were that the people of Damascus did not welcome his presence and therefore, the citadel had been purpose built as a statement of wealth and power as it towered above the city itself. With a solemn and silent look to the other; the two figures nudged their mounts forward along the final stretch of stone and entered the sprawling, dusty streets of the walled city.

****

The solitary rider dismounted unsteadily from his chestnut coloured mare and tossed the harness to the stable hand hurriedly. Weary after the long gallop, he forced his leather clad feet up the winding staircase of the citadel as fast as he could physically manage. Ignoring the waves of tiredness and nausea, he eventually reached the throne room and the guards, seeing his station as an Immortal; opened the heavy double doors instantly. The warrior rushed into the bustling chamber and as faces turned to see this travel stained member of the elite guard; they began to cease their chattering and a hush descended on the normally riotous denizens. A space was created for the silent man who staggered onto his knees before his Master, who stared at him with unconcealed impatience.

"What news? Tell me man!"

"We found the one you seek sayedy...."

The man spoke hoarsely and Al Mansir motioned to a serving girl to bring the messenger water. He gulped frantically from the silver goblet and smiled at the leader of his people.

"He fought bravely, Master but he is dead. He was slain in battle and Khalim beheaded the harbi. Khalim returns with his head for you so you can adorn the walls of the citadel with it. The others are perhaps half a day behind me."

He ceased his animated chatter as the man rose from his throne and strode towards him. The Caliph held up his hands and grinned broadly, clapping the messenger on each shoulder in a gesture of friendship and gratitude.

"Thank you my boy. This news gladdens me greatly."

Turning on the balls of his soft cloth shoes, he

addressed the quiet onlookers and chuckled loudly.

"The devil who haunts my dreams is dead. Allah is glorious. Praise be to Allah. My destiny is true!"

The coterie of guards, nobles, family members and religious leaders took up the chant, praising Allah alongside their leader.

"Send the message to the people of the city; there will be feasting tonight! The devil is dead and his head shall sit atop the entrance to the tower by nightfall. The curse is broken and Allah has chosen me. I am the Lion of Islam; no man can stand in my way. The imams were true in their words; now we can celebrate!"

The warrior was given fruit and ushered to a padded stool where he was endlessly questioned by the gathered masses as Al Mansir barked orders for free food to be sent to Damascus for his people to feast in honour of this glorious moment. Only one person remained impassive in the energized chamber and she stood, in the alcove near the fireplace wearing a frown underneath the jabaya. Nadirah slipped back out of the throne room and strode to her bedchamber. She must speak to Kalaama immediately. The prophecy had been clear and this meant that the prophecy was now broken. Had her soothsayer been wrong? Kalaama had always been accurate in the past and she had no reason to doubt her but something was not right. Picking up the hem of her long skirts, she rushed to the bedchamber to advise the prophet of the alarming news.

Chapter 26

A New Dawn

His eyes flickered slowly open and he squinted even in the dim, shimmering candlelight. His mind was functioning as if in a daze, a wall of confusion blocked his thoughts and his body ached in every conceivable area. As he attempted to sit up from his prone position on his back; immediate searing pain erupted from his shoulder and he collapsed back to the cushioned bedding in agony. Opening his hazel eyes fully, his brain began to lift from the fog and he scratched his head with his right hand; which appeared functional. His vision focused but his dulled senses were as if huge amounts of wine or ale had been consumed the previous night. The very room seemed to be moving and a soft linen covering hung over him as he lay on a soft mattress. He recognised nothing and rubbed his weary eyes in bewilderment. The room was small and was definitely moving; the noise of voices from outside drifted towards him and straining his ears, he recognised Arabic and cursed silently. Was he a prisoner? There were no chains or restraints but then again, he was in a desert; where could he escape too? Moving his legs, he re-attempted sitting upright and winced as the damaged shoulder rejected his wish emphatically. Looking at this area of weakness, he noted the care that had been taken in tying strips of expensive muslin around his upper arm and shoulder as he struggled to untie them and inspect the wound itself. Eventually uncovering the injury, his eyes narrowed as he observed the perfect stitching and dried blood. There was no sign of the arrow and pressing around the flesh, he could feel nothing alien within. The wound had clearly been cleaned and treated by someone of considerable skill and knowledge.

James shook his head as the memory of the arrow brought with it the more stressful vision of Thomas and the last moments of his life. Groaning aloud as he visualised the decapitation and elation of his enemies, he brought clammy hands to his face and remained in this position for some moments in a conflicting state of emotion; which included loss, fear, hope and the happiness of still being alive. When his mind ceased its' frantic whirring of emotive recent memory, he removed his hands from his face and considered the prospect of standing. Before his calculation of probability became action however, a figure opened the heavy cloth ahead of his bed and moved into the room; which his brain suddenly realised was a moving wagon or caravan of some type. The person approached slowly and James stiffened as he knew he was weak but was determined to fight if necessary.

"So you wake at last! How do you feel?"

The voice was brittle and rasping; belonging to an elderly male of Arabic origin as he spoke in that language. The man shuffled nearer and removed the thinly cut linen which hung over the bed in which James now sat upright. Squinting in the now fully illuminated caravan, his eyes narrowed to focus on the newcomer and the surroundings. He watched the old man shuffle across the creaking wooden boards and fasten the awning back to allow bright sunshine into the area before snuffing out the candle in between gnarled fingers.

"Allah has indeed blessed you my friend! It is a miracle you have survived. I will talk of this for the rest of the few short years I have remaining."

The man continued his broad smile and his bearded dark face was now visible. The eyes were wrinkled and weak and the way the man gesticulated and moved with his hands; the possibility of blindness was high. The face was kind however and James relaxed as he believed that he was no prisoner of hostile fundamentalist Arabs.

"Ah, you do not understand my language?"

The stranger questioned brightly and he called for another from outside.

"Halimah! Halimah? Come, come my child. I need your voice. The miraculous one does not speak Arabic; perhaps Frank?"

James was about to refute the language barrier as although certainly not fluent, he could carry a conversation in Arabic but before his throbbing mind could react; a slim, robed figure; clearly female, moved into the chamber. Fully covered in a tight fitting robe of peach silk, only two dark eyes and the very hint of dark olive skin and long eyelashes could be seen; in between the jabaya and abaya, which protected her head and face. She moved languidly next to the elderly man and spoke in heavily accented French.

"Do you understand the Frankish tongue?"

Her voice was soft and hushed behind the cloth and James nodded, as his eyes moved from the two faces that looked down on him.

"I can speak French and Arabic to a point but I am fluent in Italian and English."

His own voice sounded coarse and he realised he was desperately thirsty and he looked around for water. The woman followed his searching look and moved to a clay jug and poured some water into a simple deep bowl for him. She handed it to him and he gulped it gratefully, finishing the liquid before responding.

"Thank you. Who are you? Where am I?

Merdlan? My clothes...."

The questions tumbled from him in French and he halted as he heard the young woman translate for the elderly man, who he now knew to be her father. James allowed her to translate and then interjected before he responded back to his daughter, in their native tongue.

"I can speak your language. A little...anyway."

The woman's eyes widened in surprise and she exchanged a glance with her father.

"It appears you are indeed an interesting man. Now rest yourself; you are lucky to be alive. My daughter; Halimah, will see to your needs. I am required outside; we will be halting the caravan shortly to rest for the night."

The elderly man smiled a toothless smile and patted the young girl on the shoulder as he walked past her towards the entrance.

"Wait. Please. Where am I? How am I here?"

James winced as he moved and Halimah moved to him, gently pushing his body back to the mattress. The man smiled again and spoke gently.

"Relax please. You are very weak and lucky to be alive. Were it not for your magnificent horse we would never have found your body at all. Now, enough questions, Halimah will answer them in due course but for now, please drink water and rest."

James nodded meekly and relaxed his body as he lay down, his hazel eyes flickering towards the Arabian woman whose soft hands still sat on his shoulders.

"Thank you. Both of you. I do not understand why you would aid me but I appreciate it."

The exile whispered, barely audible even to Halimah, who sat herself on a low stool next to the injured man and poured another cup of water for her patient. Her father nodded and departed leaving her alone with the pale skinned one. As she looked back to him, he was already lost to sleep and beneath her burkha, a slow smile formed on her dark lips as she watched the man enter the deepest realm of Morpheus, a look of serenity across his drawn features.

The laughing demonic face rushed towards him without a body; a swirling haze of blue iridescent flame danced around the head; his eyes scarlet red and his skin was black as the dead of night. Burning flesh assailed his nostrils as he felt his own skin burn in the close proximity and he ducked under the flailing, cackling head and sprinted across a vast, endless sea of warm, thick blood. The blood splashed onto his naked feet but for some inexplicable reasons, he could run across the surface as if it was solid. As the demon rushed towards him again, he changed direction in a vain, stricken attempt to outrun the unnatural foe. Around him, corpses sprung up from the crimson tide; naked bodies covered in the viscous liquid as he rushed blindly onwards. In his peripheral vision he saw the bodies of Abdul and his family, of Sharla and her sons, of Jacob and of Thomas. Each lifeless body being forced out of the blood with a dull splash around him and then dropped back to the sea to lie across his path so he had to leap and dodge the corpses as he fled. The gloating, screeching head gained upon him and James could feel the searing heat on his shoulders and back; the shrill sound of his crowing increasing in volume and he dared not twist his neck. He gritted his teeth and tried frantically to pump his legs which he suddenly realised were sinking slowly into the ocean with every stride. The figure of Alessio erupted from the bloody surface and James leapt out of the way, falling to his knees in exhaustion; staring in abject terror as he saw the lifeless eyes of his closest friend. His skin

322

began to peel from his spine as the demonic head hovered over his prone figure and he rolled over in the blood to try and dampen the blue flame. His body burning, he slowly sank below the surface and he wept as the last vision he saw was the corpse of Aisha raising from the sea before him. His right hand, burnt to the bone, stretched out towards her as he drowned in the aquatic filth, the only sound being the horrendous, hysterical laughter echoing in his mind.

"Wake up!"

James snapped open his eyes as his body was rocked and he felt the mattress below him with desperate fingers, clinging onto it as he realised it had just been a vivid nightmare. The mattress and sheet that had covered his body were damp and his body was covered with a sheen of cold perspiration.

"Here, drink this...it was just a bad dream."

He turned to see the kind eyes staring at him in a mixture of pity and confusion. The girl in the burkha offered him some water and he took it, thanking her and sipping it gingerly, sitting upright as he did so, acknowledging the throbbing pain from his shoulder. Embarrassed, he averted eye contact and rested his back against the wall of the moving, covered wagon; focusing on his drink.

"Is Aisha your wife?"

The question surprised him but was asked gently and seemingly with genuine concern.

"Why do you ask?"

James replied evasively.

"You screamed her name just before I woke you; I assumed she is your wife? Is she in trouble?"

He looked at her directly now and she held his eye contact for a few seconds before shifting her hands uneasily. He shook his head and smiled fleetingly.

"No, not my wife. My daughter, well, ward I suppose."

James struggled to find the right word to describe Aisha to a stranger and he watched as the oval dark eyes opposite him now looked mystified.

"She is a girl, a young woman now who, I have protected and brought up; raised as my own although she is not of my blood."

The description was stilted and stated in a stammering fashion but his point was taken by the interested carer.

"I understand. I am Halimah, may I ask your name?"

"Sorry, rude of me, I am James."

He offered his hand and she uncomfortably and briefly shook it, although a ghostly, embarrassed smile could be seen beneath the opaque veil.

"How is your shoulder James?"

James consciously felt around the wound with his right hand and smiled broadly.

"It is healing nicely; please pass my thanks to the one who cleaned and bandaged me. He is skilled in what he does."

The smile lengthened as Halimah stood.

"I appreciate your comments and he is a she who is skilled at what she does."

"Ah, well thank you Halimah; is there any tip or shaft left in there?"

The young woman tightened the veil around her face and shook her head slowly.

"It was barbed, which is why it could not be easily removed but I managed to cut an incision in your back and extract the tip easily enough. The wound was cleaned and then the flesh sewn back up again. It should heal properly in a two to three weeks and you will be left with just a small scar on either side."

James raised his eyebrow in consternation.

"Weeks? It feels much better now; how long before I can ride again?"

Halimah paused and made a silent mental calculation.

"Gently, perhaps tomorrow or the day after but it will be sore and uncomfortable."

James made no response and the woman stood upright.

"I will tell Father you are awake, he wishes to talk to you."

James felt a pang of some deeply hidden emotion and merely nodded as she departed the moving chamber. He listened as father and daughter held a muted discussion in free flowing Arabic, which was followed by loud shouts and the halting of the caravan. Within moments, a flurry of activity and a cacophony of sounds could be heard as awning and camp fires were being set up outside. Shifting the weight to his side, he removed the sheet and set his naked feet on the wooden floorboards. Raising himself carefully, he pulled on his breeches awkwardly, which had been washed and folded and left in a pile with an Arabian designed tunic, presumably offered as a replacement for his torn and damaged one that had been removed from his body. The eastern tunic fitted comfortably and he stood falteringly in the fresh clothing, stretching his weary body as he did so. His eyes studied the room and he located the remainder of his belongings in an open wooden chest in the corner of the wagon. His short sword lay there within the battered scabbard, his leather belt, boots, goat skin pouch of coins, water skin and crossbow with the shoulder bag of quarrels. The pouch seemed to be full as he weighed it in his hands and he attached this and the belt to his person. Covering his feet with the boots, he closed the chest lid on the weaponry as he had sensed no immediate danger or threat from the strangers.

The horse trader moved cautiously to the front of the covered wagon and peered out, past the material that had been tied back to the wooden poles which created the skeletal frame of the vehicle. The wooden platform on which the driver would sit was empty and he clambered onto the polished plank of cedar wood and sat there to survey the raucous scene around him.

There were eight covered wagons akin to the one he now sat in, together with a further six uncovered carts which were all now stationary and formed a protective wide circle around which a large fire was being prepared. The sturdy horses, which were clearly purchased for stamina rather than speed and their burly strength to pull these carriages, were being corralled into a pen. Various items were being pulled from the backs of wagons and carried here and there by men, women and children of all ages, cheerfully and vocally. Although busy, each of them seemed happy with their lot; singing, laughing and chattering to each other as they set about their previously assigned duties with clarity and speed. He counted around forty people in total, which belonged to perhaps six or seven family units as Halimah's father approached him with a toothless grin.

"It is good to see you looking so alive, young man? How do you feel?"

James smiled warmly in reply and held out his right hand to shake the man's hand in greeting. The man grunted and with amusement written on his face, ignored the offered limb, instead; hugging him loosely and patting his back.

"You are with the Bedouin now James, not your French friends on the coast!"

Reciprocating the traditional greeting, they sat back against the wood and James asked for his rescuer's name and how he had come about to be in a Bedouin train and not deceased out in the desert somewhere.

"I am Halim, the elder of this community of peaceful traders but before we speak further, we are having a feast in your honour this evening; there will be dancing, music, wine and food fit for the great Allah himself. You can tell me your story then for James, I feel you have a very interesting tale to tell and then I shall continue the story to the present day!"

James nodded in agreement and noticed the three young children staring at him from across the clearing. Halim followed his eyes but his vision was too impaired to see.

"What is it James? My eyesight is failing."

"I am being stared at by the young children of your community Halim"

The foreigner smiled at the children and watched as the girl hid behind one of the boys, whose features remained stern. The younger boy, no more than six grinned affably and waved however.

"Well, we do not get such exotic guests at our table. You will be a curiosity for all my people. Some will like your presence here, some will not but it is for you to change their natural attitudes to such intriguing outsiders."

With a chuckle, he tottered to his feet and offered his arm for assistance, which James gave silently as he helped Halim down to the sand. A brief wave followed and James was left alone to his thoughts as he studied the Bedouins again and set his mind to work on what he knew of these wandering people. They were traders who travelled long distances between all peoples from the Egyptians in the south to Outremer and from the isolated Caliphates of Araby to the west and the Armenians in the north. Loosely Islamic, they cared not for wars or religious differences; trading with Christian, Jew, Shi'ite or Sunni and drank alcohol, played music and gambled. Abdul loved these people; believing his own grandparents had been Bedouins so they had been in his bloodline.

The children had been moved on by their smiling mother who nodded apologetically towards him and his eyes scanned the horses within the temporary fencing and his heart leapt as he saw Merdlan; head and neck above the other horses. Rushing down from the seating, he moved between the Bedouins, smiling and waving, nodding and greeting as he meandered his way to the animal pen. He reached the edge of it and called out to Merdlan, whose head immediately turned and he moved through the tight space to reach James. With tears in his eyes, James stroked his nose softly and whispered in Italian to his mount.

"Merdlan, I missed you boy. I think you saved both our lives you clever, clever boy."

The great stallion snorted contentedly and nuzzled into the much smaller human with his neck so James could give him more attention. Holding the horse for a few moments; he then released the stallion and stroked his forelock tenderly, elation pumping through his veins.

"Get away from my horse, infidel or do you think this is your wife?"

The voice was haughty and arrogant and before he even turned around to face the speaker, he knew that he would not like the man. The throaty chuckle after the statement was followed by more derisory, scornful laughter. James ceased his attentive display of affection for Merdlan and rotated on his heels with a forced smile, focusing his hazel eyes upon three Bedouin males in their early twenties. The one who had spoken was well dressed in expensive clothing and stood in the centre of his two companions who stood slightly behind him on either side; curved daggers clearly shown in their belt sashes.

"Maybe the infidel does not understand Arabic?"

The larger underling guffawed and James opened his hands in the Eastern fashion of peace.

"I understand your language and your ways. I believe you are mistaken with regards to the horse however, his name is Merdlan and I have ridden him since he was a young colt."

His words were softly spoken and he awaited the response; observing the surprise on all three faces yet unable to define if this was a positive or negative reaction. The leading protagonist almost snarled his retort which gave James the answer to his question.

"That horse is mine. My people found it in the desert together with a dying man."

The young man; a little taller and broader in stature than James took a step forward towards him to exaggerate his point.

"Had it been me infidel, I would have taken the horse and left the man. Think on that. My father is an old, weak man who has not much time left in this world and his affection for your kind is a mistake. I am watching you and I do not want to see you with my people for long."

James attempted to remain calm and keep his face impassive as the anger built within him. He remained silent as the three men strode away and watched them leave. Merdlan snorted and he turned to face him, nodding as if he understood the animal's thoughts.

"I know old friend; do not worry. We will not be here for long and when I have answers as to where we are and when I can use my arm properly; we will leave them and head to Damascus. It will take more than a spoilt boy with an attitude problem to stop us doing what we came to do."

With a final pat of his mount's head, he began to walk around the camp; needing to judge the mood of these people to see if he would need to leave sooner rather than later. The faces that looked back into him were in the main, welcoming if a little wary. Reassured that there would be no attempt to lynch him tonight, he walked back to the covered wagon to prepare for the evening. As he did so, he felt a presence next to him and looked down to see the young boy who had smiled and waved at him earlier. The boy looked up at James, grinning wide; showing perfect white teeth and spoke excitedly.

"My brother and sister say you are a white devil. Are you?"

James was amused by the direct childish question and he halted, crouching so he was face to face with the young boy.

"I do not think I am a devil. And if I am, I am a

friendly one so you have nothing o fear from me. My name is James, what is yours?"

The boy chuckled enthusiastically and responded gleefully.

"I am Usman and I said you were no devil!"

With this, he sprinted back across the sand and James smiled as he rushed to his older brother and sister and chattered in animation to his siblings. Waving to the wide eyed youngsters, he reached the wagon and pulled himself up into the chamber; looking around for some water to wash as he realised during his stroll that his personal hygiene was somewhat lacking. There was a small bucket of cold water from which he had been drinking and he scowled; deciding to find Halim or his daughter to see how they bathed in their constantly roving existence. At this point, Halimah entered the room and immediately held the material tight around her face as their eyes met.

"Apologies, I saw you talking with my brother, I hope he did not upset you. He seemed angry when he left you."

James scratched his chin and chose his words carefully as he replied, intrigued and being honest with himself; pleased that the woman had been watching him and was also worried about how the conversation had affected him, rather than her brother.

"A difference of opinion on the ownership of my horse, it will be sorted. I will offer your brother money in exchange for him. I feel that is fair as your father took me in, had he left me, I would have died I believe."

"I will speak to my father, the horse is clearly yours and my brother is wrong for taking something he knows to belong to another."

Her indignation was clear and James smiled warmly.

"Do not worry your father about this. I will speak to your brother this evening and I am sure it will be easily sorted and we will all be friends in no time."

His hollow words were not believed by either party yet Halimah nodded uncertainly.

"Now, a question for you; where can I bathe around here; I smell worse than my horse right now!"

Halimah nodded in agreement and giggled coquettishly, pointing vaguely to the north.

"There is a camel station to the north which has a well. That is why we stopped here; to replenish our water stocks. Many of our people will be there to collect, drink or wash themselves before the festivities start."

James nodded in appreciation and watched her lithe form leave, smiling as he saw her turn to see if he was watching her as she left the wagon. Bedouins were certainly an interesting people he mused as he climbed down from the platform and wandered northwards along a dusty trail towards water; his mind, as seemed the normality these days was a maelstrom of conflicting emotions.

Chapter 27

A Desert Banquet

James sat cross legged on the intricately woven rug; the low sandalwood table before him; laden with a vast and exquisite array of food. The aromatic smells of spiced wine, cinnamon and coriander infused barmakiyya, roasted and boned chicken glazed with olive oil and a host of other mouth-watering delicacies, which made him, salivate and his eyes widen at such a glorious display. Wooden bowls of raisins, citrus fruits and nuts; some of which he had never seen before were scattered across the table together with deep clay dishes of cous cous and hot soups of lentil, onion and murri. The tables and rugs were laid out in a perfect square in the centre of their caravan ringed clearing, with a roaring open fire in the middle to heat and cook further foodstuffs when necessary. Women busied themselves around the searing flames, serving various foods onto the oval wooden platters, which sat before all. Halim sat to his right and Halimah to his left, for which he was thankful and for the first time, he noticed only Halimah wore a covering over her face. The other women, of all ages, wore conservative Arabic clothing but none with a burkha and James wondered if Halim's daughter was more extreme in her Islamic beliefs than the other Bedouins.

With this in his mind, he waited for the feast to start and casually studied the people around him. Across the blazing flames, he recognised the grinning boy; Uzman, who waved at him happily, sat as he was between his more serious looking siblings and their mother, who was loading succulent looking chicken onto their serving plates. On the right hand side of Halim sat his son; a haughty, arrogant man who foolishly and carelessly believed he now owned Merdlan, no doubt with his underlings close by. James was careful to avoid that area as he observed the camp; not wishing to fuel further hostility. These people were Muslim and strangers; although friendly thus far, he was alone and clearly not of their kin and as such, he was nervous and defensive and wished the evening to be over and he could seriously consider how to leave with Merdlan at the earliest opportune moment.

Halimah served her father and then James with a small portion of the lamb barmakiyya and olive chicken and offered each of them wine. Such things were not allowed by the Islamic faith yet every adult male drank alcohol around him and James nodded with a wry smile as the young woman poured the cultivated grape juice for both men. The elderly man sipped the sweet white wine and stood falteringly. The noise dissipated immediately and he raised the simple cup to all present.

"Let us enjoy tonight my friends! Eat and drink to your fill; we shall have music and dancing afterwards. We have an honourable guest; who the great Allah Himself protected and brought to us. A man who survived a desert storm and whose own horse stood beside him in that raging tempest until our people spotted him and brought him here. Let us welcome him into our hearts!"

James watched all stand and raise their drinks in his direction, a flush of embarrassment rushing across his face. Raising his own cup, he stood and smiled; speaking in staccato Arabic.

"My thanks to Halim for his kindness, to Halimah for putting me together again and I appreciate all of you for showing me friendship in this troubled time."

Nodding emphatically, he sat down and felt instantly humbled as the Bedouins toasted him and immediately started to devour the feast set before them with gusto. Halimah leant close and whispered gently;

"You did well. Now relax and eat, you must be starving."

James smiled and felt his stomach gurgle; churning in response as he began to eat the spiced and seasoned food ravenously, the myriad of flavours a delight to consume. The low hum of chatter and laughter developed all around the tables as the meal was partaken by all, which eased his concerns as he sat within this circle of positivity.

"You are very quiet."

Halimah observed as he had finished his platter and was looking unconvincingly at the cous cous, debating in his mind whether to try it or partake of the dried fruits and almonds instead, which he knew he would enjoy. Scooping a mixture of dates and ripe, succulent sultanas, he turned his head to face the woman's eyes.

"My apologies Halimah, it has been a while since I have eaten or been a guest at such a table. My manners are not what they should be."

The Arabian woman giggled and touched his hand briefly.

"No need to apologise, you have more manners than most of the men around this fire! Are you enjoying the food?"

James nodded and sipped his wine, savouring the sweet fruity flavour.

"This is amazing food, you always eat like this?"

Halimah giggled again and shook her head slowly.

"Only when we have an important guest, which is very rare. Most people avoid us unless they wish to barter or purchase something. "

"I am far from important; a horse trader from Outremer, nothing more."

Halimah's laughter ceased as her eyes narrowed suspiciously but she did not question further and dropped her gaze back to her plate. James shifted uncomfortably and fortunately, the immediate silence was broken by a jovial Halim who clapped his shoulder.

"A horse trader from Outremer, are you?"

The old man cackled hoarsely as James shifted his knees, positioning himself to look into the fading eyes of the kindly Bedouin. Halim peered at him and nodded with a toothless smile, clapping loudly which brought the instant response of women and children leaving the tables; clearing away the food and accoutrements hurriedly. Halimah leant across James to pick up his platter and he smelt her perfumed body brush past him; their eyes met for a second and he knew she would have seen the instant interest and arousal in his face. It had been a long time since he had been with a woman in that way. Too long. She intrigued him however and this was unusual. He scowled as she hurried away and did not see her turn to study him as she moved away from the fire to the buckets of water for cleansing, a smile dancing around her full lips beneath the material.

"Forgive an old man's suspicious mind but I have never known a horse trader from Outremer be so far from home; alone with such weaponry upon their person and an arrow in their shoulder."

The man's opaque eyes glinted in the dim moonlight and James smiled warmly and held his hands, palms facing the heavens out towards his host.

"When you put it like that, it does sound...."

He paused to find the right wording in his alarmed mind.

"... hard to believe but I was with a group of merchants and the desert storm struck us, scattering our party. Obviously, being so far from home, I have to carry weapons to defend myself. You have seen my horse; I am a horse trader; Merdlan is the finest stallion in Outremer."

Halim studied his guest's face for many moments before replying; a stoical expression the only sign of comprehension.

"I believe you are much more than a horse trader, my friend, but that is your business. The stallion is indeed a beautiful beast and more than just a horse to you clearly. That horse remained at your side through a howling sandstorm and thanks to him; you are sat beside me now speaking!"

James nodded thoughtfully and averted his gaze to the dancing flames of the fire.

"That is the truth, Merdlan is much more than a horse to me; I have never known an affinity with any animal as I have with him. I know it is rude of me to ask a favour, after you have done so much but I will offer your son a good price. I realise that this is your world and your rules and I am happy to be governed by them while I am here, yet, the horse is important to me; I will pay your son all I have, which is more than his value..."

The old man nodded and placed an open palm towards James to cease his request.

"Of course, of course. I will talk to my son. He will listen to me; a contribution of coin is all that is necessary not all of your wealth. Now, please, this evening is for you; please enjoy it."

The guest smiled warmly and relaxed visibly, sipping his wine and tossing fat sultanas into his mouth as he watched the food and platters be taken away by scurrying women into the darkness to be cleaned; followed by a series of entertaining acts. Three girls danced rhythmically to the beat of drums, an elderly woman recited an old story about a desert dragon who feasted on naughty children, two men wrestled in somewhat frivolous fashion over a girl's attention and a middle aged man tossed a series of burning torches into the night sky to catch them dangerously in his hands in quick succession. So engrossed was he in watching such displays, he jumped when Halima slid her lithe body beside him again to watch the acrobatic fire tricks.

"Nervous?"

The woman grinned beneath her covering and James could see her dark eyes sparkle in amusement.

"You often sneak up on people in the dark?"

He responded evenly with a wry smile upon his tanned features.

"Not often."

She chuckled and exchanged a glance with her father who left the area to speak with another man on the other side of the dying fire.

"Are you really a horse trader?"

The question was direct and unexpected and James masked his surprise with a forced grin.

"Yes, why is this surprising to you all?"

The woman's eyes sparkled, which James knew meant her lips were pursed into a smile beneath the material that covered the majority of her face.

"I suppose you seem more than that somehow."

The answer surprised him and he stroked his chin as he failed to locate a suitable response to the statement. Ignoring it, he chose to ask a question that had bothered him all evening.

"How did you find enough wood in a desert to create such a fire?"

Halimah giggled initially and then her roar of laughter rocked her slight frame and James watched as her whole body shook with humour.

"I am so sorry! You are just so evasive about yourself! It amuses me."

James stiffened and nodded curtly.

"I am glad that I amuse you."

The Bedouin stifled her amusement and placed a soft hand onto his own.

"I did not mean to offend, truly. We trade for wood at any town or village; it gets cold at night in the desert and we need to create warmth."

The man nodded thoughtfully as he acknowledged the truth of her words.

"I apologise for being overly sensitive, I am afraid you do not see me at my best. I have been through..."

He paused and looked into Halimah's dark eyes for some form of security before progressing. The oval brown orbs were inquisitive yet caring and he continued in a hushed, conspiratorial tone.

"...considerable strain in recent weeks. Things have happened. Horrendous things and I am trying to make them right; to balance the wrong with right?"

The olive skinned woman nodded gently and her eyes clouded a little with confusion. James could see question after question coming from this conversation, questions he had no wish to answer and he smiled wearily.

"I am sorry, I should not burden you with my concerns; we are strangers."

Her eyes widened in dismay at his words and he rubbed his temple, draining the last of his wine.

"Where are you headed?"

James avoided her searching look and watched as the entertainers finished their skilful activities and the women take their tired children to bed. He smiled at the customary debate between child and mother over the timing of this and as soon as his smile widened; it vanished in an instant as he thought of Jacob and the many such debates he had shared. Halimah watched the man's features intently and leaned close to his face.

"You need rest I think; your wound was severe; maybe I should look after you for a few more days?"

She smiled coquettishly and this too faded as the hazel eyes that turned to face her were cold and detached.

"I am fine. I need to leave soon. Tomorrow I think. Where did you say we were?"

Halimah masked her disappointment with her robe and stood, facing the night.

"As you wish James. We are a day or two days ride from Damascus. We traded cotton there and are heading to the south west for the next week or so."

The man's heart hardened within his battered body and his eyes flashed with hate as they studied a solitary orange flame crackle in the darkness.

"Thank you for your kindness Halimah, I will not forget it but I will leave in the morning. I have business in Damascus that needs my urgent attention."

She nodded and departed into the blackness that shrouded them; confused and upset by the stranger's words and ever changing intonations. James absently watched the dancing flame as his mind reverberated with vengeful fury. Dragging his brain away from such savage imagery, he stood and strode around the fire towards the covered wagon as most of the Bedouins had also departed into slumber; the few that remained were drinking copious amounts of wine and swapping creative stories to one another of their younger years. The caravan was empty and James collected his few possessions onto his mattress and hid them under the woollen blanket, closing his eyes in pretence of sleep; he waited for silence to encapsulate the area and then he could leave under the cover of the desert night sky and head east, following the Bedouins tracks towards Damascus and his destiny.

The wait had been interminable and he damned the propensity and capacity for alcohol that some of these travellers had. Three hours or so after he had left the banquet, he now pulled on his soft leather boots as quietly as possible and hung the short sword from his belt as he left the pouch of coin on the small round table. Placing the crossbow on his shoulder and the quiver of arrows around his chest, he pulled the hood of the long sable riding cloak, tight around his face and crept out of the dwelling and onto the sand outside. The camp was quiet and dark; the ash of the fire burned slightly with a soft ruby glow and the contented sound of snoring and creaking of wooden beams were all that faced him. James moved through the shadows to the horses and stroked Merdlan's nose softly; hushing him with soft whispers as he carefully led the great stallion out of the pen. Another horse snorted in dissatisfaction as Merdlan's black flanks pushed past him but within seconds, the task was complete and James readied himself to ride the beast without a saddle; something he was no novice in so the fact did not phase either horse or rider.

"You told me you were a horse trader not a horse thief!"

James jumped in shock and turned slowly to see Halimah's slight frame behind him; her brown eyes staring at him with baleful hurt.

"Ah..."

The woman stepped closer and almost snarled the two lettered response back to him.

"Ah? That is your answer. We save your life, we bring you into our home, we treat you with respect and caring, we treat your wounds, we give you a banquet in your honour that we can ill-afford and you say ah? And what do you do? You lie to our faces, take us for fools and then steal a horse and leave without a word! My brother is right about your kind; no honour at all; you come to our lands to take what you like...."

The venomous words struck home like small knives and the tirade only ended with Halimah's voice cracking with emotion and not wanting James to have the satisfaction of her tears, she turned away and waved dismissively.

"Halimah – wait...that's not fair!"

The man stated, following and catching up with her as she headed back to the circle of wagons. He grabbed her wrist and forced her to face him. She struggled violently and slapped his face hard and James immediately let her go, surprised by her hostility. In the brief fracas, her muslin face covering had come unwound and now fell in ever growing circles from her neck. Halimah cried out and placed hands over her face, tears flowing freely now; her voice contorting into sobs. James apologised profusely, taken aback by her reactions.

"I am so sorry, I left money for the horse, Merdlan is mine and I didn't know what to say to you; I have thanked you. You know I am grateful?"

Halimah continued to hide her face and tears dripped between fingers as she nodded and pulled her hands away from her dark face to expose her hidden features from him. James tried to control his expression as he realised why Halimah of all the Bedouin women hid her face; three deep jagged scars stretched across her otherwise unblemished skin from below the left ear and across the bridge of her nose to the right side of her chin.

"Oh Halimah..."

His voice was soft but he knew he could not finish the sentence; he had no words to convey that would comfort or aid her.

"Everybody leaves me, why should you be any different? Why should you like me? Look at me....I am ugly....a poison....to any man...I am nothing more than a whore."

Before James could react or respond, Halimah was gone, fleeing into the night; fresh tears flowing down her cheeks. The man watched her disappear and lost in his own thoughts for a while; he did not hear the footsteps of far more unwelcome feet circling him as he rubbed his aching forehead and deliberated following her into the desert. Merdlan's kicking of sand and urgent snort brought his focus back to leaving these people and he turned to face three young men with knife blades drawn.

343

"A liar, a thief and a man who harms women...nobody will weep when you fall."

Halak, Halimah's brother placed the curved dagger in his belt and withdrew a scimitar from its ornate scabbard and sliced the keen blade through the air with a wild eyed grin. His two underlings who seemed to follow him everywhere flanked him with curved daggers raised in a menacing fashion.

"Kill him Halak...kill the infidel thief!"

The figure to his left spat out; barely old enough to grow a beard and James sighed audibly. All three boy-men were filled with the bravado of wine and youth and he had no wish to kill or be killed in this piece of desolate sand in the middle of nowhere.

"You have it wrong. There is a pouch of coins for you for the horse; I have told you the truth and your sister and I...had a misunderstanding; that is all."

Halak hawked and spat on the ground.

"I have heard enough from you serpent. Draw your sword or I swear, I will kill you where you stand!"

James sighed again and drew his short sword slowly, maintaining eye contact with Halak and keeping the others in his peripheral vision. Removing his cumbersome crossbow and quarrels from his back and chest, he dropped them to the ground and unbuckled his scabbard so his movement was completely free for the battle ahead.

"Okay boys, if you insist...let's do this...."

With a disarming smile, James approached the Saracen at speed, crouched low with his sword raised tip first towards his prey. He saw the fear flicker across Halak's face and felt the surge of confidence spread excitement throughout his being as he moved forwards like a wolf upon three lambs. Halak parried his first blow clumsily and James grinned as he sprang backwards, to maintain perfect balance and also to keep the knife wielders in his area of vision. The one who had urged his death shuffled forward and James swept his sword towards him, which made the youth shuffle backwards again at increased pace, sweat covering his face. The dull ache in his left shoulder was exacerbated with every sudden movement of his right arm with the blade but there was no sharp or incisive pain and he feinted at Halak again, a sneer contorting his features as the man stumbled backwards away from him. With a sudden lunge to his right, the sword crashed down upon the silent adversary's dagger and he dropped it with what could best be described as a high pitched yelp. Falling back, the men exchanged glances and seeing their concern, James pressed his onslaught and brought his weapon sharply down upon Halak's scimitar, the clash of metal ringing out in the silent night. Flicking his wrist, James pushed the scimitar back against his own sword and forced the opponent to stumble backwards, falling over and dropping the weapon. Putting a boot upon the fallen man's chest, he pointed the sword at the two retreating men who turned and fled into the darkness. Kicking the prone man on the floor hard, he pressed the cold steel against his exposed neck.

"Why should I not kill you boy. You are a pathetic excuse of a man."

Halak dared not move, his eyes filling with tears, his bladder unloading itself into his breeches. James watched the two involuntary bodily functions and sighed, removing his blade.

"Get out of here. Now."

Halak turned onto his stomach and half crawled away on all fours before sprinting away. Picking up his crossbow and quiver, James sheathed his sword and stroked Merdlan's mane.

"Thank you."

James whirled to his left and drew his sword in one rapid, fluid motion to face the new speaker from the dark.

"I knew you were no horse trader."

Halim moved into his line of sight and grinned his toothless smile.

"You can put your sword down, I wish only a few words and then you can go off like an ungrateful foreign stranger."

James relaxed visibly as the old man chuckled wryly at his own jest and smiled thinly, sliding his weapon back slowly into its worn sheath.

Chapter 28

Life Amidst the Enemy

Alessio sat cross legged on the precarious timber frame of the thatched straw rooftop and watched the city of Damascus awaken beneath him. This was his fourth morning in the Islamic city and many of his initial fears and concepts had dissipated already; growing accustomed to the sounds, sights and smells of it. In numerous ways, it reminded him of Acre with its various quarters and distinctive districts. He adjusted his position so he could dangle his legs over the edge of the three storey dwelling and shielded his eyes from the omnipresent glare of the sun by pulling the crimson keffiyah over his head, the lightweight material protecting his skin from its destructive heat. The Venetian wore nothing but the knee length breeches of the local style; his chest and abdomen exposed to the rays; his natural olive skin more deeply tanned than ever.

Looking to the west, the 'Bab Al Faradis' led to the fertile plain in which Damascus has been built centuries previously. The 'Gate of Paradise' opened out into the lush orchards and plantations where much of the populace worked for every daylight hour in the scorching temperatures of the desert lands. He watched the people, the size of insects from his position; picking and cultivating the olives, citrus fruits, almonds, walnuts, pomegranates, plums, figs and apricots that grew in carefully positioned rows. A small area of barley and corn then gave swiftly away to the miles of endless sand which surrounded the city in three directions; the other a barren landscape of rocky outcrops. It was for this abundance of fresh produce that Damascus had fallen to a huge number of invaders over the decades from the ancient Hittites, Assyrians, Greeks and Romans to the

Byzantines; who had all conquered and left their mark on this verdant desert oasis. The Byzantines who claimed the city had claimed that this fertile area was the Garden of Eden itself, believing it to be the place that God had chosen to create man. Alessio's mind examined the Biblical concept and sighed audibly; thinking of James and his belief that everything in this forsaken land came back to the divisive issue of religion.

As he mulled this thought over, his eyes were drawn automatically to the east, past the 'Gates of Deliverance' which led to the Old City; the cramped, overcrowded, poverty stricken quarter, in which he and Aisha now resided in the eaves above an artisans home and workshop. A tiny one room dwelling, rented on a no questions basis at an exorbitant rate from the smith who worked his Damascan steel noisily below them at all hours of the day and evening. The one redeeming feature of the lodgings was the fact that a latched shutter led to the rooftops and from which, Alessio spent much of his time, sat, overlooking the city and watching its' workings from up high.

Past the Old City and through the 'Bab Al Jabillah', surrounded by souks was the home of the many bazaars and market stalls, which never closed; the hawkers and traders sold an amazing array of merchandise more varied than Alessio had ever seen; from livestock to materials to precious stones and much, much more. The crumbling Roman Imperial wall was the only thing that separated the vast encampment of the army of Imad Ad-Din Atabec Zengi Al Malik Al Mansir and the city itself. The brightly coloured awnings and tents covered the rocky ground where the massed warriors slept and impatiently awaited their next campaign. Thousands of armed Saracens and hundreds of horses and camels were herded together under the fluttering banner of the man that James had decided was his mortal enemy. The army were uninvited guests and although not outright enemies of the Damascans; they were certainly not friends. Scores of disputes, arguments and even deaths had occurred between the two factions and tensions between the two sides were high. The unwanted ranks of armed warriors were seen as an occupying force by the denizens of the city who caused trouble, skirmishes and abused their hospitality; taking their food and provisions at rock bottom prices. The city elders could do little about the problem however and to provoke Al Mansir would almost certainly lead to a battle which could not be won and would inevitably become a massacre of the Damascan population.

Past the closely packed ranks of bored and listless warriors, a natural solid rocky outcrop grew eerily out of the sandstone ground and the army blocked the winding path that wound around the great stone mount; atop which a fortified tower had been constructed and where Al Mansir resided; overlooking the vast desert domain he had commandeered. The thin winding path which gradually circled the rock led to a vast gatehouse; an impressive fortification in itself with archer positions, thick walls and barred double cedar wood gates. Once inside, it was said that each of the eight floors were guarded by the Immortals; elite, experienced fighters loyal only to the self-proclaimed leader of the Islamic peoples of the sand; the man who described it his destiny and Allah's command to rid the infidel from their lands and send them fleeing back across the sea. On the top floor of the tower lay the throne room and the man who had ordered his legions to destroy the Christian city of Edessa; enraging the Western Kingdoms and the Pope himself and if rumour were to be believed; a man who had single handed caused a new mighty army of European crusaders to be formed and who would wage war again upon the Muslim.

With a deflated sigh, Alessio forced his attention to the spiral minaret of the city's great mosque; a beautiful extravagant building that had been created in honour of his own deity's enemy. He closed his eyes as he pondered this silent statement. Was Allah, God's enemy? Was every Muslim his enemy as he was Christian? In the past three days in Damascus in the company of Aisha; herself born into Islam; he found nobody he wished to harm merely people akin to the people he met in Acre or Jerusalem or Antioch. People who laughed and talked and who married and had children; just as they did in the Christian lands; were they so different? Was it actually the Pope who told the masses that God hated Allah and all Muslims should be slain and their lands invaded? Was it not Al Mansir who preached hate against every Christian; spreading lies and dictating vile creative reasons why Outremer needed to be destroyed? Were these religious leaders' simply mortal souls who sought wealth and power and used religion doctrine to attain it? Alessio had always been confused about the necessity to hate another for no other reason than his differing religious belief. He was Catholic by birth and prayed to God every morning and evening of his life and he read the Bible and knew its teachings. He thought kindly of the gentle elderly priest when he had been an altar boy in one of the many churches in Acre as a child and none of that man's stories had told him to hate and kill Muslims. The priest talked of forgiving one's enemies and of the son of God; Jesus, who turned his cheek and performed miracles on earth. Alessio smiled grimly and thought of James again; a man who refuted any religious doctrine and believed God to have left man to his own savagery and destruction yet took into his home an Islamic girl and Jewish boy and loved them as his own children.

The Venetian raised the water skin to his lost friend and murmured a prayer hoping that God would protect him on his journey. He drank deeply and surveyed the city once again. To the north, exquisite Byzantine architecture housed the rich and influential of Damascus whilst to the south; the 'Bab Al Sagir' guarded the southern trail, a classical Roman gatehouse which had once been dedicated to their God of War; Mars and with bitter irony, Alessio thought it sadly apt. His meandering thoughts scattered into nothing however as the small figure of Aisha hurried down the filthy lane from the market district towards their dwelling and wore a worried frown upon her young face. Nimbly, he moved across the wood and dropped into their room to await Aisha; concern growing as he heard her soft footfalls on the creaking stairwell. Every morning since they had arrived in Damascus, Aisha had spent time in the great bazaar; working hard for a few coins and finding out as much information as possible from the women there who loved to gossip and swap details of others private lives and general happenings. There had been no direct word about James thus far but a sharp pain in his chest now increased in voracity as he waited upon the teenager impatiently.

Aisha burst into the small chamber and closed the door behind her; tears filled her dark eyes and she rushed to hug Alessio; who responded kindly; stroking her hair as she attempted to explain; her words punctuated by sobs.

"A Christian warrior has been slain in the deserts to the west by the Immortals; his head has been brought to the tower. I think it may be James...."

A surge of panic swept through the Venetian's entire bloodstream but he forced his voice to remain calm.

"Hush...We do not know it is James....there are thousands of knights in the deserts to the west."

Aisha pushed him away and shook her head violently sending raven haired ringlets wildly around the room.

"No.....what Christian knight comes alone into the Atabeg's lands? He was killed just three days ride from here. It has to be him!"

351

Alessio stood, paralysed by the instant revelation and sat down on the worn mattress, hands covering his face momentarily before realising he had to be strong for the girl.

"It could have been a martyr or a mad man. God knows this place is filled with thousands of both."

Aisha nodded warily, her face unconvinced.

"Well the head is being placed on the gatehouse to the tower with the other traitors and criminals that lunatic has had killed. Come with me? If you hide your face and be careful; I don't want to be there alone if......"

Alessio grunted affirmation and the two hugged again briefly in silence. Aisha wiped away the tears from her cheeks and with a brave face adorning her neck; she led Alessio out in the streets of Damascus towards the army encampment, her face impassive as horrendous images floated through her brain.

****

The throne room was packed with excited faces on all sides but as the leader of the Immortals strode through them; a hush descended upon the chamber. In his left hand a small sack contained the bloody mess that was the remains of the infidel's decapitated head and with his right hand, he motioned the onlookers to step aside as he made his way easily through the massed throng towards his master; who sat upon his gilded cushioned chair like an excited child awaiting a magnificent gift. The man was barely sat on the throne; his hands gripping the ornate arms and his face peered at him; his entire body a coiled spring of nervous tension.

"Khalim...is it true? You have slain the Christian devil?"

The words were muttered yet in the echoing silence of the great chamber, the warrior heard every word as he halted before the Lion of Islam.

"My master, I give to you the head of the man who killed the great Saadiq."

Lowering onto one knee, he offered the sack to his leader and bowed his head, avoiding eye contact as was the custom. Imad Ad-Din Atabec Zengi Al Malik Al Mansir raised himself with his arms and shuffled towards the leather bag, taking it gingerly as he looked up to see the entire occupancy of the room staring at him expectantly.

"Thank you Khalim; you are a true champion. You have succeeded where even the mighty Saadiq himself failed. You have slain the one who it was prophesised would murder me."

He worked the crowd well, his voice rang out, loud and clear now as he continued, his own excitement building tangibly.

"A false prophecy in fact! Bring the witch to me – she will pay dearly for spreading her malicious lies about me!"

Five darkly garbed, fully armed men peeled away from the far wall and headed out onto the roughly hewn stairs as Al Mansir progressed with his soliloquy.

"Let us see this defeated enemy; let us prise his lifeless head atop a spike for all to see what happens to those who dare oppose my power!"

Reaching a high pitched crescendo he opened the sack and with a mixture of relief and disgust, he raised the head above his own with a triumphant cheer. The cheer was immediately taken up by the sycophantic onlookers who praised Al Mansir as Allah's chosen one and the tower's interior walls reverberated with the stamping of boots, clapping of hands and whooping of the followers of the Atabeg.

Into this scene of unabashed glory, Nadirah and Kalaama were pushed forward by the guards a few minutes later and Al Mansir thrust the bloodied head into the elderly soothsayer's face.

"This is your infidel who you say will kill me! What say you now?"
Nadirah made to make a step towards the threatening caliphate but Kalaama held up a hand to her. The old seer was confident in her abilities and two days ago when Nadirah had rushed to see her after news of the Christian Knight's death had filtered through the tower; she had checked the runes and bones once again and five times since. All portents came back the same; the assassin was alive and getting closer; the death of the Islamic leader was at hand. Kalaama peered at the Atabeg through myopic eyes and cackled throatily.

"The prophecy is not false oh great one...something else must be inaccurate?"

The insult was obvious and Al Mansir bristled at the public statement.

"Watch your tongue hag. Put this on the traitor's gatehouse to show what happens to the fools who challenge or threaten me."

He tossed the head dismissively to Khalim who in turn passed it more carefully to one of his minions who scuttled quietly out of the throne room to the stairs with his unholy burden.

"You are in grave danger! The runes foretell your destruction! The assassin draws ever nearer!"

Nadirah tried in vain to stem the stark warnings shrieked

from the elderly woman and watched in horror as the Muslim leader screamed at her to be quiet and to leave his sight immediately. The assorted guests and guards shouted at her to be silent and as Khalim drew his scimitar; Kalaama threw herself against Al Mansir's thighs; gripping them in her skeletal hands.

"You must listen to the ancients – they do not lie; you will be dead within seven days if you do nothing and believe in this false belief that you are now safe."

The Lion of Islam pushed the frail woman off his legs and kicked her across the stone floor.

"Get her out of here – the woman is insane. You all saw the head of the man sent to kill me. He is dead not I – how can I be in danger if your prophesised assassin is the one lying dead?"

Pointing a bony finger at the man who had unceremoniously kicked her, the oracle spat out an archaic curse and hoarsely whispered.

"I see a dead man in front of me."

Two immortals dragged her by force to her feet and made to take her through the enraged crowd to the stairs but Al Mansir pointed to the small balcony and the guards nodded obediently.

"Don't you dare..."

Nadirah screamed balefully as she watched the men pick up Kalaama and supported by a baying mob, approach the balcony and hold her high above the ground below. Looking towards their leader; they observed the silent nod and as the assembled host cheered, the aged woman was tossed from the tower to the rocky ground and instant death below. The woman of noble birth pulled out the ceremonial knife and leapt towards Al Mansir who stood, arrogantly smiling to the

*obsequious gathering as her oldest friend's brittle bones
shattered on the rocky outcrop of sandstone far beneath
them. Nadirah made only one step before Khalim's
great scimitar cut her down with two swift, successive
blows and a second woman died within moments of the
first; a trickle of blood oozing from her mortal wound and
heading between the flagstones towards Al Mansir; who
watched its approach with stunned trepidation.*

"Everybody get out! Leave my chamber!"

*He cried; stricken; his mind perilously close to madness.
Khalim wiped his blade on the silk clothing of the
woman he had slain and motioned for his black robed
guards to remove the congregation from the chamber
and to collect the dead body from the polished stone
floor. His master backed away from the oozing blood
and slumped on his grand chair, his vacant eyes
watching all leave the room.*

"Not you Khalim....come."
*He motioned for his champion to approach him and the
Immortal did warily; now alone in the enormous throne
room with a man barely in touch with reality and lost in a
series of lucid intervals.*

"Thank you Khalim. You are a great warrior."

*The man nodded in thanks and pushed his right hand to
his heart in a show of gratitude as the older man
continued.*

*"Tell everyone that the old woman was a traitor,
in the pay of the Christian dogs to make me fearful.
Spread the news that she is now dead and make sure
the celebrations continue with the men; explain that the
assassin is dead; killed by your hand and I am now
more powerful than ever before."*

*"Of course sire, I shall do so immediately.
Nobody will believe the ranting of an old witch. Allah*

protects you sire and nobody can deny that this is the truth in the world."

Al Mansir sat back in his throne and smiled at the warrior.

"You speak well Khalim. But...."

The swordsman tensed as he heard the three letter word and bowed his head, avoiding the penetrative stare of his master.

"But sire?"

"There remains a possibility that the old bitch was right and the man you killed was not the man from the prophecy. I want the Immortals out en masse; question and kill any infidel who rides to Damascus. I want the roads protected, the deserts patrolled and all those of Crusader blood slaughtered. I do not care how old they are or what they look like. You understand me?"

Khalim assented and bowed as he left the room; a distinct feeling of foreboding as the image of the fleeing westerner entering the desert storm a few days ago inexplicably entered his thought pattern. Muttering an oath, he hurried down the stairs, barking his commands to his men as he did so.

The head of the Islamic people grimaced as he watched the thick blood congeal on the floor and he strode from the throne room to the balcony to look down upon a small gathering of people where the broken body would have shattered on impact from such a fall. This had promised to be a great day, a day of celebration and victory and now he was unsure; it was tainted somehow by the spectre of the unknown assassin who may or may not be riding towards him right now.

Closing his eyes, he shivered in the afternoon sun.

Chapter 29

Decisions are Made

The pale orange glow covered the two figures, sat, as they had been throughout the night on a soft sand dune; the sun finally defeating the moon in its age old war for supremacy. James had agreed to the conversation with Halim and they had walked away from the dying embers of the camp fire into the cold of the desert; finding somewhere safe in the silent sands to talk. Halim had begun, telling him of his life as a boy in the east and growing up as a Bedouin trader and how he had met his beloved wife and had three children. The old man openly discussed his wife's death in childbirth with his only son and how it had affected his boy as he grew to manhood. Halimah was the oldest and he admitted she was his favourite, so alike to his dead wife that it soothed his aching soul. The middle child had been born sickly and died at three months. Halim discussed these things simply without embellishment; noting only that the world is a harsh place and everybody has burdens to bear. It is how they deal with their burdens that defines a man and at this point in the conversation; after over an hour of rambling honesty, James knew that this information was pertinent to him and that the elderly Arabian was making a philosophical point and in his own unique way; was trying to be of help. The old man spoke of how Halimah's first love was for an older married man and how he had bedded her whilst married to another. The unpleasant truth was found out and she was slashed across the face to show all others she was not to be trusted by women and 'unclean' to other men. This horrendous act had been ordered by her own father and she bore it to this day; accepting her fate as she had done wrong. The other man listened intently and patiently to the trials and tribulations that had affected the trader and as the monologue ended; he felt the opaque eyes boring into the side of his head in the darkness.

After a few stuttering sentences and broken conversation, James opened his mouth and opened his heart, unloading the harsh secrets from within the dark recesses of his weary mind. He spoke and Halim listened without response; merely a muttering here and there or a nod or tilt of his aging head. James spoke of his childhood, his brother and father dying in battle, his loss, his mother's lack of maternal love, Alessio's enduring friendship, Georges, Sophia, Maria, Abdul and his family, Sharla and her sons, Aisha and Jacob. Various anecdotes, pertinent moments and cherished memories were aired. He talked of the cabin he built, the vineyard he wanted to cultivate, the horses he adored and of Merdlan and his bond with his stallion. He choked back tears as he described the cataclysm; the immediate and successive deaths of Abdul's entire family, Sharla and her boys and of Jacob. He spoke of the aftermath of these systematic killings and how this in turn led him here and the death of Thomas.

As the tears rolled down his tanned, stubble strewn face, staining his tunic momentarily, he continued; quietly and honestly; holding nothing back from this wizened old man he barely knew; somewhat like a confessional he remembered going to in a previous life, when he was a different person; a boy with hope and emotion in his soul. Instead of informing a kindly priest of lustful thoughts for a neighbour's daughter or stealing apples from the fat Pisan merchant; he described vividly how he needed retribution and why his soul itself was being consumed by bitter hatred. James finished his story and sniffed loudly, wiping his eyes as he stared into the starless night sky.

There was a distinctive pause as both men sat in the pitch blackness and contemplated the life stories that had been shared. Eventually it was the older man who broke the silence.

"Tell me my young friend, since your boy's death; has anything you have done in anger given your soul more peace? You must swallow your pride; quench the ferocity within your self – it poisons you and will consume you whole. Take my son; he is truly lost – such a promising boy contorted by the need for some form of vengeance for his mother's loss. But at who and what for? Forever needing to prove himself against anyone and anything. He is a ghostly shade of the beautiful boy he once was. His mother would be heartbroken if she could see him now. This happens to men; we do not have the emotional capacity of the woman. If someone wrongs us or our own, we wrong them – such is the way of man and how it has been for all of time. Look at the state of the world; it burns with the destruction, pain and suffering brought by man. Man starts the wars my friend and men will never be able to finish them. I envy women; they have the power of creation. Allah blessed them with this ability and cursed us never to fully understand it."

James smiled thinly and falsely at the man's words and although he knew them to be near the truth of life; nothing could change him from his path. He remained silent and the old man progressed with his theories.

"My daughter is my most precious thing in the world; the greatest thing I ever did. Now I may be almost blind but I see the way you look at her and the way she looks at you. There is attraction, no?"

His listener groaned inwardly but remained impassive; his frame still as his eyes focused on some unknown point in the darkness; his only movement the flickering of his eyelashes as he blinked.

"I am not long for this world and when I am gone; my son will take the lead of my people. He is not equipped for such responsibility but such are the ways of my people. The future is bleak; the drums of war are getting louder and my own son will choose a side. He is not strong enough to remain on the outside of conflict. My daughter deserves more than the life she leads; she is beautiful, intelligent. I ask of you.....if you must go tomorrow; do not head to Damascus; head back to your home and your horses with my daughter beside you. You need a wife; every man does."

James turned sharply and bit his tongue before his brain instantly reacted with its' harsh rebuke. The kind old man was foolish but not an enemy and deserved no scorn.

"It may the wrong path but I have to do it Halim. Your daughter does deserve more but if you truly love her, do not pass her to one such as I. She needs a young man; the man I was before all of this maybe. A man who is not bitter and angry. A man who can see beauty and hope in this world."

He spoke wistfully and turned to face the Bedouin who returned his gaze stoically.

"It is only you who can change your path; do you really believe this will soothe your anger at the world? You fool yourself if you do and if you do, you are more blind than I. You may kill this enemy of yours although in truth you probably will not. The man borders on insanity but he is wise enough to protect himself with an army and thick walls and even if you do kill him; do you think his army will allow you to simply leave?"

Realisation struck the man as he spoke the last sentence and he shook his head violently and bowed his head to the sand.

"I am a foolish old man! This path to redemption for you brings death in whatever guise does it not? You are as bad as your dead friend; Thomas. What kind of god wishes death to their people?"

James cupped a handful of sand and tossed it before

362

him listlessly.

"I worship no god and it is not in the name of religion that I will slay this man."

Halim gripped his forearm with bony fingers; his withered hand containing hidden vigour.

"And what of your girl? She means less to you than Jacob? Your desire for revenge means more to you than Aisha's need for your love. Your thirst for this vengeance will bring only another lonely, bitter girl into adulthood!"

James stood and shook off the man's grip.

"You have said enough old man. Hold your tongue now. The light is coming and I must take my leave of you. Thank you for your kindness and hospitality. Apologise to Halimah for me if I offended her in any way; in another time I think we could have been close. "

Halim opened his mouth to speak but knew the stranger was lost to him and nodded meekly; watching the man stride down the dune towards his waiting horse, his footsteps disappearing in the sand as he walked away.

****

Aisha and Alessio walked casually with the gathering crowd as it excitedly moved through the camp of Zengi's army and slowly up the incline towards the gatehouse and the new macabre attraction. Aisha felt physically sick and flicking her eyes upwards to her companion; she sensed the same dark foreboding in his own mind. After their own journey across the desert, it could not end like this surely? Her brain processed this question over and over until she felt like screaming and as they rounded the last bend of the trail; the gatehouse loomed before them covered in the black clad shadowy figures of the Immortals who were raising fists, scimitars and spears into the air; screeching oaths and victory chants into the still air.

Her young eyes narrowed to stare at each decapitated head thrust onto the iron spikes across the crenulations; ignoring the increasing velocity of celebrations around her. Most of the heads were void of flesh; the searing heat having stripped the skin from their faces and were now a lifeless, grisly mix of bone and congealed blood. The central spike was new and the European face that had been forced onto it was now coming into her line of vision. Hurrying forward amongst the massed bodies in the small amount of space, she lost hold of Alessio who drifted backwards as the tide of people surged forwards. Allowing herself to be taken with the flood, the features became clear and she smiled broadly in spite of the horrendous scene before her. The head did not belong to James and she whirled around to share the news with Alessio.

The Venetian dilettante, although three or four bodies behind her, had also made the same conclusion but was far from happy for although not James; the twisted features belonged to the Englishman that his oldest friend had left Acre in the company of. He felt bile rise to his throat as he looked upon Thomas Holdingham's death mask and swallowed it down; moving back through the heaving mass of bodies; pushing people out of his way as the stark facts impressed swiftly upon his brain and the possible meanings of this new surprising information.

Confused, Aisha watched Alessio's face contort in recognition and fearful surprise and with one final glance back at the head; she eased her way through the crowd after him, concern raising its ugly head once again.

"Alessio?"

She whispered as she finally reached his retreating form down the scree strewn slope; grabbing his arm and forcing him to face her.

"What is it? Talk to me."

Alessio's eyes were blank and his face drawn as he shook his head and hissed his response.

"Not here."

His eyes looked past Aisha's shoulder and she saw one of the armed guards to the gatehouse eyeing them suspiciously. The young woman turned her face quickly to avoid staring and with a mumbled agreement with her friend; the two of them moved as quickly as they felt comfortable around the rocky outcrop towards the crumbling Roman city wall and the relative safety within. Keeping eyes lowered as they passed other Damascans, the duo reached the city and with a swift glance over his own shoulder, Alessio swore under his breath as he recognised the same youthful guard striding meaningfully towards them. Pushing Aisha on, he said more harshly than he meant it.

"The Old City, let's lose him in the alleys."

Aisha began to walk faster and Alessio maintained her stride pattern as they disappeared around a corner and through a narrow street which led to a myriad of confusing alleyways. As soon as they heard the man shout a warning to stop and heard him running after them; the two figures sprinted through one dirty lane and into another, ducking under awnings and washed clothing that was hanging between buildings. Turning into another and avoiding a man and his basket of oranges; they drifted left and came to a halt, standing with their backs against the rough stone wall of a dwelling as they caught their breath.

"Did we lose him?"

Aisha asked breathlessly and Alessio shrugged, pulling one of his throwing knives carefully from the leather chest belt under his clothing and peered around the corner behind him. The young woman attempted to stifle her panic and gripped the sapphire pendant around her neck; the last gift James had bought her just a matter of days ago and her heart almost wept in anguish as she thought of what had happened to their lives in this brief span of time, since that item had been granted to her by James.

"I don't see him. I think we lost him."

Alessio replied slowly, his eyes scanning every figure down the cramped alley for the young guard. Just when he thought they were safe and his breathing became more comfortable; the enemy rushed around the corner and locked eyes onto the Venetian, barking an order at him that Alessio did not understand. Darting back behind the wall, he turned to Aisha and looked into the girl's eyes.

"Head home; don't look back. I will be with you soon."

The young woman thought about arguing but Alessio's eyes were unusually solemn and the tone was serious. There was no time to debate the matter and she hugged him briefly and without a word, abruptly whirled around and sprinted along the winding sandy lane, skipping past doors and around barrels as she fled. Alessio stepped back from the corner of the house and tugged out a second throwing knife in his left hand, holding the other by the blade lightly in his preferred right and held his breath, as he heard the rushing footfalls approach.

The inexperienced guard hurried around the corner with his spear held loosely by his waist and the determined features collapsed into abject terror as he had less than a second to see the knife hurtle towards him at great speed. The keen sharpened steel blade struck him at chest height, piercing the hardened leather breastplate as if it were not there; punching the frightened man from his feet and hurling his body to the packed dirty sand. Seeing his opponent fall and drop his six foot long spear harmlessly to the ground; Alessio leapt upon him; the second dagger in both hands as he swept it across the man's throat, ending his life with a deft and deep slice. Only a brief gurgle emanated from the guard and as the hot spurt of blood sprayed forth over the Italian, the victor was already looking frantically around the scene for any onlooker. Seeing none, he dragged the body quickly behind the corner of the wall and stripped the leather armour, helmet and breeches from the fresh corpse. Kicking over one of the numerous empty barrels that sat along the lane; he bundled the dead body into it and pushed it back upright with a good deal of perspiration and effort. Tugging off his own outer clothing, he clambered into the man's garb; placing the heavy helmet onto his head and forced it into position with its hemp strap under his chin. The clothes went on top of the squashed body and the lid went back onto the barrel; sand was kicked over the fresh blood and the spear was picked up.

Everything had been done in less than two minutes and nobody besides Alessio had seen a thing and with a contented grunt to himself, he walked casually along the Old City's streets back towards their lodgings; the adrenalin rush of fear and excitement finally subsiding.

Sweat was pouring from under the uncomfortable helmet by the time he reached the door of their room and knocked three times in quick succession as he turned the handle and felt it locked from the inside.

"Who is it?"

Aisha's voice quavered, brittle with emotion and Alessio whispered through the wood and smiled in spite of the day's events as the door slowly moved ajar; to be faced with a short bladed knife and a determined looking fifteen year old girl.

"It's ok, it's me, I am alone and it is done."

The Islamic girl lowered the knife and backed away from the door so Alessio could enter and he bolted it shut behind him as he entered the room and sat wearily on the bed.

"Why are you wearing that outfit?"

Aisha mumbled, sitting beside him; tucking her legs under her chin and wrapping her arms around her shins.

"I thought it best that when the body was found; it was not wearing a guard's outfit."
The man smiled and lay the heavy spear down carefully on the floorboards and removed the helmet, tossing it onto the unkempt sheets.

"I need some air."

He said eventually as a pause developed in the room, giving the stifling chamber an oppressive feel and he opened the latch and eased his body back onto the timber frame and sat cross legged to watch the city's movements below. Forcing his mind to remain calm and blank, he focused on the figures below who were going about their business, oblivious to the on looking Venetian. As he expected, he heard Aisha move lithely across the thatched roof just a few minutes later and he smiled broadly as the young woman knelt beside him.

"Who was the man on the spike? You knew him didn't you?"

Alessio nodded slowly and spoke in a hushed, solemn tone.

"It was the Englishman who James left Acre with; he was a swordsman of some skill, a mercenary."

Aisha's eyes widened in surprise and she replied with considerable hope and excitement.

"Then James could be near; he could be alive and heading to Damascus after all!"

The man turned his tanned face to look upon the flushed, pretty features of his friend's ward and nodded again.

"Yes Aisha, James could be close."

"Oh this is so wonderful!"

Aisha gushed and almost leapt into his arms, wrapping her slim arms around his toned frame as she openly wept with joy. Alessio stroked her long, dark hair and murmured positively as his mind screamed out another option, which he chose wisely not to share

James could also be dead; his lifeless body lying in morbid isolation somewhere in the middle of the vast expanse of sand to the west.

As Aisha chattered eagerly; her whole body animated by this news over the next few hours on the rooftop; this stark image would not leave Alessio's brain and as his outer body remained constructively optimistic; his mind created haunting scenes of death and loss to torment his inner being.

Chapter 30

The Hunter is Hunted

James felt the hefty weight of his conscience lift from his very essence as he allowed Merdlan enough rein to trot through the rolling dunes of fine sand, heading eastwards towards the southern road into Damascus. The city would be within sight in a day's travel at this speed and pushing his thoughts regarding the Bedouins to one side, he attempted to focus his mind on the task in hand; as in, how to penetrate the city's defences and enter the fortified tower where his enemy resided. There was no intelligent, well thought out plan for this escapade and as the miles of desert passed under his stallion's hooves, numerous ideas appeared, were processed and then generally rejected silently as foolhardy and prone to abject failure.

After over two hours of silent contemplation; his active brain lapsed back into thoughts regarding the old man; Halim and his final conversation with him. In truth, and however uncomfortable to hear; the wizened frail trader had stated alarming facts that struck a chord but he had been wrong in one of his findings. James had no wish to die on this adventure; at all. He was not a man like Thomas Holdingham who had done horrendous, terrible deeds and wanted; almost craved retribution from a higher being. This was far from the truth indeed. James wanted revenge; pure and simple. A man who he did not know had sought to destroy everything he had ever built and cared for and no man can merely accept this as his fate. The major concern for James Rose at this time was how to gain vengeance and live to tell the tale afterwards. It was this difficult problem that gnawed at the outer reaches of his thinking as Merdlan moved with strength and grace towards the historical and fortified City of Gates.

The horse snorted, almost indignantly as James gently pressed the heel of his left boot into the animal's belly; as the gentle slope of the latest dune intensified into an almost vertical position. Even the magnificent mount struggled to reach the peak and with huge effort, Merdlan paused on the flat summit; allowing James to cover his eyes and survey the surrounding desert in all directions. Far to the west; a slight dust trail could be seen and a small number of moving dark specks on the horizon. Straining his hazel eyes, he counted five or six blurred shapes; each being presumably a horse and rider. As was the Saracen custom; this would appear to be an eight man patrol; which meant two things. The first being that there was a larger body of men behind them and the second, that they were looking for something or someone. A flicker of alarm began in the pit of his stomach and churned through his insides until it rang in his brain and then he grinned to himself. The thought was as stupid as it was arrogant that this patrol were seeking him; nobody knew who he was or what his intentions were and most likely; as with the Templars, Hospitallers and King's guard; this was merely a routine patrol of the kingdom they controlled.

Shifting in the soft blanketed saddle; his sixth sense was aroused even further as another small dust cloud could be seen far to the east and this was a problem that needed to be resolved. For whatever reason, these were Muslim armed patrols and it was only luck or fate that James had to thank for arriving in the middle of these two units. Placing his left hand back to join his right on the leather reigns, he pulled hard on them; forcing Merdlan to turn sharply and descend the steep sloping sands, away from his prone position. The stallion's hooves led them into a slight ravine, away from either force's vision and methodically went through his options; as Georges had taught him years previously; there was never a time to let panic overtake you no matter how stark the issue one faced – there was always a solution.

The Bedouins were less than two hours behind him, heading along the old merchant trail to Damascus and with them; he held a much better chance of entering the city without being captured or slain. It would be easier to apologise and stifle his pride with the desert people than try and avoid being seen in a desert for the next twelve hours with patrols on active duty. Coaxing his steed to turn around, he cantered along the ravine back the way he had came, hoping the desert train had not moved too far from where he had left them; rehearsing the lines he would need to ingratiate himself back into the old man's better nature and prayed to a deity he did not believe in that he could find them and enter into the city under cover of their wagon train.

****

"Look!"

Khalim's keen eyes followed his comrade's outstretched arm and through the shimmering heat; a horse and rider could barely be seen atop a sand dune before disappearing from view seconds later. The Immortal blinked and wiped the perspiration from his brow, before the salty water liquid entered his eyes and sought out Murzan's expression to make sure this was no mirage after the long hours of seeking for one man in the vast open desert.

"I saw him."

His shorter, muscled companion nodded in confirmation and he allowed himself to think of the glory he would gain for bringing in his Master's enemy alive. Khalim wiped his hand across his black cape and sighed in resignation. The solitary figure who had appeared in the distance for a brief moment did not appear to be an infidel knight; but it did merit investigation and the most experienced of the eight immortals barked an order to his subordinates to head at speed towards the dune.

372

In seconds, seven of the sable cloaked riders urged their mounts to gallop across the sand as the eighth released the small hooded hawk into the azure sky. The trained bird spiralled upwards for fifty metres before darting into the sun towards the next patrol; a tried and tested way of getting messages across large open spaces; borrowed from the Byzantine armies decades previously and implemented throughout the Muslim armies of the East. The hawk would then lead the second patrol to the first and if there was any plausible danger; reinforcements would arrive to surprise their opponents.
Khalim grinned and allowed himself another glimpse of possible glory as he led the elite warriors across the sea of sand and into the annals of Islamic history.

****

James crouched across the horse's back and put his mouth alongside Merdlan's flattened ears and stated simply.

"Go my friend, run like the desert winds."

Loosening the leather harness at the same time, the stallion responded by surging forward into a gallop; sinew and muscle straining under the rider's guidance. James hunched his body as close to his mounts' as he could; peering through half closed eyelids as the dust and sand kicked up had the distinct possibility of obscuring vision and causing damage to the eyes themselves. Merdlan broke from the hidden valley and burst across the open desert, retracing the now hidden shoe prints from minutes earlier, at a much more rapid pace. In less than thirty seconds, the great stallion was out of sight from the bemused Saracens who searched the series of dips, valleys and dunes to no effect and trotted westwards, after the trained hawk had brought the second eight man patrol to them at break neck speed and an embarrassed Khalim had explained the figure they had seen had somehow evaporated into the sand without a trace. The other horsemen had departed, the sound of their mocking laughter still ringing in his ears as he led his Immortals across the arid landscape; his mood darkening in tune with the dying sunset.

The slow moving merchant caravan took less than three hours to find; James had remembered they would certainly use the meandering trade road which used the flattest of routes through the desert and although a much longer route to Damascus than across the sand; the heavily laden, bulky wagons would never cope with the ever changing terrain of the sweeping dunes, hills and valleys. Forcing Merdlan to slow down to a brisk trot, he waved to the two armed outriders; who only lowered their notched composite bows when they finally recognised him; approaching as he did warily with one arm raised and shouting in Arabic. One of the outriders led him to Halim's wagon and the old man's craggy face contorted into his toothless grin upon eventual recognition and the two men embraced; James giving the kiss on each cheek as was the Bedouin custom of greeting to show friendship and concede reverence to the older man. In minutes, he was sat cross legged on the Egyptian rug within the covered wagon; Halim excitedly requesting that his daughter bring wine and a bowl of dates. Halimah hurried to her tasks, avoiding eye contact with the non-Muslim; laying the small table with the refreshments and retreating as quickly as possible out of the moving chamber.

"Ah my friend; this is great news. I knew Allah would not lead you astray; you are not a stupid man. You have thought over my words and recognised the truth of them? You are a good man, a wise man. I am pleased...no, elated at this change of heart."

James merely smiled and sipped the wine gratefully; allowing the old man to ramble; conscientiously allowing the words to wash over him and making note to nod and grin at the most pertinent

374

moments.

"We will stop to sleep shortly but I wanted to hear why you have returned? You will come with us to trade in Damascus and then return with us towards Egypt? To return to your daughter?"

Halim's aged eyes sparkled and his gurgled laughter was ribald as he thought of another reason.

"Or did you come back for my daughter?"

The man's throaty chuckle deepened and James shook his head with a wry smile upon his features.

"You are encourageable, you old rogue. That's your own daughter you are talking about in that manner!"

James slapped the old man's shoulder playfully and he could not help but feel the genuine warmth of the Bedouin's greeting and proud affection that he shared to a relative stranger and a foreigner; an enemy of his people to certain ideologies and the horse trader could not prevent himself from being emotionally touched. The two men drained their wine together; the younger man admitting there was truth in some of Halim's words and that he had changed his mind and would return to Aisha; bringing her to the Bedouins and to see if the two could live their way of life. The lie hung heavy in his heart but the words themselves sounded good; a balm to his troubled soul and James wondered if after all of this; there was a way that this lie could become fact.

A second glass of wine was shared as the two men conversed about Damascus; James skilfully extracted information regarding the city's geography, buildings and politics as the Bedouin leader wittered on about their expected profit; the goods they would then purchase and the trip that followed to Egypt; passing close by the Kingdoms of Outremer and when James could be re-united with Aisha. The early evening passed by quickly and pleasantly and the conversation ended only when the wagon came to a halt and the voices and noises from outside indicated that camp was being set up. There was to be no feast this night but there would be a fire and music and Halim left James momentarily to organise his people.

The Outlander stood and moved from the confined space of the covered caravan and jumped deftly down from the rear to avoid any uncomfortable meeting with Halimah or her brother and strode towards the horse coral, away from the huddled groups who set about their individual tasks of preparing food or fire, pulling wagons into a circle or other such jobs. James strolled through the bustling camp clad in his hooded cloak, Arabic tunic and leggings and soft leather riding boots; the hand crafted crossbow on his shoulder, short sword hanging in the battered scabbard at his waist and the plentiful supply of quarrels in the large pouch at his side. He wore no armour but his weaponry created worried glances and whispered comments as he strode amongst the peace loving traders. His easy smile and comfortable demeanour did little to allay the Bedouin fears and James wondered what Halimah or her pathetic brother had shared amongst their people about him.

"Hello friendly white devil man!"

A boy bearing a cheeky wide grin rushed up to him; his more careful siblings a little way behind him and James stopped and crouched down to face the youngster.

"Usman, I am very pleased to see you."

James smiled warmly with affection and held out his hand, which the boy immediately shook enthusiastically and waved his brother and sister over. The two siblings approached warily and he remained crouching and smiling as Usman sighed with exaggeration.

"This is Maia and Ulloch; Ulloch meet James and Maia, this is James; our new friend."

"Hello Ulloch; your handshake is as strong as your brothers and Maia, wow Usman, you never said your sister was the prettiest girl in camp."

The young girl, no more than six winters old blushed furiously but her mouth curled upwards and she hid shyly behind her brothers and James laughed aloud as Usman grunted in immediate response claiming that infidels had lower standards when it came to beauty it seemed. Ulloch stared at the weaponry in a strange mixture of awe and fear; flicking his gaze from the sword to the crossbow repeatedly.

"Can you eat with us tonight James?"

"Yes, yes, mother will let us stay up later from bed if we have a guest!"

Usman agreed with his elder brother's request and before the man could politely decline; the two boys tried to outsprint the other to their mother, who James could see had been staring at him as he had spoken with her three children. Maia remained, staring with wide brown eyes at him; a slight smile and a flush still remaining on her mocha coloured cheeks.

"Do your brothers look after you then?"

Maia tilted her head elegantly to one side and visibly pondered this question carefully before replying with a slow nod of her head; the extravagant array of plentiful curly black ringlets moving with it in all directions.

"I think so but I am the good one of the family. The boys always get into trouble, especially Us; he is always in trouble."

The girl stressed the second trouble emphatically and

James grinned; having almost forgotten how incredibly amusing children could be without knowing it. Looking over her shoulder, he watched Ulloch reach his mother first and then mock his younger brother for being slower before talking to his parent; mainly in gesticulations with his hands it appeared and the mother looked doubtful and reluctant. Usman joined in the conversation with even more hand actions and as the two brothers yelped in joy, James knew the boys had quashed their mother's initial refusal and got their own way. Usman waved to Maia and James, which led to Maia slipping her hand into the man's and leading him to their wagon. Touched by the girl's natural action, he allowed the young girl to almost pull him to the family home and he was soon surrounded by three small children asking him a multitude of questions and shouting over each other to get their question answered first. He nodded and thanked their mother, who remained hard faced and unwelcoming; her withering glare eventually ceased as she could see her children happy and only then joined the other women in preparing the meat for their meal.

The meal was as simple and as rustic as it was delicious; goat that had been smothered in various spices that James did not recognise, on a bed of aromatic edible leaves. After the meal, Maia feel asleep on his left thigh as he watched Usman and Ulloch fight with imaginary swords; making every effort to avoid the baleful stares of exposed hatred from Halak across the dying fire as the slow rhythmic beat of the musicians drum echoed across the camp. He exchanged a wave with Halim, who sat chattering to his daughter for the entire evening. James pretended not to notice her surreptitious stares and not for the first time; wondered about her feelings towards him. The scene was serene and his imagination drifted into the concept of living with these friendly people and the concept was not a bad one at all.

One of the outriders rushed into the tranquil scene and James stared intently as the man spoke agitatedly to Halim and then helped the elderly man to his feet, who shuffled across towards him. James eased Maia carefully off his thigh and passed her to her mother who wrapped her daughter in a blanket and headed to their wagon. The boys ceased their pretend fighting and watched their elder lean in close to their guest and speak swiftly. They could not hear the words but the reaction of James made them fearful of what was to happen.

"Riders, armed, in black; heading for the camp; eight of them; seeking for a Christian. Our outriders saw them; one is leading them to our camp slowly now; the other slipped off to warn us. You cannot run; they will be here any second; come with me...quickly."

James sprang to his feet; smiled weakly to the watching boys and followed Halim to his wagon.

"Under it, there is a space between the back wheels; get in there until they are gone."

Halim's voice was brittle and alarmed and James said nothing, following the directive; scrambling under the wagon and locating the compartmental space; where you could rest your feet on the axle and almost hide your body by pressing it into the alcove; two iron rungs positioned to hold your body weight above the ground. Taking up position; he heard the drum continue and conversations increase in volume again as he realised Halim was ordering his people to act normal and remain calm. Almost as quickly as it had gone back to normality; a hush descended on the camp and James heard the footfalls of horses before he saw the hooves and horses legs pass by.

"Welcome brother; you need refreshment? Out in the desert at night is unusual is it not?"

James winced as Halim's voice sounded weak and frail; the association with guilt too clearly pronounced. He condemned himself for coming back to the Bedouins and putting their lives at risk. Memories of his last encounter with the warriors of the Immortals flooded into his mind and his blood ran cold.

"We are seeking an infidel knight. An enemy of our people. We believe he is heading to Damascus."

The voice was authorative; it contained power; power that must be obeyed.

"We have seen no such knight but we shall keep our eyes open."

Halim lied and it sounded false. There was a thud as the man dismounted and a soft noise from his left indicated others were still sat on their mounts around the camp. James heart rate increased dramatically and perspiration began to break out on his palms and forehead.

"You will not mind if we take water for ourselves and our horses."

"Not at all brother."

The soft thuds of men dismounting all around the camp could be heard and the sounds of water being carried and drank followed.

"You will not mind if my men search your carts I suppose?"

The question was stated as an order and Halim's broken voice was a hoarse acceptance. James strained his ears and eyes in the darkness as wagons were being boarded and searched. The wagon he himself hid under lurched precariously as boots pounded overhead and drawers were opened and the bed overturned. There was a heavy silence that hung over the area for a few minutes until a discovery was made and James had very few options open to him.

"Sayedy!"

The one word was shouted across the camp and its forceful resonance was felt on many levels by all those within it. James swore violently in his head as he heard the noise of Merdlan's stubborn refusal to be moved and the crack of something being used to hit his horse to make it do so.

"Who does this horse belong to?"

The question was stated loudly and repeated when nobody answered.

"We bought it in Outremer brother; we are looking to sell it in Damascus..."

The protestations of Halim were cut short as a harsh slap was heard and James could see the old man stagger to the floor, holding his face in pain, from his hidden location.

"If you lie to me once more old man, I will kill you slowly in front of your people."

The scream came from Halimah and she rushed to her father, defiantly screeching at the warrior.

"Leave him be; he is an old man. We bought the horse from an infidel."

She knelt beside her father and cradled his head in her arms.

A second voice stated simple facts and James knew he had to do something drastic before more innocent blood would be on his hands.

"The horse is carrying dried food, blankets, ammunition for a crossbow and this Sayedy."

James grimaced as he realised the basic map he had been given by the Hospitallers was now being handed to a man who was clearly no fool.

"I will ask you one more time old man and remember I am a man of my word. We are seeking an enemy of Allah; a Christian knight. Have you seen him?"

The sound of a scimitar being pulled from a scabbard caused James to drop slowly to the sand and ease his crossbow from his back and as silently as he could, load a sharpened iron quarrel into the shaft of the weapon.

"Do not harm my father; the man you seek is here."

Halak's voice was recognisable and James closed one eye and pressed his other against the sight and aimed at his chosen target as he waited for the gates of hell to open once again.

Chapter 31

Desert Skirmish

The Immortal smirked and twisted his neck to view the young man shuffle forward and repeat, in a hushed voice.

"The infidel is hidden in one of the wagons; I know not which. He threatened us with our lives if we did not help him."

The warrior chuckled drily with cold eyes in response.

"One man threatened all of you. What are you; men or cowardly goats?"

He did not wait nor expect a response and hawked and spat on the ground; motioning silently for one of his compatriots to approach him.

"Shall we search the camp sayedy?"

The head of the patrol merely smiled enigmatically and bent down to pick up a piece of wood, still burning at one end in the last remnants of the fire. He offered the flaming torch to the slow witted companion who finally realised why there was no need to spend time searching.

"Fan out men and burn each wagon in turn."

Halim stared balefully at the man from his prone position on the ground and struggled to his hands and knees.

"All our lives rely on what is in those

caravans...."

The man shrugged arrogantly and nodded to his underling who strode towards the nearest wooden vehicle. Halak looked towards his anguished father and rushed to stand in front of the man carrying the burning wood purposefully. The man barely checked his stride pattern as he lifted his left hand, using the back of his strong, gnarled hand to knock the youth away from him. Halimah screamed in impotent anger, railing at the amused leader of the group.

"Are you insane? The man has clearly fled from you as you approached! Leave us alone, we mean you no harm."

The man's right hand darted forward and gripped the woman's throat and lifted her from the ground; the muscles tightening in his arm and straining her neck as it constricted within his fingers. She struggled unsuccessfully and he smiled broadly at her pathetic attempt to free herself; her feet flailing wildly for the sanctuary of the sand below them.

"Burn every wagon. These faithless dogs deserve nothing but Allah's wrath; their treachery must be punished. Kill every horse, leave them to walk the sands."

Low murmurings of concern and discontent echoed around the circular camp as men stepped forward; gripping makeshift weapons of tools or knives. The other warriors' unsheathed scimitars and tension became palpable. Adversaries eyed each other suspiciously; weighing up possible consequences of violent confrontation. It was James who broke the icy atmosphere with a simple sentence stated calmly but with confidence in Arabic.

"Put her down."

Every pair of eyes used the dim illumination of the dying embers of the camp fire to stare at the figure, who had stepped unnoticed from the shadows beside a covered wagon and aimed his crossbow in both hands towards the leading Saracen. The Saracen in turn, merely studied the newcomer and his mouth twisted into an ugly smile. His fingers released the woman who crumpled to the ground, holding her throat and coughing in a panic stricken state.

"You have one small arrow infidel; how is that going to save you from eight men?"

"They move one step, you die and then I consider my options."

James said evenly and grinned himself, masking his own increasing desperation with his own attempt at confidence. His peripheral vision was limited in the gloom and he could only count five of the eight warriors in the darkness; there was no going back and the odds of survival were extremely low.

"Who said he was alone?"

Halim stood proudly, helping his daughter to her feet and questioned the arrogance of the opponent. All around the camp; Bedouins of both sexes and all ages began to move forwards, slowly; towards each of the famed Immortals; carrying hand axes, clubs, farming tools and an array of knives.

"There are more than thirty of us and eight of you. Go now and leave us be. Nobody has to die here tonight."

The elder's words were mournful as he knew no 'Sword of Allah' as these men were known amongst his people, would step down from confrontation with traders. His heart sank and his blood momentarily froze as the raucous laughter was the response from the patrol leader, who placed his right hand to the hilt of his great scimitar as his waist and screeched to his followers.

"Kill them a........."

As the peace of the desert night was shattered with a series of vitriolic shouts, oaths and screams; the man's third word was never heard as his throat exploded outwards, showering the sand around him with blood and torn flesh; the word lost in a choking gurgle of a dying man. James crouched in the sand and rushed to reload the clumsy weapon as swiftly as he could manage in the near total blackness; his first shot having dispatched the leader of the group with a clean shot through the unprotected neck.

Halimah watched the man die before her eyes, his last mortal deed being a pitiful and ultimately pointless attempt to grasp his own throat and stem the blood loss. From the light of the dying flames of the campfire; she felt enormous pride as she saw her people take up arms against these cloaked swordsmen. She smiled at the sight of her brother rush to her side, place a reassuring hand on her shoulder and pick up the dead man's scimitar, heading towards a nearby skirmish where his two oldest friends were circling menacingly around one of the warriors whose eyes flicked from each of them quickly. A strange sound, like the fluttering of wings, zipped past her head but this was immediately forgotten as she saw one of the wagons begin to burn; the canvas shrivelling quickly under the ravenous flame; illuminating the desperate struggle between individuals and groups all around her. The scream was lost in her dry mouth as she could only observe Maloch; an older man, whom she had known since birth get slaughtered unceremoniously; a powerful sweep of a scimitar opening up the man's body from neck to abdomen.

"Halimah, come!"

Lost momentarily in the tragedy unfolding around her, she had not noticed her father's urgent tugging at her arm and he now forcibly pushed her towards the relative safety of their caravan and the enigmatic infidel who could protect them better than any other. Rushing panic-stricken through the gloom; pitch blackness covering them instantaneously like a thick blanket; they stumbled away from the fire.

James thudded the bolt into the carefully crafted groove in the shaft of his crossbow and grunted as he forced the complex trigger mechanism of the French weapon automatically and without looking; his eyes narrowed like a bird of prey as he studied the battlefield before him. He watched in satisfaction as the adversary, who had burnt the first wagon, had fallen under numerous blows from three Bedouin males although elsewhere; the valiant traders were no match for the Immortal's strength and skill with a blade. The shrill wailing of children, high pitched screams of women and threats and taunts of men coupled with the clash of weaponry were put calmly to the back of his mind as he raised the crossbow again to his open right eye, closing his left as he aimed across the fire towards an agile warrior who had acrobatically slain a petrified overweight Bedouin who had thrust clumsily with his carving knife and missed. Before he unleashed the quarrel; three children sprinted through his line of vision and he recognised them as Usman and his siblings. Cursing loudly, he lowered his crossbow and headed towards them, still crouched near to the ground, his eyes darting in all directions for any attackers.

He nodded grimly as Halim and his daughter rushed past him to the covered wagon behind him; the fear and hurt clear as day in the darkness of the night. Shouting his name over and over; the Westerner managed to gain the boys attention and motioned for Usman to lead his brother and sister towards him; which the young boy did successfully. Maia's pretty face was streaked with tears and she hugged his neck tightly as he crouched to greet them all, whispering that everything would be all right.

"Do you promise?"

The young girl stared at him intently; hope lingering in her dark orbs. James nodded and eased the small hands from his neck; placing each of her hands in her brothers.

"I promise no one will harm you or your brothers. Where's your mother?"

Usman pointed across the chaotic scene before them towards where he had eaten just a few hours ago and he nodded and stood upright; Halimah coming to his aid; ushering the three children back to the sanctuary of the wagon where Halim stood guard; his wrinkled, gnarled hands holding a wood axe with steel-eyed determination. Both hands gripping the loaded crossbow, James moved through the deadly commotion; avoiding confrontation as he raced to the covered dray, peering into the interior. The woman was shaking uncontrollably, holding out a small knife towards anyone entering her home.

"It's ok, it's James, your children are safe and with Halimah at Halim's carriage. Come, put the knife down, I will take you."

His voice was calm and soft and he held out an outstretched left hand towards the woman who was teetering on the edge of hysteria.

"Come on, please."

The slight coaxing worked as the woman tossed the knife out of her trembling hands and with tears streaming and lips quivering, the woman took his hand and stepped down to the sand beside him, hiding her face in the cloak he wore at his shoulder. His left hand hooked under her elbow and as his right hand gripped the weapon firmly; he moved alongside her and led her through the anarchic pandemonium towards her offspring. Flicking his eyes left and right, he ignored the hand to hand melee and skirmishes, looking out only for an enemy assault and was thankful when none were forthcoming and he reunited mother and children. Nodding to Halim, who promised to protect them with his life, he turned to view the battle and moved forward to join the conflict, where the tide was slowly turning against the Bedouins.

Nearest to him, the three youths including Halak had one of the Immortals surrounded but his scimitar was raised high and the poise of his stance caused concern; as he waited patiently for them to make the first move enabling him to do a counter attack. There was no chance to shoot as the youths constantly moved around their enemy and James winced as the youngest of them leapt forward with purpose, only to be slashed across the chest; which erupted in blood and he staggered backwards; causing alarm for his companions, who lowered their guard for a second and the skilled warrior flicked his wrist and rolled his body sideward; the sweeping arc of the scimitar slashing open the stomach of Halak's friend and ending the teenager's short life instantly in a grotesque fashion with his guts and bowels emptying onto the blood soaked sand.

Halak took the split second opportunity and thrust his sword into the exposed flesh at the back of the hardened leather breastplate and placed his left arm around the Immortals' neck as he used the pressure exerted to force the blade into the body; slicing through tissue and muscle. The warrior dropped to his knees, releasing his weapon and Halak placed both hands on the pommel of his scimitar and drove it through him, ending his life. Halim's son rushed to his wounded friend and James focused his attention elsewhere; the desperate battle continuing around him; the bright orange flames from the various fires enveloping the deadly scene in grotesque luminosity.

The acrid stench of smoke, blood and other bodily fluids pervaded the atmosphere and James felt a wave of nausea wash over him, which he gulped down fervently and watched in increasing frustration as a woman in her thirties was hacked down with ruthless aggression as she vainly attempted to protect her children. Dropping to one knee, he brought the crossbow up to his chin and aimed at the attacker before a girl's high pitched scream made him instantly whirl to his left as the sound of thundering hooves approached him rapidly. His eyes widened momentarily as he watched an enemy horseman bear down on his position; his great scimitar whirling in the air above his helmet as he shrieked a blood oath. James regulated his heart rate and breathing pattern and closed his mind to the maelstrom that raged around him and he calmly released the bolt which fired straight and true, through the ineffective leather breastplate and into his upper chest; tearing through internal organs and punching him from his brown and white dappled mare. The Immortal landed heavily on the ground, convulsed briefly and died. The skittish mare continued her gallop through the camp and was rapidly lost in the blackness of the night beyond.

The battle was continuing all around him but the Bedouins were no match in hand to hand fighting and he cursed as another of them was slain before his eyes. Dropping the crossbow as there was no time to reload, he drew his short sword from his battered scabbard and whistled for Merdlan; unable to spot his stallion in the chaos of the night. Another of the wagons burst into flames to his right, revealing the grim efficiency of these elite warriors as the lithe shape of one of them danced athletically around a fearful family; slaying the man with a skilful thrust and hacking the boy's arm clean off at the elbow as he foolishly rushed to his dying father. Merdlan appeared at his side and he deftly mounted the beast;

digging his heels into the horses underbelly to make him rush towards the killer with a shout. The man turned and James saw in his eyes there was no fear and in that split moment, wondered if his own eyes betrayed his own. The tearful mother grabbed her wounded son and ushered him swiftly away as James leapt from the flanks of the horse onto the Immortal, his body crashing against him at pace; causing both men to hit the ground with force; the impact jarring the weapons from their hands as they rolled over landing heavy blows with fists onto each other. James winced as the realization struck him at the same time as a third punch drew blood from a split lip that the man was heavier and stronger. The salty taste of blood entered his mouth and he charged into the Saracen; unwilling to stand trading punches with a bigger man. The man staggered backwards, losing his helmet and James forced his own forehead forward, head butting the man on the nose; shattering bone and tissue with a sickening crunch. As the Muslim cried out in impotent anger; the Westerner brought his knee up sharply into the opponent's pelvis and he crumpled to the sand in a heap. James picked up his hand weapon and while the man lay prone and in agony on the ground, he ended his life with a powerful two handed downward thrust of the metal into the man's neck.

Spitting blood onto the fresh corpse, he turned to view the combat situation wearily as Merdlan moved to his side again, nudging his shoulder with his enormous chin. Slightly dazed and close to exhaustion, James could not even clamber onto his steed's back and he merely rested his body against his horse; seeing that the battle was almost at an end. Only three of the enemy remained alive and one of those was clutching his blood soaked arm in consternation and they stood now, next to the blackened shell of one of the burnt out wagons. Across from them, the Bedouins had huddled together; the older boys and surviving men stood in front of their women and children; a host of injured scattered on the sands behind them. The battle had subsided; the only sounds now were of sobbing and the cracking of wood from the second wagon, flames eating away at the structure; casting eerie shadows across the carnage strewn camp.

Forcing himself to remain in control and strong for the traders, he withdrew the sword from the dead man's broken body and led Merdlan to where they congregated; speaking quietly to Halim with authority.

"They have lost their leader and lost their thirst for blood. We can finish them or let them go. What do you wish to do?"

James looked at the frightened faces of the merchants but saw determination and pride. There were still at least six of them who could aid him in a battle should one arise which meant seven versus three.

"I do not know what to do."

Halim's voice was cracked with emotion and he suddenly looked like a weary, frail old man; the grisly series of events clearly damaging him emotionally. James nodded and turned to face the three remaining Immortals, striding three paces in front of the Bedouins.

"You can go or you can die."

The sentence was barked like an order and it was the tallest one who stepped forward and smiled enigmatically.

"You are a worthy opponent infidel but we do not run from wagon traders."

James forced himself to smile in return and replied evenly.

"You are outnumbered and outmatched today. Be on your way. There is nothing to be gained in losing your life for pride."

The man raised his scimitar and whirled it slowly to the night sky that surrounded them.

"It is you who is outnumbered and outmatched infidel."

James looked into the blackness and watched a small bird, perhaps a hawk, land on the arm of the man who stood behind the talkative Immortal and all three warriors grinned as one.

"James!"

He turned as he heard Halimah's shriek and heard the unmistakeable sound of galloping riders hurtling towards them; the shadowy fleet footed figures heading towards them at speed. His heart sank and he cursed inwardly as he knew the battle was over.
He rushed towards the elder and barked out orders knowing that at least he could save those innocents he had dragged into this nightmare.

"Get the injured on your wagons, pack up what you can and head west. They are after me; I will take Merdlan east towards Damascus."

"That is madness, you will never survive alone."

Halimah gripped his arm, tears flowing down her open face; the scars and covering material forgotten in the madness.

"We have no time to debate it. Save yourselves. This is my war not yours."

Chapter 32

Damascus Awaits

Several of the frightened and shocked Bedouins immediately started loading themselves and their wounded kin onto the three remaining carriages and Halim nodded gravely at James, pulling his daughter away roughly. Her vacant, wide eyes wore a haunted, desperate look and he could not read them. He mouthed an exasperated apology and with a final, lingering look at Usman's mother who was cradling her tearful children, he ran to Merdlan and heaved his aching frame onto the beast, picking up his crossbow as he did so. With hazel eyes fixed on the nearest of the Immortals, he loaded the weapon casually and efficiently, subconsciously aware that neither hand trembled. The three warriors made no attempt to move or intervene in the panic stricken rout of their foes and their apparent lack of concern bothered the horse trader immensely. The reinforcements would arrive in a matter of minutes and all knew the heavily laden wagons would not be able to outrun the Immortals. Merdlan, however, most certainly could, so the plan remained a sound one in theory. Positioning him and his horse between the traders and the three stationary enemies, the crossbow now loaded and held firmly in both hands at his waist, he waited for his moment to dictate the next stage of this battle in calm contemplation.

The small overburdened caravan train began to leave the campsite painfully slowly and James flicked his head leftwards, straining his eyes to peer into the night as the whooping of the new arrivals was getting louder with every passing second but the impenetrable wall of blackness made it impossible for him to make out the onrushing Islamic warriors. Merdlan snorted his unease and moved his forelegs slowly; the stench of the battlefield and the palatable tension itself causing the animal's senses to heighten; initiating James to stroke his mane softly, whispering to him in a soothing tone. His own anxiety was acute and the dawning realization that the plan he had hastily hatched was intrinsically flawed caused the anxiety to deteriorate into unease. On the surface he remained stoically composed and his unwavering gaze continued on the three men opposite him; suddenly and subliminally aware that it was the exact moment to make his move as his opposition were merely relying on the numbers of reinforcements to gain victory. Merdlan's mane was matted with dust and sand but the coarse hair created a degree of comfort he craved and this simple, prosaic action stifled the increasing turbulence within his psyche. He sighed deeply, regulated his ragged breathing and acted.

In one fluid, swift action, he brought up the crossbow; aimed and pressed the firing mechanism within a second; immediately tossing the unarmed weapon onto his back via the leather strap and drawing his sword at the precise moment the central Muslim clutched his abdomen; the sharpened quarrel penetrating his stomach wall and causing him to stagger in writhing agony to the sand. As the two incredulous men, either side of him peered into the blackness in abstract fear, Merdlan burst towards them with a burst of incredible power and speed, crossing the dying campfire in a blink of an eye; one Immortal bringing his scimitar up to eye level belatedly as a downward thrust from the ebony beast's back ripped apart the soft exposed skin of the neck; almost decapitating the horrified man and ending his life with a low gurgling cry. The remaining swordsman; already badly injured from the previous fighting; fell under Merdlan's front hooves; iron clad violence breaking numerous bones and shattering his skull as James allowed his war horse to inflict deadly force. The trio of Immortals dispatched convincingly and in deadly fashion, James ignored their ghastly, inhuman death throes and whirled his stallion away from the unseen howling horsemen and galloped off in the vague direction of Damascus; the first trace of sun rising in the east, a hint of crimson cutting through the night sky.

The high pitched screams caused the rider to pull hard on the leather reins and force the disgruntled horse to decrease in speed dramatically and turn around in an acute angled arc. The bawling became more frantic and as the screeching emanated from children or women; they were clearly coming from the wagons. Kicking his heels into Merdlan, the stallion; breathing hard through his long nostrils; picked up his pace quickly into a gallop to head towards the stricken caravan. Realisation was as sudden as it was dismaying as the reason for the alarm became clear; another group of horsemen were streaking across the desert sands from the west towards the wagons.

The harsh choice screamed through the echoing chambers of his inexplicably empty mind and he made it instantly as he allowed himself a swift glance behind; the slight illumination of the breaking of dawn permitting him to see the shadowy figures in pursuit, still around one hundred yards away. James gritted his teeth and narrowed his eyes as the particles of sand battered his facial features, the black hood bouncing at his neck; his unkempt hair and beard protecting his skin only a little. The magnificent horse increased the distance between the hunters and the hunted and he reached the first caravan easily and shouted at Halim who stared into his eyes with pools of pitch acquiescence.

"If I head into the desert, will they let you live? Tell me the truth Halim!"

The old man puffed out his wheezing cheeks; his frail frame belying his inner strength and he stated without emotion.

"We shall all die today."

James felt the harshness of undiluted blame like a heavy blow to his midriff and he pressed on, tears welling behind his stinging eyes.

"The women, the children....?"

Halim nodded and closed his eyelids to the inevitable conclusion.

"No!"

James roared in defiance and kicked Merdlan to reach the second covered wagon where he saw Usman, Ulloch and Maia huddled into their fraught mother who anxiously sought his features for some iota of comfort.

"Usman, come...."

Holding onto the reins with his left hand, he trotted adjacent to the slow moving vehicle and offered his right hand to the boy; who looked in wide eyed bewilderment.

"Please, you can save your children...please...there is no time."

Tears streamed from his blinking eyes as he choked on the words, attempting to explain his idea and unable to prevent the fearful emotion that was rapidly overwhelming him. The frantic mother nodded meekly to her son and he held onto the outstretched forearm and jumped into it, struggling to clamber onto the horse's back; gripping hold of James's waist as he called for Ulloch to do the same. The less confident boy scrambled across and sat behind his sibling as Maia was thrust from her mother's chest and into the offered strong arm. James clasped the young girl as gently as he could and brought her slight frame in front of his body so she almost lay upon Merdlan's neck, her small arms wrapping themselves around the sable mane to cling on awkwardly.

"Now, you. Quickly!"

James shouted, more harshly than he anticipated to the stricken mother.

The woman looked quizzically at the fervent man who called her on-board.

"There is no room!"

She argued pitifully as she staggered upright on the moving wooden boards of the carriage.

"Trust me. Jump."

Unwilling to lose her children, the woman leapt into James, almost knocking him from Merdlan's back and he held onto the woman's body as he brought Merdlan away from the wagon train. Trotting a few yards into open desert, he extricated himself from the plethora of limbs and dropped to the soft sand; helping the woman onto the horse to be with her family.

"What are you doing?"

It was Usman who asked him the question and James kissed him briefly on the forehead and slapped Merdlan hard on his hind quarters. The horse moving his legs in response as James screamed into the air behind them.

"To Damascus, hold on tight. You will be safe."

All four sets of eyes stared at him in astonishment before Merdlan came into his great stride pattern and galloped away eastwards, into an empty gaping hole between the enemies who could now be seen clearly; such was the closeness of fate. Only Maia's frightened wide eyes remained on James as they disappeared from view, leaving the horse trader to breathe hard and turn away to face his destiny; whispering the words.

"I promised."

Wiping his tear stained cheeks with the sleeve of his cloak, he pulled the crossbow from his back and loaded the weapon; a sense of providence pervading his acute brain as he studied the beautifully bleak landscape of this alien land; observing the warriors from the west descend upon the wagon train; which was already slowing to a halt in front of the impossible odds. Before him, two of the horsemen had wheeled from the group in a vain attempt to intercept Merdlan and heartfelt pride bathed his battered soul as he knew the family would be safe upon the greatest horse he had ever known. The six remaining Immortals bore down on his isolated position on foot in the sand and somewhere within his sub conscience he remembered Thomas Holdingham's last moments on earth and hoped he had at last found peace; as he closed his left eye and aimed at the leading Muslim warrior; he wondered if his soul would do the same.

The black clad riders came towards him at pace in a well-practised parallel line in close ranked formation and as his perspiring right hand pressed the release mechanism; he cursed inwardly; intrinsically and acutely aware it was a misdirected shot. Whether it was due to his subconscious fear of impending mortality or not, he could not be sure but the iron bolt fired through the air, merely clipping the enemy's shoulder and causing no decrease in the velocity of the charge. Adrenalin pumping through his veins, he tossed the impotent weapon aside and sprinted to the nearest dune, pounding his legs up the incline to reach the summit and unsheathed his short sword; positioning his feet well apart ready to leap onto the back of the first warrior as he would inevitably slow down to force the horse up the slope. The four horsemen turned as one, their steeds' stride pattern barely altering as they followed their prey with grim determination.

James held his sword like a knife; the blade

brought up to his chin; its metal edge towards the hunters and as the first sable cloaked warrior emerged, he threw himself upwards, jabbing the weapon into the Arabian thigh; twisting the metal into tissue and sinew; creating a deep gauge which erupted in blood; accompanied by a pained cry. The wounded man slashed wildly with his scimitar and James leapt back deftly onto the balls of his feet and dived to the side as a second opponent's horse forced itself up the hillock of compacted sand and into the fray. Pushing himself acrobatically with his left hand back to an upright position; halfway down the sloping, sinking ground; the third and fourth horsemen forced their mounts to approach him and with low levels of energy reserves, James knew his time was near. Unable to parry the surprisingly powerful swing of a scimitar, he staggered backwards and lost his footing, his weary legs buckling beneath him and his body rolled swiftly to the horizontal ground at the foot of the slope. The sword had been lost in the fall and as he attempted a frantic search for the weapon on all fours, he stopped as an authoritative voice called out from behind him to the four Islamites, who readied themselves for the final onslaught around him.

"Alive! Our Master wants the assassin alive!"

James moved cautiously upright to a standing position and turned slowly to face the owner of the voice. Trotting towards him were another group of black clad riders; six cowled faces in a perfect line behind two foremost; one stroking a small hooded hawk tenderly and the other; a swarthy man with cold eyes who clearly held a position of power; his dark eyes fixed upon him as a mother who looks upon one who has hurt her child. Aware of the four horsemen in an arc around him; he held the cold one's eyes and watched him dismount and approach him; the black leather breastplate hugging his muscular frame as he walked up to the captive and looked over him without speaking; appraising the horse trader with his eyes only. Uncomfortable, James awaited his certain death in silence; his own eyes flickering to the trail where he could see all the remaining Bedouins being unarmed and forced to kneel in a line in the sand.

"You are the man who has been sent to kill our illustrious leader; Allah's chosen one; the great Imad ad-din Atabec Zengi al Malik al Mansi? The infidel who killed my oath brother; Saadiq?"

James did not answer immediately although he understood the accented Arabic clearly. He needed a few seconds to allow his cognitive processes to work and he nodded slowly; his brain too tired to find the most appropriate response.

"I expected....more."

The leader of the Immortals smirked and his followers, now closely packed around them on horseback chuckled at his words. James remained composed and stoical, his eyes flickering once again to the merchants who had aided him. The orator turned to follow his gaze and he nodded to the man of European blood.

"Traitors to our people. To our race. They killed their own kind to defend an enemy of Allah Himself. They must place their misguided trust in your God to help them in the afterlife now."

The words were harshly spoke, almost spat out; the vitriol seeping from each pronounced syllable.

"They are innocent; you have me? What more do you need?"

James was aware his voice was weak and pleading and it was abruptly halted with the man's back handed slap to his face; the leather gauntlet stinging his cheek.

"Do not speak again. You are only alive

because our leader commands it so he can watch you scream and beg a thousand times before you die."

He turned on his heel and marched towards the kneeling Bedouins, motioning to the four men behind James to bring their prisoner. Pushed roughly to the trail by two dismounted warriors who held each arm and shoulder, he stumbled and staggered in growing anxiety to where the traders knelt in a line with armed Immortals scattered around them. All faces were staring downwards as ordered; their hands behind their backs and James was at least grateful that he could not see their eyes as his soul screamed in silence as all knew what was to come.

"Kill them all."

The leader spoke sharply as he looked at James with a sickening smile and strode to stand beside him.

"In less than twenty four hours, you would give your very soul to die this quickly and painlessly."

James snapped his eyes tightly shut as the first screams, sobs and pleading shattered the all-consuming silence of the desert and he wished more than anything he could close his ears to block out the sounds of the brutal atrocity. Trying in vain not to imagine Halim and Halimah being beheaded, he failed miserably and gritted his teeth to stem any tears that may fall; he focused his anger at the man who had ordered the deaths.

"We will meet again and I will kill you as I killed your 'Saadiq'; he died sobbing like a child; begging for me to let him live....."

His provocative lies were ended as a fist smashed into the side of his forehead and his world sank into blackness; a feeling of weightlessness washing over him as he fell against the men holding him; losing himself to unconsciousness.

"Calak; ride like the wind to Damascus; tell our Caliphate that we have the one he seeks and we will be with him soon."

A thin rider with a weak chin and pot marked skin nodded in response and wheeled his medium brown gelding around and galloped off eastwards, leaving a trail of dust and sand in his wake.

"Tie him in front of you; Allochi. We shall all ride with him together to the city. Leave the traitors bodies where they are; take whatever coin you find and distribute it equally to the men."

Khalim looked in disgust at the headless bodies that adorned the sand and walked back to his brown and white stallion in an elated mood. The assassin had been captured alive and easily and he knew his status as his leader's right hand was now assured. The honoured memory of the great Saadiq had overshadowed him since he had been elevated to the position as Head of the Immortals and now, this would be no longer the case. In great spirits, he mounted his horse and pointed towards the direction of the Gated City and the considerable force of warriors headed there as one in a defensive arrow formation; their prize in the very centre of the arrow head; incapable of escape and ready to meet his fate at the hands of the most powerful man in all the states of the East. Unable to prevent his grin, Khalim took his position at the tip of the arrow and allowed his horse to trot quickly; his mind savouring the moment of triumph to come.

Chapter 33

Hope and Despair

Alessio sat cross legged on the flimsy roof top and watched the city busy itself beneath his vantage point; his listless blue eyes unable to focus on any particular person or event as they were as restless as the remainder of his body. Aisha had departed the shared chamber early, as was her want of late; to gain information and watch the Western Gate, where she believed James Rose would come riding upon his great steed; Merdlan; in a blaze of heroic glory at any time. The Venetian shuffled his legs to a more comfortable position and yawned profusely. Where Aisha held hope in her heart, Alessio found only despair. His oldest friend; a man he loved as a brother was gone; an isolated corpse decaying somewhere in the miles and miles of desert to the west. There was no hope at all in his heart; the adventure had been as dangerous as it had been insane and the only surprising thing about any of the past seven days was that Aisha and he were not also in a shallow grave somewhere or adorning the city's walls with their decapitated heads.

The dilettante was bored and afraid. Neither of these emotive activities could be handled well by a man who could not remember being either before. A social animal since childhood; he had always craved company; be it in the form of James or a multitude of other drinking and gambling companions or one of his numerous lovers. He enjoyed life and believed implicitly that life was to be lived and not wasted. In Acre, he lived his life and here in Damascus; he merely existed; a spectral form of his own being. Unable to mingle with the local populace for fear of being recognised as a Christian; his blue eyes were rare and his accented Arabic was abominable; he spent more and more time alone cooped up in a small bedchamber or on the roof; where at least he could live a vicarious existence by watching others. Aisha was too young and too naive for meaningful conversation and as Alessio was becoming more self-aware; his needs were simple; good food, alcohol, games of chance or cards and sex. Aisha had no concept of any of these things and so their communication was drying up and they both seemed more content to be away from the other to avoid a confrontation or heated debate.

As a Venetian; as he classed himself, despite being born on Outremer; he was a typical representative of his native realm. Venice was a grandiose city of wealth, trade and debauchery and the plentiful populace of the city state loved it as a baby loves its mother. Venetians had no interest in outright war; bravery was over rated and could very easily get you killed and what point is there in life, if one is dead? Venetians were interested in gaining wealth and enjoying life and Alessio was no different; although personally speaking; he was excruciatingly bad at the former and incredibly talented at the latter. The very idea of a dangerous, almost suicidal mission to avenge the death of a family member did not remotely enter Alessio's head. Had a member of Alessio's family been slain; he would arrange for an assassin to regain the family honour or wait until a suitable opportunity arise; be it years later, for a chance to stab the man in the back or push a rock on the man's head. Alessio smiled thinly at his own thoughts and admitted to himself that he was making Venetians sound cowardly and this was far from true, they were just sensible and calculated the odds of success before embarking on anything in life. If the odds were favourable, the people of Venice would do whatever was necessary to succeed in their chosen event.

His oldest friend however, was only in part Venetian as his father had been a minor nobleman from England and a knight of the crusade at that. To the

English, from the little Alessio knew of them; bravery was important and honour even more so. This somewhat serious race also believed in fair play and this made every Venetian roar with laughter and it was something of an anomaly to every Italian that so many Englishmen still existed in the world with their bizarre belief systems. A distinct and palpable pang of pain erupted in his heavy heart as he thought of James and crossed himself, wishing that if he was in fact dead; the Lord Almighty would forgive him his foolish irreligious ways and look after him in heaven above. Mouthing a silent prayer, he looked across the alien city and never felt more alone in the world.

As a down hearted Alessio sank deeper into the chasm of isolation, Aisha was wrestling with her own inner demons as she trudged through the 'Gate of Paradise'; leaving the dusty, cramped streets behind her and entering the verdant pastures and orchards of Damascus on the Western edge of the city. Ignoring the plentiful crops and pastures, her young legs felt weary as she headed to the central area where the trade routes from the desert entered the city and the stall holders and water sellers set up their wares to sell to the hungry and thirsty travellers at exorbitant prices. Waving away the first water seller with a dismissive gesture, she sat cross legged under the parallel rows of citrus fruit trees and lost herself in her own thoughts; depressingly realistic as they were.

Her overriding feeling was one of guilt, closely followed by fear and then a great expanse of numbness; her youthful brain chose to call despair. The guilt was due to the declining state of Alessio; a man who was the epitome of a fun loving adult male had become a sulky child; incapable of positive thinking and abrupt and sullen as opposed to bright and cheerful as he had commenced their adventure together. It was clear he saw the 'adventure' as a foolish and lost quest. Implicitly and however much it decimated his mood; he believed James to be dead. Alessio wanted to return to Acre and it was only a matter of days before he would begin to talk of this departure; a departure which Aisha could never do without knowing one way or another, the fate of James. The guilt was acute as she knew Alessio had never wanted to leave the Christian port and he was less of a man now being a foreigner and infidel in a foreign land.

Her fear was becoming an increasing issue, especially as she tried to sleep in the cramped room with its creaking bed and Alessio's nasal snoring. Images of yesteryear replayed over and over in her mind; happy, beautiful scenes that were now lost forever; ending always with the death of her stepfather and her entry into an ever increasing void of nothingness; a black hole of impending doom. As each day passed, her own hope wavered a little more without any news of James and her own confidence was failing; contorting into despair as the reality of what he had attempted was debated riotously in her fervent psyche. Her feelings towards her guardian fluctuated wildly as she struggled with his loss; she still could not forgive him for leaving as he did without talking to her; for treating her as a child who could not understand his need for vengeance. She bit her bottom lip as she dwelt briefly in this uncomfortable realm of blaming James for causing all of the fear himself, since Jacob's death. His handling of everything after that heinous event was unnatural; his usual persona had been abducted and a stranger had been installed in his body and mind. She wondered if she would ever see him again and if so, would she even recognise him. This thought stung and she bit her lip more, promising herself she would not cry. Enough tears had been shed.

The teenager tucked these thoughts to the back of her brain and considered her future. If James were gone, she would have to make it in this world on her own; a difficult thing for a fifteen year old girl but not impossible. Her brain was acute, her body fit and her face attractive and she would cope; she would be letting

James and Jacob down if she did not and that was something she would never do. Her fingers of her left hand first touched her necklace and then the bracelet, sighing audibly, hoping beyond hope that he was alive and she would be with him again because although she would cope, the very concept was a horrible one.

She stood and made a clear decision; she would rid herself of guilt by telling Alessio to head back to Acre without her, she would tell him that James may have gone back to his sister's, which of course was possible, but improbable as she knew the sheer stubbornness of the man more than any other person alive. Alessio would argue and protest but ultimately, she had no doubt he would go and welcome the chance to get away from Damascus, a city he despised. She would tell him she will wait one more month; the little coin they had left would just about cover that if she were frugal in her needs and then she would make her way back to Acre. The Venetian would believe her too or at the very least, pretend to believe her.

The girl who was becoming a woman looked around and seeing nobody looking in her direction; skilfully and discreetly plucked a plump orange from the nearest tree and tucked it within the folds of her dirty tunic. She did not belong here but nor, without James, did she belong amongst the European Christians. Her heart was heavy, as with every internal thought process that ended in a future without her guardian; she felt lost. He may be a man of prodigious stupidity when making impulsive decisions but she loved him greatly and if he was truly gone from this world, the world lost a little of its light. Ignorant of the incredible oasis of plenty in the vast expanse of sand around her, she strolled back through the gate determined to put a smile on Alessio's face and readied herself for the lonesome days ahead.

The stroll became more of a trudge by the time she reached the main western thoroughfare of the city; the stench of horse manure affecting her nostrils as this part of the city housed the various stables and wrinkled her nose as she hurried through this busy quarter. She almost fell over as she stopped suddenly; her mahogany brown eyes fixed on a large black stallion being led into one of the less expensive stables. Aisha's heart skipped a beat and her stomach churned as she rushed towards the crowded stall where the horse was being tethered by a young boy. With every step, the recognition was clearer and by the time she reached the animal she knew that it was Merdlan.

"Merdlan!"

The word was a high pitched squeal of excitement which made the youth who had tied the rope tether jump. Almost leaping on the stallion in animation, she curled her slim arms around his neck and planted kisses upon his nose. The dark skinned boy looked on in amusement as he watched this older girl act as if she was in love with the animal. Stroking his nose and repeating his name over and over in soothing whispers, she turned to the boy and grinned.

"Forgive me, I thought he was lost. Where is his owner, the man who rode him here?"
The stable hand's smile disappeared, replaced by confusion and replied slowly.

"No man rode him, a woman and three small children; they look like they have travelled far; they went in there."

He pointed a spindly, malnourished arm towards a traveller's house; a building similar to a tavern in Outremer but without the alcohol and where people could eat and rest. It was not a place with which she was familiar and wondered if she should get Alessio first. Her excitement and need for answers immediately negated that idea and she almost barked at the boy.

"Do not let this horse out of your sight!"

The boy, used to being spoken harshly too by older men nodded and pulled a face behind Aisha's back as the woman, who was not much more than a girl herself, headed into the traveller's house.

The wooden and thatch building was two storey with beams holding the second floor in place; smoke filled the chamber from the fires of the cooking pots in the far corner and the smell of lamb cooking made her stomach rumble as her eyes scanned the open room. It was a large chamber filled with low tables and straw mattresses to sit on cross legged and eat and it was only half filled with patrons. She had no trouble recognising the woman and three small children as there were no other children in the room. All four of them looked like refugees with filthy faces and dirty clothes and the woman looked harassed as she tried in vain to seat her two sullen boys down opposite her as she struggled to keep her other child asleep in her arms; from this distance, Aisha could not tell if the sleeping child was a boy or girl and she took a deep breath and approached the table.

The mother saw her draw closer and stared with cold appraising eyes; the woman clearly prepared to defend her family against any unwelcome interference; which Aisha fully felt as she halted next to the table and smiled her warmest smile.

"May I speak with you please?"

The two boys turned to look up at her but she did not avert her eyes from the woman's glare and added another please. The woman nodded curtly and Aisha thanked her, seating herself next to one of the boys, who stared fearfully at her. She flashed him a smile and turned to face the mother who was now hushing her youngest who had woken and was sniffling into her neck.

"I am sorry to trouble you but I could not help

410

notice your horse...."

"You want to buy it, give me a fair price, it's yours."

The woman interjected, her accent was unusual but her Arabic perfect.

"Well yes but I was going to ask how you got it...."

"None of your business."

The mother spoke with an air of brusque finality and Aisha maintained her composure, looking into her eyes pleadingly.

"Please, I know the man who owns this horse, he is my father...."

"Impossible."

Aisha flushed, struggling with the urge to slap this woman hard.

"I have travelled far, we lost each other. I need to find him. He is a white man, from Outremer; I think he is coming here. Have you seen him?"

"The friendly white devil...."

The larger of the boys whispered hoarsely and then stopped as his mother shot him a withering stare.

"Please...his name is James...please...if you know anything...."

The tears came in spite of her mind promising that she would not and she sniffed loudly, wiping her nose and eyes with the sleeve of her tunic and looked every inch a young girl in need of help. The mother softened instantly, as was her instinct and the smaller boy shuffled beside her and placed his hand on her shoulder, stroking her awkwardly. The gesture caused her to stare at the boy and when she saw his tears, the emotional damn welled inside her and burst open. Her body heaving, she wept before them all.

Chapter 34

More Hope, More Despair

Alessio rested his chin in his hands and sighed deeply; his mind a maelstrom of very differing emotions. His tired eyes flicked from the expectant face of Aisha to the three children who ate the freshly picked orange segments noisily; juice covering their dirty faces as they squabbled over the last piece; which the girl eventually gave to their mother who tried in vain to quieten them all down. Alessio cleared his throat and thanked the woman for her kindness in repeating all she knew of her meeting with James. Avoiding Aisha's wide eyed stare, he fixed a soft smile on the smaller boy who looked across the cramped room into his Venetian eyes with barely disguised suspicion. After the boys' experiences in the past forty eight hours; he could hardly blame him for not trusting another stranger. He smiled wider and the boy hid his face behind his mother who immediately apologised for his rudeness.

"Don't worry, it's very understandable. You have all had the worst of days. Please, stay here; the rent is paid on the room for a further three days. We do not have much money but when we leave, we will give you as much as we can towards food while you sort out what you will do."

His voice was authoritative yet even; in an attempt to brook no opposition to this act of kindness and Aisha nodded and smiled warmly in agreement. The woman thanked each of them prodigiously over and over as they collected their meagre possessions; including the Damascan guard's uniform and weaponry. Alessio left half of his remaining coins on the small, rickety table and departed a few moments later; Aisha rushing after him; delaying only a brief minute to hug the Bedouin woman and receive the mother's blessings.

Aisha blinked in the glare of the midday sun and attempted to read Alessio's thoughtful expression as he rested his back against the wall of the archaic run down apothecary on the opposite side of the street; its' torn awning offering scant protection from the heat.

"I told you he was alive!"

Aisha gushed excitedly and Alessio wiped the beads of perspiration from his forehead and nodded absently.

"I want you to stay here; I am going to take Merdlan out along the trail she described."

The authority was back in his voice and Aisha blinked in astonishment; immediately attacking what she saw as the most ridiculous plan ever set out.

"That's just stupid. We need to stick together for a start as you cannot speak Arabic well. I am also the better rider than you and Merdlan won't even let you ride him; at least he knows me...."

Alessio shook his head firmly and looked deep into Aisha's eyes.

"Please do not make this harder and please do not make me spell this out to you Aisha."

"I don't understand; we find out he is alive and you push me away now. I am not a little girl!"

Alessio placed his belongings down wearily beside him and lowered his body to face her, crouching in the hot sandy street. He pulled her to him and hugged her tightly, whispering in her ear in soft, hushed tones.

"I need to know if they have taken him prisoner or if they killed him out there. If they did kill him, I do not want you to have that as the last image in your head of James. If they did take him prisoner, they will bring him here. You will watch the western gate which is where they will come in with him and see if they take him to the tower or the Damascan main square. When I return, we will then together try and get him out of wherever it is they take him to...."

His voice trailed off as he felt Aisha's body heave a little as the tears streaked down her cheeks at the realisation of what Alessio was saying; striving to protect her. Aisha wiped the tears from her cheeks as they fell and stepped back from the embrace; composing herself as she cogitated her thoughts. She knew she had to hold herself together; Alessio was emotionally exhausted and his nerves were on edge and no matter what obstacles lay in her way; she would find a solution and reunite herself with James; no matter what the cost.

The Venetian studied the young woman's face and prayed that she was seeing sense and hoped that his words were sinking in for as much as he loved James; it was time for this madness to cease once and for all. He longed for the relative safety and comfort of Acre but if James had managed to live through any of this insanity; he would do everything within his power to make sure they all made it back to Outremer alive and well. The two people looked into each other's eyes; neither of them capable of reading the other's thoughts. It was only the sudden sense of excitement and surge of locals pouring out of shops and houses that stopped Alessio from condemning the annoying teenage attitude he faced. Aisha turned to stare at the swell of palpable curiosity of a continually growing crowd, who all streamed towards the main thoroughfare from the Western Gate and she felt a deeply sickening feeling of utter dread as she heard snippets of conversation as Muslims rushed past. The words were all different but held only one meaning for

her.....'Infidel'....'Knight'....'Christian'...'Captive'.....'Priso
ner'....

Gripping Alessio's free hand instinctively, she
tugged the bemused Italian into the wave of Damascans
and the duo from Outremer were carried away with the
heaving procession to the central area; the one main
paved street which linked all of the many quarters and
gates of the sprawling ancient city. Taller than most,
Alessio saw the scene first and his dark eyes studied
the event which was unfolding before him with a kind of
dreamlike attitude; not quite believing if what he was
seeing was real or one of those famed mirages
travellers spoke about after spending weeks in the
desert. Aisha jabbed her elbows into those near her and
craned her neck to get a better view of what everybody
was looking at and her young eyes widened at the
beautifully sad vision before her.

A line of sable clad horseman; their weather
worn capes falling down the flanks of their mounts
making them look at one with their steeds; creating a
feeling in the onlooker of these 'Immortals' being
inhuman somehow. In the middle of the silent
procession; a prisoner was pulled on foot; his arms
bound together in front of him at his wrists and the thick
rope in turn tied to leather bounding by a metal ring
fixed to the pommel of one of the horsemen's saddles.
He looked absolutely exhausted, wearing only loose
Arabic breeches; the tight fitting tunic little more than
shreds of material; torn and damaged beyond recovery.
Various bruises, cuts and scars were visible on his
torso. The man stumbled a little; fatigue and pain
adorning his European features; his eyes fixed ahead,
ignoring the mockery and derision hurled at him from
the animated crowd. The man remained passive, noble
and proud and in spite of his precarious predicament;
Aisha's heart instantly healed a little and the constant,
intangible pain that had consumed her soul and
enveloped her in sadness illuminated slightly.

"James...."

Her hoarse whisper was caught in her throat and Alessio's perspiring palm gripped her hand tighter. Alessio's dark eyes studied his friend and could not prevent the smile from adorning his handsome face; sheer amazement mixed with pure undiluted joy at seeing the man he loved like a brother living and breathing once again. He heard Aisha gasp that she knew he was alive and all he could do was to nod; words completely lost as James staggered and stumbled past them; his head aloft staring into empty air as the baying crowd hurled insults and scorn on the captive man. Grasping Aisha's hand tightly, he pointed with his eyes to the Old City and forced a passage through the bodies to the alleyways beyond; his mind alive and active once again to the clear and present danger to his oldest friend.

"I thought he was dead Aisha, I thought he was lost...."

Alessio spoke hesitantly through tear filled eyes as they reached a deserted lane behind a row of market stalls. The young woman hugged him tightly; her brain unable to find the right words to respond correctly.

"We have to get him out of that tower...fast."

Aisha nodded, peering up at the man who wiped his eyes quickly with more than a hint of embarrassment.

"I know...but how? There is an army camped at the base of that place and only Immortals are allowed inside...."

The Venetian nodded vigorously and began pulling off his tunic, waving away the concerns.

"I know but I have a plan; it's simple but I know it will work. I have that guard's uniform and all we need

417

to find you is one of those hood things some of the Muslim women wear..."

Aisha was taken aback by the dramatic change in Alessio's personae but his infectious grin was back on his features for the first time in many days and she smiled warmly in response.

"Okay; tell me more about this plan of yours...."

****

His ravaged mind could not distinguish which pain was greater; the ravenous hunger that literally begged for food in his churning, empty stomach; the need for water to quench the thirst in his dry, cracked throat or the plethora of cuts, injuries and wounds which decorated his aching body from head to toe. The sheer exhaustion that caused every step to be a monumental effort added only more misery to the bleak mood into which he could barely break from. Death would be relief. Four words which had remained constantly in his thoughts for over twenty four hours now. He shut out the baleful stares and the contemptuous scorn that was spat out at him from the hostile crowd on either side of the narrow Damascan streets by staring ahead of him; focusing his mind on placing one foot in front of the other and not stumbling; the stark concept of being dragged through the sand and dirt added only the extra incentive to maintain his footing more intense.

Some form of rotten or soft fruit struck him on the leg; thrown by some unknown assailant, to be swiftly followed by raucous laughter and further derisive abuse. Ignoring the growing rumble of intimidation around him; his brain flickered through the past twenty four hours; attempting to converge his thoughts into a semblance of reality amidst the sheer swell of madness which threatened to overwhelm his fragile sanity. Intermittent images of fighting, screaming, sobbing, bleeding, dying bodies drifted through his head and he closed his eyes;

a simple fact which failed completely to stop the pain within his soul. It seemed like he was living in a bizarre lucid interval and he hoped fervently that at some point soon; this nightmare would end. He was so weary; every fibre and muscle in his body ached and it took all his effort to place one shaking foot in front of the other; the rope and metal chains almost pulling him off his stuttering feet along the city's main thoroughfare.

The grim procession headed right into a litter strewn, narrow street; blocked entirely on one side by the backs of badly built dwellings. The packed throng of hostility thinned out now as the horses filled most of the thin pathway through the city. There was no worked or paved stone now so the ground beneath him was merely rough compacted sand, dirt and other less desirable material, which made the movement even harder for James to remain upright. The thinning crowd of onlookers made less noise however and for that; the man from Outremer was thankful. Half dragged and staggering through the alien environment, the ground began to rise and he trudged through another three streets before a great expanse of tents replaced the rickety buildings and he strained his eyes in the sunlight to study a vast amount of Muslim warriors. As he stumbled through the enormous encampment of the army of Islam, he could not count the sheer number of temporary dwellings and as the hard faced men watched the slow procession; there was hardly any sound at all; just various emotive looks; ranging from derision, open hatred but also ones of interest and incredulity.

The incline steepened and the dusty trail became narrow as it weaved around the great block of sandstone that stood proudly before them; a meandering, twisting trail that would make it almost impossible for an attacking force to defeat a defending army here as only two horses or four men could march or move adjacent to one another at any one time. The progress was slow and arduous; even for the powerful horses as they moved forwards for over a mile; the entire circumference of the rocky outcrop before the fortified gatehouse loomed into view; the black clad armed veteran troops defending the parapets opened the gate and portcullis for the line of bedraggled travellers. As James lurched unsteadily through the dark gatehouse; silence descended on the guards who watched with respectful if baleful stares but the man of European origin did not make eye contact with any warrior; his hazel eyes widened in open despair as he surveyed the decapitated head of Thomas; his flesh decaying in the sun, ravaged by birds or insects, both eyes lost in the empty sockets, fragments of white skull shining; bleached by the powerful rays of the all-encompassing sun. As the portcullis dropped shut behind him, he forced his eyes away from the grotesque scene on the battlements and wondered if that was to be his immediate future. Would death be a welcome release; an end to the torment in his soul or had his mother always been correct in her unyielding beliefs; his body would forever burn in the lake of fire for his lack of faith. As the captors allowed their horses to be taken by the young grooms, the chain was removed and the rope cut; freeing his wrists from their binding. He watched, as if in a form of daze or dream as members of the Immortals hugged each other as if some great mission had been accomplished and he stared upwards as he was pushed forcefully towards a narrow stone staircase which led into the rock itself. James looked upwards and realised that the rocky outcrop itself became a tower; immaculately crafted out of the sandstone itself as if it had grown out of the natural stone itself. As he stared in awe at the great structure; he blinked in the sunlight and suddenly the ground beneath him collapsed and he fell forwards; the world becoming cold and black all around him.

Chapter 35

Meeting with the Devil

"You are absolutely positive this is the man who crosses my destiny? This pathetic husk of a man is the one in the prophecy of that damned soothsaying corpse?"

The man spoke softly but the authority of his voice resonated deeply through the empty catacomb walls of the dungeon. The prison guard said nothing; masking his fear as best he could and hoping that the leader of the Immortals; the esteemed Khalin would respond. This was the King of Amirs, the Falcon Priest, the Atabeg of Mosul and Aleppo, the Fighter of Jihad, the Tamer of Atheists, the Destroyer of Heretics; the Lion of Islam – he was not a man to be crossed in any way, shape or form and the young prison guard knew this. There were hundreds of stories about the man with many names and some were most certainly true. It was said he had skinned and scalped Turkish enemies in the north, hanged people he deemed as traitors, crucified his own warriors for the most ridiculous of 'crimes;' trampling of crops, not showing enough bravery, losing a battle; the list was long and made friend or foe fear as one. The guard remained impassive, motionless; unmoving and only when the tall, muscular Khalin replied did he breathe a slight sigh of relief.

"This is the most definitely the man who killed Saddiq and the others you sent to Outremer; this is the man who crossed the ocean of sand with merely one other; this is the man who befriended Muslims and they aided him; this is the....."

"Yes, yes, I get it!"

421

Zengi snapped, stifling the monologue and flicking the flies from his nostrils; the stench of various bodily odours from the overcrowded cells offending him. Turning his head slightly to glare at the head of his elite fighting force; he continued disdainfully.

"You sound as if you admire him, do you?"

Khalin chose wisely not to look into his Emir's eyes and bowed his head slightly as a sign of servility and obedience.

"With respect my Lord, I believe he deserves a modicum of honour for his bravery. He fought with the ferocity and skill of a beast; fortunately; very few of the infidel invaders display such talents."

The elder man clicked his tongue against the roof of his dry mouth and for the eighth time today wondered why the Koran forbade wine. It had been one of his greatest pleasures and since the death of his beloved Mahmud and his subsequent murder of the treacherous Nadirah and her poisonous witch; he had brought in the Shi'ite Imams to rid the court of its taint of disease. Adhering to the strict scripture was the only way that he would become the greatest Islamic warrior of all time. The man who would go down in history for not only defeating the Franks at Edessa and destroying the first of the foreign states and the cradle of the Jerusalem dynasty but the one man who took Jerusalem itself and destroyed the infidels in Acre, Antioch and all the other towns of Outremer until not one Christian man was left in the chosen realm. Realising he had spent a few seconds staring into a dark empty corner of the dungeons without speaking; lost as he was in his own triumphant thoughts of glory; he whirled theatrically about and moved swiftly out of the distasteful domain and into the corridor beyond and into air of a more pleasant aroma. Pausing at the door, he half turned his head and spat out some orders at the greatest of his warriors.

"Get him upstairs; prepare one of the

bedchambers for important guests of honour, bathe him, see to his injuries and clothe him in the Frankish manner. Tomorrow at noon he will be publically executed in the city in full view of the rabble. I need him to be seen as a legendary warrior not an injured peasant. Send word to the people that he was the best of the Christian knights; a trained assassin sent to kill me. A hero of the enemy if you will."

He allowed himself a sardonic smile, warming to the theme of his subject matter.

"I need the masses to witness a great hero vanquished by me; how even the best of their knights are no match for me; the same man who took their Edessa's walls so easily. By sunset, his head will adorn the battlements of my gatehouse with the rest of those that dare to oppose me."

"Certainly, my Lord."

"Send word to the kitchen to prepare food; locate wine for him if he wishes it; a woman or girl; a boy if he prefers. Let this brave fool enjoy a final day before his reckoning with Allah tomorrow. Guard the chamber of course and keep the door locked at all times and tonight when the throne room is empty with the exception of me, bring him to me. I will speak to him to find out who did actually send him to slay me and why; I need to know my enemies for with knowledge; there is power."

Khalin nodded his head and assented, watching his master depart; he turned to view the broken, beaten figure that lay in his own filth in the tiny, dank cell.

"Call two guards and get them to bring this unfortunate soul to the guest chambers; I will make arrangements and meet them outside one of the rooms."

****

James woke with a start; sitting bolt upright and pressing the palms of his perspiring hands to his aching hazel eyes. The soft, luxurious silk blanket was tossed angrily aside as he looked down on his naked body; covered in a sheen of cold sweat. For the second time in a matter of weeks he observed Arab medicine and poulces had been applied to the plethora of cuts, bruises and contusions which littered his chest, abdomen, legs and arms. His mind struggled to reconcile the past few days and weariness washed over him as he struggled to sit upright on the feather filled mattress. His eyes scanned the chamber and wondered if this was the most beautiful prison room in the world; exquisite tapestries depicting Saracen hunting scenes and victory celebrations adorned the tiled walls, a thick, lush rug of Arabian design covered what appeared to be a marble floor and on the rosewood table; a clay bowl of ice and jugs of water and white wine rested with a carved drinking vessel made of some shiny white material he had never seen before. Shakily, he poured some water and added ice; pausing to feel the refreshing, numbing sensation of the ice on his skin. Sipping the water he observed a standalone looking glass edged with silver and stood; feeling the soothing wonder of the rug under his feet. Striding to the glass, he felt the strength returning to his body and stared intently at his naked body in the mirror. He was clean; his body had an aroma of spices similar to those he had smelt at Abdul's family home months previously. His wounds were many but were cleansed and purified; none of the injuries particularly severe and even his shoulder was feeling better again. Swinging his arm to prove to himself that he was back to physical fitness; he felt his stomach growl and he looked around the room for any food. There was none so he drained his glass of the water and meandered back to the table to place a melting piece of ice into his mouth. The chamber had one door; closed and presumably locked and one window; barred with an iron grill and he smiled thinly. A beautiful cell but a prison cell never the less.

Noting that there were no clothes either in the room; he headed back to the bed and pushed the delicate blanket over his manhood and sat to conjugate his thoughts. The images and visions of the past few weeks threw themselves unhappily through his brain and his face crumpled into a snarl as he realised that he was so close to the man who had inflicted such atrocities upon him and had changed the course of his life eternally. Death was near and he presumed that it would be public; knowing the Islamic world as he did. This was the day of reckoning; he had walked his path to redemption and now he would know what lay beyond man's understanding. The beautiful, smiling face of Aisha entered his head and he closed his eyes in shame; he had let her down; the one human being left in the world he had to look after and he had failed her with his pride and anger. Sins that could never be washed away; he looked down at the jug of wine and thought about drinking it all and losing himself for a while but he did not. Instead, he took the jug and threw it hard against the wall; the clay smashing on impact with the tile and showering the tapestry with its contents. The door immediately opened and two black clad armed guards stared at him with contempt; calling to others beyond to hurry into the cell. James steeled himself for his demise, attempting to block the palpable fear that was rising slowly in his guts and threatened to overwhelm him.

Three serving girls bearing huge silver platters laden with foodstuffs were ushered into the chamber and laid their burdens at the foreigner's feet before shuffling out in their covered burkhas; frightened eyes all lowering before the enemy. Two more serving girls appeared with clothing and piled the tunic, pantaloons, shoes, undergarment, mail shirt and belt on the hard floor near the platters. A third girl entered and silently cleared the shattered pieces of the jug from the corner of the chamber and all then left James alone in silence. The two guards casually pointed to the clothing and food and then slammed the heavy door shut.

The man looked over the vast array of eastern delicacies including; citrus fruits, dried fruits, almonds, nuts, honey cakes, skewered lamb and a spiced goat dish. Ravenous with hunger; and without acknowledging the clothing; James ate his fill; randomly stuffing fruit, meat and cake in his mouth in quick succession; barely chewing the immaculate food as he swallowed and filled his stomach swiftly. Pausing to drink more water only after over half of the sumptuous banquet had been consumed; he began to eat more appropriately; savouring the food in his mouth, surprised to be given such treats. Feeling bilious from such over indulgence, he sipped the water and moved to the clothing; dressing himself in the white undergarment and tan coloured breeches; both of French design. The white tunic was expensive and tailor made and fitted him adequately; the belt was Byzantine workmanship and he clipped it around him; looking again at himself in the large mirror. Apart from the stubble on his face and thinner than he remembered; his appearance was not displeasing and leaving the chainmail sleeveless mail shirt on the floor, he sat back onto the bed and awaited the inevitable entrance of the guards in due course. This incredible hospitality would not clearly last and James planned to fight at the earliest opportunity; the concept of being killed within the walls was preferable to being beheaded or worse in a public square in front of the populace of Damascus.

Picking on dates as he waited, the waiting became tedious and unbearable so he paced around the chamber, straining neck and eyes to study the world outside the room; he saw the camped horde below and judged there to be thousands of warriors and horses. In his life, he had never seen such a vast army or display of military power and he wondered how those few hundred pious Templars and their like could believe Outremer needed to grow and expand; the sheer numbers of Arabic, Egyptian, Turkish and other Muslims were impossible to defeat without massive reinforcements from Europe. It was rumoured that a new army was coming east; mainly French and German to defeat the unclean and James wondered how many were coming and how many would actually survive a battle with the massed ranks of the Damascan based force below. He remembered his father and brother talk of the Saracens; uneducated savages who were an affront to God and the Pope Himself had offered all Christendom the opportunity of forgiveness of all sins and entrance to the gates of heaven in exchange for a holy war against the Arabs. Living on the edge of Outremer had taught James that the Muslim was not an uneducated savage but actually one who had advanced medicine and culture and trade between the two sets of peoples would bring wealth and happiness to both parties; war was totally unnecessary yet was also the future for this realm. No man could stop it; it was an inevitable reality like the sun rising up every morning. He sighed and bowed his head just as the door opened and the hulking figure of the man who captured him entered; flanked by two armed Immortals.

"Feeling refreshed infidel?"

James nodded and refrained from speaking to a man who carried himself with the calm demeanour of confidence in his abilities. The idea that this was to be the man who beheaded him was not a comfortable one.

"The Ornament of Islam; Imad Ad-Din Atabec Zengi Al Malik Al Mansir respectfully awaits your presence in the Throne Room."

A trickle of excitement rippled through the veins and arteries of his body as he responded evenly.

"You treat your prisoners very well."

He rose from the bed as the silent warriors with scimitars drawn and held at their sides, the gleaming points of the blades in perfect line with their chins stationed themselves either side of his body.

"You were a worthy adversary, it is almost a shame that you will be slain tomorrow. Follow me."

The horse trader wiped the back of his hand on his dry lips and swallowed the bile that rose in his throat.

"You are a very courteous executioner."

The leader of the Immortals twisted his head to gaze upon James and smirked.

"What do they say in your book of lies; the Last Supper has been eaten and now you face Allah's wrath for your irreligious ways."

James stifled a response and followed obediently up the winding staircase; past black clad servants and guards; ever higher until a great door with the Arabic words carved upon it; *Fighter of Jihad.*

"Remain here."

Khalin ordered to the two swordsmen and he entered the great throne room of one of the most powerful men in the known world. James followed him, feigning an aura of confidence which had slowly deserted his body with every step up the stone staircase of the tower. If the dungeon had been opulent; the throne room was the most gaudily extravagant place he had ever stepped into. The chamber itself was circular; a polished wooden floor covered the central area; heavy wall tapestries depicting Islamic victories covered garishly painted walls. A raised dais at one end of the room had a great golden throne upon which the figure of Zengi sat; back straight and staring with stark interest at the prisoner. James moved into the centre of the empty wooden floor; the larger armed man a yard behind him; his face illuminated by the many bronze candelabras and wall mounted torches; all burning brightly. The rest of the room held no significance for the man from Outremer as he locked eyes with the powerful leader of the Islamic forces.

"Khalin; fetch the man a drink; I have need of conversation and his lips do not need to be parched."

The great warrior began to move towards a low table in the eastern side of the room but James replied loudly; responding in Arabic so that every one of the eight half hidden armed guards stationed next to each of the large pillars in the room could hear his words.

"Do not concern yourself Khalin, I am choosy who I drink with...."

A flash of anger crossed the seated man's face but he controlled it well; forcing a throaty chuckle.

"You are angry; it is understandable. You are my prisoner; you have failed to do whatever it is you have come here to do. But please, try and be civil; I realise you Christians struggle with manners or I shall be forced to kill you now....slowly and painfully rather than give you the swift death I am told you deserve."

James remained stoically quiet; preferring to stare blankly at the man who was older than he had believed; his body; which presumably had once been muscular was now fat and the saggy flesh could be seen under his colourful robes.

"Now, is it true that you were sent to kill me? By whom? The boy; Baldwin or his mother; Melisende; the Templars? Egyptian court?"

Zengi spat out the words in quick succession and James shook his head slowly in a theatrical fashion.

"I was not sent by anyone; although it is true many people want you dead."

The man guffawed in response, bringing his flabby hand down onto the edge of his throne.

"I am not afraid of enemies who send one man to slay me as I lie sleeping; they should be afraid me who will send ten thousand to destroy their towns; burning them to the ground."

James cocked his head to observe the Atabeg and wondered if the rumours of his madness were not in fact truth.

"I was not sent by anyone. I came to kill you of my own free will."

Zengi peered through the brightness of the flickering torches and candles, squinting as he considered the words.

"May I ask why? Are you some sort of Christian fanatic?"

The man of English and Venetian blood forced a brief laugh before answering coldly.

"Far from it. I have no interest in any religion; it is not because of an old man in robes in Rome that I came here for your blood."

Khalin's hand twitched involuntarily on the ornate handle of his great scimitar; the insolence shown by this prisoner was unknown and to his master in the throne room of the tower was almost too much to cope with. The muscled body of the warrior placed one step towards the white man but halted immediately at the briefest shake of Zengi's head. James turned his attention briefly to the man behind him who literally bristled with indignation and his dark eyes swam with molten fury. The self-proclaimed Lion of Islam smiled widely; showing perfect white teeth as the infidel focused his blank stare back upon him.

"Forgive the man Khalin; the dogs of the sea lack courtly etiquette and respect no one."

James tossed his head back and laughed loudly; his confidence returning as a dead man walking had no need of fear.

"You speak of manners? You; who sacked a city and slaughtered hundreds of unarmed men, women and children in Edessa. You speak of manners yet embark on genocide. You can keep your courtly etiquette; I do not respect a filthy murderer of innocents....."

The angry tirade was halted as he was struck hard on the back of his neck with the bronze hilt of a weapon and he sprawled unceremoniously onto the animal skin rug before him. As he turned to face his attacker; his eyes narrowed as the tip of Khalin's scimitar touched his exposed cheek.

"Speak another word in anger and I shall remove your eyes right now!"

The tension was removed as Zengi dropped softly in cushioned shoes to the floor from the magnificent throne.

"Enough Khalin; he will be dead soon enough. Let me educate the barbarian on the history of my land."

James rose to his feet cautiously as the scimitar was removed from his face and the hostile warrior stepped backwards, bowing to his superior.

"You are too young to remember how your people rejoiced in the slaughter at Jerusalem some forty years ago. Over ten thousand of my brothers and sisters were lost. Burnt alive, decapitated, cut down as they begged for their lives; the city streets ran with the blood of my people. None were left alive; not a woman or a child was spared. This is war; a holy war; jihad. You are my enemy, your people are my people's enemy; Allah has decreed it so that you must all die and our lands be cleansed of your defilement."

Wisely, the man from Acre remained silent; attempting and failing to control his heavy breathing. His hazel eyes watched the man intently as he strode around the throne room, gesticulating with his hands; his eyes flashing with exultance as he warmed to his theme.

"Now, tell me who sent you to slay me and why? My patience is not my greatest virtue and the concept of watching you die slowly and painfully in front of me is becoming more appealing by the second."

James straightened his back and looked deeply into the man of power's eyes.

"Some weeks ago, some men, dressed as he..."

He paused for dramatic effect to incline his head towards the towering Khalin.

"... Murdered a seven year old boy, an elderly woman, her two sons who worked for me together with one of my oldest friends and his entire family; including his wife and children. I found out you ordered these massacres. I made an oath to myself that I would not rest until the man who had ordered such deaths would be killed himself by my own hand."

The antagonistic words resonated in the throne room and Zengi's response surprised all in the circular chamber. He broke out into raucous laughter and settled himself back onto the cushioned, bejewelled high backed chair; only managing to speak after the ripples of laughter emptied from his chest.

"So you came here alone across the sea of sand to kill me; surrounded as I am by my warriors in my tower, blessed as the chosen one to lead my people by Allah himself. You came because some of my men killed those that were close to you?"

James seethed with impotent fury; realising that he would not ever get within a few yards of the man before he would be cut down from all sides. He swallowed his rage and remained mute in the face of the mockery and scorn.

"So you were the man who saved that traitorous bitch Nadirah; aah…it all becomes clear. Foolishly your gallant saving of a woman from assassins sent by me; a woman who deserved death for allying herself to another man behind my back caused me to send out more men to slay those that had saved her. I believed you were Christians who she had allied herself to and would bring an army to my gates. Now of course, I realise my mistake; you were being a knightly hero saving the poor defenceless woman."

The chuckling in between the words poured more heat onto the flickering flame within the soul of a man who had nothing to lose. James leapt forwards as he heard the footfalls of the armed guards all around him. His opponent merely grinned as he could see the scene before him and knew the guards would catch James before he came within reach and the horse trader was closed in on all sides by raised weaponry. He brought his body to a standstill; surrounded by a mass of sharp metal. The wall of steel opened and Khalin strode towards him; his face contorted into a snarl of hatred.

"We kill him now my lord?"

Zengi shook his head firmly.

"No no, this is a good day. Let the man have one more day in the sun. The man is brave if perhaps short on brains; I believed the false prophecy that a great Christian knight shall cross my path; not one man with a vendetta to pursue. He shall be publically executed tomorrow and then only one more problem remains to be resolved. You have informed the army we move to deal with the traitor who conspires against me; tell my two sons they shall ride with me at the head of the Immortals to defeat The Kurd general; Naim al-Din Ayyub – the actual traitor who the bitch; Nadirah was allying with against me. Once that thorn is removed; we march on Jerusalem."

James was pushed forcefully towards the door and he turned to face the enemy once again.

"You can send me to hell tomorrow but I will be there waiting for you and your soul is hell bound; I know that for a fact and maybe I will not kill you in this life but in the next I will kill you; over and over and over. You can have my body but I will have your soul."

The head of the Islamic forces watched as the angry young man was forcibly removed from the great throne room towards his bed chamber and his last night on earth and his grin disappeared. A cold shiver touched him and he looked to the window but saw not a trace of breeze or wind. His body shook involuntarily and he felt suddenly very isolated and alone; a feeling of morbid desolation blanketing his body.

Chapter 36

A Plan Unfurls

Ishmael yawned unflatteringly and rubbed his tired eyes. He loathed guard duty at night. The gatehouse was bleak, cold and it stood at the top of over a mile of a winding track that wound around the craggy outcrop of sandstone; which dwarfed the ancient city of Damascus beneath it. At the bottom of the trail lay the sleeping encampment of the great army which was gathering to defeat the renegade Kurdish general; who had been called a traitor to Islam by the illustrious leader of the Arab peoples; Zengi himself. From there; the rumour was that they would lay siege to the centre of the world; the Holy City; Jerusalem, which had lay in Christian hands for almost half a century. Due to the simple fact that thousands of faithful warriors were camped on the eastern edge of the city, at the base of the tower; Ishmael did not fully comprehend the logic of guarding the gatehouse from enemies. However, he was a proud supporter of the Lion of Islam and the great man had enemies within Islam and without; even yesterday, a Christian assassin had been despatched to slay him and had been caught and would be publically executed in the city tomorrow; a sign that Zengi's star was rising and he would embark on a series of battles which would defeat the traitors, the Christians and bring rebel towns within his sway and more importantly; the crescent would be raised in the Holy City once more.

He puffed out his chest in pride and smiled in the darkness; proud to be a small part of this history making campaign. Born in the northern Seljuk territories; known as the Sultanate of Rum, he was like many of the chosen Immortals; the same race as Zengi. The army below was a sprawling mass of bodies from all over the Islamic world but only those horse warriors

435

of the northern territories could wear the black cloaks and black leather breastplate of the Immortals; the Atabeg's personal and elite guard.

The low snoring of his comrade; Al-Dair brought his attention back to where he sat with his back against the half open gate. Ishmael smiled wider as he thought of kicking the idle Anatolian harshly awake but thought against it, on balance; Al-Dair may be very indolent by nature but his temper when raised; was like a wounded, vicious camel so he turned away from the sleeping guard and focused instead on two shadowy figures moving towards the gatehouse from the sloping trail. Gripping his scimitar, he stepped forwards slightly; peering into the darkness to try and make out who the newcomers were. Again, the thought of kicking the Anatolian awake flickered through his mind but he chose against it as the figures came into view; a smaller burkha clad female was being pushed roughly by one of the Muslim warriors who bore the helmet and cloak of the Syrian contingent who excelled at the use of the spear which he carried in his right hand and used his left to force the woman ahead of him.

"Halt and state your reasons for entry into the tower."

Ishmael held his hand up palm outwards and held his weapon in his right hand.

"Can you tell this man to stop pushing me? I am a servant here at the tower and he calls me a thief because I had linen to be washed with me as I walked down the trail. Please, help me. Don't let him hurt me...."

The woman rushed pleadingly at the guard who lowered his weapon as she removed the material from her face to show that she was in her middle teens and very attractive. He turned his head momentarily to watch the man stride towards them both and he smiled at the girl.

"Don't worry! I am sure we can come to some arrangement young one."

Ishmael sheathed his sword and directed his attention back to the warrior who was heading towards him just that slight touch too fast, his sixth sense failing him badly at the very moment he knew that it was wrong. It was also the moment that the helmeted man grabbed him roughly by the throat and pushed him against the wall of the gatehouse; winding him; the strong hand restricting his windpipe; not allowing any air or sound to erupt from his constricted oesophagus. His eyes widened in growing terror as burning pain erupted in his abdomen and he felt his knees sink to the ground. The hand now twisted over his mouth and nose as he watched impotently, as if in a dream, as the knife viciously stabbed him again. With his life force draining away, his last realisation was that the attackers' eyes were sapphire blue.

"Look away."

Alessio ordered sternly; perspiring profusely under the awkward heavy helmet and cloak; unused to such apparel as he hissed at Aisha who was staring incredulously at the fresh corpse. The Venetian moved silently in his soft leather boots across to the snoring second guard and sweeping the hushed gatehouse with his keen eyesight; he gripped the man's mouth to stifle any sound and as the frightened man's eyes bulged in horror; Alessio slit his throat with exceptional skill he was not proud of having. Easing the heavy body to the ground, he looked at both dead men and moved back to the first killing and began to disrobe the deceased's prone body.

Aisha headed to the half opened gate and looked beyond, across the flattened courtyard towards the low building beyond; which she believed to be the guardhouse. There was no sign of movement and no sound; with the exception of her erratic breathing; which was so loud she thought the whole tower would hear the frantic beating of her heart inside her chest. Placing the keffiyah in place, so only her eyes were visible; she craned her neck to see Alessio hurriedly exchange clothing to become one of the feared 'Immortals'. Attaching the breast plate and cloak; he struggled with the turban styled head ware and she rushed to help him in making it look authentic and wrapped it firmly in place. They exchanged a grim nod and strode through the gatehouse with the false confidence of a troubadour; sweeping through the courtyard and up the stone steps to enter the tower itself.

A snoozing guard started as they stepped into the first cold stone hallway but managed only a bored glance at a serving girl and fellow Immortal, before closing his weary eyes again. A few flickering torches in iron rings high up on the walls were the only illumination and they headed to the landing; where the staircase headed upwards or downwards. In every civilization known to Alessio; dungeons were always underground so he pointed silently downwards and Aisha nodded in agreement as the two furtive figures padded down the steep steps. The stone steps came to an end a few yards below ground level at a heavy door and gripping the handle; Alessio strode inside; happy that the door was unlocked. Stepping inside a long, narrow room; he studied the rough-hewn rock floor; the walls bare and unadorned; a simple wooden table in the centre of the room where the remains of a meal on a wooden platter sat. The stench of human excrement, urine, body odour and blood assailed his nostrils and he motioned for Aisha to remain the other side of the door as the sounds of violence could be heard behind one of the numerous closed doors which opened out from the chamber.

Placing the ungainly spear on the table, Alessio unsheathed two if his throwing knives and moved swiftly to the door which was the home of the unwelcome sounds. Placing his foot against the door, he eased it open; holding the tip of his first knife in his right hand.

As the wood slowly swung open, the scene in the small dungeon cell became alarmingly clear. A large man in a leather tunic was abusing a smaller, frail looking man; who was naked and on his knees. The kneeling man failed in his rather pitiful attempts at defending himself from being struck with some form of wooden club and now he simply begged for mercy, as his body and face was awash with fresh blood. Alessio hurled the perfectly balanced knife at the protagonist who whirled around in surprise only to have the blade embed itself deep into his shoulder. Dropping the blood splattered club to the filth and straw strewn floor, he grabbed at the bone handle to try and withdraw the dagger but a second knife tore through flesh as it struck his left cheek, causing him to crumple to the ground. Leaping deftly beside the stricken enemy; he calmly ended his life by slicing through the jugular vein at his throat and gripping his mouth shut to avoid any final death cry. The whimpering man scuttled away on all fours to the corner of the tiny cell and began jabbering in Arabic. Alessio cursed and headed back outside; whispering Aisha's name and the worried looking teenager appeared; following the Venetian's hand directions and entered the dungeon. Shuffling in; the young Syrian woman's eyes widened as she observed yet another fresh corpse and then allowed her companion to hold either side of her head and looked into his soft blue eyes.

"We have no time for fear. Ask the man if he knows where James is; there are twelve doors; the dead guards could be discovered any second and if we are here; we will be killed. Be strong for me...for us all...please?"

His breathless urging informed Aisha of his own urgent concerns and she nodded, her dark eyes darting to the beaten prisoner and crouched to be alongside the forlorn, frightened man and spoke in a soft intonation. The man from Outremer retrieved his throwing knives, wiped them on the dead man's breeches and sheathed them; moving into the main room again and picking up the spear; wondering which of the many cells his friend would be in and what state he would be in, when they discovered him. He felt the cold sensation of perspiration dripping under his clothing and armour; his hands were clammy and his breathing ragged; fear was an odd numbing feeling and he waited impatiently for Aisha to reappear with some good news. The seconds dragged on into minutes and with the seconds seeming like minutes and the minutes seeming like hours; his awareness of the situation they had gotten themselves into was becoming unbearable.

"He is not here. He was. The man heard them speak and he was taken to the bedchambers upstairs; those for guests. They are on the floor below the throne room; as in the top of the tower. What do we do now?"

Her voice was shrill, high pitched and laden with emotion. Alessio gripped her shoulders and looked deep into her eyes.

"Go tell that poor wretch to unlock all the prisoners' doors and allow them all to escape in a few minutes. We will need a diversion. Now, breathe deep, we go upstairs. Stay close."

Aisha almost instantly argued against the insanity of the course of action; she could feel tears welling within her but after the immediate swell of terror, she knew they had to continue. To be this close and to flee in panic was clearly not an option for either of them at this final stage in their arduous journey. She darted back into the cell and relayed Alessio's positive message to the terrified blood covered man but as she returned to her companion; she saw hope flicker in the captive's eyes and she set her jaw in a determined fashion and rushed up the stone steps after the oldest friend of the man she saw as her father.

The dilettante from Acre moved cautiously up the steep winding flagstones; attempting to look normal without creating suspicion. He ignored three floors; which all seemed to be kitchen areas, store rooms or sleeping barracks but on the fourth landing; an alert guard stood with his spear across the carved archway which led to the hall and doorways beyond. The young man in his early twenties scrutinised the newcomer; clearly not recognising him and placed his spear across the entrance as he and a serving girl strode forwards.

"You know the armoury and weapon smith's quarters are restricted, what......"

The harsh stated words were lost in an anguished gurgle as Alessio punched him viciously in the throat without breaking his stride pattern or giving any hint of the impending assault. Deftly, he caught the spear in one hand before it struck the floor and elbowed the guard in the bridge of the nose; hearing the sickening crunch of bone. Tossing the spear gently to a shocked Aisha; who caught the quivering shaft in both hands, he grabbed the dazed Muslim roughly by his hair and brought his knee swiftly up to the broken nose to inflict further damage. Losing consciousness, the guard did not feel the knife blade ending his life.

"What did he say; I couldn't understand the words?"

The assassin whispered and Aisha placed the heavy spear against the wall and repeated what the man's last words had been. Alessio swore and pointed upwards, Aisha nodded in return and both climbed to the next landing in grim determination. Nearing the top of the tower; both sets of lungs were working overtime and both sets of legs were getting weary and as the landing appeared; two guards sat either side of the archway and one of them immediately enquired about their appearance.

"Why are you here? Nobody but our Master is allowed in the harem!"

Alessio attempted to understand the words but his rudimentary Arabic, taught in a few days was deserting him already and the unintelligible words hung in silence.

"He is taking me to the Christian prisoner...."

Aisha intervened swiftly; feigning disgust in her voice. Her agile brain saving the situation instantly. The man chuckled drily and winked at his comrade who grinned lasciviously.

"Well he dies tomorrow; I guess he deserves a good last night on earth. Next floor; guest bedchamber; it is the only one guarded."

Aisha nodded her thanks and rolled her eyes as the two men clapped each other on the back and made crude comments as she headed upwards with Alessio now in tow; slightly confused and more alarmed now than before at the lack of understanding   . Reaching the next stone landing; Aisha leant close to him and explained what she had said and the response she had received.

"Clever girl. I am impressed."

Alessio grinned and with a nod to each other, the two began to head down the passageway into the guest bed chamber area with the animal skin rugs covering the floor, lit torches in ornate bronze brackets and papyrus maps and drawings on the walls. A show of riches and power for all of his guests; be they diplomats of enemies, important neutral powers or allies. Only one of the numerous doors had a guard stood outside and the unlikely couple shared a swift knowing look as they approached it. The guard stiffened as the two figures moved towards him and asked the obvious question.

"What are you doing here?"

Aisha bowed her head and said distastefully.

"I am from the harem; the infidel's last wish."

The man smiled broadly at Alessio who responded in kind.

"And you get to watch I suppose? Lucky man! The dog is asleep I think; but I am sure you can wake him up in your own sweet, special way."

With a soft laugh he turned and unlocked the door, opening it to make sure that the occupant was well away from the immediate vicinity. The guard never turned around. The white hot bolt of pain tore through his body and he tried to scream but a powerful hand clamped over his mouth as he tottered and then collapsed inside the chamber with a hefty weight on his back; a second thrust of steel into his upper abdomen crushed major arteries and a third deep stab ended his life. Dragging the body inside; Alessio looked upwards as Aisha followed him into the room and closed the door behind them.

James sprang from the bed where he has been pretending to sleep, waiting for this last slim chance of escape or being killed in the attempt; either fate, he believed better than the one that awaited him tomorrow. He gripped the engraved, glazed clay jug which had housed the Syrian wine he had emptied out under his bed earlier that evening and he balanced on the balls of his feet, hunched and ready to leap forward against the Immortal. His eyes; accustomed to the gloom of the chamber; widened in incredulous surprise as he watched the newcomer stab the guard to death before his eyes. The murderer stood upright and stated simply in Italian:

"James! Praise God you are alive!"

The recognition of the voice registered into the whirring of his confused mind and he peered in the darkness.

"Alessio?"

The man removed his helmet and James dropped the improvised weapon to the thick rug and stared open mouthed; no semblance of a coherent sentence could be managed; just words uttered through the sheer astonishment.

"How? Why? What the.....I don't understand...."

Alessio sheathed his knife and embraced his stunned friend briefly.

"You have no idea how good it is to see you alive....now; no time for explanations; we have to get out of here quickly; there are dead guards littered all over the place."

James nodded and stepped back from the embrace as he saw a woman move from the darkest shadows of the walls and remove the black keffiyah which hid her face. He could manage only one word before tears welled in his eyes.

"Aisha!"

The young woman bolted into his opening arms and she almost crushed him with her tight, emotional clasp. His hands stroked her hair and kissed her cheek tenderly.

"What the hell are you doing here and let me look at you. Are you ok?"

He fussed and she scowled in response and slapped him hard across the face; his cheek stinging from the harsh smack.

"Don't ever leave me again, don't ever not share your thoughts, don't ever...."

Her condemnation choked in her throat as the tears

rolled down her dark cheeks and James made soothing noises and cradled her head against his chest.

"I am so sorry Aisha; I promise never to do this again."

Alessio grabbed his friend's arm and urged frantically.

"Dress in the dead guy's clothes and let's get the hell out of here – we have no time for explanations or recriminations. Let's go – please!"

Aisha nodded and reluctantly let her guardian go and refitted the material across her face as James swiftly exchanged clothing. Once he had finished, the three of them looked at each other in turn and managed thin smiles; heading out of the door and closing it behind them. With Alessio leading them; James and Aisha held hands behind him as he made his way down the illuminated corridor; their footfalls cushioned by the straw mattresses that covered all the stone floors of the thoroughfares on each level.

"I cannot."

James stated suddenly and stopped, releasing his grip on his young ward. Alessio looked behind and swore under his breath as Aisha literally pulled on his arm towards the last two guards and the relative safety of the steps which led down. Just as Aisha was about to plead earnestly to James; a metal gong peeled out from many floors below them and all eyes swept downwards towards the echoing warning noise; which was followed by the sounds of doors opening and shouts.

"Must be the prisoners...."

James looked in bewilderment at his oldest friend who uttered the explanation that meant nothing to him; his response was equally cryptic.

"I have to finish this. Once and for all."

Aisha cried out in anguish as James blurted out an apology and rushed to where the two guards had been but now; there was no sight of them. With a last glance to Aisha, he rushed past the bemused Venetian and bounded up the stone steps to the throne room above; tugging the scimitar out of the leather scabbard as he did so.

"Alessio....?"

The girl; whose tears had begun to flow again sought out some form of solution from the desperate looking Italian; who shrugged in resignation and followed the other man up the steps; barking at Aisha to stay there and look out for any trouble. The teenager considered berating Alessio for stating such a stupid remark as clearly all three of them were in about as much danger and trouble as they could be already but wisely thought not to mention this at this particular juncture. Her hands tightened into fists as she waited impatiently; a wave of panic about to crush her small shore of hope and using one of Alessio's many colourful expletives; swore profusely as she strode around the small landing; staring at the now empty steps which led to the top of the tower. Unable to stand still, she cursed again and followed the two men up the flight of steps into the unknown.

Chapter 37

The Final Battle

James strode meaningfully into the throne room; the torches and candles still lit; illuminating the great circular chamber in a dim, shimmering light. Fully expecting to find the room void of life completely or heavily guarded as it was earlier in the day, he was both surprised and grateful that the only figure in the area of his vision was Zengi himself, hunched over the throne; empty wine bottles, bronze goblets and silver jugs lay scattered across the animal furs before him. Gripping the ivory handled scimitar, he rapidly approached the man who had damaged his very soul, a man who had crushed the beauty of life, replacing it with the destructive forces of hatred and unquenchable vengeance. His footfalls echoed softly around the expensively furnished room; causing the Lion of Islam to raise his weary, drunken head.

"Wake up; time to die!"

The man of European ancestry raised his blade and slowed his stride pattern to savour the moment; his eyes focused on the man who had to die to allow him to live a more normal existence; or at least; this was the hope. His attention fully on the man who commanded thousands of troops, he failed to see the blur of movement to his left until the very last moment, managing to avoid the swinging scimitar by bringing up his own sword but the power of the attack was too much and ill-prepared; his own hand weapon clattered to the ground and he leapt backwards, away from immediate mortal danger. The rasping chuckle of the wine laden leader radiated menacingly from the throne as James retreated from the athletic frame of Khalin; clad in his hardened leather armour but without the cape. He wore no helmet; his bull like neck and unattractive features contorted into a snarl as he tossed the handle of the enormous scimitar easily from left to right hand, following his prey around the vast area as a prowling wolf before a lamb.

"You have to be a man of honour and skill to wear that uniform infidel...."

A twisted smirk closely followed the mocking statement and James responded evenly; grinning at the angry man.

"I will tell that to the corpse I took it from...."

The goading worked and the larger man stormed forward; his scimitar rose for a downward stroke. James moved his position, balancing on his toes as he prepared to dodge and then kick out at the midriff of his opponent. The ferocious attack never came however and in mid stride pattern, the leader of the Immortals grunted and twisted his body, as if struck by an invisible assailant. A second, more pitiful cry erupted from his throat as he stumbled and dropped to the lion skin and James smiled broadly as he watched Alessio dart forwards from the doorway. He then noticed the two throwing knives embedded in the upper and lower back of the unfortunate Khalin as he lay, struggling to breathe on the ground, gasping for air. Working at speed, James gripped the bone handle of one of the daggers and removed it from his bloodied back before stabbing it deep into the back of the prone man's neck, ending his life in an instant. Whirling around, he grinned at the man who cowered now on his ornate throne; the mocking laughter immediately ceasing with the death of his second champion to this man in a matter of weeks.

"Guards! Guards!"

He shouted; his voice shrill and hoarse with terror.

"Watch the door Alessio! Let no one past."

James boomed and keeping his body low and the knife in his right hand poised; he sprinted forwards. Zengi struggled to lift his bulky frame from the elaborate chair upon the raised dais and he gripped one of the silver candelabra; throwing it towards the assassin. Ducking comfortably under the poor attempt at stalling his advance; the lit candles struck the wall and the sparks of the hot wax set light to the tinder dry tapestry; setting fire to the costly piece of art. Falling unceremoniously from the throne, Zengi moved as quickly as he could to the far wall and pulled out a burning torch from the bronze bracket and swung it wildly before him as James moved ever nearer; his eyes as cold as ice and a look of pure hatred adorning his features.

Once, not so many years ago, the Atabeg had been a skilful warrior and he reined in his fear; using the torch as a make shift weapon, he circled this mortal enemy; taking care to remain just outside the man's reach of his short bladed knife. Alessio watched the two men from across the room; his senses heightened as he expected a tidal wave of Islamic warriors to rush up the stone steps as he heard rapid footfalls behind him. The alarming thought of how he was supposed to not let a host of heavily armed men past rode roughshod through his mind. He unsheathed another knife and aimed the perfectly balanced blade at the as yet unseen figures but the only entrant onto the landing was a tearful and frightened looking Aisha. Scurrying to the Venetian, she huddled into his lithe frame and both watched the room in silence.

Consumed by molten hatred and blinded by ferocious rage, James dodged and weaved through the heavy yet clumsy swings of the ornate torch, the burning wood scattering hot embers and ash around the room. The cold hazel eyes followed the tiring, corpulent older man, waiting for the exact moment to strike. Zengi cursed and kicked over the gem incrusted silver table, sending the remaining bottles and assorted wine containers flying, the alcohol merely adding fuel to the growing blaze. James chose that moment to dart forward, slashing the blade of the knife across the larger man's left cheek as he was slightly off balance. Zengi dropped the weapon and staggered backwards, bouncing off the wall and ripping an ancient papyrus map from it, in his stricken haste to retreat. The thin wound opened up on the flabby cheek and the sight of the crimson blood flowing through the flesh brought a satisfying, icy smile to the horse trader's lips, a shiver of excitement rippling through his body. He moved fluidly to block off the man's exit, grinning maliciously as he could see the fear in the opponent's wide eyes, revelling in the sheer sense of abandonment from morality or conscience, losing himself completely to the delicious all-consuming feeling of vengeance.

Alessio patted the girl's shoulder reassuringly and turned back in increasing apprehension as he watched the scene unfold before them in the throne room, the fire was spreading rapidly across the chamber, the various wall hangings acting like tinder to the flames that devoured them hungrily, burning everything consumable in its path as it sought more and more nourishment. The Venetian murmured something unintelligible in a soothing tone to Aisha who gasped in growing panic as she watched the rugs, skins, paintings and furniture begin to burn throughout the room as the two men circled each other like sinister dark shadows in the smoke that was beginning to cloud her vision.

Zengi swore under his breath and wiped the blood and perspiration from his face, the disorientating cocktail of too much wine, the increasing swirling strands of smoke and the palpable fear of his own mortality causing increasing concern. Fumbling for another torch from the wall, he grasped one in both hands and released it from its metal cage, waving it frantically in a semblance of an arc before him, to keep the omnipresent assailant away. Panic began to swell and his chest tightened as he wondered where his guards were, who must have heard the sounds of battle and the acrid stench of burning and he had himself heard the gong that sounded the alarm minutes ago. He wondered if they had betrayed him too, flashes of faces of all the traitors he had executed passed before his mind's eye and before the seemingly endless array of visages could be exhausted, intense pain erupted from his chest. His thoughts scattered like birds in a desert storm as he watched with an agonised scream, the knife tear through material, skin, flesh and arteries. The blade was instantly yanked roughly out again, causing greater torture as it sliced open his chest again. The man of many titles lurched backwards against the wall again and his shaking hands dropped the burning torch to the floor as he slumped to his knees, his wide eyes recoiling in fear from the white devil that had haunted his dreams for so long since that damned old crone and her prophecy.

James thrust the dagger into the man's abdomen and twisted the lethal blade into vital organs, ignoring the hideous squelching sounds or the warm rush of blood that flowed onto his own hand. Gripping the dying man's oiled hair, he forced the self-proclaimed Lion of Islam to have his last vision on earth before his descent to the netherworld as his own mocking sneer. Again the blade entered the prone body and again, thick viscous blood spewed forth over expensive silk robes. Oblivious to the smoke and increasing intensity of the blaze, lost to the temporary madness of man's lust for death and the power it provides, the once placid family man looked to the heavens and mocked the man's god. Bending down, he pressed his face close to the Atabeg's and listened to his final gasping, frantic breaths and smiled in grim satisfaction as the man whose actions had destroyed so much of his life died in front of his eyes.

"See you in hell...."

James whispered and dropped the blood stained knife to the floor as Alessio called from across the smoke filled, burning room, and the sound of shouting and plentiful footfalls clearly moving up the stone steps. The killer took a last lingering look at the fresh corpse and swiftly exited the burning room as Alessio gripped his shoulder and exclaimed feverishly;

"The guards are coming; we have to get out of here...now!"

James pulled a helmet onto his head which covered most of his face and he instructed Alessio to do the same, immediately rushing down the steps to meet the enemy just as the incandescent flames of the fire licked out of the throne room and began to burn the woven straw rugs which covered the landings of each floor within the tower. Grabbing Aisha's hand, Alessio fixed his helmet clumsily into place and left the fire behind him, following his friend down the many stone steps, fearful and confused as to how they could possibly escape this nightmarish predicament. His face and heart sank as he saw James rush towards a group of Immortals and began jabbering at them frantically in Arabic.

"Our Master has been attacked but Khalin has taken him to safety, the slaves who escaped have set fire to the tower. His orders are to evacuate everybody – immediately. Now move!"

The warrior no more than nineteen summers old took in this information and looked dubiously up at the entrails of smoke now wisping towards them from above. A harsh shove from James secured his acquiescence and he nodded, screaming to his comrades who clamoured on the stairwell behind him. The men began to retreat backwards down to the next landing but the murmurings of discontent were clearly heard by the three fugitives and James took control of the situation forcefully again, screaming to all of the congregated Immortals, now numbering more than ten.

"If you need to check on my orders, head upstairs but may Allah protect you from his wrath."

A larger man moved the youthful warrior out of his way with a single wave of his hand and with a dismissive glare at James, he pounded upstairs, calling for buckets of water to be gained from the kitchen. Taking advantage of this sense of confusion with warriors hurtling themselves down the steps to deal with a 'slave uprising' below, others heading upstairs to the burning throne room or following the 'Atabeg's' orders to exit the building, James led Alessio and Aisha down the steps, barking out guttural orders as he did so, knowing full well that the real alarm would be raised soon enough when the dead bodies of Zengi and Khalin were found and his lies would be uncovered. Before they were down to the fourth landing, shouting and cursing could be heard above but in all the bewildering perplexity, the screaming of 'stop him' and 'He is dead' was lost amidst the chaos, only a few understanding the truth of the developments at this moment in time.

With so much mystification tossed around, James continued to spread misinformation as he moved down each level of the tower, doing everything his quick witted mind allowed him to create further disorder. Alessio followed with his head down, Aisha close behind him, almost not daring to believe that they could get out of this alive. James was more positive, his brain whirled faster than his aching feet and yet he knew getting out of the tower would be the first step of a number of problems to resolve and he wondered if fire and chaos would work a second time. In the sickening absence of any better concepts, his mind fervently hoped they would as the three of them hit the ground floor level of the tower, the bustling inhabitants of the building all around them. Servant and warrior alike bore the look of fear and flush of excitement as the noise of the clamour and mayhem enveloped the fortification. Clipped sentences were caught as the three figures rushed through the mass of bodies and James was satisfied with the sheer scale of upheaval he had induced with the most prolific words being; slaves, escape, assassin, fire, traitor and murder.

The gong sounded again, the low rumbling sound reverberating around the cylindrical, dense walls and James turned to look into his two more fearful looking companion's eyes.

"Stay close....."

Pushing through the confounded congregation of hushed Muslims, James strode arrogantly, continuing to bark orders indiscriminately, forcing a path through the milling crowd and through the gatehouse, heading down the slope and walking swiftly around the first corner of the meandering dusty trail. A scattering of serving girls, servants and warriors moved haphazardly towards the city as well as towards the tower. The sense of foreboding, concern and confusion hung heavy in the night sky above them all and with every passing yard in the comforting cloak of pitch darkness, their hopes rose little by little.

Aisha quickened her stride pattern to keep up with the two men who marched in silence on either side of her. She could hear the beating of her heart in her ears, it sounded like some crazed drummer was beating it for all he was worth and she tried to make out each of the man's faces in the gloom. James looked drawn; he had lost weight and bore cuts, bruises and scars but most importantly, he wore a more ethereal burden she desperately needed to help him carry. He looked as if he had aged years since she had seen him last. She saw the simple chain and the pendant which bore Jacob's name was still around his neck and it warmed her a little but her very essence hurt as she looked upon that face and swore inwardly that she would never let him out of her sight until he was back to his old self. He had spent years protecting her, being a father for her and now it was her turn to repay that debt. James needed her and she would be there for him no matter what. Alessio in comparison looked alive, his senses were heightened and his nervousness was obvious to any who cared to look. The Venetian was afraid but determined and strangely, she felt a sense of pride for the man who had helped both James and her so much in the past few incredible weeks. Before all this madness had commenced, she had known and thought little of Alessio but he had proven to be a man of honour and worth and she was determined to say so to his sister when they returned safely back to Acre. Her mind dwelt on the word 'when' in that sentence and refused to use the word 'if', as her brain strove fervently for positivity, her left hand reached for James in the dark and smiled as his palm closed around hers, the fleeting flash of his teeth in a brief smile illuminated the night more than he would ever know.

James dropped his gaze to Aisha for a moment and then turned to look ahead, the trail was sloping and uneven and he had to be careful at the pace they were walking not to lose his footing. His heart sang as he looked at the girl he loved as a daughter, the sickness in his soul lifted in her presence and to know that Alessio and her had come looking for him and indeed, saved his life and enabled him to rid the world of a man who had almost succeeded in dragging his very spirit into the unfathomable depths of the abyss was nothing short of a miracle.

The lanterns, torches and cooking fires of the great army blazed ever nearer as their steps followed the winding path towards the base camp of the late Zengi's massed army. Through the murk of the early sunrise, which was slowly breaking through the blanket of night, creating a sliver of light on the horizon, James could make out the shouts of alarm and a cacophony of noise commencing ahead of them as the muezzin rang out from the tower, warning the faithful of danger. He knew not whether this was the raging fire or of the death of their illustrious leader and he cared little in truth. Stay calm his head urged, they did not look out of place and under cover of darkness and with the hysterical confusion around them, they had every chance of getting into the maze of narrow alleys and back streets of Damascus alive. A flicker of hope ignited in his chest and he suddenly realised that he had not experienced that feeling for some considerable time. He also realised very clearly that he liked it.

A trickle of frightened refugees from the tower were now mingling with the waking members of the army and frantic, puzzled exchanges were taking place with many pointed fingers outstretched towards the flames that flickered in the distance atop the stone tower, smoke billowing from the windows and balconies. Entering the camp, the three figures drifted through wraithlike, James and Aisha occasionally mentioning slave uprising and traitors within the elite bodyguards of the Atabeg to any Muslim who approached them. The swathe of confusion stretched over the massed ranks of the army just as it had done in the tower and the flicker of hope began to erupt further within all three of the escapees.

Dawn was breaking as the trio finally picked their way through the tents, cooking fires and weapon racks of the camp and entered Damascus through the ruins of the archaic Roman built wall, quickening their pace as they rushed through the dusty lanes and filth strewn alleys of the Old City, avoiding the great bazaar and its souks, the city's traders already waking in their droves. Sprinting through the less salubrious quarter of the ancient city, the three characters came to a standstill behind a clay pot stall and James grinned at his two exhausted companions.

"Damn it all, I feel alive!"

Aisha hugged him energetically and held her slim weary

body close to his own. She winced inwardly as she could feel how thin he had become and she kissed his dirty, bloodied cheek.

"You need to eat something."

Her admonishment was accompanied with a genuine smile and Alessio interrupted the conversation by joining the embrace. His toned arms held each of them at the same time and chuckled.

"Can we all eat back in Outremer – I am not sure we can stay in this city in daylight with the Immortals crawling every street shortly!"

James kissed Aisha's forehead briefly and then kissed his oldest friends cheek.

"You are right my friend, let us get to a stable and get us some horses; we need to be out of here as soon as we can."

Aisha issued an excited snort and both men looked with amusement at the teenage girl.

"Merdlan is here – we can take him!"

Her rather bedraggled looking stepfather studied her flushed features and raised an eyebrow.

"Merdlan is alive?"
"Yes! I can take us there right now; we stabled him as soon as we saw him."

"And the woman and her children who rode him, did they live too?"

Aisha smiled and nodded and James thanked a deity he did not believe in.

"Come on for God's sake!"

457

Alessio interrupted them and shoved both backs in the vague direction of the stable.

The stable was a basic establishment a mere few minutes away and James studied the scene in contentment. The plan was as void of intrigue as their pouches were void of coin. With no option to purchase, the object was to steal Merdlan and another sturdy, healthy looking horse for the intense, interminable and hazardous journey westwards over the bleak ocean of sand for hundreds of miles and the relative safety of Outremer. Clad as they were in Immortals' black, tight fitting leather armour, soft under tunic and baggy Arabian style pants which were tied just below the knee, at the exact point where the leather boots began. Only two of Alessio's throwing knives remained in the wide belt of sheaths under his outer clothing and he carried the unwieldy large bladed scimitar. James had one of the daggers tucked in his belt and this was his only weapon, the eight foot long iron tipped spear had been lost somewhere in the tower in his rush to escape.

The Islamic city was slowly waking as the sun's powerful rays began its eternal battle with the night and as in the usual cycle of life; it was winning the war at dawn. The stable doors were open and the three outlanders hurriedly scurried across the compacted sand and entered the rickety, badly constructed building. Two boys were brushing and washing two horses in their separate hay strewn stalls. Aisha nodded to the one whom she remembered from their first meeting and spoke directly, explaining in a rather rude, succinct fashion that they were here for Merdlan and pointed to the great ebony stallion and as the boy nodded in understanding; James was already opening the flimsy wooden door and stroked his neck, the animal responding with a nuzzle of his cold nose and an excited snort of recognition. Bringing Merdlan out of the stall, the boy helped with the blanket and partial saddlebags; the last remnants of anything James had brought with him from Outremer. The youth was suspicious but more frightened of the weapon laden men so worked quickly and in stoical silence. Alessio studied the other mounts in the stable but gave up swiftly; he had no concept of a 'good' horse and motioned to James to choose one for him. A cursory glance followed with a nod of a head to an Arabian white and brown mare in the next wooden booth was enough for the Venetian dilettante to open the door and bring the healthy looking animal into clear view.

James checked over hooves, teeth and eyes, moved his hand across the flanks and under the taut stomach and nodded again to Aisha who advised the nervous stable hand that both animals would be made ready and taken. The second youthful worker rushed to prepare the other beast as Aisha mouthed the word 'coin' to James who shrugged with an apologetic grin. His ward closed her eyes in mock despair and deftly mounted Merdlan.

"I will ride him, you can be my guest."

She smiled with an over exaggerated blinking of her naturally long eye lashes and James gripped the pommel of the soft, Eastern style saddle and positioned himself behind Aisha, loading six full water skins across the small iron hooks on the bright red horse blanket.

"Fine by me, you do know how long we have to ride for don't you?"

He whispered in her ear as he placed his hands around her waist and kicked Merdlan's flank gently, adding with a wry grin.

"Alessio – pay the boy will you?"

The Italian smiled easily at the teenage workers as he checked for his leather money pouch, knowing it to be empty and watched his companions trot out of the stable in the direction of the Gates of Paradise and the bountiful orchards, meadows and pastures which lay beyond. Watching Merdlan gather speed to a brisk pace, Alessio clambered ungainly onto the back of the skittish mare and unhooked his pouch from the belt at his waist, tossing it to the freshly brushed wooden floor of the stable and urged his mount onwards. The nearest boy picked up the pouch and immediately began to complain as he felt no coin, shaking the emptiness furiously into his palm as if money would magically appear. This brought only a reaction of a swift, sharp kick to the mare and the sauntering horse began to trot and then canter and within seconds, was galloping through the awakening city and past Merdlan at pace. Hearing the warning cries behind them, Aisha could not repress a chuckle as she skilfully urged the stallion to follow at the same pace and the three companions bolted past puzzled and enraged Damascans whooping and laughing as relative freedom could be seen in the form of the 'Eden' esque gardens of plenty, which fed the tens of thousands of denizens within the city.

Workers stopped to stare in the early morning sun as the two horses galloped out of the city walls and through the orchards, taking their riders into the great desert trail which stretched for as far as the eye could see across the distant horizon.

Chapter 38

Return to the West

Aisha snored gently on his shoulder, her arms wrapped tightly around his stomach. In truth, James had been uncomfortable for hours but he had not the heart to wake the girl. The journey had been long, tedious and arduous. They had eaten precious little food until they had eventually reached the dangerous border town of Safed and only then did they eat their first hot meal in three days. The unknown, unrecognisable badly cooked meat, vegetables and herbs of the stew had been one of the best meals he had ever tasted. The water had almost run out by the time they had traversed the calm waters of Lake Tiberius and managed to thankfully refill their skins and stomachs. Travelling by night in the cooler temperatures and sheltering in dunes when available during the worst of the sun, had made all three frustrated, weary and on edge. The constant fear of being followed, caught or intercepted weighed heavily on all and incessant bickering or heavy silence had been the main diet of the journey. Without coin, they had threatened, stole, lied and deceived throughout the four days of hard riding but now, well inside Outremer's ever changing frontier, the two exhausted mounts cantered along the Merchants Trail south of Acre, merely minutes from the home of James, which he had not seen for weeks. His thoughts and feelings were mixed, as they had been for most of the return journey through the hundreds of miles of desolate desert, rock and scrubland. He knew deep inside that life would never be the same and that his quest had changed him fundamentally and permanently as a man.

Before the cataclysm had inexplicably exploded into his world, he had been a contented man; striving to build something worthwhile for his ever expanding family. Now, part of him knew that this would not be enough for him and that part was a dark, sinister side to his personality that he had allowed to exist over the past few weeks. It was as if he had made a covenant with the devil and once made, he feared that it was an eternal agreement. The house he had built with his own hands would always bear the ghost of those he had lost and Aisha had already advised him gently, yet strongly that she would never be able to live there again. He knew he would have to sell the small holding and the few days with the Bedouin people had shown him that a travelling merchant's life could be considered as an option. Aisha was less keen on this idea when broached initially; the girl wanted and required stability and security right now for her to mature into a woman. There was then the stark fact that he was tired, achingly tired of the religious and political issues of Outremer. War was coming again, perhaps his own very personal involvement bringing that war closer and more inevitable.

He shunted the thought away from his whirring mind and he traversed instead through the hours of conversation between the threesome; their shared experiences, the reasoning behind their individual actions, the tears, the laughter, the sorrow, the pain, the necessity. Discussions about how James became embroiled in the first place, in the paranoid, political machinations of the Fatimid Egyptian woman he had saved from assassins and the powerful, somewhat psychotic Islamic leader were held and the potential enormity of the results of the subsequent actions taken were analysed. All these things had been spoken and the path to redemption had been long and harsh for all three of them and each bore the scars; both physical and intangible. All would do so for the rest of their days.

He did feel more human again, almost whole once more but he was very far from naive and he knew deep within his being that he would never be the same man again. The road he had travelled had been tragic, intense and emotionally draining. The past six weeks had been the worst in his life, surpassing even the macabre days that followed his father's and brother's deaths. However, the veil of darkness that had descended upon his soul had now lifted a little and his thoughts were of the future more than the past, a healthier approach to life. He chided himself immediately; he wanted the present to be the most important time; a time to enjoy oneself as nobody could foretell what the next sunrise would bring. That simple fact, if nothing else, had been learnt on his journey.

Aisha unleashed a soft, contented sigh as she slept against his shoulder and he twisted in the blanketed saddle so he could look upon her pretty, youthful face and he felt genuine elation. There had been many times, particularly towards the end of his adventure that he had believed he would never see her face again, let alone be able to hold her and tell her how much he loved her and that he had been wrong to leave as he did. He had been wrong to embark on his path without discussing with her first. All this, he had informed her in the past few days and thankfully, she had forgiven him unconditionally and accepted the reasoning behind his decisions.

James glanced beside him to look upon Alessio as he rode the young mare, which had shown exceptional stamina during the hundreds of miles and the two men of Venetian descent exchanged warm smiles. His friend had shown immense character and fortitude in recent weeks and he was intrinsically proud of him; an emotion he had not often felt towards the man who had never held a real job or any form of lasting relationship in his life.

"Looking forward to getting home?"

Alessio rubbed the perspiration from his brow with the sleeve of his grubby, travel stained tunic as he mulled over the question in his head.

"Yes, I think so. Am looking forward to seeing Maria anyway and to the simple things: ale in a tavern, a card game, tupping a serving wench or two....."

The sentence ended with a throaty chuckle as he watched James grin and roll his eyes in response.

"And here I was, thinking how much you had changed and matured on this adventure of ours!"

The dark haired man's chuckle became a full bodied laugh, waking Aisha from the shoulder of James as Alessio flicked his eyes to the female of the group.

"Sorry Aisha, James here was making me laugh with his thoughts!"

He exclaimed, unable to prevent a further eruption of mirth from himself.

"What were your thoughts?"

Aisha asked wearily, rubbing her eyes and looking to James every inch an innocent child as she did so.

"I was telling the childish one over there how much I thought he had grown up and shown maturity of late...."

His step daughter giggled herself before James had the chance to conclude his explanation and responded with gusto.

"Maturity? On occasion perhaps but definitely more child than man!"

Alessio grinned and bowed his head extravagantly in jest.

"You see, for a man who does not wish to mature and spend all of his life having fun like a boy, that my lady is a compliment."

James smiled at the duo's amusing discussion which broke down into the trade of jovial insults and pretend scorn for the other as they guffawed and exaggerated about the various escapades they had endured on their travels together. For the horse trader, it was a lovely piece of escapism before the serious decisions that would have to be made about the future and he laughed with his companions, enjoying their tall tales which increased in bravado and splendour with every telling.

Merdlan picked his way along the trail, familiar with the trade routes in The Kingdom of Jerusalem, especially this close to Acre and his home and his hooves trotted happily along the dusty road before picking up a scent he recognised. The stallion halted and snorted, whinnying in alarm as his nostrils flared.

"What is it?"

Aisha asked as James stroked his favourite mount softly and replied in trepidation.

"He is not happy about something, a smell or noise perhaps?"

Alessio drew alongside them; his own horse unperturbed by whatever it was affecting Merdlan.

"How far is your cabin from here?"

James scratched his considerable growth on his face, acutely aware his beard was scratchy and itchy and he needed to shave it from his skin as he gently dug in his heels into the great flanks and urged Merdlan onwards, a growing feeling of unease emanating from the pit of his guts as he replied darkly.

"Less than a mile I would say, just beyond that ridge and then a little way through the two hills you can see. Meet you there."

Alessio watched the ebony stallion break into a gallop and covered his eyes from the cloud of dust which billowed suddenly into his face, before digging his own heels into the horse he had yet to name and followed suit. Aisha clung to James as he allowed Merdlan to gallop over the sandy ridge and give full rein to the powerful animal enabling him to gain and sustain his incredible stride pattern, his ears pinned back to his head and his nose snorting as he sprinted towards his home. As the homestead came into view, James swore under his breath and unleashed an enormous sigh, bringing Merdlan to a shuddering halt. In direct response, Aisha craned her neck and strained her eyes as the dust cloud dissipated around them. Her young, mahogany coloured eyes immediately widened in shock as they took in the devastation before her. The place she had called her home for years was now utterly destroyed. The stables, compound, vineyard and cabin were blackened, burnt husks of what they had once been. The buildings that had been lovingly crafted had been wilfully demolished and tears rolled down both cheeks as she watched James dismount and trudge towards what had once been the house he had personally built.

Gripping Merdlan's neck for comfort, the teenager buried her salt water stained face into his mane as Alessio trotted alongside her to survey the burnt, broken and charred remains.

"Revenge for the death of the Damascan?"

Alessio shouted after James as he heaved his aching body off the mare.

"No."

James responded grimly as he studied the ground and looked down on where he had buried Jacob. Crouching down he touched the hallowed ground which had been desecrated and ruined and he rubbed his temple as the knowledge of this depravity reached his mind.

"Oh my god...."

Alessio stated in hushed tones as he placed a reassuring hand on his friend's shoulder and then crossed himself. The Venetian blinked in the sun, aghast and confused.

"If not Saracens, then who...who else would do something like this?"

Aisha slid from Merdlan's neck and rushed to James to hold him tightly, hugging her slight frame across the left half of his body and placing her forehead gently against his cheek. Staring at the slight hillock, which hid the log cabin from the trail, James stroked his ward's hair and through gritted teeth, he replied to Alessio without any hint of doubt.

"Templars..."

The Italian man in his early thirties shook his head, his lank, unkempt hair shaking as he did so.

"Such depravity, I don't believe it. They have standards, God's Law."

James eased Aisha away from him and whispered in her ear.

"Go stand by Merdlan, if things go wrong, you ride like the wind to Acre and go to Maria."

Alessio's look of confusion exactly mirrored that of the young woman. Only then did his friend comprehend, following the unblinking glare at the raised ground to the south and made out the shimmering figures of two men; clad in shining plate mail armour, their tunics and iron shields bearing the holy cross insignia of the Knights Templars. The two knights could be seen conversing and then both nudged their horses, cautiously approaching the huddled trio.

"Give me the sword."

Alessio nodded imperceptibly and handed over the unwieldy scimitar hilt first, unsheathing one of his throwing knives and positioning himself in front of Aisha so that the youth was protected between Merdlan and himself. James took five paces into the centre of his shattered homestead and swung the scimitar twice, loosening his shoulder; his hazel eyes never moving from the two heavily armoured knights who trotted casually towards him. Their faces were covered in the full metal helmets and only when the armour plated destriers pulled up a few yards away from him that the two men flicked up the visors and one man spoke in aristocratic French.

"You are the one they call James Rose?"

James studied the man who spoke and smirked. The man was over forty summers with a clipped grey beard and was clearly a French nobleman, a typical member of the elite holy knights.

"Are you responsible for desecrating my son's grave and destroying my home?"

The reply was shouted across the small, desolate landscape in fluent French.

"Then you have answered the question. You are charged with treason, for striking a brother knight of the Poor Fellow-Soldiers of Christ and of the Temple of Solomon, for aiding our enemies and the enemies of Christ the Redeemer and our Lord God Almighty. You are to come with me now and be judged for your crimes by the Grand Master where you will be allowed to explain your treacherous actions."

James stared intently with simmering hatred and repeated his question. The French nobleman shifted in his saddle and exchanged a worried glance with his younger companion, whom the landowner now focused on and recognition ignited in his brain. He looked an atypical young Templar; arrogant, pious, self-righteous and filled with extremist doctrine. A picture of a young goat herder with blood on his face and an arrogant knight with the same blood on his mailed fist came into his mind and his features contorted into that of a she wolf when her cub is attacked. All these knights seemed to be one and the same and James had had enough. The younger Templar's eyes also flickered in recognition and he grinned coldly, calling out to the human imitation of a lupine.

"This is a good day. The owner of this hovel is a traitor to God and an enemy within Outremer – therefore, it was right to be burned off the face of the earth and there can be no desecration of the dead if the family of the dead are a disgrace to our Lord."

James nodded solemnly and turned to Alessio and the Venetian knew what his friend's cold eyes said without the need for words to be passed. Staring back to the two knights, he set his stance and brought up his sword above his head.

"I am the man you seek, now come, and take me to your Master."

The younger man chuckled drily and pulled down his metal visor.

"Wait!"

The more experienced Templar Knight attempted in vain to hold back his more emotive comrade and cursed as he watched him kick viciously at his gelding who responded submissively, charging forward skittishly. James held the scimitar aloft, its blade pointing towards the armoured rider, his body tense and mind active. Noting the young knight thunder forward, his long sword in his right hand and shield attached to his left, James smiled thinly at the impetuosity of youth. Waiting for the perfect moment to side step the charge with a fluid motion of ducking and weaving his athletic frame, he swept the scimitar through the dry air, the sound of clashing metal ringing in the valley as blade struck shield. The knight unleashed a stricken cry as the heavy pointed shield was forced from his forearm and clattered to the scorched earth. With a quick glance in the direction of the more experienced Templar, who remained stationery in his saddle, James brought the keen blade one hundred and eighty degrees around and scraped the weapon across the heavy plate mail armour which protected the enemy's back.

Shaken, the young Frenchman pulled desperately on the reins and his frightened mount whined, twisting his neck in panic and reared, sending the armoured figure hurtling to the sand. Darting forward, James placed a boot solidly against the man's chest as he lay prone on his back; the weight of the plate mail making it almost impossible for him to raise himself. The helmet had cracked and his face was exposed, showing an exact image of fear. The edge of the scimitar rested under the man's pot marked chin and James wondered if the youth was even old enough to grow a beard and he looked to the other Templar who shouted anxiously.

"Please...he is just a boy! A stupid, proud, arrogant boy. I promised his father back in Breton I would look after him..."

The pungent scent of vengeance receded as he stared into the eyes of Aisha, whose own pupils were wide and her face aghast at what James would do next. James swore and removed the blade, turning to face the older

470

opponent who had dismounted and was walking his horse towards the trader, his left hand at his side; his blade sheathed.

"I have enough blood on my hands; I have no desire to kill a misguided boy today. Take him away and ride back to your Master – tell him you killed me or tell them nothing at all. Let me and my family be. I have no fight with you. I care not for your holy war; you are more than welcome to be killed by the Islamic hordes that lie in wait for you in the East."

"You have my appreciation. I will say nothing and neither will Guillame. You have my word as a Frenchman."

"Like that is reassuring...."

Alessio smirked, moving languidly beside his friend, placing a hand gently on the other's forearm.

"Come, let us get to my sister and decide what to with our lives in the comfort of friends and with a cup of good Venetian wine in our hands."

Aisha moved forward and hugged him as he waved away the knight's heartfelt thanks and guarantee that he would do as he asked. The younger man struggled to his feet and staggered to his gelding, his body shaking in fear, tears on his cheeks, his legs covered in his own urine. Alessio watched the two knights depart and he nodded at his companion, pleased that the man he had known all of his life was returning to the man he used to be and silently prayed for God to look after him. The three figures stood as one as they watched the new enemies trot into the distance, the heat of the present day sun on their backs as the cold embers of the past lay scattered under their feet.

Chapter 39

Return to Acre

James listened to Alessio's peaceful slumber, his soft snoring a comfort more than an issue and he smiled warmly in the darkness. Distrustful of the French Knights in spite of their acquiescent words, they had travelled into Acre under the cover of the starless sky and like thieves in the night; they crept swiftly and silently to the relative safety of Alessio's sisters' home. Waking and surprising the two women who lived there, they watched Maria's fearful expression change instantly to unbridled joy as she saw the two men she loved more than any other smiling in her doorway. The images of the excited tears, honest recriminations, tear stained embraces and emotional words floated ethereally through his mind. Steaming, scented baths were offered and gratefully taken by the weary travellers as a bountiful meal was hurriedly created by the bustling Maria and Jaeda and this was consumed ravenously by all. Animated conversation followed long into the night and as an emotionally exhausted Aisha slept peacefully in a swiftly prepared bed, Maria's finest Venetian white wine flowing amongst the four adults as stories were shared and explanatory information gained.

Maria and Jaeda listened intently to the men who narrated their individual events and the incredible journeys they had experienced. The women in turn, eagerly shared the gossip and news of the port; advising that business was booming with the influx of pilgrims and mercenaries from Europe, a German army led by the Emperor Conrad III himself had reached an agreement with the Byzantines and was marching currently through the land of the Turk and a French army, led by the youthful, pious Louis VII and the enigmatic Eleanor of Aquitaine was to arrive by sea into

Acre itself within the next few days. The Templars were exerting even more power over Baldwin and an apparent accord with the Hospitalliers had come into existence with the latter holy army taking up a stronger position in the Principality of Antioch and what remained of the County of Edessa whilst the former gained further power and prestige in the Kingdom of Jerusalem. More of direct interest to James was that Sophia's father and henchman had been murdered and that his one-time lover was now the sole and wealthy owner of one of the most popular hostelries in the city.

Feeling relaxed for the first time in weeks, helped at least in part by the copious amount of sweet white wine, he drifted off to bed but found sleep hard to come by. His mind whirled with the opportunities and problems that faced his return to Acre and he knew that in the morning, he needed to visit the Knights of the Order of Saint John the Hospitaller and claim his reward for his successful mission and also compensation for his ruined home which the Knights had sworn to protect. Of course, he was actually unsure if any payment at all would be forthcoming as no written contract had been signed and a Frenchman's word was hardly his bond, as Alessio had pointed out numerous times this evening. He then needed to talk to Aisha and see if she was ready to leave Outremer and make a home for the two of them across the Mediterranean in Cyprus or perhaps even beyond. In his heart, he knew that the Holy Land was no longer a place he wished to live and a fresh, clean, new start at life was necessary for his soul to be at peace. Peace. It was a word which resonated within his psyche and the realisation that he longed for it more than anything else was clear. He closed his hazel eyes and longed for sleep but still, it would not come.

The visage of Sophia materialised in his mind as he thought of her father and Aldo; his violent underling, being killed and the fact that it was she, and not Maria or Jaeda as he had initially believed, who had

473

repatriated the remains of Jacob and given him a second decent burial. He made up his mind to thank her after he had been to see Du Puy and he nodded to himself in the darkness that this was the correct and proper thing to do. Pushing the warm memories of sexual conquest to the dark recesses of his brain, he rolled over to find a more comfortable position and attempted to find Morpheus for the hundredth time yet he remained awake and in exactly the same repose when the sun sent its unwelcome rays through the wooden shutters four hours later.

Leaving the other occupants of the house asleep, James crept through the store before his fast had been broken. In his finest claret tunic and tight fitting black breeches, with the pitiful remains of his coin in a leather pouch at his waist, he strode purposefully through the sleeping port as the sun rose; a few traders and fisherman the only men he passed and he did that without looking or speaking to anybody.

His face was set firm, his eyes cold and his mind focused as he was ushered into the small private office of Louis Atrente; one of Du Puy's most trusted advisors who resembled a large bird of prey. Small dark eyes, positioned close together above a large, hawk nose and merely the smattering of tufted white hair on a balding plate made him a somewhat pathetic looking Knight of God but it was well known that Du Puy respected his wisdom above all others within the Order and with the Grand Master attending to the expansion of their new Temple in Antioch, James was pleased to be meeting Atrente rather than the odious Francois D'Agostin; the overtly pious, sensitive weak chinned Hospitaller whom he had met on his first meeting with Du Puy. The two armed guards, wearing full armour and bearing the insignia of their Order on their finely woven tunics and shining kite shields looked ahead impassively as the tall, emaciated Atrente closed the door behind them and motioned for his visitor to take a seat.

"A drink? And apologies for not meeting with the Grand Master himself. You may have heard that we are relocating our base of operations to Antioch so we have much to do. Outremer is changing young man and we must all change with it."

James seated himself gently on the exquisitely hand carved chair and shook his head to the initial question and murmured that he had indeed heard the news as Atrente continued talking with barely a pause for breath.

"The Grand Master passed on his congratulations to you on the incredible success of your...errm...err....mission?"

The Frenchman struggled momentarily to locate the right word and smiled knowingly as James nodded that 'mission' was an acceptable term.

"It really is a remarkable achievement and we have much to discuss with so little time."

The listening man cocked his head slightly and his quizzical expression clearly humoured the narrator.
"Well, there are one thousand Bezants in a chest to be given to you by the Sergeant as you leave the building for the success of your 'mission' and a further five hundred Bezants compensation for the destruction of your home, which we had sworn before God to protect in your absence. A princely sum you admit? You are a rich man James Rose."

The man shifted in his chair and it creaked slightly as he did so, belying its actual age and no doubt grandeur.

"It is most generous....I was not expecting such an amount..."

The Hospitaller cut across him with genuine warmth.

"Not at all, not at all. A trifle in comparison to

what you have done for the Holy Land. Our spies have told us that there is already unrest amongst the Saracen's army. Zengi is dead and his two sons are fighting over his men and his land. Egyptians are moving into his territories from the South, the Kurd; Naim al-Din Ayyub, from Baalbek; their most feared general has made noises of independence from the Seljuk army itself. The death of Zengi is perfect timing – the enemy of God is in chaos and the Pope himself has sent us two armies united under the banner of Christendom to defeat them and extend the boundaries and area of God's law, creating beauty out of evil."

James remained silent as his mind railed against the religious sermon of a naive knight and allowed the excitable Atrente to continue.

"Most thrilling of all for you Monsieur Rose is that the Grandmaster himself has offered you the rank of knight in the brotherhood. Join us in our fight for glory!"

The one time merchant of horses smiled warmly and held up the palm of his left hand.

"Thank you but I fear I cannot accept. A most generous offering but I am leaving Acre and Outremer itself for a new life, beyond the sea. My daughter and I will be heading for Cyprus as soon as I can gain passage on a ship. I am no knight and am tired of death and all I see is the impending war coming again at pace and I want no part in that."

"Not part in it but my man, it was you who made this possible by killing Zengi? You are already a part of it and a heroic one at that."

James blanched as he saw the confusion in the eyes of one of the faithful and apologised again.

"I am sorry. I must protect those that I love. This

'mission' cost me dearly, please understand that. I thank you Monsieur for your most munificent offer and please give my heartfelt gratitude to the Grandmaster for his generosity but I must humbly decline."

The tall, thin man nodded curtly and indicated that the meeting was over; disdain oozing from every pore of his body now that the glorious offer of brotherhood had been refused. James masked his smile, stood and offered more profuse apologises, bowed his head and exited the chamber; the grin unmasking with every step towards the main doors of the Chapter House and the vast amount of gold which awaited him.

When he exited the building and blinked in the dazzling sunlight of an early morning in the city port of Acre, he was a much happier man that when he had entered. At his belt, his leather pouch bulged with coin and he imagined the faces of his loved ones as the Hospitallers delivered a casket of hundreds of coins to Silk Street in around an hour's time. His grin broadened and he bowed to a French noblewoman and her maid as they looked at him on the cobbled street, winking to them as they giggled together at his boldness. Unable to wipe the smile from his face, he strode towards the grand market and the traders stalls and shops of the Merchants Quarter with a veritable swagger in his step.

It was three hours before James opened the door of the fashionable store which Maria owned; his arms and hands laden down with a whole array of assorted merchandise. Aisha almost knocked him over in her rush to get to hug him and she babbled incoherently about visitors from the Knights of the Order of St John the Hospitaller and the locked chest that had been brought to them. Maria, who stood behind the wooden counter hurried to lock the outside door and stare in confusion at the man. Struggling with the packages, James made his way past the clothing and bolts of variously coloured and differing types of cloth and with an excitable Aisha in tow, moved to the kitchen area where Alessio and Jaeda sat side by side, talking in soft tones to each other in Italian, which Jaeda was rapidly learning. The elegantly carved oak casket sat on the roughly hewn cedar table before them; iron hinges and lock adding strength to the skilled workmanship of the box.

James grinned and displayed his acquisitions around the chest as he felt all eyes upon his visage.

"Is that what I think it is?"

Alessio beamed, leaning forward to slap his friend on the shoulder as he joined everybody in seating himself around the table.

"How much?"

He pressed as James merely winked in response.

"So it is filled with money?"

Aisha's eyes widened in a look of incredulous wonder and James nodded and pausing to tease the four flushed, excited faces around the table, he slowly opened a smaller pouch, hanging from the new leather belt at his waist and pulled a small iron key, holding it up as if it was some holy artefact.

"Let's see shall we?"

He smirked and unlocked the casket carefully, opening up the heavy lid to show the interior to be velvet lined and filled almost to the top with gold and silver ducats and bezants. There was a combined sharp intake of breath and then the room descended into raucous exclamations, cursing and all manner of disbelief.

"Do you know how much is in there exactly?"

His oldest friend asked placing his gnarled hand

amongst the coins and scattering them through his fingers, his mocha eyes staring at each coin as it dropped amongst the hundreds of others.

"Well there were 1500 bezants but I must admit, I have spent a little this morning!"

Aisha began picking up and peering through the procurements, giggling as she did so.

"So we can see!"

James passed her a carefully wrapped object and grinned.

"You will probably like this one best."

The teenage girl's dark face illuminated with excitement, unmasking her naturally pretty features and she tore open the wrapping with youthful enthusiasm, revealing a small ornately carved ebony box with a silver bracelet inside. Holding the gift to the light, the exquisite, detailed inscriptions became apparent; beautiful words stylised on the precious metal in Arabic. Aisha peered closely, straining her eyes to read the lettering as she moved the item carefully between the tips of her fingers and told the room what it said.

"To the one who is a part of me always."

James flushed under the gaze of the others around the table and spoke awkwardly.

"I admit I am no poet...but...you understand my meaning..."

The words came clumsily from his mouth and Aisha laughed loudly.

"Hush please. It is the most beautiful thing in the world!"

479

Jaeda helped her clasp the bracelet and it fixed around her delicate wrist, nodding with a smile flashing at the embarrassed male.

"It fits perfectly."

Maria, as was her way, came to his rescue and bustled around the table to look upon the jewellery and whistled in admiration.

"Why don't you ever buy your female family members such amazing presents and tell them such beautiful words..."

She playfully slapped her brother who grinned wolfishly and grabbed his sibling, planting a wet kiss on her cheek.

"You do not need expensive gifts to know I love you Maria!"

James and Aisha exchanged the look a child and parent share when families are in a perfect moment and then the horse trader found his tongue and focused his attention on the pouting seamstress and handed her a package of her own.

"You get an expensive gift anyway Maria.....as does Jaeda...."

Passing out the presents, he smiled warmly as effusive thanks and kisses were exchanged as the two ladies opened up amulets of bronze skilfully shaped into a figure eight with minute precious stones inlaid into each. The workmanship was incredible and all guessed James had been to see his old friend, Zacharias in the Jewish Quarter of the old city who was renowned for being the best jeweller of all of Acre.

"It is the symbol of eternity, or so Zacharias informed me so when you wear it, you will always think of me."

James confirmed the store he had made the purchases from and then passed out some purple and azure bolts of silk to the women, explaining that he had met a Syrian trader of silks in the market and the merchant had advised they were of prodigious quality, which Maria affirmed by stroking the material softly.

"Hold on...back up a moment. Why will we always think of you – are you going away?"

Maria spoke, her eyes clouding as she dropped the silk which floated gracefully to the table.

"All in good time..."

James said evasively and tossed a wooden box to Alessio who caught it in his left hand deftly.

"I thought you had forgotten your old friend!"

He winked and James grunted an equally playful retort about trying to for many years as the Venetian lifted the lid to look upon carved ivory dice.

"For you to gamble at home and not get in any more trouble when I am not....."

The flashes of interest from the others stifled his last words and he forced a smile, turning to Aisha.

"Walk with me?"

The young woman nodded with a worried expression and James stood languidly and nodded to the chest of coins.

"Half of them are for you....so get counting Alessio...."

The look on the three faces was a picture of total astonishment and James chuckled as he placed an arm around Aisha's shoulder, drew her near and kissed her head gently, leading her from the kitchen, through the shop and out into the busy street beyond.

"Let's go to the docks and watch the ships awhile."

The two figures departed leaving the remaining three to their own astonishment and both smiled at the other as the whoops of joy could be heard behind the closed door. The walk was casual in all but the hazel eyes of James which remained on the alert, the Templars were not going to let him alone if they found him and it appeared that the Kinghts of that particular holy order were the new law in Acre and in the whole of the south of Outremer. Making it to the port district, they sat on an empty quay, the fishing vessels who moored there bobbing out in the harbour.

"Did you not buy anything for yourself?"

Aisha questioned, almost afraid of what James was about to say and needing time for her mind to adjust from the happiness of the past few hours.

"Yes, I bought a new short sword, Damascan steel and a good balance to it and I pick up a crossbow tomorrow, I wanted one that was akin to my old trusted one so the armourer had to make some alterations to one he had in stock, mainly to realign the spring mechanism, it was too tight. I also bought us some woollen cloaks for riding. I was going to purchase some clothes but I thought that depended on where we were heading and to be honest, you are old enough to choose what you wish to wear from now on; I have realised you are no longer a child."

He allowed the statement to hang in the air and looked out across the water at a large, Genoan galleon of enormous proportions and watched the vast amount of crates being shipped onto the dock.

"So you are not leaving me? We will be going together?"

James brought his knee upwards to sit in a more comfortable position and nodded, twisting his neck to look upon the rather pathetic looking face of his ward.

"Yes Aisha, I left you once, I will not do that again until you get married or can bear to live with me no longer!"

The amusement twinkled in his eyes and Aisha merely smiled broadly and shrugged in a typically teenage fashion.

"I can put up with you for a while, you're not that bad and as for marriage....who wants to get married?"

The man raised an eyebrow but left the comments for the wind, preferring to ask questions of his own.

"I don't want you to be scared. We just need to leave Acre, for so many reasons and I am tired of this Kingdom, there is nothing left for me here anymore but bad memories. You understand?"

Aisha nodded her head emphatically and replied evenly.

"I want to leave, it will be exciting, an adventure...our adventure. There is nothing left here for either of us. But, where do we go?"

James rubbed his chin and cocked his head to the side, giving an impression of a thinking man.

"Cyprus first, there is passage tomorrow at noon on the tide. From there, I was thinking Venice maybe or perhaps even England. See the lands my ancestors came from. What do you think?"

The young woman tittered and stated her answer with a cheeky smile.

"Will all the men in Venice be as attractive as Alessio?"

James turned his head sharply and exaggerated a look of horror across his drawn features.

"Well that is settled then easily enough. We travel to England."

Aisha sniggered and both joined in the mirth as they sat side by side on the dock, laughing raucously as the sun shone above and the sapphire sea lapped gently against the stone quay, oblivious to the ordinary looking man who stood in the doorway of a derelict house, watching them closely. The merest glimpse of a fleeting smile passing over his full lips as he stood perfectly still, at one with the house; his eyes fixated, never moving from the figure of James.

Chapter 40

Sophia's Choice

The morning had been a good one. Passage had been booked on the English merchant ship; '*The Lady Amber*' at reasonable rates, which departed from the southern quay at noon tide tomorrow. An excitable teenager was now spending a sizable portion of his money on clothing and equipment for their departure with Maria and Jaeda in the many shops and stalls of Acre, whilst Alessio trudged alongside him towards the tavern for a farewell drink. Personally, he was elated but his friend had misery pouring from his very essence; in his walk pattern, in his demeanour, in his conversation, in everything.

"For a man who has been given a small fortune, you are the most ungrateful bastard I ever met."

The curse was stated in a jovial fashion to lighten the mood but the taller man merely hawked and spat into the compacted sand which made up the ground beneath his shuffling feet.

"Oh come on, talk to me. I need this. Aisha needs this...."

James continued in appeasement and tugged on his friend's tunic as Alessio turned wearily to face him and they both stopped in the street to look upon the other.

"I know James, I know. Look, just get me drunk and then I can celebrate with you okay. I just feel we did something amazing – it was some kind of miracle we survived out there and now, you are leaving me alone."

The man of English blood chuckled and apologised

through his mirth.

"You are such a spoilt child. Once we are settled, you can come and stay with us any time you like. Come on, let me get some ale inside of you so you cheer up – you are seriously ruining my celebratory mood!"

Alessio swore again but managed a thin smile and walked after his companion, looking for the entire world like a small boy who had lost his favourite toy. The two strode in silence for the next few minutes until they reached the Genoan Quarter and stood opposite the sandy trail, which served as a thoroughfare and looked at the city state flag of Genoa which fluttered in the slight breeze under the creaking sign bearing the words: *Il Caravel.* The proud Venetian's features collapsed into an explicit expression of disgust.

"Really? Here? Are you serious? Venetian ale houses not good enough for you anymore?"

James opened his arms and had the graciousness to flush momentarily.

"I have to say thank you and goodbye, that's all. Then we can go to a Venetian tavern and get as drunk as you want!"

Alessio shrugged and murmured something unintelligible about a dead man's inn and followed his friend across the dusty trail, past the overtly muscled guard and into the smoky gloom of the interior.

Memories flooded through both minds of the men who entered the relatively quiet chamber beyond, which had been freshly painted and the walls were now adorned with maps and paintings of all things Genoan. For Alessio, Genoa and Genoans would always be an inferior version of Venice and Venetians and he scowled at the artwork of the bar room. Although smoky, the nauseous stench of body odour, stale alcohol and urine, which used to pervade the nostrils upon entering the establishment, was missing and for that, both were thankful.

"Looks better than the last time I came here."

James remarked as he scanned the area for anybody of note and pointedly ignored his friend's derogatory remark. He saw none, merely an amorous couple in one corner of the room and a group of artisans in the centre of it, who sat drinking around a large, circular table. The affluent man smiled as he approached the long bar and recognised the girl behind it from the last eventful time he had been there as Francesca, Sophia's youngest sister.

"Good day to you young lady, two of your finest ales please."

The young woman smiled warmly and pushed her dark fringe out of her eyes and spoke as she busied herself getting the order.

"I recognise your faces...."

She peered from James to Alessio and lingered her gaze on the Italian's face, finally remembering why he used to frequent the inn.

"It's not that kind of establishment anymore. We only offer food and drink here now, food downstairs and drink here. The rooms upstairs are for patrons to sleep only. We are a respectable hostelry now."

The words were directed at Alessio and James grinned at his discomfort, turning to face the bar maid and smirked, paying for the drinks and offering to purchase one for herself, passing the first wooden tankard to his embarrassed comrade.

"Thank you for the information, I shall pass it onto my friend here..."

He sipped his ale and ignored the hefty shove of his shoulder from Alessio as he continued.

"Is Sophia around?"

Francesca's eyes widened with interest as she reverted them back to James.

"Oh I am sorry sir, you know my sister? I thought I recognised you with your friend here, I know he was a regular to the girls and the gambling tables, I didn't want you disappointed in your stay at 'The Caravel'...."
"Too late for that....."

Alessio grunted harshly and lifted his tankard from the bar and wondered to a free table, where he lowered his frame down onto the stool.

"Sorry again sir. I will go and tell Sophia she has a visitor. Who shall I say is calling?"

James shrugged off her concerns and said his Christian name to which the waitress's nose wrinkled and eyes sparkled, showing recognition and he wondered if that was a good or bad sign as he sauntered over to seat himself opposite his grumpy friend.

"So just how much of a regular visitor to the 'girls' were you then Al?"

He grinned at the oath that was the stark response to his teasing question and drank deeply from the drinking vessel. The door opened and a dark haired man with swarthy skin entered, made his way to the vacant bar and waited for the girl to return. James watched him idly and reverted his attention back to his scowling drinking partner and chuckled throatily.

"To think I used to defend you against your sister's comments about your maturity levels......"

A further curse was the only response and the chuckling deepened before a familiar voice brought the familiar feeling and he twisted his neck to view the owner of it.

"So, what brings you two rapscallions to my tavern?"

The woman was striking, her curvaceous figure seemingly poured into a tight fitting simple pale blue dress and her sleek black hair tied back from her face, which enhanced her high cheek bones. The deep ocean blue eyes sparkled as they focused on James and smiled warmly, standing to gently hug his previous lover who returned the embrace lightly. She languidly slid into the only empty chair at the small table and thanked her younger sister as a large goblet of red wine was placed carefully before her.

"Well, a few reasons actually..."

James stated seriously and sipped his ale as Sophia tilted her head and stared into his eyes with interest. The man shifted uneasily under her unwavering gaze and forced a smile.

"Mostly, to thank you for what you did for my boy....."

Sophia's face softened and smiled in sympathy, placing both of her hands onto the man's arm.

"Please James...it was something that had to be done, it was wrong...and had to be righted. You do not ever have to thank me for doing what is right."

Alessio watched the exchange and softly excused himself, heading to the long bar to stand beside the newcomer and ordered ale. James flicked his eyes to the Venetian as he departed the vicinity and he continued in a hushed tone.

"I know but I wanted, no, actually needed you to know that I appreciated it. You see, I am leaving."

The soft fingers retreated from his arm and Sophia stifled her fleeting look of disappointment with a casual smile.

"Well, I do not blame you heading out of Acre; I have heard...numerous things about you James Vittorio or is it Rose now? People talk in taverns...there is little I do not know about what goes on in this city."

James nodded and gulped another swig of the bitter ale.

"Not Acre...I am leaving Outremer."

The Genoan woman's eyes widened and she placed the glass delicately down onto the table slowly.

"Because of the Templars?"

The question was muttered as her eyes scanned the chamber for any listeners and James sighed softly, mulling over the question in his mind.

"Partly perhaps but after what happened with Jacob... and I have to think of Aisha and life here...I am not sure I can be happy here again. I need peace...for my soul...do you understand?"

His explanation was clipped and stated in a staccato fashion and Sophia cocked her head to observe his battered, weary face and nodded her head.

"Well you do look terrible...."

A smile flickered across her lips and James held his breath a little as her beauty was unmasked momentarily.

"You don't....."

He whispered and she snorted, placing a stray hair back behind her ear.

"I feel and look old and this place, running it is not easy..."

Sophia dropped her eyes and looked forlornly around the chamber as the conversation became suddenly awkward with it being more about what is not being said as opposed to what is.

"I heard about your father...I will not lie to you and say he was a good man and I mourn his loss but he was your father and for that I am sorry...for you."

A barely perceptible nod was the only response and he knew as she stared at a painting on the wall absently, her thoughts were elsewhere and he could not guess where in her life she was right now.

"So is it true? The stories about you?"

James drained his ale, the conversation drifting from his control and he shrugged listlessly.

"It depends what they say about me?"
The woman in her early thirties smirked and sipped the blood red wine slowly, her tongue sliding over her lips to savour the full flavour.

"Oh there are many...You hate the Templars, you hate God, you hate Christianity, you attacked the Templars, you went to Cyprus, you went into the desert, you killed the man who took Edessa, you are an assassin, a killer, a hero, a traitor....."

He held up his hand to stem the list of rumours and he

laughed drily.

"People talk too much. Some of those are true, some of those are false. Choose whichever you want to believe about me."

Sophia's eyes narrowed and her lips pursed, leaning towards him slightly.

"I don't think I want to believe any of them. I like to think of you as that handsome young man who was so earnest, so sweet, so funny...the one man I made love to that I did not learn to detest..."

James stroked his chin in discomfort at the distant memories meandered into his brain through the fog of yester year. The slight, unconscious movement halted the woman's chain of thought and she sat upwards once again, flushing briefly, continuing her conversation in a much more superficial sense.

"Whatever you have done or not done, did it give comfort to your soul? Is your mind at peace now...after Jacob I mean...? Whatever you have done since his death...are you happier now? Have you found contentment in your heart?"

The man stroked his stubble strewn chin more fervently and looked upon Sophia with a pained expression on his gaunt face. The wide hazel eyes glistened with emotion and his former lover placed her hands back upon his own and stroked the skin of his wrist tenderly as he managed to shake his head and hold back his tears.

"Listen to me; you are a good man James, no matter what you have done. They took the boy you loved; they took your home, your friends. Whether they were Islamites or Templars – whoever they were...they were just misguided, stupid murderers who believe in a different God to the one my mother taught me about. Go find yourself some peace and happiness James, look after your girl and your soul....please?"

James forced a weak smile and stifled his emotion, choosing humour instead.

"Maybe God has mood swings, maybe God's a woman?"

Sophia opened her mouth wide in mock horror and slapped his wrist in admonishment for such blasphemy.

"You will never go to heaven!"

She exclaimed in genuine concern and the man opposite her just smiled knowingly and stated simply:

"No, I don't think I will."

Sophia removed her fingers from his warm skin and eased herself upright to stand over him.

"I think about us sometimes? You know, what would have been....do you?"

James breathed in deeply and nodded, sitting upright on the stool.

"Sometimes...but you would have got bored of me even if your father had not undertaken his defence of his daughter....I was way too young...."

The Genoan dark haired woman ran her fingers through her hair and looked deeply at his face, taking her hand and gently pushed his wayward fringe from his eyes. The brief, simplistic act caused a stir within his body and he wondered if it was due to history alone.

"I don't think I would have you know. I wish you luck...and may my God protect you James."

She leant in and kissed his soft lips briefly and departed swiftly, quickening her pace as she headed across the bar towards the staircase which led to the erstwhile gambling tables. Alessio placed a second tankard of ale down in front of his friend as he observed him watch the woman he had loved walk away from him with something resembling loss etched upon his face.

"You ok?"

The Venetian slapped James on the shoulder and sat down in the seat Sophia had just vacated.

"All good, life is good."

James lied and smiled without humour. Alessio smiled thinly and allowed his friend to lie to him in the circumstances.

"Let's get out of here."

He added and drained his fresh tankard of ale in a series of deep drafts as Alessio watched, grinned broadly and nodded, supping his own beer quickly and following in the wake of the man he thought of as a brother as he strode from the bar into the busy street beyond.

"Has he gone?"

Sophia asked her sister as she stood with her back to the departing men, brushing a solitary tear from her cheek. Francesca confirmed and whispered conspiratorially, stressing the final of the three words with feeling.

"That was *him*?"

The elder sibling tied her hair back and blinked away any further tears, hardening her face before looking upon her sister.

"Yes."

The younger girl's eyebrow quirked in response and asked if she needed a drink, feminine understanding in his eyes.

"No, thank you. Business is quiet today..."

Sophia said matter of factly and stared around at the few patrons within her bar room, sapphire eyes scanning the room as a desert eagle scans for prey, focusing them on the man who was watching the main door swing shut. The man immediately left his unfinished ale on the polished bar, moving casually towards the exit. The sheer impact of the recognition of the man struck the innkeeper with considerable, ethereal force and it took a second for her to retain her usual calm exterior.

"Excuse me sir?"

The man pulled his hood over his head and receding hair line and half turned his head, hiding his features as he answered.

"Yes, madam?"

The voice was rasping and forced, yet totally confirmed her realisation and she shot a warning glance to her sibling, who retrieved a curved dagger from behind the bar and passed it to her eldest sister, who unsheathed it carefully and spoke loudly, so her three armed guards could all hear; Gennaro outside, Alfonso downstairs and the giant Lorenzo who was in his bedchamber above.

"I know you stranger."

The loud cacophony of lewd banter, blasphemy and raucous laughter decreased in volume and almost immediately died down completely on the artisans table, as the drinking workers all turned to watch the tense scene unfolding before them with interest. The young lovers in the corner detached their limbs and mouths from each other and peered through the smoky gloom as the man turned to face the woman and chuckled sardonically.

"Are you sure you know me madam. Think carefully."

The words were laced with derision and he removed his hood so she could observe him clearly. Sophia heard the creaking of the wooden stairs behind her and smiled with confidence as Gennaro opened the door from the street, sword already in his hand as he looked at his employer and asked simply,

"Trouble... Sophia?"

Setting her eyes upon the murderer of her father and Aldo, she nodded to her henchman.

"Oh yes...Meet the man who killed my father, Gennaro."

A soft murmur of excitement exuded from the onlookers as the man known to very few individuals as 'Il Falco' bowed theatrically, untying his cloak to reveal the tight fitting interwoven chain mail shirt beneath and a multitude of weapons which adorned the three soft leather belts he wore across his waist and chest.

"What do you want with those two men who left just now?"

Her voice cracked slightly as she felt the discomfort of isolation, as every eye in the chamber was focused on her.

"It is merely my work...Are you sure you wish to do this...I gain no coin or enjoyment from slaying women..."

His eyes scanned the two stairwells behind the annoying distraction of a woman and watched the two men rapidly approach to aid their pay mistress and he listened intently as the latch was bolted across the only exit door in the room behind him.

"You don't understand Genoan women do you..."

Her sentence died on her lips as she watched, almost mesmerised as the man suddenly unfurled his cloak in his left hand, using it as a whip to lash Gennaro across the face and as he raised his hand to pull the cloak from the opponent, a small knife flashed from the assassin's right hand and embedded itself deep into the guard's exposed neck. The bar room erupted into anguished shrieks, curses and sudden movement as patrons leapt away from the killer or behind stools, tables or onto the floor for some relative form of security, tankards bouncing off flagstones and various liquids splashing on the floor. The bounty hunters mouth curled into an arrogant sneer as he observed the female bar owner standing in shock, the dagger in her hand held limply at her side as she tried in vain to mask the horror of the situation and he basked in the moment of glory as the woman instantly realised the helplessness of fear.

Using surprise as a deadly weapon, the man who originated from a small village in the mountains in Sicily, leapt forwards deftly, unleashing a second knife into the panic stricken face of the smaller guard who had barely had time to unsheathe his blade. Moving fluidly to his right, he manoeuvred his frame behind a small table as he slid the Damascan steel bladed sword from his waist and grinned as he watched the chaos he had caused. The shocked innkeeper was tending to her guard who lay on his back screaming in pain, blood oozing through his fingers which splayed across his face, pulling at the twine laden bone handle of the knife. Crumpled in a heap with his back to the locked door, a second guard was breathing raggedly, his life force

497

draining from him second by second. A huge man roared in indignant rage and approached him with a heavy bastard sword in both hands. Every other figure in the bar cowered on floors, against walls or behind any piece of furniture to hand.

The assassin was absolutely confident of victory but knew he had to be swift and decisive; he had no wish of Templar or Royal guards' interference or interest in him and his target had eluded him yet again. Time was no friend of his right now and so he calmly kicked the flimsy round table into the onrushing seven foot tall cursing beast and as the ogre crashed to the stone, he bounded onto his exposed back and thrust the blade of his sword through the flesh, tendons and blood of the guard's neck, slaying him in a brief instant. Standing to his full height with a triumphant grin adorning his lips, he stared at the woman who had stupidly initiated this carnage and strode towards her crouching form, tears upon her cheeks and horror in her eyes.

His menacing stride pattern was checked as suddenly as it was unexpected as a bottle of wine struck him fully in the face and he staggered slightly backwards. The bottle did not break on impact with his cheekbone, only when it bounced onto the stone floor and after a moment of confusion, his cognitive processes reacted and his head twisted to view the perpetrator. The young woman behind the bar shouted something unintelligible but blatantly hostile at him and hurled another bottle in his direction. Infuriated by this pathetic attempt to derail his actions, he advanced swiftly to the bar, ignoring the brief moment of pain as the second bottle impacted on his chest, shattering against his armour, the scarlet wine staining his torso as if blood. The girl shrieked and backed off against the oaken barrels of ale behind her and he drank in her fear with utter delight. Hopping onto the counter with ease, he raised his blade to his shoulder and positioned himself for one of his favourite killing moves.

It never came. As he prepared for the death blow, his right ankle collapsed and he looked down in absolute disbelief as the woman who had initiated the whole drama balefully stared up at him, grim determination in her face and a bloodied dagger in her hand. She scurried backwards as the blood spurted from the back of his calf, his tendons slashed and the weight of his body too much for the damaged leg, he teetered on the polished bar and he dropped like a stone, his spine smashing into the heavy counter on the way to the flagstones where he crashed onto his skull. Excruciating pain burned through every fibre in his being as his head split open on the shuddering impact. His vision blurred and his consciousness began to fail as he managed to watch the woman furtively approach and place the cold steel of the curved knife across his neck.

"I said you didn't understand Genoan women, stranger."

The broken bounty hunters mouth contorted into a half smile as his last feeling on earth was one of ironic amusement. Mortified, Sophia slid the weapon's sharp edge clumsily across the killer's neck and hurriedly stepped backwards as the man died before her eyes. The heavy weight of relief flowed through her and she dropped the dagger to the floor and staggered backwards, steadying herself with one hand on the bar as the other masked her open mouth. Francesca rushed to her side and hugged her emotionally, stroking her elder sibling's hair and allowing her to sob into her shoulder. As her sister wept, she stared at the patrons of the tavern who were only now standing shakily to their feet and she yelled at the men angrily.

"Get out you cowards. Get out of our inn. Go! Now!"

The last word was barked out and the artisans filed past the two women in silence, their eyes not daring to look into her own; instead, flicking from corpse to corpse. The door was unlocked and the customers welcomed the cleaner air of outside and drifted out into the streets of Acre, away from the fetid stench of death. The young lovers were the last to depart and the frightened girl shut the heavy door behind her with shaking fingers.

Francesca kissed her sisters forehead as the tears stemmed and smiled lovingly into her eyes.

"I am not sure we will have any trouble in here when word of this gets out."

Sophia sniffed loudly and wiped her tears and nose on her sleeve unceremoniously in response, looking at the four men who lay scattered about the chamber, all dead.

"Christ, look at the state of this place...."

Her sister shrugged and kissed her forehead again, whispering.

"You did good Sophia."

A thin smile was attempted and her voice was hoarse as she replied.

"As did you, Fran."

The siblings stepped back from the other and straightened their clothing, faces and hair, as if these simple actions were required to calm their nerves.

"Ok, go to the guardhouse, tell them what happened. Don't mention James though..."

Francesca nodded in understanding and scurried to the door, pausing as she opened it and turned to her sister.

"Did you kill the man because he had killed

father or because you thought he was going to kill James?"

Sophia stiffened a little and took a moment before replying.

"Because of father."

Her sister nodded and headed out into the street, leaving Sophia to mull over the reasoning for her lie. She gazed at the room and prayed for the man she had once loved and wondered why trouble seemed to follow his every move. Shaking her head to herself, she closed the dead, glassy eyes of Lorenzo and sighed deeply.

Chapter 41

A New Life

James groaned loudly in response to Aisha's continued admonishments about the obvious results of drinking so much ale the evening before. His stomach churned in time with the cog's lurching movements in its anchorage at the southern quayside. He waved away her condemning tone listlessly and wondered which of the quarrellers was the parent and which the child as she chided him again. Perspiring fingers rubbed his aching temple as the teenager's tone changed as she used the emotional tactic which had always stood her in good stead with her protector.

"I just wanted to enjoy today, I am so excited! Maria promised to wave us off, come on...."

He nodded in resignation, his brain throbbed and nausea swept in waves throughout his internal organs. Grunting, he blamed Alessio for his pathetic condition and this brought only a snort of indignation from the lecturing female.

"Oh please! So Alessio forced you to drink so much did he? Poor, defenceless, easily manipulated James...."

Standing opposite him with hands on hips, she looked every inch the disappointed parent and he smiled in spite of his condition. His smile was infectious and the teenager's features broke into a beaming grin, her white even teeth breaking through and she giggled as she knew his defences were failing.

"Ok, ok, let me lock the chest and cabin door and we can wave to the others."

He had not the strength, nor the inclination to prolong an argument, he knew he could not hope to win and he shook his head in mock indignation as the young woman clapped her hands in victorious triumph. The simple action of locking a chest proved trickier than it ought to have been with shaking fingers and was concluded with an exasperated, impatient young woman taking the brass key from his hand and performing the action for him. Avoiding eye contact, James handed Aisha the iron door key also and stumbled out of the small cabin as she secured the room behind them. Using each wall as support in the narrow corridor, he followed it up the small set of steep steps and onto the lower deck, which was mercifully shadowed by the steep towers at the fore and aft of the single masted vessel.

Typical of many northern European designs, this merchant ship was a cog; which were developed to carry huge amounts of cargo, their flat bottoms allowing them to load and unload easily in shallow harbours. Although unable to carry large amounts of crew as there was limited room for cabins, their high sides made it more difficult to be boarded by enemies or pirates and many, including the 'Lady Amber' had towers built which had both been fitted with heavy ballistae, which could inflict massive damage on any possible attacker. Aisha eased past him and gripped his palm, urging him to the starboard side of the anchored ship and strained her eyes in the morning sunshine to find the familiar figures of Alessio, Maria and Jaeda on the dockside. The frantic waves of two women on the quay attracted her attention and she grinned and waved back, chuckling in delight as she observed a sullen Alessio hunched over with his head in his palms, sat gingerly in between them. James eased himself slowly beside Aisha and rested his elbows on the low rail and nodded his head to his friends, amused by Alessio's pained expression as he raised his weary head and managed to force a thin smile onto his unshaven face. The two men exchanged eye contact and the emotion was transferred ethereally in almost imperceptible nods, which only other adult mature men could ever wish to understand. The weary, bloodshot hazel eyes of James flickered over to Maria's tear strewn face and he smiled to reassure her.

Unwoven thoughts of the past floated through his mind as he stared at the people he loved and the city port he knew so well; shimmering images of himself as a boy growing up in the streets of Acre, with Alessio; having fun, getting into and out of mischief together, fighting, loving, laughing and all the other emotional angst that every boy has as he grows and develops into a man. The ship lurched slightly and his sentimentality cleared, replaced by the sweeping nausea and aching in his guts. The shouting from the crew directed his attention to the anchor being lifted and the heavy oiled ropes being untied from the great iron blocks on the quayside, resulting in another unsteady heaving of the shallow bottomed vessel. Aisha chattered excitedly, pointing out the young sailors unfurling the great white sails from the netting on the mast; their athletic bodies swinging high above the deck in the rigging. They called to each other in English and it reminded James of his father, another memory tugging at his heart strings on this emotive day.

"I thought I would sob my heart out but I am so thrilled, so happy, a new life, our new life!"

Aisha hugged him happily and leant her cheek on his chest. He stroked her hair and cradled her face gently as he responded honestly.

"I am scared Aisha but yes, I am excited; it is exactly what I want and what we need. What does Outremer hold for us? Nothing that I have done in the past few weeks has eased the pain of Jacob's passing, revenge is a myth I think...."

The introspective words were lost as Aisha moved onto

her tiptoes and kissed him gently on his cheek.

"Hush James, there are no words needed. Jacob will always be here and here."

She smiled and pressed her right index finger to his forehead and his chest and he looked at his pendant which bore the lost one's name. The man forced a smile, nodded and no more words were required. More shouting from various members of the crew reverberated around the small ship and the 'Lady Amber' began to drift slowly towards the centre of the bay, moving effortlessly on the slight tide towards the open Mediterranean Sea.

"Do you think Merdlan will be ok in the hold?"

Aisha suddenly asked as she cried out a final farewell across the broadening expanse of water between cog and harbour wall. James held his right hand aloft and waved goodbye to his friends and the land he had called home for all of his life; the emotional strands of memory tugging at his heart; images of his mother, father, brother, Georges, Jacob, Abdul, Sharla and fleeting glimpses of familiar faces soared through his aching brain ending with a smiling Sophia. He crushed the sentimentality and turned away from the receding port of Acre and eased himself to the deck, resting his back against the low railing and smiling at Aisha.

"Merdlan has been through much worse, he will be fine, he's a born survivor."

"Like you?"

The young woman grinned, adding with a less certain tone;

"Will we be fine? Where are we going exactly?"

The man of English and Venetian blood chuckled

505

throatily, reminding himself to locate some fresh water and re-hydrate as he replied hoarsely.

"We will be more than fine. England... eventually, the land of my father. This ship docks at the Byzantine port of Famagusta in Cyprus; first to load and unload its wares and then onto Sicily. After that, the captain was unsure if they would port in Spain – there is war between the Almohad Muslims and the Spanish and Portuguese Christians there too. Regardless, it is bound for an English port called Dartmouth on its south coastal shores and that is our final destination. It will take some weeks in total but there are various stopping off points along this journey. It will be an adventure!"

He ended his monologue with an exclamation and smiled as he saw Aisha's young eyes widen in wonderment.

"It sounds amazing; I cannot wait to see all these places!"

James nodded and looked around the bustling ship for water and stood gingerly, holding the rail for support.

"Will you miss Acre and Outremer?" He hesitated and turned again to see Aisha resting his elbows on the wooden beam, her chin resting in his cupped hands as she watched the trail of white foam leading from the port.

"Of course and it's not going anywhere, we will come back and visit...."

His voice trailed off as the crew of the cog began to shout and point out to sea, agitated commotion and enthusiastic chatter filling the air. James strode to the aft side of the ship and looked out at the calm azure waters and blasphemed under his breath as he saw the reason for the enlivenment. A great flagship, bearing fluttering colourful banners of the French court; the blue and gold Fleur de Lys billowing from each of the three enormous sails looked magnificent in the distance, heading for them from the opposite direction. Behind this leading war ship; a dazzling array of hulks, cogs, galleys, galleons and other types of ships he did not even recognise appeared on the horizon. Even at this distance, straining his eyes through the reflections of glittering sunlight off the surface of the sea, the flags and glinting metal informed him that this was the great crusading Christian armada from France. The army of King Louis had finally arrived in the Holy Land.

Aisha stood beside him, unable to count the number of vessels as they bobbed and weaved their way towards the small English merchant ship. They looked on in silence as the sheer magnitude of the force drew nearer through the water, the decks crammed with knights in full battle armour interspersed with holy relics and crosses of all sizes in carved wood and various precious metals. As the small merchant vessel bobbed precariously in the lapping waves caused by the French invasion army's plethora of ships, James could hear the religious mania and anti-Islamic sermons being spread to the grim faced, determined knights. On the poop deck of the enormous flagship, surrounded by flags, banners and religious artefacts sat the young, pious King Louis VII; a man in a hurry to distance himself from his father's advisors back in the court of Paris and to prove to the Christian world that he was a man to be admired and feared, a powerful King in his own right. He sat on a makeshift throne, self-confident and devout, staring ahead at the land mass of Outremer; the Holy Land.

"Is that the King of France?"

Aisha asked with an unnecessary hushed tone and James nodded, gripping the side of the railing as the 'Lady Amber' lurched in the wake of the war ships that sailed past; the crew of each ship waving to each other as their rows of knights stood taciturn and serious, looking ahead.

"He looks too young to be a king...."

Aisha observed and James broke into a smile in response.

"He is out to prove himself, a dangerous thing; a young man seeking glory for his country, for his god, for himself. "

His voice hardened and he imagined the hundreds and thousands who would die for the vanity of a monarch's need for pride.

"I have never seen so many knights...."

Aisha continued, a little in awe of the show of power from the West and James shrugged to show his lack of concern.

"They may win some battles, maybe even take back Edessa in the north but then the knights will return home; their vows completed and then the waves of Zengi's armies will defeat the farmers and traders that remain...."

The woman looked unconvinced and whispered surreptitiously.

"But Zengi is dead....you killed him."

James twitched slightly at the memory of ending the Islamic leader's life and he snorted indignantly.

"There will be other Zengi's with different names and the same ideals. What then, a third crusade, a fourth....is this how it is to be here, forever? Wars fought by men for their Gods for eternity?"

Aisha stared backwards at the shimmering, hazy outline of the coastline now far in the distance and shuddered involuntarily.

"Maybe the wars and hatred will never end in Outremer. I don't know, I am just tired of the religious politics which always ends in death. The land is tainted I think; maybe cursed by the Gods themselves and fought over by men who know no different. I am glad to be leaving it Aisha; I hope that we find peace in England, a home, without the need for my sword..."

His hazel eyes stared poignantly westwards, across the empty sea and his spirits lifted a little, the warm breeze ruffling his hair as the cog picked up speed. Aisha nodded in understanding and agreement and took his gnarled hand in her soft palm.

"Let's go see if Merdlan is okay in the hold, he is probably going crazy down there."

The owner of the stallion chuckled drily and nodded, leaving the past far behind him and the future way ahead of him; content finally to be living and enjoying the present.

THE END